Adva

"Brian Wilkinson's debut is an exhilarating celebration of the imagination."
— Scott Carter, author of *Blind Luck, Barret Fuller's Secret*

"Brian Wilkinson has one of the best reps in the online community... respected by the pros and the fans alike."
— Mark Millar, Writer, *Marvel Comics*

"As if I were actually reading how a teenager would react... an amazing read!"
— Ashley Nicole, *Bookshelf* Book Blog

"An epic read which I enjoyed thoroughly... a must read for YA paranormal fans."
— Fizza Younis, *Book Eater* Book Blog

COPYRIGHT INFORMATION

PARAMNESIA

The Deadish Chronicles

Brian Wilkinson

BlueMoon
PUBLISHERS

FOR NORA

I hope your passion, your smile, and your love will always lead you to the same kind of happiness in this life that you have always given to me. I love you to the moon and back.

TABLE OF CONTENTS

Paramnesia
(par·am·ne·sia):

*A disorder of the memory or the faculty of recognition
in which dreams may be confused with reality.*

PROLOGUE

The wind rushed in through the dark, open doorway, causing an unearthly howl that sounded like screaming. As the young woman dressed in her sparkling pink prom dress rushed through it, she was briefly grateful the doorway could manage what she herself could not. Her terror was so great that she couldn't have screamed even if she wanted to. She tried several times to yell and call for help, but the barest of croaks were all that she could manage.

She was angry at herself for this weakness. She was angry that she was running for her life in the middle of the night through some stupid abandoned hotel from God knows what. She and Jeremy had thought it would be cool to get away from the prom after-party and hook up in this dead place. Now she was running for her life and Jeremy... well, she'd have time to think about him later. She hoped.

She ducked into the next room, an office, and quickly ran over to hide under the desk. It was a poor hiding place, not to mention the *only* hiding place and the oldest cliché in the book for bad horror movies, but it was dark and she hoped it would be enough. Despite being angry at herself for not being able to cry out only moments ago, she now felt relieved that she could barely breathe and hoped that the silence in the room would hold and whatever was out there would forget about her and move on.

From the belly of this beast of a hotel, a scream came. It was loud and faint all at once. It sounded like Jeremy and didn't all at the same time. It was a pleading, moaning, totally terrified cry. It was something that could have come from him, but it was so primal, it could also have been a brutally tortured animal. She plugged her ears and felt her eyes well up with tears.

It increased in pitch and fervour until she thought she was going to lose her mind as well.

And just as suddenly as it started, it stopped completely. There and then gone. The total silence was back, even louder than before.

Quietly, patiently, she waited. Seconds passed, then a minute. Two minutes. Eventually, she could feel the panic start to subside, and a low sob emerged from her throat. She adjusted herself so that she was on her hands and knees in the cramped space and slowly lowered her face down to the floor so that she could look out under the desk into the space beyond.

As slowly as possible so as to avoid making noise, she shifted herself into place. Every movement seemed to shatter the stillness of the room and fill it with her labours. Finally in place, she took a deep breath and lowered her face to the floor.

Her eyes were wider than they had ever been before. Even if she wanted to blink, she doubted she had enough control over the muscles to make them move. She stared deeply into the inky blackness beyond the doorway but could see nothing other than the still-swirling dust motes her own passage had made.

She willed her eyes to adjust to let her see better, but the darkness was near total. She tried to listen for signs of movement, but the blood was pounding in her ears from the position she was in, and her imagination started to fill in what the darkness refused to give up.

Waiting. Looking. Breathing. Nothing.

And then a faint shuffling sound in the room beyond. Her breath would have caught had she not already been holding it. Fearing it was her imagination, she almost called out to the noise to challenge it and just be done with it when the shuffling came again. Then out of the blackness came a mouse padding toward her. Normally terrified of the things, she breathed a sigh of relief at her error, relieved that the noise had been just this small creature going about its business.

It came closer to her, cocked its head, and then twitched its nose.

Tears came unbidden to her eyes. "Will you help me?" she asked it uselessly, her voice making clicking sounds instead of words, because she was speaking so faintly.

A heavy-booted foot suddenly slammed down on top of the mouse, crushing it instantly and sending its small, pulsing organs flying into her face. She screamed, trying to back up, and found she was trapped by the same place that was moments ago a safe haven. The desk was wrenched up and over her head in an instant and was flung to the side, where it shattered a window and took down part of the decrepit wall with it.

Wasting no time to look up at the monster, the girl dashed for the open space and dove through the shattered opening to the outside world and the woods beyond, slicing her leg open in the process. Her attacker reached an arm through the opening, too small for it to get all the way through itself, and snagged part of her dress. Screaming, the girl pulled away, until the only thing left in the monster's hand was a piece of her dress.

Crying freely now and panting hard, she limped through the small outcropping of trees, desperate to reach the roadway beyond. A few headlights drifted past in the distance, far too quickly and too rarely to be of much use. She didn't dare pause often, though when she did she strained to hear any signs of approach. It was all quiet; even all the night noises had fallen silent. That could mean she was safe, but silence hadn't meant anything back in the old hotel. She moved on.

She gasped and panted as she broke through the last of the thick underbrush and stumbled onto the side of the road. She looked left and right for any signs of life that could help her, but the cars that had been around moments ago had deserted her as well. It was the middle of the night, and all of the good prom parties were happening far from this desolate stretch.

Forcing herself to her feet, she cried out as she put weight down on her injured leg. Blood was flowing much too freely from the gash, and much of her pretty pink dress was now crimson. If she wasn't killed by that monster, she feared that the wound would see her bleed out if she didn't get help soon.

The relief was incredible when the headlights rounded the corner up ahead. "Here!" she shouted and waved her arms. "I need help! Please help!"

As the vehicle got closer, she felt her luck finally turn around. It wasn't just any old car but an actual ambulance. Not only would it stop, but the people inside could help her. Could fix her. The night was survivable. Maybe they could get help quickly enough to go back and see if Jeremy was still alive. Hope sprang in her chest.

And then it faded quickly as the vehicle suddenly sped up. Fearing that it was going to drive past, she waved her arms even more frantically and pleaded for it to stop. The driver hit the gas, and as the ambulance was about to pass, the driver suddenly jerked the wheel and smacked right into the girl with enough force that it severed her injured leg entirely and sent the rest of her flying a good twenty feet through the air before she came to crumpled heap on the ground.

The wheels on the ambulance ground to a halt, the lights on top spinning mockingly as the driver calmly exited and walked over to the girl, still alive for the moment, but the light quickly fading from her eyes. She tried to move her head, to look up, to ask 'why?' and to beg for help… but her head wouldn't move. Nothing would move. She couldn't even flinch when that heavy, familiar boot landed in front of her face.

"A bit ironic, don't you think?" asked a quiet, soothing feminine voice. Too quiet. Too soothing. It was a voice that should bring comfort at night, tuck you into bed, and tell you that it was all going to be better. It was the wrong voice. A terrible voice coming from the monster who had done this to her. "I mean, really. You need help, and you get hit by an ambulance? There's a certain kind of poetry to it."

The voice sighed and bent down, the face stilled concealed by shadows. "I take only the pleasure in this that I must in order to survive," it said.

A cool, clammy hand touched her forehead, and finally she felt her eyes begin to close. She felt like she was falling toward the hand, like her whole being was pulled out toward it. It was soothing. It was pleasant. She *wanted* to be taken in by this act. At the same time, she revolted against it, pulled back from it with everything she had been before and hoped to be in the future. She fought to stay, to breathe, to *be alive*.

Finally, she gave one last heaving sob, and then her eyes closed all the way for the last time. The creature dusted off its hands and stood up.

"If it's any consolation," it sighed as it headed back to the ambulance, "you look really pretty in that pink dress."

PART 1: DENIAL

CHAPTER 1

"You have the ability to wake the dead, you know."

The voice was angry, dark, and suggested danger or violence was imminent. Despite the warning bells going off in her head, Nora Edwards could do nothing about them. Instead, she closed her eyes and clumsily forced another mouthful of Cheerios into her dry mouth as she tried to block out all of the intruding noises. The television, the rustling of her mom and dad as they got ready upstairs, and now this twit. Let her idiot brother go and do whatever it was he wanted do. Or say. Whatever. She was way too damn tired to put up a fight today. Instead, she went for the witty retort.

"Guhh whay," she muttered. She dribbled a bit of milk down her chin and then flicked the lone surviving Cheerio off her face and onto the floor, where the family dog, Rorschach, so named for the overlapping patterns of black and white on his shaggy fur, snatched it up immediately. No one in the house ever attempted to honour the ten-second rule considering how fast the dog was. If it left your hand, it was your own stupid fault. No wonder the dog was getting fat.

"Oh, very intelligible," mocked her brother, Tom, from behind her. "Your stupid snoring is getting out of control, *Snora*. I would very much like to finish that dream I was having last night. It was me and Casey. I finally asked her out to prom and I think she was about to say yes and then you opened your mouth and tried to swallow the world."

"First, it's not my fault that I snore. Second, it's closer than you're likely to get in real life, so I wouldn't complain if I were you," she said.

"Oh, funny," sneered her brother as he hopped up and sat on the counter and rummaged his hand around in the cereal box before pulling a mitt out and stuffing it into his face.

"Sorry," she said.

She really wasn't. Snoring wasn't something that Nora could easily control. Her mother actually took her to see the doctor about it because of her brother's constant complaining, but instead of fixing it, the incompetent doc thought it was time that she and her brother occupied different rooms. After all, she was seventeen, he was eighteen, and they were both too old for that sort of thing. Nora had to sheepishly admit that they hadn't shared a room since they were little kids and that her snoring was penetrating the wall between their bedrooms. The doctor coughed uncomfortably and suggested she try a nose plug. She did, with little success, and then tossed the thing altogether when her brother started calling her Pluggy. With that gone, he went for the play-on-words brilliance of Snora and other half-assed attempts to rhyme with her name. At least that name didn't sound like an animated pig.

Going back to the doctor hadn't solved anything. When they looked closer, they saw that she had a deviated septum and that snoring was going to be the norm for her. Her brother was not pleased at the news and asked to be assigned to another family.

"You *should* be sorry," he said. He looked over her shoulder into her bowl of mushy Cheerios and raised an eyebrow. "Clearly you had a rough night, if you put that thing in your bowl and didn't take it out."

Snapping to, Nora blinked heavily and looked into her bowl. In the past, other oddities had made their way into her breakfast when she wasn't looking closely. Barbecue sauce instead of ketchup. Drinking a bottle of vinegar instead of water. That sort of stupid thing. She looked closely but couldn't see what error she'd made this time.

"I don't see…" she began, until all of sudden her face was immersed in the bowl. Her brother lifted her up and shoved her face in it again to drive down his point. "You are SUCH a jerk!" she screamed at his retreating back. He laughed maniacally as he backed away from her and grabbed his backpack. Give it to Tom, he knew how to prank and run.

She picked the Cheerios off her face as her best friend, Veronica, let herself in the front door. Tom worked his way past her, doffed an invisible cap to Vee's rolling eyes, and headed out for school. He had his own car, an early graduation gift from their parents, and never waited for Nora to give her a ride, even though they were going to the same school. He said it hurt his "cool points," though he sometimes relented if Veronica was present and in need of a ride. He'd never admit it out loud, but he'd always had a little bit of a crush on her.

"Oooh, new look?" Vee asked as she raised an eyebrow toward the Cheerio still dangling from Nora's chin.

"He is a hemorrhoid," Nora complained. She attempted to wipe the Cheerio off into the bowl but instead it made its way down to Rorschach and his wagging tail.

"Lovely image," Vee said.

"I haven't even gotten started," Nora said with renewed energy. "He is a festering boil that is ready to pop. You only need to apply the slightest pressure, and the thing will explode. I hope it happens in front of Casey."

"Who's Casey?" asked Vee.

"You know her," Nora said. "Grade 12. Super-smart. Glasses. She's the head of the prom committee."

Veronica nodded as she made the mental connection and helped herself to the carton of milk in the fridge. "You're just jealous," Vee said with a chuckle.

"Who's jealous?" asked Nora's mom as she entered the kitchen. She was rushing around, as usual, trying to put in her earring while carrying a folder full of real estate contracts under her arm.

"No one…" Nora began.

"Nora," Veronica said at the same time. "She's got a lack of dating prospects at the moment."

"Shut up, Vee! I don't care about that!"

"Oh, Nora," Mrs. Edwards, said pausing midstride and looking at her daughter with pity. "Some people take longer to… *flower…* than others."

Veronica laughed hysterically as Nora turned beet red. *"Mother,* I am in no need of *flowering."*

"Of course not, sweetie," said her mother apologetically. "It's just that you're so amazing, no matter what."

"I get it, Mom. Self-esteem is fully engaged. Feelin' good. Confident. Now can we please be quiet?"

"Sure, sweetie," said her mom, who had turned a lovely shade of red. Her relief was obvious when the car horn sounded from the driveway. "That's your dad!" she said with too much enthusiasm. "See you tonight, okay? I may be late! I have a showing for the Beyer-Roys."

"No worries, Mom, I got it," Nora said. "Though you may only have one child to come home to if I get my hands on Tom."

"Sounds good!" called her mother absently as the door shut behind her.

Veronica pulled up a stool beside Nora and put an arm around her. "You know I'm just teasing you, right? Your mom is right. You are smart, funny, cool, and will eventually take over the world."

"With you as my minion?" Nora asked.

"Partner," Vee corrected, rolling her eyes. "Now go fix your face so we can go to school. Cheerio-brown is not a good foundation colour."

AS THE radio blared and Veronica chattered, Nora shifted in the car seat, because she was always uncomfortable riding shotgun with her best friend. It wasn't that she didn't love and adore Vee, it was that machines did not. Nora had been in the car with her when she took her driving test and was shocked when she was awarded a license despite hitting two trash cans and parallel parking more than three feet from the curb. The examiner happened to be the son of an elderly woman whom Vee visited twice a week as part of her volunteer work at a senior's retirement community. After all the good she'd done, he couldn't say anything to disappoint her, though he'd clearly been conflicted. He just said "pass," and Vee gave him a thousand-watt smile.

Nora tightly gripped the side of her seat as Veronica jammed on the brakes and came to a screeching halt mere inches from the car in front of her. The driver ahead of them checked the rear-view mirror with a panicked, annoyed look and allowed the car to drift ahead a foot. Clueless, Vee took her foot off the brake and matched him inch for inch, chatting the whole time.

"Anyway, I told them that if we bring in more board games or something then the residents will have something to do. Maybe they'll get a little more sense of belonging, at any rate," she finished. There was a silence that told Nora it was finally her turn to speak. The only problem was she hadn't been listening, so she didn't know what to say.

"Uhhh," Nora began.

"I know, right?" Veronica chimed in. "Oooh, I love this song!" she squeed when "Royals" by Lorde started booming out of the radio. Without waiting for any further comment, Veronica cranked up the volume and then continued to chat away about improving snacks at the home as well.

Nora knew she should be a better friend and pay attention, but she was dead tired. Her snoring, as much as it was an irritant for her brother, actually kept waking her up at night. She had become so self-conscious about it that even a hint of a noise escaping her mouth woke her up, and it was happening a lot. She yawned and hoped that Vee didn't see it and take it personally.

As Vee talked, Nora took in the little world passing by her window. They lived in the small city of Guelph, just an hour away from Toronto, but sometimes it felt like the middle of nowhere with how sleepy it could seem at times. It wasn't that quiet in reality, considering there were more than a hundred and thirty thousand people living there, but it could feel like it if you were used to the day-to-day of the city. Compared to a lot of other cities in the country, Guelph was practically a metropolis. They had a great mall, movie theatres, a university, and some great places to hang out. It was a comfortable place rich in history, beautiful parks, old buildings, cool places to chill, good people, and pretty great Chinese food after the clubs downtown closed up for the night. Neither Nora nor Vee had been to the clubs, but they'd taken advantage of the Chinese food. The chicken balls in particular were amazing.

"Sad, huh?" Vee asked beside her. Nora had been too busy daydreaming to realize that both the song had ended and that Vee had finally taken a break from narrating her own life. Nora was about to ask her what she was talking about when she clued in that the DJ was talking about the infamous dead prom girl and her date.

"It's been nearly a year since eighteen-year-old Isabel Clarke and her prom date, Jeremy Vettoretto, were killed under gruesome and mysterious circumstances late last May," said the DJ. All of the local outlets were whipped into a frenzy now that prom season was upon them again. The bodies were barely cold and the media were salivating with the idea of fresh tragedy ready to evolve into urban legend status in order to boost ratings.

"Witnesses found Isabel, her leg viciously severed, lying dead in the middle of the street after 3:00 a.m. on the night of her senior prom, her beautiful pink dress torn and coated in blood. Investigators traced her path back to the old Guarida Hotel, a popular destination years ago that turned into a bar hangout for a short time before it closed its doors for good. Inside, they found her date dead on the floor. His back and neck had both been broken with multiple lacerations around his face and torso.

"What happened to this young couple? Was it a spat gone wrong? Did Isabel murder her boyfriend and run? If so, what happened to her in her last few minutes? Was it an accident, a hit-and-run, or was it done deliberately? Police aren't saying, and given the amount of time that has gone by, few in the community have any faith that they'll get answers.

"What's more, several groups, both parent and student-led, are suggesting that prom this year be cancelled for all of the high schools in the city in consideration for the feelings of those affected."

"I don't know how I feel about *that*," Vee butted in. She slapped the button on the console and turned off the radio. "Going to prom is something we've always dreamed about. Getting to dress up, get our hair done, stay out late and party… but at the same time, I can see how hard this must be for that girl's parents. I feel bad, but I still want to go."

"I know what you mean," Nora said. "I guess it's all about having some compassion for the family."

"I *do* have compassion. No one should have to go through anything like that. At the same time, it wasn't the prom itself that killed that poor girl. In trying to honour her life, I just don't know if putting a halt to things for the rest of us is the right thing to do."

"It's not like we're being punished," Nora said. Vee slammed on the brakes once again, and Nora jerked forward. There was no need for the harsh stop since the actual stop sign they were approaching was at least twelve feet ahead. It was doubly annoying because once they actually got to the stop in question, Nora knew Vee would just probably roll through it anyway. For all of Vee's good qualities, driving was not one of them. How could someone who gets straight 'A's with notes about her attention to detail in her work be so awful at the practical application of her skills?

"Well, it feels like it," Vee said a minute later as they slowly pulled into the parking lot at the school. Kids milled about as they made their way inside.

"People at this school need to celebrate. There has been a lot of time and effort put into planning things. Kids have bought outfits, tickets, and are so excited for this. It's a rite of passage. To think about taking it all away just seems wrong," Vee said.

Vee went silent for a few seconds and then her eyes lit up and she turned quickly to face Nora. "I know! We can dedicate the prom to that girl's memory! Maybe do a fundraiser or something!"

Not that Nora didn't appreciate the thought, but in her excitement it seemed that Vee had forgotten that she was still driving, albeit very slowly, but it mattered a great deal to Nora, especially since they were about to hit a guy.

"Vee! Look out!" Nora screamed.

Vee jammed on the brakes and pulled the car to the side. As a result, she only clipped him rather than bump into him head-on. He turned to see the car at the last second and managed to hop a bit and absorb some of the impact. He still dropped off the hood and landed on his butt.

"No!" yelled Vee. "Is he okay? Please tell me he's okay! I didn't see him!"

Nora didn't bother to answer this. In a flash, she was out of the car and ran to the boy on the ground. He was sitting on the ground in a daze and not moving. A small group of kids gathered around to watch, none of them quite sure what to do.

Kneeling by the boy, Nora hesitated. She had never seen him before and was certain she would have remembered. He was absolutely gorgeous. He had a tousle of brown hair, a soft, kind-looking face, and a body that suggested he worked out and looked after himself. She was so taken by him, she almost forgot that she and Veronica had just hit him with a car and that she was checking to see if he was dead or something.

"Is he dead or something?" Vee asked behind her.

Nora came to her senses and reached out to gingerly touch him. Just as she did, his eyelids fluttered open and his beautiful deep blue ocean eyes focused right on her.

"Are you an angel?" he asked quietly.

"What?" Nora answered, confused.

"Are you an angel?" he repeated.

"No, not last time I checked. Why?"

"Because you look like you fell from heaven."

It was super-cheesy. It was totally ridiculous. It was the wrong time and the wrong place. It was also kind of cute, she had to admit to herself.

"You must have hit your head," she said to him, then cursed herself for being too quick to brush off the compliment. She helped him sit up, and the crowd, disappointed that it wasn't a fatal encounter, got bored and made their way inside. "You okay, otherwise?"

"Just fine, thank you," he said. He tossed his chin toward Veronica in greeting.

"I guess we didn't see each other. Most of me is fine. My butt, however, is probably going to have a nice little bruise on it."

Relieved that the guy was okay, Vee finally pulled her hands down from her mouth and leaned around Nora to take a better look.

"I am SO sorry," Vee said. "Do you need to go to the hospital? I can drive you!"

Nora was about to, politely, try and find a way to point out that more of Veronica's driving was probably not the solution.

"I'm fine, or least I will be. Promise," he replied, saving Nora the awkwardness of trying to keep him away from Vee's car. He slowly got to his feet, Vee barely offering her arm as support for fear of doing more harm than good. Nora wanted to help as well, but hesitated too long.

She got up herself and walked past them. Nothing more to see here.

Just another lost opportunity. Show's over, folks. A hand gently touched her arm to stop her.

"Whoa, slow down," the guy said with a smile. "We haven't officially met. What's your name?"

"Me?" Nora asked.

He nodded. "Of course, you. I'm Andrew. Andrew Manes. I'm new here."

"Oh," she said and then mentally kicked herself once again for her lack of ability to flirt. "I'm Nora."

"And I'm Veronica," put in Vee with a weak little wave. "Sorry I almost killed you."

Andrew turned to look at her with a little laugh. "It's okay. Doesn't seem to be any major harm done." He turned back to Nora. "It's nice to meet you, Nora. I didn't expect to meet a guardian angel today. See you later?"

"Um, sure," she said, tucking her hair over her ear.

"Perfect," he said. He waved to both and headed in. Nora could feel Vee staring at her and didn't have to look to feel the broad grin on her friend's face. Nora couldn't help it. She grinned, too. It was nice to be noticed.

"Ready to go inside, *Angel-kins*?" Vee gently teased with a laugh.

Nora smiled and shoulder-punched her friend.

Ahead, Andrew stopped and turned around. "Are you sure this isn't heaven?" he called out to them.

"Oh, you are in trouble," giggled Veronica to Nora, who was too busy blushing to answer.

CHAPTER 2

I t had been far too long since the last meal, and the Revenant was hungry. Deep-in-the-gut hungry. The kind that takes over every waking thought and impulse. The kind of hunger that sees meals in anything and everything from pencils to shoes, let alone the kind of food that would truly sustain a thing like her.

It was her own fault. Needing to feed was important, but secrecy trumped food. It was a kind of messed-up logic that demanded you never be found out, because to be known would mean you were hunted and killed, yet not to feed meant you were starved and would die. Either way meant death, so the decision was made long ago to feed on the sly. Sneak a meal, so to speak.

That was why the Revenant had become a paramedic. She kept her brown hair closely cropped, wore flattering but largely unassuming clothes, and did little to attract attention to herself. She specialized in becoming just another body in a crowd. She was no one and everyone. Eyes passed over her as if she weren't even there. No one bothered to talk to her, not even her coworkers. Her partners talked more with the dispatchers than they did with her. New people often tried to strike up a conversation but gave up quickly. The job was a brilliant idea as well. Why not position yourself in the best possible place for meals? She was called out to attend to the dead and dying. No more than normal died under her care, but those who did might have had a little less to them after she was done with them. It fuelled her. It made her greater and increased her power. She let it into her and even let it change her features from time to time. The small changes would be so gradual that not even the people she worked with on a regular basis would ever be able to accurately identify her. She was totally unremarkable and worked to keep it that way.

That was the plan, anyway. Then came that frustrating night when she had nearly undone it all. She had gotten greedy when the two teenagers stumbled into her home. A late-night snack (an opportunity for a bonus meal) had turned into near disaster when the girl ran. As it was, the very public death of the girl led them back to her home in the old hotel, where the body of the boy was still cooling, so she had no choice but to run. Luckily, she kept nothing incriminating that could lead back to her, but still, living there was out of the question. Too many looky loos would want to check out the grisly scene.

What did that leave her? To run and to hide and to starve. If it had just been her on her own, that would have been bad enough, but The Others had been angry. More than angry — they demanded penance for the way she had broken their code. Once you were of them, you followed the path or you were stricken from it. And oh, did they like their punishments, as did she before she found herself on the receiving end. Death, torture, and mutilation were all options on the table, but forced fasting had won out. She was fairly new to their ways, after all. She had to learn. Besides, death was something they delivered to the living, not to each other.

And so she had been told to keep her belly empty for one year. No new souls, no living energy to fight against the endless deep in her body. She withered under the punishment. Her already slim and sleek features were running close to gaunt. It became harder to live under the rules and thumb of the humans, but her position was so perfect to feed her that to let it go simply wasn't an option.

She thought she could sneak a little and get away with it. The Others weren't omniscient. They didn't see everything. So why not? What better place for an opportunity to feed than the frontline of life and death? In a bigger city like New York or Los Angeles, it would be a buffet of epic proportions. In Toronto or Vancouver, she could eat out nightly and enjoy the choicest cuts. But that was not where she was allowed to go. In sleepy Guelph it was a beggar's banquet.

And beggars can't be choosers.

So few opportunities. Everyone she had been sent for was either too healthy or too stubborn to die. Her partner was normal, a young buck, too eager to see every detail for himself which in turn meant no time alone. He had been off that night, and she rolled the dice and lost. Since then she'd been saddled with Captain Eager and no opportunities to get a little taste. Until tonight.

Tonight, the Revenant finally got lucky. They'd stopped at a cheesy car-themed diner on Wellington, and the Young Buck was on his second helping of the early morning breakfast special when she stepped outside. There was a low moaning coming from the alley beside the diner, where she saw her first opportunity in ages for some scraps.

It was a homeless man hunched over beside a garbage bin. He was clutching at his chest and there was a sheen of sweat on his face. Not needing to be a doctor to read the signs, the Revenant could tell a full-blown heart attack when she saw one. He couldn't breathe, only gasp and look at her wildly.

It was beneath her, really, even to consider consuming this soul. He was pathetic in a brown ripped coat, woollen hat, and years of hair and grime plastered over his stupid-looking face. It was homeless dumpster-diving. But she was a beggar and he was a meal. When you're this desperate, anything will do. It was like the James Bond villain in *Quantum of Solace* who was left out in the middle of the desert with nothing but a quart of oil to drink. To do so meant death, but desperation would drive a man to try anyway. The villain had consumed the oil and died.

She would consume her meal and live.

Something like gratitude passed over the man's face as his soul slipped from his body and the pain went away. Something like relief mixed with revulsion washed over the Revenant's face and reminded her what she had been denying herself. Something, now that she had this taste, she wasn't sure she could resist indulging in further as soon as possible, even though there was still a month to go until her punishment was over. She had broken the seal. Opened the floodgates. Set her stomach to rumbling now that she had reminded herself of what she had been denied. It was so good.

And she was still hungry.

CHAPTER 3

Surrounded by her "Honey Hive" of Vee's Bees, Veronica was in her element as one of the senior advisors of the School Cares Committee. She had dispatched several kids to work on aspects of the various outreach programs they were doing while imparting little bits of advice and worldly wisdom. Though well-intentioned, many were simply too in awe of Veronica to do much more than blink in wide-eyed astonishment and hope that some reflected glory would come their way because they were hanging out with their highschool heroine. Vee had just finished yet another pitch for more volunteers at the retirement home.

"You are *so* nice, Vee!" Kia said.

"Incredible, really!" Kapalini put in, not wanting to let her friend be the only one throwing out compliments. Nora had to roll her eyes at this adulation and then suppress a laugh when Kapalini started to muster tears. *Actual tears.*

"Guys, you're being silly. I just like helping out," Vee said modestly. It *was* modesty, Nora had to admit. Vee really did do a lot of good. It was a hard act to follow. Not that Vee ever made anyone who did less than she did feel bad. Instead, she'd just be happy that people were doing something.

"But you're *so* good at it," teased Nora gently with a smile. Vee shot her a look that warned her against making fun of the others, but Nora just grinned at her. Vee tried to keep up the fierce look, but a small smile touched the corner of her mouth.

"Anyway," Vee continued, turning her attention back to the others. "Please think about helping out. We'll get to do it together!" She rummaged through her bag and frowned.

"What's wrong?" Kapalini asked.

"Forgot my water bottle," Vee muttered to herself.

"I'll get you a drink!" Kia said quickly.

"No, I'll do it!" Kapalini put in almost shrilly. The two girls quickly scampered off out of the room in search of a beverage that would best satisfy Veronica as Mr. Elrick, the advisor for the School Cares Committee, walked into the room for their noon-hour meeting.

"Oh, for the love of…" Veronica said as the girls practically ran out of the room.

"You are terrible," Nora laughed. "Those poor girls will do anything for you."

"I didn't mean for that to happen!" Vee laughed. "Were we ever like that? Super eager to please the older girls?"

"Sure we were, Vee," Nora said. "We were in awe of them. They were like gods. So wise, so experienced. Plus, they'd survived so much hardship… like English class."

"Well, maybe I won't feel too bad then," Vee said. "They are doing a service of sorts, aren't they? Even if it is for me!"

"You are too kind, Veronica," Mr. Elrick said sarcastically as he put his bag on the desk at the front of the room. "Just remember that being on the SCC is about giving back and making people feel welcome at our school."

"Hey, I didn't ask 'em to do it, Captain," Veronica said with her hands in the air. "They ran out of here before I could stop them. Don't worry, though, I have plans to take them both out for coffee later."

"You do?" Nora asked.

"I do *now*," Vee whispered to her before speaking loudly again to Mr. Elrick. "They've been doing an awesome job. When I was a junior member the seniors did similar things for me, so it only seems right. I'll even drive them!" Nora cringed.

"Okay, okay, enough," Mr. Elrick said in an attempt to move them along. "In addition to the upcoming prom, which our principal assures me is still going to happen despite the media coverage about the deaths last year, our ongoing mandate is to make people feel welcome and safe."

Nora's ears perked up. This was the Elrick speech about making people feel at home in their school, and he'd then go on and on about community, caring, pride, responsibility and blah, blah, blah, just before asking them to take on a new job, create a poster, volunteer, or maybe even look after a new student. Most of those were no big deal. As for the last one, this late in the year there wasn't anyone new she could think of except...

"...Andrew Manes," finished Mr. Elrick. He gestured to the door, and Andrew walked in looking slightly embarrassed at having a fuss made over him. He barely made eye contact with anyone until he caught Nora's eye.

She held his gaze longer than she dared and then looked firmly down at her desk so he wouldn't see the rising colour in her cheeks.

"Hey," Andrew said with a small wave and an awkward grin. There was a bit of gravel in his voice, which made him sound a bit mysterious. Nora did her best to avoid looking at him and instead stared at an old doodle that someone had drawn on the desk that looked like Optimus Prime.

She waited for Elrick to ask for volunteers and was steeling herself to put her hand up. But that would make her look totally desperate. Any cool factor was already in question as a member of the school welcome wagon, despite the fact that it looked great on university applications. She wrestled with what to do until the decision was made for her.

"Kapalini," Elrick said, picking out the girl as she re-entered the room with a bottle of water, a Coke, and a juice box. She nearly dropped all three in surprise at being addressed by the teacher. "Do you mind showing our new student around?"

Nora gulped and immediately tried to pin down her feelings of jealousy. It was completely unfair to be mad at someone who looked terrified at the idea of showing someone around and who hadn't actually asked for the job in the first place, but there it was.

"Actually, sir," Andrew said politely, "I met Nora earlier and she promised me a tour, if that's okay."

"Really?" Elrick asked, the surprise evident in the way his eyebrow arched up. Nora was annoyed, because it wasn't really that much of a stretch that she would volunteer. She was on the verge of indignation when it hit her that this cute boy had just lied to be with her and was now looking to her for support.

"Absolutely," Nora stammered. She could feel Vee grinning off to the side and wanted to punch her on the shoulder, but she kept her eyes focused forward and gave Andrew her best smile and was rewarded with one in return.

"THIS IS our Grotto space," Nora droned on as she gestured to the enclosed forest-like area in the middle of the building. "A few years ago, students here undertook a project to make the school more green, literally, and transformed the small space in between the two wings of the school into a living classroom. There are park benches, trees, flowers, and other beautiful things here. Even a little statue of a fairy, though it's pretty ugly and the teeth look a bit messed up. Anyway, it's a preferred spot to hang out, and students are surprisingly respectful of it and never leave any garbage."

"Well, I suppose there are some things that were worth preserving that people don't need to be told about first," Andrew said. "Kids, of course. Any kind of true beauty. And love, of course. Always love."

It was silly and true all at once. Nora didn't know what kind of response was called for here and still couldn't quite believe that this guy wasn't trolling her. "Love is important," she said, nodding. "Shall we move on?"

They took a look at several parts of the school that she thought he might find interesting or useful: the cafeteria, where she warned him never to eat the food unless he wanted crippling diarrhea (he laughed at that); the school pool, which never rose above hypothermia in temperature (he shivered at that), the Radio Room; where the cool kids hung out and did everything except put on a radio show (he wrinkled his nose at a familiar smell that had baked itself into the fabric of the beaten-up couch); and, most importantly, she showed him where the bathrooms were.

"Have you ever noticed how important bathrooms are?" she asked rhetorically. It was a thought she often had and didn't realize she'd spoken out loud.

He laughed. "No, how do you mean?"

"Oh," she said, surprised. "Um, well, whenever you go somewhere, it's like the first thing you're told. Movies? Bathrooms are here. Stadium? Bathrooms to your right. Someone's house? Down the hall to the left. It's like people are constantly worried that you're going to crap yourself right then and there. Our society is built up to spare us all having to wear Depends."

He laughed heartily at this. "I get that," he said. "And it's important."

"You sound like you have some experience," she said and gently nudged him. It struck her as absurd that she had chosen potty talk as her moment to start flirting in earnest.

"I might," he admitted. "But it's pretty embarrassing."

"Tell me," she teased.

"Maybe on our second date," he said.

Date. There it was. The word to end all words. All possible appropriate responses and possibilities rushed through her head at that moment. Kissing? No. Laughing? No. A handshake? Definitely not. Witty banter? The only thing playing in her brain was a circus theme. This was not going to go well.

"What's this?" he asked, breaking the spell and sparing her a world of awkwardness.

In front of them was a collage of photos lovingly arranged on the wall. Some were in colour, others were black and white. Beneath each one were two dates. The day they were born, and the day they died. It was a sad place but also a hopeful place where the school honoured those who had lived and died in service of their country or community before they were taken too soon. It was meant to inspire people to live to the fullest. Though it had no official name, the kids called it the Hall of Heroes.

Andrew was appropriately solemn and even bowed his head in silence for a moment. It was sincere and beautiful. She liked him even more for that. When he looked up, his eyes scanned photo after photo like he was trying to understand them, hear them, or know them again.

"Tell me about some of them," he said, nodding at the more recent additions.

So she did. There was John, cut down in the twelfth grade by cancer. Tyler in a car accident. Tom in the war in Afghanistan. A kid named Reno, who died rescuing a little boy trapped in a fire.

"All lost," whispered Andrew.

"But not forgotten," Nora said proudly. "The room beside the Hall is called the Heritage Room and is the pride of the school." She led him into the spacious room, and he had to marvel at how cool it was. The room had high ceilings and bright, tall windows. Oak bookshelves filled with old volumes lined the walls, with modern tables and chairs taking up one half of the room. On the side were leather couches, lamps, and reading tables. In the back of the room were bleachers, actual bleachers, where large audiences could pile in to watch the massive television fitted above the stone fireplace in the middle of the room.

"This place is amazing," Andrew said breathlessly.

"And infamous," Nora said.

"How so?"

"School legend has it that this room is haunted," Nora replied with an exaggerated raised eyebrow.

"Haunted? Seriously?" Andrew had on his sexy grin again.

"Yup," admitted Nora. The stories had been circulating the school for years and even popped up on Internet searches. Tacky reality TV shows dealing in this kind of bunk had been trying to get into the school for years, but it was always blocked by administration. Nora doubted the admin believed the rumours but rather blocked the attempts because it was against the school board policy to allow strangers into a building with kids. "There are two ghosts here, supposedly. One is the former librarian. People report feeling as though they've been tapped on the shoulder in here, or else they smell little pockets of perfume in the air."

"Wow, really?" Andrew asked excitedly. "That ever happened to you?"

"Yeah, but it was just Veronica. I'll admit that I may have screamed slightly."

He laughed at the image. "And the other ghost?"

"Yes, the other one," Nora said. "A custodian who hung himself in the back stairwell. It's pretty high up in there, though rumours disagree as to whether he killed himself or fell off a ladder. It's supposedly in the public archives, though no one has ever bothered to go look themselves. Apparently the promised 'true story' is good enough for most."

"You don't believe in ghosts, do you?" Andrew asked with a grin.

"Afraid not," Nora said with a shrug. "Though that doesn't stop kids from sneaking in here at night to try to get a look. They block the door open downstairs and slip in. It's a big dare-thing that's silly."

"Sounds cool to me," Andrew said. "I wish my old school was that awesome."

"Tell me about it," Nora asked.

Andrew shrugged. "Not much to say, really. My parents and I are from Brantford, and we moved here because that's where my dad got a new job. I went to a boring school in a boring city. All I really left behind was the track team, though I wasn't so great a runner that my leaving hurt my chances at winning a championship."

"That sucks. Just so you know, Guelph isn't necessarily any less boring. So... your girlfriend must miss you," Nora said in a way she hoped wasn't totally awkward but was of course totally awkward.

"She does, terribly," Andrew said. Nora's hopes began to dry up. Of course he wasn't single. A guy that good-looking had to be snatched up. "She's imaginary, you know, so I figure she'll get over it. No double-date for us, I guess."

Relief! And now the ball was in her court. "Just the three of us, it is. You, me, and my boyfriend here..." She put her arm out around an invisible figure in the air. "Claude Invisibly. Claude, say 'hello.'"

Andrew came over and shook the invisible hand. He leaned in as if to whisper in Claude's ear. "Just so you know," he said quietly. "I'm going to take your girl from you."

Nora felt the heat rush to her cheeks. "Oh, are you now?" she asked playfully.

"Yes, I am," Andrew said confidently. "Are you free tonight?"

"I am," she said with a smile, surprised at her own boldness and confidence. "Claude has another engagement."

"His loss," Andrew said.

SHE LIED to her parents and told them she was going out with Vee to the mall. Her parents would have been fine with the date, but she didn't want the hassle of them making her drag Andrew in before them while they poked and prodded. Not only that, she didn't want her brother getting in the way. She would be mortified if he used the name "Snora" in front of Andrew. That was more of a third or fourth date kind of humiliation. Or a tenth date. Or never, if she could manage it.

Besides, it was only really a half-lie. She went to the mall and met him in the food court. She put on a super-nice summer skirt that had a floral pattern and tied her hair back in a half-braid. It was a cute and flirty outfit designed to show that she had some style. He managed the same kind of look with a button-down shirt and cargo shorts. His hair was still mussed, but she suspected that was less bed-head and more carefully arranged bed-head. It worked wonders, because her heart was instantly a-flutter.

Neither of them was flush with cash, so a date on the dime had to do. It was a food court mash-up of treats that they shared between them. All of it was the kind of food designed for sharing or accidental touches. Nachos, French fries, or anything like it that could result in a brushing of fingertips. They went to a movie next, a light Canadian film about a town on the East Coast trying to lure in a handsome doctor. It was that or the latest Marvel movie, but Nora didn't want to be distracted.

And it worked! If you asked her later, Nora wouldn't be able to give any details about the plot. Their food sharing continued with warm, buttery popcorn, their fingers brushing and resting in the mix before he got up the courage to put his arm across her shoulders and she dared to rest her head against him. They left the movie before the end, too eager to talk and see where it was all going between them. He reached for her hand as she reached for his, and their fingers intertwined as though it was meant to be.

They walked from the theatre back toward her house. Their walk took them through the school property, which lay still and quiet in the warm night. Odd shadows played across the surface of the old brick from streetlights. If she listened closely enough, Nora could almost hear the echo of conversations, laughter, and learning that the school had housed only hours before.

As they rounded the corner by the base of the building where the Heritage Room was, Andrew got a mischievous look in his eyes. "Are you ready?" he asked. Nora's heart leapt, sure he was asking about a kiss. She was about to close her eyes and lean in when he motioned to the propped open door.

"You're kidding me, right?" she asked with a nervous laugh.

Andrew walked over to the door and removed the small stick he had wedged in there hours before. "I couldn't resist," he said. "You told me how to do it earlier, and I thought it would help make our first date more memorable."

Even though she didn't believe in ghosts, she didn't relish the idea of walking into a dark place in the middle of the night, no matter how many times she had been there during the day. It wasn't much different from how creepy your own house could get at night. More than once she had run up the stairs in her house after being mildly convinced something was staring at her from the dark.

"It's kind of creepy in there, isn't it?" she said.

"Please," Andrew asked. "I'll be with you, so you don't need to be scared. We'll go up there for five minutes, tops."

Okay, so maybe it would be kind of cool. It would certainly give her bragging rights in the years to come that she had ventured into the Heritage Room at night. Nora allowed Andrew to take her hand, and she laughed as they slipped through the doorway, up the old stairs, and into the room. She was steeling herself to go in, take a quick look, and get out just in case ghosts turned out to be real after all. Instead of seeing ghosts, Nora found herself swept away.

Andrew moved to the middle of the room, where a small table was set up already. He lit a match and put it to a candle. The faint light glowed on the decorated table to reveal a small box filled with pastries that he set out on plates. He pulled back one of the chairs and gestured for her to sit.

"When did you..." began Nora. She was speechless and in that moment quite possibly in love.

"Before we went to the mall. I set all of this up and hoped our date would go as well as it has. Do you like it?" He seemed as nervous as she was, and there was hope in his voice.

"It's amazing," she said breathlessly.

They ate and talked for what felt like an eternity. Andrew then pulled out his phone and plugged it into a music dock, and the air filled with slow music. He offered his hand to her. "May I have this dance?"

"You may," she answered formally. They started out clumsily, unsure of each other's rhythms or paces, but finally they fell into step.

"You smell amazing," he said. "I love your perfume."

Nora smiled at him sweetly. "You too," she said before stammering to correct herself. "You smell amazing. You look amazing." Whoever they had been separately before, they seemed to find out who they were as one. It was simple. It was incredible. It was a perfect moment.

And then he kissed her.

No ghosts came to visit while they danced or after when they packed up their secret meal and stole back down the stairs. She was giddy from the moment and happily accepted Andrew's compliment about her perfume. It wasn't until later that night as she lay in her own bed, smiling from ear-to-ear as she thought about their date, that the comment came back to her.

He must have made a mistake. She hadn't been wearing any perfume.

CHAPTER 4

The homeless man had been the Revenant's first indulgence in ages, but not her last. Like an addict who convinces herself that one more hit won't be a big deal, the Revenant had fallen into a similar trap. If one small indiscretion wasn't an issue for her control, then why not one more? So she had one more. Then another. And another. She was in control, and it was no one else's business but her own. That's what she told herself, anyway.

She found the drunk man stumbling through Exhibition Park, a pristine parcel of city land except for one small patch off to the side of it marked for construction that had become a temporary haunt for drunks and the dead alike, especially around the old circus pavilion. Singing loudly to no one at all in the middle of the night, the drunk finally stopped to relieve himself into the water. The Revenant was watching disgustedly from the shadows, but the hunger flared and it was not to be ignored.

The man finished, shook himself off, and then fell over. The bottle he had been clutching slipped out of his hands and rolled toward the edge of the water. The man rolled toward it himself, touched it with his fingertips, and then watched it slip into the water and bob downstream, out of sight.

"Bye, bye boozy bottle," he slurred as he waved goodbye. Then he said nothing and stayed perfectly still. Within moments, it became clear that he had passed out. It was the combination of his indiscretion and his position near the water that gave the Revenant the permission she was looking for. Bodies created attention that she must avoid. Drunks who fell into a river and drowned themselves didn't deserve pity, much less an investigation.

She came out of the darkness and hovered above the still man. He smelled like tequila and urine.

Hungry as she was, his foulness smelled divine and tasted better. At least that was what she told herself to make it more palatable. She wouldn't have to settle for scraps much longer. The year-long punishment was nearly up and prom night, with all of its excesses and lost inhibitions, promised many opportunities for her first meal of freedom.

And wasn't it nice of her to volunteer for an extra shift that night?

CHAPTER 5

The next month passed for Nora in a whirlwind of love and bliss. Every night before she went to bed, she and Andrew would text each other sweet nothings and see who could hold out the longest before falling asleep. She would wake bleary-eyed in the morning, and the happiness would be so strong that it would block out everything, including her annoying brother. Tom still complained about the snoring, but when she wouldn't even react to the teasing, he became even more incensed.

"Don't 'ignora' me, Snora!" he teased. She just smiled and passed down a piece of toast to Rorschach below. He happily snatched it up. The dog had gained nearly two pounds in the last month alone from these absent-minded feedings.

Nora's mother and father just smiled at each other. They were surprisingly cool about the whole thing, especially once Nora finally agreed to bring Andrew around to the house. Thankfully, her brother was out for the evening. He went to the movies on their parents' dime, and she was grateful they had the sense to get him out of the way so he wouldn't embarrass her.

The only awkward moment came the next morning in the laundry room. Nora skipped in to grab a skirt from the dryer, and her mother quietly told her to "be safe." Nora knew what she meant, remembering their talk from years before.

"We're not there yet, Mom," she said. "But I promise I'll be careful."

And that was that.

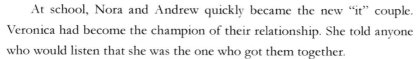

At school, Nora and Andrew quickly became the new "it" couple. Veronica had become the champion of their relationship. She told anyone who would listen that she was the one who got them together.

"I could tell from the first moment they were meant to be," she gushed. Kia and Kapalini echoed the sentiment and claimed they were there to see it all. They weren't, of course, but gossip has a way of becoming truth if you tell it enough times. Really, the facts of the meeting didn't matter to Nora; the eventual outcome was all that she cared about. Let people reinvent history, she figured. She was loving the present.

It didn't affect her schoolwork... much. Mostly she would be overly distracted in any class or club if Andrew was there. Elrick would get annoyed at having to repeat himself in SCC. The science teacher, Mr. Symington, had to yell at her to stop before she mixed two chemicals that could, would, sorta, slightly *explode* and possibly blind people. Mr. Javeed, the geography teacher, would just chuckle at the two of them and gently encourage them back to their studies.

Though it was taken for granted the two of them would go to prom together, Andrew didn't disappoint in the grand gesture department. He solicited the aid of Mr. Tufford, the art teacher, in getting supplies together to create a large banner with a painted angel on it and the name "Nora" stencilled into the halo in flowery script. Next to it was the simple question, "Prom?" and then it was hung from the ceiling in the Heritage Room. A cute little romantic table was set up in the middle that recreated their first date, but now it was filled with donuts for all of her friends who were lying in wait.

She had been having lunch with Veronica that day, and Vee said she had left something in the room and asked Nora to tag along to get it. When the door opened and all of her friends were there standing under the huge banner, each holding a small halo cut out of glossy wrapping paper, she was shocked. They cheered and clapped and waved, but the group disappeared from view entirely once her eyes focused on Andrew in the middle, already wearing a tuxedo, holding a bouquet of roses.

He smiled and shrugged as if to say *I didn't know about all of this and I'm as surprised as you are* and then held the roses out to her. "Well, Angel?" he asked.

As if there was any doubt.

And that was it. They were going to prom, which was actually going to happen. Despite the constant doomsaying from the media about proms getting cancelled or all the other horrific possibilities, the event was going ahead as scheduled.

A drunk man had been found dead in the Speed River a few weeks ago and became the new hot topic, with some suggesting he was murdered despite the obvious evidence that it had been nothing more than an accident. There were a few parents who boycotted the prom and forbade their kids from going, but for the most part the mantra of the school and the town had been that life moves on and is deserving of celebration, not mourning. The politics of the piece had no shape in Nora's decision. For her, love was the deciding vote. She and Vee had gone to nearly a dozen shops to find just the right dresses to wear. Vee had settled on a sleek red that had a single strap and a classical look. It flowed outward nicely at the bottom and allowed her to move like she was on a cloud. Nora, on the other hand, went with a deep purple gown that plunged at the back. She loved the idea of Andrew's hands roaming up and down the open space on her back. It felt electric when she tried it on, and she could only imagine the voltage it would crank up to on the actual night.

Though several others had asked her, Vee decided to go to the prom with Peter Tieri, a fellow SCC member. To splurge, they had all decided to share in the cost of renting a limo for the big night. None of them were particularly rich, but getting the cash together between all of them was doable.

"It's going to be *amazing*," Vee said for the hundredth time as they were getting their hair done. The dance was hours away, but perfection takes time, and Vee demanded that they be perfect. They were worth spoiling, she insisted. Nora normally didn't go in for such a pampering, but it was prom and she wanted to look good.

Nora smiled and extended her hand to the attendant, who was putting on purple nail polish to match her dress.

Veronica raised an eyebrow and leaned in to her. "So... have you and Andrew..." she whispered and let the unfinished sentence hang in the air.

Nora turned sharply to her friend and shushed her. "Not yet," she said.

"Hmmm," Vee mused as she appraised Nora's expression. "But soon? Tonight, maybe?"

"I refuse to answer the question."

"I think you kind of just did."

"I did no such thing!"

"Denial," Veronica said. "That's what I'll tell people later. 'The poor girl is just out of her head. She can't see what's right in front of her. She claims to be able to see it, but I can tell she's making it all up.'"

"You're crazy," Nora laughed. "I know what's going on. We just haven't gotten there yet. Maybe tonight. Maybe next month. Maybe never. Who knows?"

"Never?" Vee said. "Seriously?"

"Okay, that's a bit much."

"A lot much."

"Fine, not never. Maybe tonight? Let it go! You're making me nervous."

Vee laughed and dropped it.

After getting their hair and nails done, the girls went back to Nora's place to get ready. Tom was already out the door in a cheezy t-shirt tuxedo outfit that he claimed was cool because it was cheap. He actually managed to get Casey ("Dreams do come true!") to agree to go, a small miracle, but Nora figured that her brother had at least one good thing coming to him, considering he was graduating this year and heading off to university. Tom might be intolerable at times, but she knew that when push came to shove he would have her back. Nora's mom fussed over him and tried to get him to wear a suit, but he wouldn't hear it. He also refused to parade Casey in front of the family and said that he was going to her house instead. He promised to take pictures to show the family later and was gone. Nora's dad reluctantly passed him his keys after eliciting a promise of no alcohol.

Nora, however, was not going to get off so lightly. Since it was her first prom, her mom made her promise that Andrew would come over and that she would get to take as many pictures as she wanted. She even allowed Veronica to get prepped at the house as well so that Nora would have a friend for support and to spread out the attention.

Her dad called out that Andrew had arrived, although he wasn't alone. His parents had driven him over to see their son and their "future daughter-in-law" in their prom get-up. He blushed furiously the first time his mom had called Nora that in her presence, though Nora noted he hadn't objected. Marriage was a far-flung idea not meant for the likes of a teenager, especially one with a whole year of high school to go, but the idea that he hadn't ruled it out was incredibly romantic.

As best she could, Nora put up with the snapping photos, the sighs between moms, and the wary glances the fathers cast at each other. Vee ran over and joined in to get pics snapped with Nora, and then the three of them lined up together.

A car horn sounded the arrival of Peter in his long, sleek limo. He emerged out of the roof panel like a heroic soldier returning home from war, and he beckoned them to come. It was all for naught, however, as Nora and Andrew's mom immediately hauled him out of the car and the photo session continued.

Finally, the kids were able to tear themselves away from the parents. They loaded into the limo, toasted each other with the complimentary, though not entirely legal champagne, and headed off to their magical night.

This year, the prom committee decided to really get into nature by making the whole event at the Grasslands, a nature preserve and group facility in the back end of the university. It was a beautiful place lined with trees, a gazebo, and even a river. The main hall was filled with fairy lights, the nature accents exaggerated with a mixture of real and fake plants, and the ceiling was made to look like a thousand stars thanks to the LED lights the tech crew had spent the past week stringing up. When Nora walked in, she felt like she'd been transported away to another world in which every fairy tale or literary imagining had been made real. It was breathtaking. It was wondrous.

She felt Andrew's hand slide into the space in the back of her dress. It was magical.

The rest of the night was a blur of dancing, hugging friends, and incredible food. The music flowed seamlessly to allow for dancing, celebrating, and slowed down often enough to get in close and personal. The teachers watched from the sides and tried to hide their smiles when the kids got a bit goofy or carried away. There were a few speeches, a few toasts, and a highlight reel of the kids who were graduating thrown up on display. Nora even found herself clapping and applauding when Tom showed up with the silliest expression on his face in one of the photos. Veronica got slightly tipsy on the small bottle of champagne that Peter had snuck in for the two of them and was laughing at everything. Nora needed no extra help to feel good that night. Not when she had Andrew by her side.

Gradually, the crowds thinned out as kids moved on into the woods or to the after-parties. The police and paramedics were around outside, looking bored, but paid to be there just in case. Their presence was a concession the school had made to worried parents after the events of the past year that extra help would be on hand in case of emergency. From the look of things, the expense was wasted.

Veronica laughed wildly as she wobbled slightly over to Andrew and Nora, who were sitting at their table, chatting and laughing. She whispered loudly in Nora's ear that thanks to her small drink she wasn't feeling too great and that Peter wanted to make sure she got home safely in case she got sick. Andrew assured her that they would be fine and get a cab. Veronica turned around and beckoned to Peter, and they exited the hall.

"Shall we go, Angel?" Andrew asked.

"Do we have to?" Nora said. She sighed and leaned into him. "I don't really want this night to end."

Andrew laughed. "I didn't mean home, sweet girl. I meant shall we go for a stroll on these lovely grounds?"

"Are you taking me away into some dark corner of the woods?" Nora asked playfully, matching his tone. "That sounds quite scandalous, good sir!"

"That's the plan," Andrew said with a grin.

"In that case, I heartily accept."

They passed groups of people and promised to see them at one or another after-party. Andrew became quite formal as he passed the teachers and even shook Elrick's hand and offered a salute. Outside, they fended off a cab driver who hopped out to open doors and passed by the police in the direction of one of the many footpaths. One bored officer cautioned them to be careful, and Andrew told the man he had a bodyguard and squeezed Nora's shoulder. The officer laughed and waved them away.

As Nora and Andrew headed down the path, a young EMT hopped out of the back of her ambulance and watched them walk out of view. She was alone that night, her partner not interested in the extra cash, and none of the officers on duty noticed when she disappeared.

The path hadn't been a random choice, Nora found out. Before coming, Andrew had done his homework yet again and set up a romantic space for just the two of them in one of the old cabins that during the day served as one of the nature tracker stations. It all sounded very formal and stiff to Nora, but it was a stark contrast to the intimate setting on the inside.

Andrew had set up a bed with a bottle of wine next to it, and his hands shook as he lit the candles set up around the room. Nora could tell that all of his hopes and fears had been put at risk by setting this up, so she wasted no time in letting her actions show which emotion was going to be his reward.

She moved behind him and rested her head on his back while sliding her fingers down the front of his shirt. She tugged at the hem until the fabric was loose and her fingers felt their way through to his bare skin. She kissed his back gently. He turned around, and their eyes met through the flickering light. With the barest of pauses he kissed her deeply, allowing all of his love and passion to flow out into that one kiss in such a way that suggested he was daring anyone in the world, past or present, to try to match its intensity.

Nervously, clumsily, but with passion and purpose, they fell into each other and onto the bed. They kissed each other deeply and though the moment was ripe, they went no further. It was perfect just as it was. It was a sweet and beautiful moment shared between them.

They were watched the entire time.

OUTSIDE, THE Revenant watched and waited. Allowing the teenagers their moment added a sweetness to the whole event. They got to experience joy, and soon she would savour that joy like the cherry on top of a sundae. As long as she wasn't seen, it would be perfect. There would be no fuss, no struggle, no cries.

Here, in the middle of the Grasslands, there was no one watching and the darkness would allow her to move the bodies unseen. She made a mental note to sign up for more events at the venue. How conveniently her meals were served to her!

Patiently, she waited. Gradually, the talk slowed and stopped. The breathing evened out. She watched a further five minutes even then, just to be sure, before reaching one hand out to the handle at the door. She prepared herself for the meal, felt the features in her face shift to accept the soul energy as her eyes swirled grey and slits opened on her cheeks and rippled with the soft sound of a rasping breath. She began to push down on the handle.

"Hey there!" yelled a young, drunken voice behind her. "Wanna dance with us unner the stars?" Startled, she turned quickly to see a teenage boy, obviously one of the kids from the prom, as he stumbled over to her. His eyes widened when he saw her face, and he squinted to try to understand what he was seeing through his drunken haze. "Whas wrong wit' your…"

Before he could finish the sentence, the Revenant snapped a hand out and brutally punched him in the head. He wasn't dead and whenever he woke up or was discovered, it was likely he wouldn't remember what had happened or what he had seen if he could think at all past his inevitable hangover. More voices could be heard approaching as the rest of the group this idiot was with was moments away from seeing them both. She grabbed the body, stuffed it into a bush, and looked around wildly to make sure she hadn't been discovered. The first teen rounded the bend but hadn't seen her yet. Just as she was about to run into the woods, she tossed a disappointed look at her abandoned meal in the cabin and felt dread as her eyes locked with the boy inside, who was staring out at her with wide eyes.

BEFORE HE could make sense of what he was seeing, the woman in the window was gone. It was so quick that Andrew was sure he was seeing things. In fact, now that he was fully awake and could hear the voices and laughter outside, he was convinced of it. Looking down at Nora, whom he was surprised to see (and hear) was snoring, he shook her awake and put a finger to his lips when she began to question him.

They giggled as they fixed their clothes and blew out the candles. The laughter and voices grew louder until they passed the cabin and slowly faded away. Then the two snuck out and ran back down the path toward the prom, filled with a deeper awareness of themselves and each other, as well as the joys of young love.

Once they were back at the main pavilion, Nora and Andrew could see that they were one of the few couples still on the property. The teachers were cleaning up and shepherding a few stragglers out the door. The cabs had all gone, and Nora wondered how they were going to manage to get home.

Elrick solved the problem for them by agreeing to let Nora take his car. He said he would get a ride with Mr. Symington and that she could just drop the car off at the school the next day. Normally it wasn't something he would do, but considering that he had known her for a few years and her brother was one of his star pupils, he figured she was a safe bet. Keys in hand, they got in the car and headed home.

As they drove through the quiet night, Andrew asked if she wanted to go to one of the after parties, and she politely declined. "This night belongs to us," she said. "This was perfect. I don't want anything more from this day. If I had to die now, I would be content forever."

"Morbid," Andrew said with a chuckle. "Are you kidding me? I'm just getting started. I feel like tonight is the night my life began!"

"So sweet," Nora said and leaned over to kiss him on the cheek.

"You are my Angel," Andrew said. She looked at him adoringly and was about to kiss him again when the light around his head grew brighter and brighter. Too late, she yelled to look out for the vehicle speeding toward them. It connected with a sickening crunch, and Nora's whole world exploded in toward her. Glass and blood showered her face as the car reeled back from the impact beside Andrew's door. The car turned over and over until it came to a stop and they hung suspended in the upside-down car.

Nora was sure she was dead or otherwise horrifically injured, because all she could see was red out of her left eye. She gingerly felt around her face and let out a gasp of pain when she touched the edges of a nasty gash. A quick mental accounting of the rest of her body told her she was more or less fine. Andrew, beside her, was bleeding profusely and not moving, but there was a slight rise and fall to his chest. He was still alive. Thank God for that. She reached out for his hand.

Before she could grab it, Andrew's door was wrenched off entirely, and he was pulled out so viciously that the seatbelt, still connected, snapped. Nora screamed for him and fumbled to get herself out of the car. Finally able to get the belt undone, she collapsed in a heap of glass and moaned from the pain. She then began to drag herself out of the car.

Outside, beyond her field of vision, she heard Andrew moan and then scream. When Nora shakily got to her feet she saw something that looked like a woman, only twisted and grotesque, standing over Andrew and pulling a blue mist from his body into the gills on her face. Aware and crazed, Andrew looked to Nora and beat at the creature to try and get away from it.

"Go!" he screamed at Nora. "Run away! I'll hold it off." Gallant of him, but saving her own skin just wasn't part of her DNA. She was definitely more of a Buffy than a Cordelia.

Gathering all her strength, Nora ran over to the thing and jumped on its back. Its actions temporarily disrupted, the creature howled as some of the mist faded back into the boy and into the street. The creature reached back and pulled Nora off by her hair before tossing her away. She rolled until she came to a stop and roughly hit her head on the curb. Nora tried to call out and to stand up, but her vision had tripled, and even trying to think hurt.

Satisfied, the creature looked back down at the boy, half dead, and drank further.

Finding strength within herself she didn't know she had, Nora pushed herself to her feet and began to stagger toward the creature. It noticed her the way a man notices a fly around a meal, ready to dismiss her once again, but utterly unconcerned about it in terms of a threat. Nora would correct that assessment. As she took another wobbly step forward, she heard the crunch of glass under her feet. Without taking her eyes off the creature, she reached down and felt her fist close around a shard. She gripped it so tightly that the edges cut into her own hand.

With renewed vigour, the creature consumed Andrew's energy. Nora's wobble became a shamble, then a trot, and with an incredible effort she lunged at the creature, which only now saw it had made a mistake by ignoring her. It let out an ear-splitting shriek as Nora plunged the shard into one of the gills on its face.

Rearing back in pain and anger, the Revenant clutched at the shard with one hand and grabbed Nora by the neck with the other. Nora battered uselessly at the creature as she yelled and cursed at it. The creature pulled the shard out with great force and the energy that it had been taking in cascaded out like air from a burst balloon and slammed full force into Nora's face before wafting into the air. The creature rammed its forehead into Nora, ending all resistance before it once again tossed her to the side of the road.

Angry and in pain, the creature gave a long look at Nora to make sure she was watching and then it brought its foot down on Andrew's neck, which made a loud and simple snap. The action had been an excessive and unnecessary gesture, Nora knew hopelessly.

After all, Andrew was already dead.

Nora whimpered with the knowledge of it in her gut and tried to yell out in defiance at the thing approaching her. No noise would come out, just a breathing whisper. She wanted Andrew back. She wanted this thing gone. More than that, she wanted to know *why*.

This much she got an answer to. "I was seen," the woman said to the unspoken question. "That must not happen."

When? Where? How? What are you? Why? WHY? All of her questions went unanswered as the creature bent down, grabbed her, and began to drink. It was red hot at first, and then a cool wave slowly replaced the searing heat. The feeding had only just begun, but Nora felt sure that something of herself had been lost but couldn't have named it if she wanted to.

Turning her head as best she could to see Andrew, Nora began to give up, though she could swear she heard his voice yelling at her to fight. She saw him again, though incomplete, standing near her and gesturing at her to get up. That didn't make sense, though, because he was still lying on the ground.

Car horns and sirens washed over his voice in that moment, and the creature hissed in frustration. Instantly, the cooling sensation faded and she felt her strength returning to her. Before she could question what was happening, the creature had let go of her and ran out of view.

Flickering lights filled her peripheral vision. She tried desperately to stay awake and to hear Andrew's voice again. She willed her eyes to focus on his body and watched for any sign that she was wrong about him being dead. She watched for him to move. To stand. To smile at her. To slip his hand down the length of her back. To kiss her one last time.

She watched until gentle hands began to pull at her and she was lifted up and away where she couldn't see him. Only then did she allow herself to drift away.

CHAPTER 6

"You have the ability to wake the dead, you know."

Anger and hurt flashed through Nora's mind, along with the pain of sitting up. She'd been stuck in a hospital bed for two weeks already and had been subject to pokes, prods, questions, and fawning over by anyone and everyone who came in contact with her. They all wanted to know about Andrew. The media had already dubbed them the second coming of the prom massacre, and they were constantly finding their way into her room. Tom had grown tired of the incursions and one day bodily lifted one of those clowns out of the room.

Now she had to contend with smart-mouthed nurses and orderlies who didn't have the sense to avoid using certain phrases so close to Andrew's death. She wanted to get up and scream at the idiot, but instead she went for icy cool.

"I beg your pardon?" she said evenly.

"Your snoring," he said, apparently oblivious to the social blunder. "The first time I heard it I ran in here thinking you were flatlining. Once I was in the room, I thought for sure that it was an earthquake or something. Then I just saw that you had your mouth open and were sucking in air like a black hole. It's an impressive skill."

"Wow," Nora said incredulously. "Not only are you insensitive, you're kind of a jerk, too."

"Thanks," said the man jovially. "I do my best. My name is Charlie. Charlie Ignis." He walked over to her and held out his hand. He had a big grin plastered on his face. Nora expected him to be embarrassed or even angry before he left quickly. She was so flustered by his acceptance of her criticism that she actually shook the guy's hand.

His grip was strong, but not crushing. He was at least six feet tall, close-cropped brown hair, well-muscled, and the dimpled look that you normally only got to see in movies.

"What are you doing in here, anyway?" she demanded.

"Working," he said. "It's what you do to get money. I'm an orderly here at the hospital, though I'm actually doing a bit of job shadowing as well, because I want to go to school to become a nurse. I'm just here to pick up your lunch tray."

"Well, take it and get out," she said. She leaned back and closed her eyes. The effort was dizzying even now. When she first woke up after the attack, she had been confused by the comfort of the bed. The curb on which her head had lost consciousness was a soft pillow. The gravel of the street had become a firm yet yielding mattress. The blankets on top were the smoke and blood. She remembered a lot of voices, some tears, flashing lights, and mass confusion. She couldn't make heads or tails of what was happening around her. The only coherent thoughts were about Andrew, and each time she remembered he was dead.

Now that comforting bed was a bit of a prison. Her butt ached constantly, her arm movement was restricted because of the IV, and nothing that had been brought to her was of any comfort. Reading was an effort. Watching anything on the tablet that had been brought was an effort. Going to the bathroom was a full four-stage process that involved sitting, resting, walking, and fumbling with cords to pull down her pants. On top of all that, there was barely a moment's peace. Everyone wanted something from her, and she had little to give.

First came the police to ask what happened. She told them about the attack and the creature and they all nodded politely. It wasn't until the third or fourth round of questioning that she started to pick up the condescending looks. It was clear none of them believed her. She raged at them at that point to find the killer. Finally, a kindly female police sergeant came and sat with her and told her that there was no evidence of a third party at the scene. The car, from the looks of it, had spun out of control and was partly wrapped around a pole. Both Nora and Andrew had been found outside of the car, but there was no sign of foul play. The so-called attack had been ruled an accident.

That's when she understood. They thought she was making it up. Maybe they believed he was drunk or they were distracted. Maybe they thought she was trying to capitalize on the media attention so she could ride that wave. They asked her the same questions over and over until Nora refused to answer any more.

Before the media arrived, Nora's mother and father sat with her and listened to her story. They told her they believed her, which was a kind but obvious lie. Nora ignored their pleas, telling the story from start to finish to anyone who would listen. The media, she thought, would get her story out. Instead, the media twisted it into a horror story and frequently had guest panellists cast doubt on her mental state.

It didn't help that she looked a bit crazy now as well. The gash next to her eye had turned a bright purple and looked like a stylized make-up choice rather than a wound. It made her look like the offspring of a rock star gone wild or a rich kid with daddy issues. Pretty or not, now she had to wear her loss for the rest of her life out in the open where everyone could see it. The unfairness of it all was too much.

And now she was here in the hospital dealing with this idiot who wanted to rub death and dying in her face while criticizing her for snoring. He was still looking at her oddly, holding her lunch tray and waiting for her to say something else. He opened his mouth to speak, then closed it and nodded at her before heading toward the door.

Just before he left, he asked her if she had a good visit.

"With who?" she asked, exasperated. Between the meds and the attention she slept a lot and people were constantly coming and going. Today, however, had been quiet so far. Veronica told her she planned to come after school, but it was barely past lunch.

"The guy," he said quizzically. "I walked by an hour ago and heard you talking to a guy in here. He sounded kinda lovey-dovey."

"Look, just get out. There was no guy, you are a jerk, and my snoring is something you need to shut up about, okay?"

"Fine, fine," he said surrendering. "Just maybe get a nose plug or something."

"Get out!" she screamed.

He ducked out of the room, and she could hear him chuckling in the hallway. He was clearly toying with her, and getting a rise out of her was his twisted idea of fun. The next time a doctor or nurse came by, she would complain. For now, she would sleep.

Wait, she thought as she drifted off. *What guy?*

THE NEXT few days at the hospital went from frustrating to strange to frustratingly strange. She spent most of her time in her room wanting to avoid the seemingly crowded hallways beyond her door. Day and night, people walked by. Some talked, some complained, a few moaned and groaned. For a smaller city like Guelph, the hospital was doing big business.

During the day she could put it up to the hustle and bustle of the living going about their business. At night, it was strange to have it continued nearly uninterrupted. The nurses were far less frequent, but the voices of people she assumed were the other patients were louder and more insistent. She was grateful in some ways for the distraction from her thoughts as the snippets of conversation were always interesting.

"Where is my family? Why haven't they come back?" one voice said.

"It hurts! Goddamit, it hurts!" yelled another.

"I'd go out, but I'm afraid. I've been walking these halls for nearly sixty years," another put in.

Sometimes the voices were conversational, and other times they came across as crazy people talking to themselves. The footsteps went up and down the hall without ending. No one in this place apparently slept.

Once or twice in the night she would awaken with the belief that there was someone else in the room with her. By the time her eyes focused, the room would be still with the barest of hints that perhaps something was off. Maybe the bottom of a curtain would move slightly, or she would awaken to what sounded like the bathroom door closing. She would look, and the door would be closed, but she could never remember if she had closed it herself before going to sleep.

Her best nights were the ones when she woke to Andrew's voice. She could hear him tell her that he loved her, missed her, and wanted to be back there with her. She would awake to these sweet nothings in a haze of bliss, sure that the nightmare was over, only to die inside again when she remembered what happened. She stopped opening her eyes after a while, instead allowing herself to hover in between awake and asleep, listening to his voice. It was harder to hear in these moments, but it was all she had.

When dawn came, she was already awake. She had taken to watching the sunrise through her window. The rays cascaded through the leafy branches and reminded her that life moved on, whether she wanted it to or not. She would look out and think of all the people out there who were just waking up and getting ready to go about their days. For most of those people, there was no tragedy in their lives they were dealing with right now. Life was a routine they were going about. They had no idea how good they really had it. She would look out at them and try to better appreciate their lives for them.

Her moment of peacefulness was ruined when she heard the idiot orderly talking outside of her door to another patient.

"Look, I told you, stop following me," Charlie said.

"But you can help me," pleaded the other voice.

"I can't help you, and you know it."

"You can. Just deliver the message."

"Look, man, you know what year it is. They're all gone. *Gone*, gone. You need to go too. Hanging around here isn't doing anyone any good, and all you're doing is driving me nuts."

It sounded rude to Nora. This guy was just an all-around creep. This other man, whoever he was, needed help, and instead Charlie was giving him excuses and telling him to get lost.

"Where do I go? Where is my Adelaide?" asked the voice pitifully.

"Is there a light?" Charlie asked. "If so, go into it. See if she's there. If not, I don't know." Nora was horrified. What a terrible thing to tell someone!

Seconds later, Charlie pushed into Nora's room and flashed his smile. "Hey there, super-snorer, I have your morning grub. Undercooked eggs and a side of bacon-flavoured grease. *Yum*," he added for emphasis.

"You're a real creep, do you know that?" she said.

"I do," he said. "But you'll have to specify in what area for me. I'm a bit of a renaissance creep. I spread my talents around."

"That poor man in the hall," she said. "Just help him find his family."

The grin on his face faltered, and he looked unsure. "Oh, you heard me, huh?"

"Yes, I did," Nora said. "You want to be a nurse? Learn some compassion. You told that man to go into the light! People come here to get better, not to be encouraged to drop dead."

Charlie began to look sheepish. "You don't have the full picture. Without context, you don't understand. Besides, he was fine with it."

"No, he wasn't," Nora said. Charlie just nodded and put the food tray down and began to busy himself. He had apparently dropped the matter and was going on with his day as though she wasn't there. "Can't you find her?"

At this, he paused in mid-step and looked at her, as though he was only just seeing her for the first time. The smugness and cavalier attitude were gone in a heartbeat. "Find who?" he asked cautiously.

"Adelaide, or whoever," Nora said. She wasn't sure what had just happened, but a change had come over Charlie.

"Where did you hear that name?"

"Like I said, from the man in the hall."

"No," Charlie said. "You only heard me talking. Right?" He seemed to be encouraging her to accept this version of events.

"No," Nora pushed back. "I heard you both talking. I hear everyone in this stupid place. They walk around jabbering twenty-four seven."

His eyes flashed over her, and Nora knew she was being evaluated. He focused on the purple scar beside her eye. "How long have you had that?" he asked.

She reached up self-consciously. "Since my accident," she said.

"How did you get it?"

Before she could answer, Vee spilled into the room with a Tim Hortons bag and a fresh coffee. She squealed at Nora and ran over for a hug. Only then did she turn around and give Charlie an appraising look.

"Who is *this*?" she asked.

"This is a jerk," Nora said.

"Oh, really?" Veronica said. "Nice to meet you, jerk." She then leaned in to Nora and to talk in a whisper clearly meant to be heard. "Are we sure he's a jerk? He's kind of cute."

"He is definitely a jerk," Nora responded.

The Charlie of old seemed to reassert himself, and the serious tone was nowhere to be found. "I am not just a jerk," he said. "I am Sir Jerk of the Ward, and I must take my leave of you. I have jerking to do elsewhere."

Vee laughed out loud. "Good luck with that."

Charlie's eyes widened as he realized his mistake and in attempting to leave he banged into a table and knocked over the empty can of Wild Cherry Pepsi on it. Veronica laughed at him, and even Nora allowed a small grin. "Yes, right," Charlie stammered. "As you were." With that, he went back out of the room.

"Oh, I *like* him," Veronica said playfully. "Dibs."

THAT NIGHT, as always, the voices in the hallway continued. A major difference was that instead of being outside her door, this time one of them came inside.

When the little man with the too-big glasses and comically large bowtie came bustling into her dark room, Nora was sure she must still be sleeping. She felt wide awake and couldn't bring herself out this obvious dream, but it wasn't until he stopped at a chair, concentrated fiercely on it, and then dragged it over to her with a large screech that she knew this was actually happening.

There were elements about it all that suggested maybe she had lost her mind. The man wasn't all there, for one. She meant that literally. It was just the dark playing tricks on her, but parts of him seemed to dissolve and then reform in the gloom. He was pale blue and gave off a pale blue light on top of that. If she stared at one spot it seemed to swirl and reveal transparencies that she could see right through.

It had to be a combination of the light from the street and the darkness in the room. And her head injury, of course. She pinched herself to make sure it wasn't a dream.

"What are you doing in here?" she demanded. "Who are you?"

"Can you get in touch with my Adelaide?" he asked in a high-pitched voice as he blinked at her hopefully. "He won't do it. Can you do it?"

"Who is Adelaide? Who are you?"

"I heard you talk about me. I heard you say her name. Do you know her? You must know her. I told everyone that you can help me. I wish I had some cheese."

"No, I don't know her," Nora said dumbfounded. "And who is everyone? Cheese?"

"You don't seem very smart," he said as he shook his head. "And you make a lot of noise with your mouth. Very unpleasant. Very distracting to people in the hall."

Nora's surprise was fading, and her annoyance was in full gear. "Listen, whoever you are, please get out of my room right now." She was fumbling around in the dark for the call button. The nurses would get this weirdo out of here for sure.

"You can help me," he said. "You can help the others."

"What others?" Nora demanded loudly.

As if it was an invitation, Nora's door flew open and a half dozen more bodies entered the room, all with the same qualities as this little man. They all began to shout questions at her. More voices filled the hallway, and the doorway became crowded. There were shapes beyond all those who were still jockeying to get in. Nora felt like her eyes were going to pop out of her head.

"Lots! But I suppose you can start by helping *him*," the man said.

"Who?" Nora asked.

The little man turned and pointed as another body pushed into her room. She could never forget that face, those eyes, that smile. Her heart fluttered. Andrew opened his mouth to speak.

Then the light snapped on, and a nurse entered the still and empty room. Nora whipped her head back and forth, looking for all of the people who were just there and felt the panic rise in her chest.

"What can I do for you?" the nurse calmly asked.

"What the hell!" Nora yelled. "Where did they all go? Where did all of those people go?"

The nurse looked bewildered as he took in the room a second time. There was no one there. "Where did who go?"

"All the people!" Nora said. "They were in here. Where are all the people in the hall?"

"There's no one here," the nurse said. "It's the middle of the night. Everyone is sleeping."

"No!" insisted Nora. "No one sleeps in this place. People are always walking out there and talking. They were in here! There was a creepy little man in a bowtie harassing me just now!"

The nurse walked over and checked Nora's chart. He gave a little "tsk" and looked softly at Nora. "Do you need some medication to help you sleep?" he asked.

"What?" Nora yelled. "No, I need help!"

"You just had a bad dream," the nurse ventured.

"I didn't have a dream! There were people."

"Well, they aren't here now, miss. I don't know what to tell you."

Nora didn't have a good response to this. She wanted to get the hell out of the place but was still too weak to go. Putting up more of a fight wasn't going to get her anywhere either. No matter what this nurse said, though, she knew that those people had been here. *Andrew* had been here.

"Try to go back to sleep," the nurse said as he left the room. "Do you want me to turn off the light?"

"No!" Nora shouted. "No, please leave it on." The nurse nodded and left the room.

She watched and waited and looked and listened for as long as she could before the need for sleep took her again. The voices in the hallway didn't return that night.

WHILE THE voices might not have come back, that didn't stop tongues from wagging. When Nora's mother entered the next morning, she could tell that the nurses had told her about what happened the night before. All of the statements from Nora's parents that they believed her and supported her were called into serious question the moment it was suggested Nora see a shrink. When she refused, her mother told her in a sad voice that the hospital was demanding it because of concerns for her mental health. It turned out that telling the truth can get you locked up. First the police didn't believe her, then the nurses, and now her own parents. It wasn't fair.

"You all think I'm crazy," Nora said.

"Not crazy, sweetie," her mother said, patting her hand. "Just concerned."

And that was how Nora found herself in Dr. Westlake's office that afternoon. The man was pudgy and clearly under the impression that he weighed twenty pounds less than he did from the way he preened. The room was filled with objects and items that suggested this man thought highly of himself, even if the vision was slightly clouded by reality. He had his degrees framed and placed with care, African masks hung on the wall, obscure pieces of art stood out on bookshelves, and every furniture item was a deep brown mahogany frame with seats covered in taut leather. Books lined the shelves, and a strategically placed picture of his family, or perhaps a solid Photoshop job with the family picture the frame came with, sat on his desk. He kind of reminded her of Patton Oswalt but without a sense of humour.

"I believe that what we are dealing with is a by-product of your accident," he said in a smooth voice. Nora suspected he probably had to practice in front of a mirror to get the volume and tone just right.

"It wasn't an accident," she said acidly. She hated that everyone referred to what happened to her and Andrew as an "accident." "He didn't 'accidentally' get murdered."

"My apologies," he said as he clicked his pen and wrote something down. He clicked it again and looked back at her. "Still, I suspect that there may be a few by-products of... *the event*... that are affecting your mental state."

"You think I'm crazy," she said, translating. "I'm not crazy."

The pen clicked again. "Not at all," he agreed in a way that meant he really didn't. "But the brain is an incredible organ that we rely on for everything. It's how we see, smell, taste, think, and feel. Our body carries out the directives from the brain. But in many cases involving some sort of injury or trauma, it's not uncommon for the brain to shape our awareness or perception of things in order to help us cope with reality."

"That sounds like you're saying I'm crazy."

Click. "Think of it this way. A soldier goes into combat prepared to fight for home and country. What that soldier sees and experiences is vastly different from what they expected. Movies and television show us one version of the world, but real life shows us another. I call it the *American Idol* effect. When you watched people on that show, most of them arrived thinking they deserved fame because they could imagine it. When others, especially the judges, didn't share that viewpoint the contestant was bewildered, frustrated, angry, and confused. 'How can they not see what I see?' they asked, and yet almost every single viewer at home was asking the contestant 'how can you believe what it is you're saying?' It made for engaging but heartbreaking television."

"I'm not deluded. I know what I saw," Nora insisted.

"And I believe you are being sincere," Dr. Westlake said, leaning back. The leather made a slight squeaking sound. "But is there a possibility that what you're experiencing is not actual reality? You must admit there's a chance."

Nora seethed. No matter how nicely you put it, this quack was suggesting she had gone crazy. Arguing the point, however, was a risky proposition. Things had gone south with the media, the police were watching her every move, and even her parents didn't believe her. At the shrink stage, fighting meant the possibility of getting put up in some place for kids who had gone loco. Wisely, she held her tongue.

The pen clicked in the silence. "Based on what I've been told from all the parties involved," (traitors, more like it) "I'm going to offer a preliminary diagnosis of paramnesia."

"That sounds like you're saying I have cheese."

"Clever," Dr. Westlake said blandly. "Very funny." The lack of laughter and the click of the pen suggested he didn't actually find it amusing.

"Paramnesia," he continued, "is a real but rare condition. Since you have reported that your… events… happened either late at night or close to points when you have woken up or are about to fall asleep, paramnesia seems plausible. It is a disorder of the memory or the faculty of recognition in which dreams may be confused with reality. Most people experience this in minor bouts on a regular basis. You might wake up, and a dream has been so vivid that you confuse it with a memory. My wife was once angry with me for a whole day after having a dream that I was cheating on her. I had done nothing wrong but still had to sleep on the couch."

Nora felt her resolve fade just a little. For the first time, doubt began to creep into her mind. Despite the fact that the man was a quack, he was right about a couple of points. She had no clear, lasting memory of what happened with her and Andrew. A hardcore concussion muddied her thoughts and perception. The voices were louder at night and in the dark. Could it be true? Was she just a little bit crazy?

"Okay?" Dr. Westlake asked, sensing a potential victory. He continued to talk about medications and regular consultations, but it was all background noise to Nora's own doubts and fears. She nodded glumly and sat back as he paged for an orderly to take her back to her room.

She was still so caught up in her thoughts that she didn't notice when the orderly who arrived was Charlie. He simply helped her into the wheelchair and pushed her out of the room and toward the elevator.

"You're not crazy, you know," he said quietly as they rode up to the eighth floor and her room.

"Huh?" she asked. "What do you know about it? Just shut up."

"I know because I know," he answered.

"You know what?"

"I know things," he said. He pulled up his sleeve and showed her a raised purple welt in the middle of his forearm with two long trails reaching out of it: one toward his wrist and the other toward his elbow. "You aren't crazy."

Before she could ask him what he meant, the door opened and her whole family was waiting in the hallway. Her mother had Nora's bag packed, and her dad had a big grin plastered on his face.

"Time to come home, sweetheart," he said.

Nora turned to look back at Charlie, but she only caught a glimpse of him as the elevator door shut.

CHAPTER 7

O h, it was painful. More than that, it was excruciating. Every bone felt brittle. Her blood felt like it was on fire. Her skin felt as though it had been torn off her body and then sewn back on. It was what she deserved, but she still howled, screamed, and cursed at her tormentors endlessly.

She thought she knew what punishment was when they forbade her from eating for the year. How smug and clever she had felt when she grabbed a snack or two in the month before her time was up. How delighted she was that it was so easy on her first night of freedom to eat and sup in secret. How arrogant the Revenant had been, and now the bill for that arrogance was due.

She had been so careless in the woods. If she had been at the top of her game, there was no way she would have allowed herself to be caught off guard like that. By a drunk human, no less! Then, foolishly, she looked back into the window and knew her true face had been seen. It didn't matter how much or how little the boy inside actually understood, because it was forbidden ever to be seen. Even if no one would believe him, and in history no one ever had, to be seen was the greatest taboo of them all. It was not tolerated. If the witness was not caught in time, there was no telling what the fallout damage might be. There was no escaping the consequences of being seen for either party. One must die, the other must be punished or killed as well.

The Others made it clear: *you were not to be seen.*

Luckily for their ilk, history was full of fantastic and silly accounts of supernatural beings, along with a shocking lack of proof. People were extremely interested in the stories; they were great around a campfire, but heaven help you if you claimed to witness something directly. Witnesses were shamed, subject to treatments, were harassed, or killed outright for colluding with the devil. It was a dangerous thing to peek behind the veil and then speak about what you supposedly saw. These sorts of people were relegated to the *Weekly World News* or other tabloids that mocked people who spoke up. It did help that a lot of the stories in those rags were actually made up, but every now and then one of them was actually true. All of the noise around the supernatural made hiding the truth all that much easier. Still, truth or not, speak and the real monsters would come for you in the end. And if they didn't, then chances were the person's own family would.

There were stories of vampires, ghosts, werewolves, sasquatch, wendigo, aliens, or other such creatures in cultures all over the world. There was no proof of any of them other than blurred or doctored photos. The first fakes had been put up by The Others themselves on the Internet as soon as they were capable doing so. They disseminated lies and mistruths amongst the population. They were the first to point fingers at witnesses and suggest they were liars, frauds, or insane. It spoke ill of humanity that they were all too willing to believe the worst of themselves or others. It seemed as though they only believed in possibilities in fiction, and even then they either glorified it or put it on a pedestal. Get someone like Joss Whedon or JJ Abrams to cover things up for you, albeit unwittingly. Call Sam and Dean and put them on the case. Where was John Constantine when you needed him? Get Rick Grimes to clean up your mess.

And this was a mess.

Humanity was made up of fools, to be sure, but a fool had seen her, and the laws of her kind demanded a response. The girl had to go as well. Who knew what the boy had told her. What a disaster.

The pain was exquisite now. Stars flashed behind her eyes, and her body shook uncontrollably. While deserved, the Revenant's punishment had been more severe than it was for others like her. For one, it was the second year in a row that she had been caught. For another, she was in the process of cleaning up one mistake, only to commit another, bigger mistake. The boy who had seen her was dead, and they were pleased, but she had revealed herself to the girl in the process, and she was still very much alive.

And she was talking to anyone who would listen. It was what had, ironically, saved her life, as The Others had not wanted to send another to claim her. To have her die so quickly would be to cast suspicion upon them. It wasn't to say that she would be spared — that was a step too far, but enough time must pass so that it didn't gather undue attention. When it did happen, it must happen smoothly and without incident. A tragic coincidence, perhaps. A sad twist of fate.

They watched the news coverage with dread and fury at first as the girl talked and talked. The Others took their anger out on their captive. The Revenant was tortured around the clock, only to be healed before having the cycle begin anew. She was their unwilling Prometheus. The Greek God had been chained to a rock for giving fire and knowledge to mankind to help them. The Revenant was chained for giving knowledge as well, and they would see to it that she existed as long as Prometheus was still a name known to humans so that she would understand the severity of her folly.

Then the tone of the media coverage shifted. There were questions raised about the night the boy died. Others suggested that the girl was not in her right mind. Late-night talk show hosts like Fallon and Kimmel began to make jokes. Soon, it all faded to noise. The torture eased at that point before it finally stopped. The anger spent, she was allowed to wallow in her pain and misery. The fear of discovery passed, and new judgments and assessments were made about the future of the Revenant.

The final decision came when the media announced the girl was being released from the hospital. It was almost a trivial bit of news and one of the last stories presented at that, buried at a time when most viewers had already switched off their televisions or clicked away to another website. More quickly than expected, the girl had been tossed aside as a nothing kind of story. None of the Others were eager to risk exposure when the damage had been done, but still, she was a witness and none must live to continue to tell the tales.

And so…

Who would take care of this for them?

With some hesitation, only then did the Others decide to release the Revenant. She was to be sent back to clean up her mess and resume her job. Before they had taken her, the Revenant had put in a request for a leave of absence at her cover job as a paramedic, so no one would be surprised to see her come back or wonder too much at where she had been. At least the Revenant had been smart enough to use a stolen truck to do the assault, rather than her own vehicle. She had made it back to her ambulance in enough time to get the call that went out asking for assistance. She had laughed at that, and it was the last laugh she'd had since. Her speed and forethought had at least spared her from suspicion. It was the only reason she was still alive and being given yet another chance. She had no doubt what a third failure would mean.

The news mentioned the girl was still getting treatment, so it was likely the Revenant would have a convenient excuse to come in contact with her. That was another stone cast in her favour. It was a mess, but at least she had the right equipment to clean up after herself.

The chain around her neck was shattered, and she was brought beaten and bloody into the dark spaces the Others dwelled in. It was called the Margins, and it was there she healed and recovered. She was not given anything for the pain. She screamed as each bone reset itself and settled. She moaned as her cuts stitched themselves together with needles made of ice and fire. She vomited up the poisons she had been made to ingest. She listened to the darkness and could hear the scurrying of creatures, Groundlings and worse, that watched and enjoyed her discomfort.

Her assignment was her last chance to redeem herself, though she honestly wasn't sure what she wanted to do. She was insane with pain at the moment and would have lashed out at anyone she came in contact with. She was not so wild, though, that she forgot what they could do to her or what they would do to her if she failed. She had to succeed and hope they would let her go about the business of invisibility once again. She had to earn her freedom.

Perhaps there was a way, once she was released, to finish the job she had started but also to ensure that she could not be caught and contained like this again. She would not allow herself to be subjected to torture and cruelty at their hands. No, this was the last time she bowed to what they wanted her to do. One last job, and then she'd be free to do as she pleased, and there were many things she could think of that were pleasing.

As she healed in the Margins, the Others in the darkness disappointedly wondered why her screams had suddenly stopped.

The Revenant was too busy plotting to notice any pain.

CHAPTER 8

Nora heard her voice being called gently in the night and worked it into her dream. She was at a cottage her family sometimes rented in Crystal Beach. She and her brother were out in the shallow water that seemed to stretch forever. Tom was busy hopping up and down and then flopping down onto his bum in the water, which made Nora laugh in delight each time. It had to hurt, as the water was only a foot and a half deep, but Tom dutifully got up and did it again at her insistence. They must have played like that for hours.

There it was again. Her name. Her father calling them from the water to the beach. He was holding open a big towel and getting ready to wrap her up in it. He would delight in this as much as she would. It was a ritual between them. She loved the sound of his voice.

A voice, a third time, more distinct. Now she wasn't so sure it was part of the dream. Tom glanced over his shoulder back at her as he headed back to shore, and he smiled as he held up a small shell he had collected. She reached out for him, but the space grew farther and farther apart.

Her name was called a fourth time. She woke up in a daze in her own bed for the first time in nearly a month, and there was a tear in her eye. The curtains floated lazily in the moonlit window thanks to an unseen summer breeze. It was quiet in her house to the point of being deafening. She had gotten used to the noise and thrum of the hospital. She sighed and rolled over, determined to get comfortable and go back to that perfect beach. She was bone-tired and ready for the rest.

Then she heard her name for a fifth time, and her eyes opened into the dark room. It was the same sound from her dream, and she wondered if she was still sleeping. "Hello?" she whispered, more to herself than anything.

"Hi, Nora Angel," Andrew replied as the darkness receded and his pale blue glow began to fill up the room. She knew that voice and that face. She had seen it in her mind a thousand times. Unbidden, tears came to her eyes, in direct contrast to the small smile on her lips. She *was* crazy, she knew now. She was hearing voices and seeing things. The quack had been right, and now she was crazy. She was ashamed that she was grateful to be crazy, because it meant she could still be near him.

"Hi, Andrew," she said with a sob. "I miss you."

"I miss you, too," Andrew said.

"I think I'm going crazy," Nora said as she wiped a tear.

"Nah, you aren't crazy," Andrew said. "But you do snore a lot."

Nora perked up a little at the insult. It was just like her to be crazy and self-deprecating at the same time. If she was going to be nuts, however, she was determined that it be on her terms.

"No, I don't," she insisted. "Go back to being nice."

The rude voice laughed at her instead. "Sure, you do. But I don't mind. It was my favourite part of being next to you that night. To watch you sleeping. You're the girl I fell for, snoring and all. I was enjoying watching you sleep just now."

"You're making fun of me."

"I promise I'm not."

She reached out to touch him, and he smiled sadly at her. Just as her hand was about to caress his face, it fell through, and small tendrils of his essence floated and swirled about her hand like bubbles in a pond. "It's not fair," she said as her voice caught in her throat.

"I know, Angel."

"Why did you leave me?"

"I didn't want to. I didn't mean to. I fought with everything I could to stay with you. I think it's why I'm still here."

"Why didn't it take me, too? Then we could be together."

"No, don't say that," Andrew said, suddenly serious. "Don't even think that. Besides, I'm here with you now."

"But I can't even touch you. I need to touch you. I need to hold you. I need to kiss you."

"I know, Angel. I want those things, too."

"I must be crazy," Nora insisted.

"Why?"

"The nurse," Nora said. "She couldn't see anything. The lights came on, and there was nothing there. But now you're here."

"You aren't crazy," Andrew said reassuringly.

"Then why couldn't she see you?"

"I don't know," Andrew admitted. "So far, you're the only person who I've been able to talk to. Well, the only one who's still alive, anyway."

"What does that mean? How many are there?" This waking dream was getting strange and off-topic. She didn't like it. She tried to fight off the grogginess of sleep.

"More than I ever imagined, to be honest," Andrew said. "But enough about that. I don't know what kind of time we have here, so let's use it to be together. Move over," he said indicating the bed.

She obeyed and made room and watched as Andrew gingerly arranged himself so he was lying next to her. She tried to put her arm around him and pull him tight, but all she saw was dust swirling in the moonlight.

"I miss you so much," she said, her eyes starting to close.

"I miss you too, Angel," Andrew replied. He looked at her and smiled. "Now hush, baby. Get some rest. I'll still be here tomorrow."

"I don't ever want to sleep again," Nora mumbled.

"Hey, don't knock sleep. It's the thing that I miss most, next to you. And cheeseburgers."

She laughed, yawned, and pulled the blankets tight around herself. "No, I think I'll stay awake all night and just look at you. No sleep for me."

Sleep came regardless, and it was the first night in ages that she didn't snore.

WHEN NORA woke the next morning, she rolled over to look at Andrew, only to find her bed empty and the boy gone. It had been nothing more than a dream after all ... a side effect of the paramnesia diagnosis that Dr. Westlake had given her. So be it. It was a small price to pay to be able to see Andrew again. There were worse ways her mind could cope with the loss she was still feeling.

Besides, all of her episodes happened at night when she was alone. No one else was around to bother her or to contradict her. What she experienced last night was like a waking dream, and no one was usually harassed because of what their imaginations conjured up. She could live with the paramnesia. Today, for instance, was the first time she had woken up since the accident and not felt like crying herself right back to sleep. So what if dreams and reality were hanging out and having lunch? It was working just fine for her right now.

So much so that even though she had resisted her mother's suggestion she go back to school, despite the fact that there were less than two weeks left, Nora decided to go. She texted Vee and asked her to pick her up and then shuffled off to the bathroom.

She checked the bags under her eyes and judged them not terrible considering she hadn't slept much the night before. She considered putting some foundation on the purple scar by her right eye, which was as vivid now as the day she got it. After a moment's consideration, she decided to leave it. Whenever she saw it, she remembered Andrew. Rather than hide the mark, she would own it. The rest of her was up for debate, however. Her hair was a mess of tangles that matched her scrunched-up pajamas and the redness on her cheeks. Hopefully when Vee got there she could work a little magic so that Nora didn't look as dead as she felt.

Yawning, Nora dropped her pants, sat down on the toilet, and propped up her chin with her hand. It was going to be an exhausting day, no matter what she did. It was her first day back, so people at school would stare, no doubt, but she would have to endure that sooner or later, so best to get it over with. Vee would shelter her, anyway, and probably wrangle Kia and Kapalini to run interference. It could be worse. She relaxed and started to pee.

"Hi, Nora Angel!" Andrew said merrily as he phased through the door.

"OH MY GOD!" Nora shrieked. An extra-loud splash of water could be heard beneath her as she scrambled backward, away from the ghost that had just appeared in front of her. She slipped one foot into the toilet and pulled the shower curtain off the rod in a desperate attempt to find something to cover herself with before toppling over and falling into the bathtub.

Then she screamed.

Andrew, alarmed, tried to calm her down and was trying to get her to shush. "What are you doing? Calm down!" he yelled, but Nora just kept screaming. Outside the door, Rorschach started to bark and paw to be let in.

"Nora?" came her mother's worried voice from downstairs. "Are you okay? Nora! Answer me!"

"What is going on?" Nora asked her hallucination in a panic. "I've lost it!"

"What are you doing?" Andrew asked again. "Why are you freaking out?"

"Nora?" called her mother again, the panic rising to a fever pitch.

"Answer her!" Andrew said.

"Guh, bah, huh?" Nora replied.

"NORA!" came her mother's voice, this time from the other side of the door.

Andrew put his finger to his lips and then gestured for Nora to say something to her mother. Warily, Nora turned her head toward the door without letting her eyes leave Andrew's face. "I'm fine, Mom," she called out. "Um, I saw a spider?"

"*Oh, for...*" she heard her mother mutter under her breath. "You scared me half to death!"

"Sorry?" Nora said.

"Why is everything a question? Are you okay?"

"I'm fine, Mom. Sorry. I'm just getting ready for school."

Her mother softened instantly, but Rorschach kept barking. "You're going? Okay. I mean, good. Great! Can I make you some breakfast? *Rorschach, hush!*"

"Um, just some Cheerios, thanks."

"Okay, sweetie! Rorschach, come!" The dog sniffed under the door a couple more times before it padded off down the stairs after Nora's mom.

Meanwhile, Nora's eyes had yet to leave Andrew's face. "How are you here?"

"Didn't we go over that last night? We talked for quite a while."

"Yeah, but I was crazy last night. I have a condition."

"I told you that you weren't crazy."

"But I am. I'm talking to a ghost while my foot is in a toilet."

"Yeah, you might want to flush that," Andrew said, nodding toward the contents. Embarrassed, Nora scrambled to her feet and flushed the toilet. Then she turned on the shower and started to wash off her legs and feet. "Cute, by the way."

"You aren't here," she said.

"Why are you having such a hard time with this?"

"Because you're dead!" she yelled. She shot a look toward the door, fearing her mother had heard her. When there was nothing on the other side, she looked back to Andrew and dropped her voice. "Because you're dead," she repeated in a near-whisper. "And I'm not Haley Joel Osment."

"Why didn't you freak out about this last night?"

"Because I was asleep! Or I thought I was. Or I have paramnesia."

"Isn't that a kind of cheese?"

"No!" she snapped. "Clearly, you are ignorant about mental health conditions. That's a very insensitive comment."

"Sorry!"

"Apology *not* accepted!" she said. "At night, I'm crazy. That's what the doctor said. But I am awake and you are here and this is not normal and not all right and you are still cute but dead and I have pee on me and I need to go to school goodbye."

Nora really wanted to storm dramatically out of the room, but Andrew was in the way. Finally, deciding that if she really was crazy there was nothing really blocking her, she ploughed forward and sent his essence scattering into a fine mist.

"Listen…" he began as he reassembled himself in her room.

"There is nothing to listen to. You aren't here. I can't hear you."

"Then why did you answer me?" he said smugly.

"I didn't," she said, then cursed herself for replying. "I'm not going to. Not anymore. You aren't here. You don't exist. You died."

"Only one of those is accurate," Andrew said. "You can't ignore me forever, Angel!"

But she tried anyway. She got dressed and did her best to look past him or away from him with whatever she was doing. She got dressed and at first tried to cover herself up before she remembered he didn't exist. She took off her shirt with a flourish and then decided that even if he didn't exist, she was really modest at heart, so she went behind her screen to change anyway. Downstairs, she walked through him to get the milk out of the fridge and added it to the bowl on the counter. Rorschach, however, was a traitor in her cause, because he barked at Andrew wherever he went. Nora decided that Rorschach was just seeing a mouse. A very tall, cute mouse.

Stop that! There's no one there.

When Vee showed up, it was clear that she was expecting a frail, emotionally crippled Nora to shepherd to the school. She had on her solemn, considerate face that she often had after visiting the senior's home. Vee was shocked when she barely had time to step out of her car before Nora came barrelling out of her house and down the steps toward her. Vee kept trying to change her expression to try to match whatever vibe it was that Nora was giving off.

"Hi, Vee!" she said in a too-cheery voice. "Let's go!" Then she opened the car door, got in, and closed it behind her. At the door, Rorschach was still barking his fool head off at that giant mouse.

"Hey, Norie," Vee said in an overly sympathetic voice as she got in the car. "How are...?"

"Let's go!" Nora said, too chipper.

"Okay, babe, relax," Vee said as she backed out of the driveway and they headed off for school.

Nora kept checking back over her shoulder. She could see Rorschach, still barking but muted at Andrew, who was standing on the porch. Tom came out a second later, shooing away the dog, and then he walked right through Andrew and sent his form scattering.

Andrew didn't re-form. Only then did Nora turn around and start to relax. Veronica got her caught up on the things happening at school and beyond that she had missed. It started out with a lament about Peter Tieri, whom she said was great the night of the prom but had wanted more of a relationship than her busy schedule at school combined with all of her extra curriculars allowed for. Since then, Peter had started dating Kia, and now they were a thing. Nora could tell that it stung Vee even though she had been the one to call it off. As a result of the awkwardness of the new relationship, she wasn't really speaking to either Kia or Peter. She didn't know what to say, but knew eventually she'd have to talk about it or lose a couple of good friends. She sighed loudly and then leaned forward to flip on the radio. It was a Radiohead song called "Give Up the Ghost." It was a little too on the nose so Nora reached out to change the stations.

"No, don't!" Andrew said from the back seat. "I love this song!"

Nora screamed, and Vee jerked the wheel up onto a curb. She got control again quickly and went back out into the street. "What the hell, Nora?" Vee yelled. "Are you okay? What is your problem?"

"Yeah, what's your problem?" Andrew echoed. "This is a great song! It's kind of ironic now, but that makes it cool."

"It's not cool!" Nora yelled at the back seat before turning to Vee. "I mean, that wasn't cool of me. Sorry. I saw a spider?"

"Good one," Andrew said. "Nice cover."

"A spider?" Vee asked incredulously. "Where?"

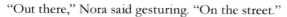

"Out there," Nora said gesturing. "On the street."

"Okay, terrible cover," Andrew said.

"Seriously? How big was it?" Veronica asked. Nora was pleased that Vee could sometimes be a bit dim.

"Huge," Nora said. "Really big. Annoying, too."

"That hurts," Andrew said.

"It's gone now," Nora said. "Went away. As in it will stop bothering me. *Us.*"

Andrew rolled his eyes from the back seat. Veronica looked appraisingly at her friend. "Are you okay, babe? You seem kinda crazy."

"More than you know," Nora replied quietly to herself.

Walking the hallway, Nora got all the stares and whispers she expected to receive, much of it directed toward the strange purple mark by her eye, but she was too distracted to pay it any attention. Andrew walked beside her, ghosting through anyone and everyone in his path, all the while talking to her about nothing.

"I forgot to hand in my culminating to Mr. Tufford," he was saying. "Think I'll still get the credit?"

It was so asinine! Here he was, a dead figment of her imagination, and talking about schoolwork. "Shut up," she hissed at him.

Vee, walking on the other side of Nora, thought she was talking about the kids in the hallway. "Just ignore it," she said. "Let them look, and then they'll go away."

"Ignore it," Andrew agreed. "Easy to do, right?" Then he stood in front of her and forced her to walk right through him. The shower of blue mist forced her to shiver a little, and she was mad at herself for giving in to the illusion. As hard as Andrew was to ignore, however, she was more alarmed by the fact that she kept seeing other forms and figures out of the corner of her eye that shared Andrew's ghostly hue.

"Please, Nora Angel," he pleaded in frustration. "Just talk to me!"

"Bathroom?" Vee asked her and pointed to Kapalini, who waved eagerly from the doorway.

"Can't," she said gruffly, answering them both. "Time for class."

All of her energy was spent that morning ignoring Andrew while trying not to upset Veronica. She mixed the wrong chemicals in chem class because Andrew was waving his hands over the labels so she couldn't read them. She couldn't listen to Shakespeare in English because he kept performing, badly, at the front of the room. Finally, during the SCC meeting, she begged Elrick to let her go to the bathroom just so she could get a moment of peace. Andrew and Vee both stood up to go with her.

"No!" she yelled. "You stay here. I need to go alone."

"Okay," Vee said, clearly embarrassed. "Whatever."

"Sorry, I, uh," Nora said, trying to find a smooth transition out of the room, "I have to go poo."

"Gross!" Kapalini said.

Elrick closed his eyes and rubbed the bridge of his nose. "If only I had quit yesterday," he mumbled. "Just go, please."

In the hallway, Nora was relieved to see that neither of them had followed and that she had a rare moment of peace. On her way to the bathroom, she passed the Hall of Heroes, and her breath caught when she saw the latest photo that had been added to the wall.

It was Andrew, full of life and smiling that gorgeous smile of his. She recognized the picture, of course. She took it during one of the brief times they shared together. They had gone out to Guelph Lake to sit by the beach during Hillside, an annual music festival. He brought a blanket and a picnic basket and set it up under a tree. He leaned back, looking so at peace, and smiled at her. She pulled out her phone and snapped the pic, making it her lock screen and wallpaper at home as well. It was a perfect moment, she said, and she wanted to capture it forever.

And now here he was, on this board in a hallway in a school he barely went to. Few kids had even had the chance to get to know him. In a few years he would just be another name, another legend, to the kids who passed by. Maybe he'd become a ghost walking the halls. Maybe they'd even make up another name for him.

"Nice picture," a guy said beside her.

"Yeah," she said. "From happier times."

"Did you know him?"

"He was mine," she said sweetly. "For a time."

"You're a romantic. I like that. Of course, I like just about anything these days. Especially people who actually talk to me."

"Why wouldn't anyone talk to you?" she asked, turning to look at the stranger.

What she saw, or didn't see, was a blue-hued form of a teenaged boy, seventeen or so, with a shaved head and muscles poking out from under the sleeves of a t-shirt. He faded in and out, just as Andrew did.

"You're the first person to talk back to me," he said with a grin. "You know, since I died. I'm Reno. Do you like *Star Wars?*"

She screamed and startled a girl down the hallway who was studying at the foot of her locker. A couple of classroom doors opened, and irritated teachers stuck their heads out to see what was going on. She quickly backed away from the ghost boy and ran down the hallway, away from him and everything else. She turned a corner and ran right through two other ghosts. When she apologized to them, they looked at her in wonder and started to follow. She ran farther down the hallway, and when she saw they were still coming, she grabbed the handle on the first door she found and let herself in, while slamming the door behind her.

"Can I help you, miss?" a woman demanded angrily.

"I'm sorry," Nora began before looking up at the ghostly form of the librarian who was standing in the middle of the Heritage Room. Through the door at the back, the form of a janitor materialized as he walked in to see what was going on.

Nora screamed again and ran back out of the room. Reno and the two ghosts from the hallway were waiting for her, so she ran off again. Every twist and turn revealed more ghosts until she was herded toward the middle of the school and the nature classroom that had been set up there. All of the commotion had staff and students leaving their rooms to see what was going on, and all they could do is stare in wonder as Nora ran up and down the hallway, yelling at things to go away and leave her alone.

Finally, backed up against a tree, the crowd of dead and living alike stood watching her with a kind of fascination. Andrew and Vee pushed their way to the front and stood looking at her with a mixture of pity and horror.

"Good job ignoring it," Andrew said wryly. "I think you can safely say you flew under the radar."

CHAPTER 9

Nora tapped her foot impatiently as she waited for Dr. Westlake to be free to see her. After the incident at the school, both the guidance staff and her parents thought that a regular visit to the shrink was a good idea. The worst part of the whole incident was the way that everyone just stared at her like she was some sort of wounded animal. One girl in the back chimed in that she "called it." That loser even sounded proud of herself. Who takes pride in trying to predict someone else's downfall?

Nora couldn't really blame any of them for being concerned. Hell, *she* was concerned. Seeing and hearing things at night was one thing, but since that day in school the floodgates had opened, and now she saw things all over the place. Even her brother, who had driven her to the hospital this morning, gave up trying to make small talk and was actually being nice to her. That was really weird. During the drive, she made the mistake of looking out the window at a traffic stop and saw a lot of misty blue people wandering around. Once they realized she could see them, a few pointed at her and started to approach. Before they could get to the car, Tom was off again. After that incident, she kept her eyes on her feet.

Sitting in the hospital wasn't much better. The place "skeezed" Tom out, so he decided to go grab a sandwich while she waited for Dr. Westlake to be free. That didn't mean she was alone, though. The little ghost man with the big glasses and bowtie who had first shown up in her hospital room lit up when he saw her come in and was now sitting on the bench beside her, chattering nonstop.

"Did you find Adelaide?" he asked for the thousandth time. "She hasn't come to visit me in a while. Sometimes she gets confused. Boy! She can be funny sometimes. I'm trying to look my best so that when she sees me she'll be reminded of me when we first dated. I was quite the looker!"

Nora didn't respond.

"Oh, yes," the man responded to some unheard question. "I had to push the ladies off. They liked my bowtie. Do you like it? I wear it all the time. I tried to take it off once, but it wouldn't come free. It's stuck with me. But Adelaide likes it, so that's a good thing. Say, have you seen her?"

Nora didn't respond.

"She likes flowers, my Adelaide. Not just any flowers, though, but orchids. Very expensive tastes, she has. It's what won her over, mind you. Just some flowers from me to her, and that was that! Why, she even would send me flowers sometimes when I was in here! I haven't gotten them in a while, though. Have you seen my Adelaide? She might have been carrying flowers."

Nora was about to snap at the oblivious ghost when he suddenly went very quiet. His eyes were fixed on the far entrance to the emergency ward. Nora could see the lights of an approaching ambulance flickering through the doorway but not what was causing the ghost's discomfort.

"What is it?" she asked.

He didn't answer. Instead, he shuffled his little butt forward and hopped off the bench. He glanced again toward the entrance and gave a start. Nora followed his gaze but could only see the back of an EMT who was helping pull a man out of the back of the vehicle. She looked back to the little man, but he was already trundling down the hall.

When she looked back to the entrance, the EMT, a young woman, was staring directly at her and ignoring the patient under her care. There was something off about her face, Nora thought, but it was hard to tell at this distance. Just when she thought she could focus on some sort of detail, it all became blurred and murky again. In the back of her brain an alarm bell sounded quietly, but for what reason, she couldn't say. Her Spidey sense was tingling, but with every nerve already frayed and on edge, she wasn't going to label it as something more than it was. The receptionist spoke up from her desk and shook Nora from her reverie.

"Ms. Edwards?" asked the receptionist. "Dr. Westlake is ready for you now."

Before she followed the receptionist, Nora strained to look back toward the EMT. Though the lights were still flickering, the woman was gone. Nora decided to throw the encounter in the overflowing box labelled "crazy" and call it a day.

As she entered Dr. Westlake's office, Nora began to ask him questions before he even had time to greet her. "Can I get some medication? I need some."

Maddeningly, he ignored her question and went to the pleasantries. "Hello, Nora," he said evenly. "How are you feeling?"

"Not good, obviously," she said impatiently. "The meds?"

"Why do you want medication? What's the problem?"

Nora was about to answer and then considered what it was she was going to say. Admitting that you were seeing things was usually a ticket to the looney bin, but not admitting that you were seeing things meant you weren't going to get the meds to make it stop. "I'm having trouble at night," she said.

"Oh?" he said as he clicked his damn pen. "What sort of trouble? Please. Sit."

"Well, you know," Nora said hesitantly as she plopped down in a chair opposite him. "Paramnesia kind of trouble."

"Ah," he said. "Is that what led to the incident at the school?"

"What? No. I was just tired. I couldn't sleep, and there were people staring."

"Then why were you shouting at invisible people to get away from you?"

She was annoyed at this. People should mind their own business. Whoever ratted her out to this guy would get an earful later. "They weren't invisible. I just wanted kids, you know, and teachers to go away."

"You were alone in the hall when it started."

"No, I wasn't. There was a kid. He ran away when I yelled at him." It was kind of true. Reno, the ghost of the teen she met, had his form buffeted all over the place when people came to stare. It was kind of like he ran away.

"Okay," Dr. Westlake said.

"Okay?" Nora echoed, surprised.

"Sure," he said. He put down the pen and notebook and looked at her. "Listen, Nora, I'm not here to judge you or make you feel bad about yourself. You've been through a lot, and it's going to take time to get over everything that's happened to you. Heck, you might never get over it.

"You look surprised to hear me say that. Well, it's true. Parents who have lost a child never really recover from that loss. Husbands who lose wives tend to die earlier than wives who lose husbands. The reason for that is that women are much better at building a community around themselves for love and support. Having supports doesn't take the pain away, but it can help to manage it.

"Right now, your brain is trying to manage the pain, but perhaps you aren't getting the support you need, or you aren't accepting the support that's being offered to you. Were people at the school actually bothering you?"

Nora considered this. She assumed a lot was going on, but truthfully, most people either kept their distance or were really nice to her. She had been kind of rude to Kia and Kapalini and probably took Vee for granted. "No, I guess not," she said. Instinctively, her hand moved to the scar by her eye.

"And don't worry about that, either," Dr. Westlake said. "It's a mark that doesn't define you. Actually, I think it kind of makes you different. Memorable in a positive way."

"What about the medication?" she asked. "To help me sleep or not have those dream-things."

"Well, that's something we can talk about," he said. The brief bout of humanity he showed her seemed to have taxed him. The pen and paper were back in his hand, and he was writing furiously to make up for lost time. "But not right now. I think what you need is just good old-fashioned sleep."

"And that will cure me?"

"I don't think you need to be cured. I think you're just fine. You need time."

Nora sat back and sighed deeply. She wanted to believe what he was saying, but so much had happened in so little time. Whatever she was, she wasn't fine. But maybe Dr. Westlake was right. Maybe with time, she would be.

"Okay," she said.

"Good!" Dr. Westlake said and dropped the pad. He stood up, which Nora took as a cue that their session was over.

As he walked to the door, two forms suddenly flowed through it and were in the middle of a heated argument.

"She's fine!" Reno said. "Just give her some space, dude. You don't need to haunt her."

"She's not fine," Andrew snapped back. "You saw her! Everyone saw her!"

Nora felt the colour flow out of her face, and Dr. Westlake frowned when she suddenly stopped midstride. "What's wrong?" he asked.

"Yeah, Nora Angel, what's wrong?" Andrew asked, full of concern. Nora flushed. It was always amazing to see him, but she was torn right now between talking and being committed by the doctor staring intently at her.

Reno rolled his eyes and with half of his face being transparent, the effect was a little disorienting. "My god, you are cheesy. Nothing's wrong! Just ease up!"

"Nothing, Doctor," Nora repeated. She turned and forced a smile that she was sure either made her look crazy or evil. "Are you sure about the medication?"

"Medication?" Andrew asked. "What medication?"

"None of your business," Reno said.

"I'm sure," Dr. Westlake said, but he didn't sound sure at all.

Out in the hallway, Nora quickened her pace as she tried to get away from both Andrew and Reno. They followed relentlessly, since apparently ghosts don't get tired or take hints. They argued and bickered with each other. Desperate to get away, Nora called out for an orderly to hold the elevator for her, and she ducked inside before either Reno or Andrew could follow. She exhaled in relief as the elevator its slow climb.

"Rough day?" Charlie asked behind her.

Nora actually yelped when he spoke and cursed her stupid luck. She had just gotten away from two problems, only to wind up with a third. This one, at least, she was reasonably sure was alive.

"Sorry," Charlie said. "Didn't mean to scare you."

"You didn't scare me," Nora lied.

"If you say so," Charlie said. An uncomfortable silence followed. "Besides," he ventured, "I figured you'd be done with scares by now."

Nora dreaded asking the question for fear of what the answer would be. "Why wouldn't I be scared?"

"Well, all the dead people," he said nonchalantly, as if he were talking about the weather. "Once you've seen 'em and get used to them being all over the place, it kind of takes the edge off of the dark, you know what I mean?"

Nora closed her eyes and started counting to ten in her head to slow her beating heart. This was not what she needed to hear, and even if it were true, this was not the person she wanted to be hearing it from. Why, in all the world, did the one person who might know what was going on with her have to be such a pain in the ass?

"Why do you have to be such a pain in the ass?" she asked.

He laughed. Nora turned around to look at him questioningly.

"Maybe it's my gift," he said. "In addition to the Vision."

"Vision?" she asked. "What, like twenty-twenty eyesight or that dopey blue eye colour you have?"

"It's not dopey, it's amazing," Charlie said, winking at her. "Very popular with the ladies." Nora fought a mental gag reflex. "And it's 'Vision' with a capital 'V.' At least that's what Graves calls it."

Great, Nora thought. *This guy gives the kinds of answers that only lead to more questions.* Rather than get him off-track, she opted for a single-word question that ideally would lead to clarity. "Explain," she said.

"I hardly understand it myself," he said with a shrug. "All I know is that your ink, that scar by your eye and this mark on my arm, are what let us see them. That's what Graves thinks, anyway. He found me after I got my mark and gave me the dime tour."

Nora rubbed her eye and stared at the sleeve covering Charlie's arm. "How long?" she asked. "How long have you had it? Will it go away?"

The elevator door dinged and opened, revealing a group of patients and at least one ghost looking to get in. Charlie gestured for Nora to get out, so she did. The ghost, an elderly woman, looked like she was about to ask a question, but Charlie gestured that it was not the time, so she got on the elevator with the living and disappeared from view with the rest when the door closed.

"Are you just making fun of me?" Nora asked when they were alone.

"What do you mean?" Charlie asked, the grin dropping from his lips.

"You told me I wasn't crazy the other day, and now you're talking about Vision, and while I wish it was, I'm assuming it's not the android Avenger. How do I know you're telling me the truth? How do I know I'm not being used?"

Charlie nodded like he'd been expecting this. "Come with me," he said. He gestured down the hallway, and though her first instinct had been to brush him off, the gentleness caught her off-guard. It was protective, not forceful, and she found it was nice to feel like someone was looking after her since she had been feeling so alone lately.

He led her down the hall until they came to the auditorium. It was a sad place, filled with dust and loose paper. There was a stage and lone piano that looked lost and abused. Charlie led her to the front and sat her down before vaulting up to the stage and sitting at the keys.

"Listen," Nora began, wanting no more nonsense.

"No," Charlie interrupted. "*You* listen. And watch."

It was then that he began to play the opening notes of a song she recognized. It was "The Scientist" by Coldplay. It was a slow, dramatic song about endings and beginnings. It was romantic and sad all at once. As he played, she was aware of a few patients finding their way into the auditorium to listen. She saw an old man and an old woman take their seats. A nurse ducked her head in from the level above.

And then *they* came. Ghosts began to fade into view all around her. They didn't walk in, they just appeared. All of them quiet, all of them focused on Charlie and the music he was producing. It was beautiful. Nora saw the ordinary magic that Charlie was creating and the mood he was setting. He gave these people, living and dead alike, a moment away from their current reality. It was a short peace but a peace nonetheless. When he finally finished, the ghosts faded and the elderly couple politely clapped. Charlie stood, took a bow, and hopped back down to Nora.

"Did you see them?" he asked her.

"Yes," she whispered. She wanted to say more, but the words wouldn't come.

"Do you want to take a ride with me?"

"Where to?" interrupted Andrew rudely. Nora had forgotten that she had ditched Andrew and Reno somewhere down below. Reno was nowhere to be found, but Andrew had caught up to her at last. He took up a protective stance near Nora.

"Nowhere you'd be interested in, Casper," Charlie said casually. "It's not really dead-friendly."

"What did you say to me?" Andrew snapped back. "Listen, just because I'm intangible doesn't mean I won't slap your ass silly."

"Guys, enough!" Nora snapped. "Andrew, stop it."

"What, you're speaking to me now?" Andrew said with a sulk.

"I don't know what I'm doing," Nora said calmly. "I don't know what's happening to me. I'm pretty sure I'm crazy, but if I'm crazy, then Charlie's crazy too. Or else he doesn't exist either. I don't know what's happening!"

Nora slumped down onto the bench and began to sob. Charlie looked uncomfortable and suddenly found the ceiling very interesting to look at. Andrew sat next to Nora and tried to put an arm around her, only to have it pass through harmlessly.

"Hey," he said. "I'm sorry. Really. It's a lot to take in, I know. I don't know what's going on, either. I'm dead, I know that much."

"Fine," Charlie said, clearly exasperated. "I'll take you both to meet him. Damn newbies."

"Meet who?" Nora asked. "Who can help us?"

"His name is Victor Culshaw," Charlie said. "I call him Graves. As in 'one foot in.' He's... kind of *odd*."

"That's fine," Nora said as she wiped away her tears. "Odd is my specialty these days."

CHAPTER 10

Despite everything she had seen and been through in the past month, Nora never felt at any time like she was in serious jeopardy. Weirdly, she kind of felt invulnerable. Maybe it was because she was young and her whole life was in front of her. She had been in a horrific accident, had the love of her life murdered before her eyes, and then had to endure the encroachment of the afterlife on her current life but she was still here and among the living with the future ahead of her. That optimism for the future all changed as she approached Charlie's van. The thing was rusted so badly that the underlying white paint job bled red all over the place. One of the taillight covers was broken, a side-view mirror was missing, and one of the tires was the spare donut. Sitting there in the parking lot like that made it look like it had come here to die instead of get better. Nora had serious misgivings about getting in. She didn't weigh much but feared it was going to be the straw that broke the camel's back.

"Is this the part where you murder me?" she asked, only half-joking.

Charlie pretended to be deeply wounded. "How dare you?" he said. "This is a thing of beauty. It's a work of art."

"It's a death trap," Andrew said grumpily. He hadn't taken it well when Nora agreed to go with Charlie. Part of it, she suspected, was wounded pride at having another man who could possibly help her. Boys were so silly. Women did not need a man to solve their problems for them. In her experience, it was more often the other way around. In the time they were together before the incident, Nora and Andrew acted and thought as a team and there was no way that was going to change now.

She mentally checked herself at this point. It was also possible that she wasn't being entirely fair. His whole world had collapsed. He lost his family, his dreams, and every connection to life except for her, and even then he couldn't hold her any more than she could hold him. Crazy or not, she felt a responsibility for him and a duty to see what this guy Charlie was talking about could perhaps do for them.

It didn't mean that she had to put up with his nonsense, however. She stopped midstride and turned around to face him. Andrew didn't have time to slow down and wafted right into her. He pulled himself back and faced her. "Listen," she said as his face settled into view. "I don't know what's happening to me. I don't know if you're here or not. I have no idea what is real or if I'm crazy. This guy might kill me in his murder van, and if so, that's fine with me at the moment. All I know is that you…"

"Me, what?" Andrew asked petulantly.

"You *died*," she said as tears crept into the corners of her eyes. "You *died* on me, all right? I love you, and you're *this* now. It's not fair, not any of it. First I lose you, then you're back but I can't touch you, and I don't know what is going on. So let me have this. Let's at least hear what they have to say."

"This is crazy, Nora," Andrew said, attempting to calm her. He reached out to touch her and realized the futility of the gesture. "You don't want to go with him."

"Look, it's my life, okay?" Nora shouted at him. Andrew looked wounded, more so than she expected, and she reviewed what she had said. It was the "L" word that must have done it. "I'm sorry…" she began.

"Hey, there you guys are!" yelled Reno as he trotted out through the hospital doors. Seeing ghosts run through solid objects was not something Nora was going to get used to any time soon. "I've been looking all over for you," he said as he caught up. He took the temperature of the situation and shifted awkwardly. "Am I interrupting something?"

"Yes!" snapped Charlie. "No more room in the van for you guys. It'll be cramped as it is."

"That's stupid," Reno shot back. "I have no mass. There is no possible way I can take up room. That's like saying you have too much air."

"Well then, I have too much air," Charlie said. "Deal with it."

Reno shrugged. "We're still coming with you."

"No, you aren't."

"Yes, we are."

"No, you..." Charlie paused. "Wait, we?"

Reno nodded. "Yeah, man. Me, these two, and my man Peepers back there." He gestured over his shoulder as the little man with the giant glasses and bowtie shyly pushed his way out of the hospital doors and slowly waddled over to them.

Charlie was rubbing his eyes and forehead as though he had a serious headache. He looked to Nora to back him up, but she and Andrew were still having a staring contest, so there wasn't going to be any support there. "No, no, no," he mumbled to himself.

"It'll be fine," Reno insisted. "We're pals now. I have friends all over this city. I also have membership in an exclusive club. If you're nice, I'll introduce you to them later."

"I'm sure they're a lively group," Charlie said sarcastically.

The little man grinned up at her once he arrived. "Are we going to go look for Adelaide now?"

"Sure, Peepers," Reno answered, ignoring Charlie's glare. "Hop in the back with me."

"Fine, whatever, I don't care," Charlie said in disgust. "Everyone get in the car. Let's go to the man with the answers."

Nora looked at Andrew long and hard. "Look," she said. "I don't want to fight. I just want to figure all of this out."

Andrew nodded but didn't look back at her. "What does that even mean, though? For us, I mean." Nora couldn't answer him, though. She didn't know how to. She wanted to pull him tight and say that they could make it work, somehow, but that seemed wrong and unrealistic. How could they ever have a normal relationship? A family? She loved him so much, but was love enough? Short of him coming back to life or her dying, they were short on options. All she knew was that she couldn't let him go, but deep in her gut she also accepted that she couldn't keep him.

Instead of talking, Nora walked over to Charlie's van and wrenched the door open, which sent a shower of red rust to the ground. She looked at Charlie and arched an eyebrow.

"What?" Charlie said with a grin. "I'm telling you, Betsy here is a *classic*."

She fought against it, but a small chuckle came out of Nora as she sat down. In the back, Reno, Andrew, and "Peepers," as Reno insisted on calling him, drifted in and out of each other's space.

"And hey, listen," Charlie said. "Graves is a good man, but he's had to deal with a lot. He's just lost so much and… well, it's part of the reason he's so out there." He paused as if considering what to say next. Nora got the sense that something was being left out. The pained look on Charlie's face, though she still could barely stand the guy, told her that it was not the time and the place to press him for answers. "Anyway, just keep that in mind. I'm sure it will be fine, but try to be kind just in case."

Nora was only half aware of the ambulance parked near the entrance as they passed by it. A few moments later, the driver started up the vehicle and pulled out to follow behind them.

CHARLIE'S FRIEND and "expert" turned out to be a clerk and live-in resident in a small historical building close to downtown. Nora had visited the place when she was in primary school and had marvelled at the collection of artifacts that celebrated the lives and achievements of people with ties to the city. One display was focused on the famous poet John McCrae. She grew up with his poem, "In Flanders Fields," and like many of her classmates had memorized it after reciting it on Remembrance Day year after year. It was a powerful call to remember the toll of war and the lives of the soldiers who fought and died bravely in service of their country. There was a lot to admire about McCrae. In his life, he had been a soldier, a poet, an author, and even a doctor.

It seemed fitting, almost dignified, that an expert on the afterlife should make his living in a place like this. Nora felt better about meeting this man.

Or at least she did until she opened the door and he knocked her over. Out charged a man, easily in his late seventies or eighties, with a wild tuft of white hair that bounced merrily on top of his head. He wore round glasses, though one of the lenses was cracked in the corner, an old tweed jacket, dirty moccasins, and was brandishing a badminton racket. "Back off, you fiend, or else I'll bash your brains out!" he screamed at her. Nora, on her butt, scooted back while Charlie rushed in front of her to block his advance.

"Graves, calm down!" Charlie shouted. "She's with me!"

"Then I'll bash your brains in too!" Graves shouted. "Bashings all around!"

"Stop it! Graves, dammit, I don't want to hurt you!" Charlie shouted. Finally, he managed to wrench the racket out of the old man's hands and chucked it into the bushes.

"Why the hell did you do that?" Graves demanded angrily. "Now I'll have to go get it! What gives you the right to take my things and throw them? Have you no manners?"

"You were going to hit me with it, you crazy fool!" Nora said as she got to her feet. She looked back to Peepers, Andrew, and Reno, who were all fighting the urge to laugh at her. "And you guys were no help, either!"

Graves looked at her as though he'd never seen her before. "There are no fools here! And who are you talking to? If you want that van to help you, then you'll have to get behind the wheel. Shouting at it won't do any good. Are you on 'the drugs'?"

"What? No!" Nora protested.

Charlie reinserted himself in the situation. "Graves, it's me. It's Charlie." He stood in front of the old man, and they looked at each other for several seconds. Finally, the light seemed to go on in the old man's brain.

"Charlie!" he said merrily, all aggression now abruptly gone out of his system. "Good to see you. I had to chase off some ruffians a moment ago. I was ready to bash their brains in!"

"Great, Graves," Charlie said as he beckoned Nora forward. "I'm sure you would have as well."

Graves looked at Nora and smiled broadly. "And who is *this?*" he asked with a sly laugh. "Charlie, m'boy, she's lovely! Careful, now, or she'll get jealous!"

She? Nora wondered who he was talking about.

"Yes, she's very nice, Graves," Charlie said patiently. "This is Nora."

"Pleased to meet you, my dear," Graves said as he shook her hand politely. "If he doesn't treat you right, you let me know!"

Nora was thoroughly confused. A moment ago, this old man had tried to kill her. Now, he was being totally friendly. Between the dead boy, the jerk orderly, the little man, and this old fart, she was batting a thousand in gathering a list of mentally unstable associates.

"No, no, no, no, no," Charlie said dismissively. Nora thought there were one too many "no's" in that sentence to be polite. Just because he was a jerk didn't mean she wasn't offended that he was so against the idea that she was girlfriend material. "It's not like that, Graves. *She has the Vision.*"

Just like that, all traces of confusion or befuddlement left the old man's face. If it could have turned to stone, Nora was sure it would have done just that. It was the death of humour and light talk. "Come inside," he said as he turned and headed for the door. Charlie gestured for Nora and the others to follow.

"Is Adelaide in there?" Peepers asked quietly.

Graves poured her a strong-smelling cup of herbal tea. It had elements of vanilla and berry in it. As she sipped it, she felt warmth returning to her limbs. The inside of the house, though cramped, was warm and inviting. Most of the pictures were clearly vintage, though a few of them showed a much younger version of Graves in what Nora hoped were better days. There were lots of faces in the pictures she didn't recognize, but one of them looked like it had been taken not terribly long ago, considering it had a younger version of Charlie standing there beside a beautiful young woman with long, flowing hair. Nora made a mental note to ask Charlie about her later to find out if this was the "she" that Graves had been referring to earlier.

Graves hung a closed sign in the window and then shuffled into the kitchen to make the tea. A few moments later he came back with the steaming and clinking cups and passed them around before he sat with a heavy sigh on the sofa opposite her. Charlie, uneasy, stood in the doorway to the dining room while Peepers, Reno, and Andrew did their best to occupy the empty spaces in the room without encroaching on the living.

Though half of her acquaintances these days were dead, she still gasped when the ghost of a man in his forties entered the room. He wafted over to Graves, said something in his ear, and patted his knee gently. Graves smiled, whispered back, and then the ghost drifted away after nodding a greeting to Nora and her friends.

"Was that...?" Nora began.

"John, yes," Graves said. "He stays here with me."

"But how is he here?" Nora asked as she searched her memory for her lessons from history class. "Didn't he die at Boulogne in France?"

"Very good," Graves said, impressed. "Pneumonia got him in the end. How about that? Went through the war fighting and surviving against other men, only to get taken down by a bug in the end. Good man, though. A good friend."

"How is he here?" Nora repeated. "How are any of them here?"

"Any of whom?" Graves asked. He raised an eyebrow at her and Charlie. "Can you see others right now? Other ghosts?"

Nora was confused. Clearly the old man had seen the ghost of John McCrae a moment ago, so he had the same ability that she did. Was he testing her? "Yes," she said cautiously as she indicated the others. "This is Andrew, Reno, and..." she hesitated. "'Peepers?'" The little man nodded and smiled, not seeming interested in corrections or clarifications. "Can't you see them?"

Graves nodded as though he could. "Yes, yes, I suppose." He turned to his right and the empty space on the sofa and addressed Andrew. "Pleased to meet you, Andrew." The only problem was that Andrew was sitting behind Nora. It wasn't a case of mistaken identity since none of the ghosts were actually sitting on the sofa with him. Nora looked to Charlie for answers, but he didn't return her gaze. Then the old man looked to the fireplace and shouted a warm welcome to someone named Harold. Nora looked but couldn't see anyone there.

"What's the matter?" Graves asked sharply, startling Nora. "Can't you see him?"

"Um..." Nora began but was cut off by his laughter.

"It's okay," he said. "I'm not all there, you see. Not what I used to be when I was younger. To answer your question, no, I can't see your friends. My Vision has gotten a bit cloudy with age. Call it 'supernatural astigmatism.'"

"But you saw Mr. McCrae," Nora pointed out.

"True, but not like I used to," Graves said wistfully. "And even then, I see him because I'm used to seeing him. We've been friends here at this little place for more than thirty years. I look after both the house and him. It's our retirement home. The rest we earned for our service."

"You fought in the war as well?" Nora asked. She took another sip of the tea and did her best to ride out the visit. So far, very little of what she was hearing included anything resembling an answer, but before she went back to Dr. Westlake and demanded every pill he had, she was determined to hear him out.

"I fought," Graves affirmed. "But not in the war you're thinking of. I fought in the war that really matters, though no one knows about it or honours it the way they should. Kind of a family business, you see. We fought, and now I have my time here to rest. I'm too old for it, anyway. I walked through that doorway once, held my golden slate, and closed the page on that story in my life."

Charlie cleared his throat from the doorway. Graves looked up at him through his bushy eyebrows and nodded meekly, understanding that he needed to get on with it and not let himself be distracted.

"Yes, yes," Graves muttered. "The young, you see. They like to get on with it. They don't realize that time is not on their side. Not ever. We think of our lives as long and eternal while we're living them, but the truth is that we are nothing in the grand scheme of things. Millions of years happened and we weren't there. Millions of years from now will happen and we will be long gone. So what's the rush with the here and now? Why not slow down and appreciate it? Soon enough we'll all be gone." He sighed wistfully and glanced at the old pictures for a moment.

"Except they aren't gone," Nora said trying to get his attention. "I can see them."

Graves looked away from his pictures after a while and nodded. "There's no textbook for this sort of thing, you know. We never had a guide. We called it the Vision. Kind of a pretentious name for a simple ability. But to us it sounded more grand and mysterious. We would feel superior because we could see what others couldn't, and wasn't that great? We would aid and direct events of the world because we had vision! We could see ghosts because we had vision! We would be masters of death because we had VISION!

"Ha! Nonsense. What we have is the ability to see things that we shouldn't. How is it a gift to be able to see the ones you love but not be able to hold them? How is it a gift to try and live while those around you are dead?" There was anger in him, Nora could sense. It was old, muted, and buried, but it was there beneath the surface waiting to break free. When he'd threatened to "bash" them outside a few minutes ago, it had bubbled to the surface. Whatever this man had been through had been tough. It may not have broken him, not entirely, but the damage had still been done.

Nora nodded and willed herself not to look at Andrew as she considered what Graves had said. She couldn't face him for fear that something in her face would add to his own misery and confusion.

"It's awful," she said in agreement. "I thought there would be a heaven."

Graves put down his cup and looked at her thoughtfully. "Who said there wasn't?"

"Well, I just mean that I see ghosts all over the place," Nora said.

"Yes, you do. But how many do you see? One? Two? Maybe a small group here and there? My dear, think about it. Given the number of people who have lived and died, if there was no heaven you would have waded through the fields of Asphodel to get here like a busy night at a country fair. I can't confirm the existence of a heaven, and neither can John or any other of your dead friends, because it remains elusive still. One of the horrible by-products of a God, if there is one, who wants us to believe in Him."

"What do you mean?" Andrew asked, intently curious. For the first time since he died, Nora sensed, he had hope for the future. She had been so focused on herself that she hadn't really considered what his life, such as it was, must look like to him. For all he knew, this was all there was ever going to be. It was a wonder that despite what he was going through, his only thoughts were still about her. It made her love him even more and broke her heart more just when she thought it was done breaking. "What's going to happen to me? Why am I here then?"

Graves looked at Nora and then to the empty space beside her, since it was clear she was distracted. "Does your friend have a question?" he asked with a raised eyebrow. He didn't seem surprised or annoyed. She knew then that however crazy he was, Graves was indeed a kind man. For once, Charlie had been right about something.

Nora repeated the question, and Graves sat back with a sigh. "I'm sorry," he said. "I do have some answers, but not to *that* question. That's the ultimate question, I'm afraid, and not one I think we're supposed to know. Or that we can know. I won't get us off track, but I think the point of faith is to believe and hope for the best. It doesn't mean that there is or is not a heaven or that there is or is not a God. It's infuriating, isn't it? Not knowing, I mean. Ever since humans could think about their own fleeting existence, the question of 'what next?' was the first to pop up in their minds. Many people vow on their deathbeds to find a way to come back to the living and let them know about what lies beyond the veil, but I have my doubts that any have actually done it. If you think back to what I said about the temporariness of our lives and how brief they are in the cosmic sense, I will explain. If our souls get to exist forever, time without end, then why, for the sake of a handful of years, would the dead spoil the surprise for the living? I have to wonder what that existence is like, being truly gone from this world."

"But you don't know," Charlie said from the doorway. It was the first time he spoke, and Nora sensed that there was some deep pain hidden behind the question.

Graves looked at him sympathetically. "No, I don't know," he admitted. "The answer may well be '42' in the end."

Andrew edged forward on the couch toward the old man. "What does he know?" he asked. "About why I'm still here?"

"Where is Adelaide?" Peepers asked sadly.

Nora repeated the question.

"Ah, well, to that I have some answers, or at least some educated guesses. Ghosts are here for a variety of reasons and are created under a variety of circumstances. It's hard, if not impossible, to predict what kind of elements need to be in place to make it work. Think of it on a grand scale once again. Life on Earth, scientifically speaking, is so unlikely as to be impossible. Things were randomly occurring that resulted in life and yet were so random that it probably shouldn't have happened at all."

"Can you be more specific?" Nora pressed.

Graves nodded and then shook his head. "No, not really. The best way I can put it involves special circumstances that are emotionally charged. In life, we often leave emotional 'stains' on a place by exerting our emotional energy. Some researchers believe that poltergeists, for example, are an example of powerful emotions marking a space and causing it to skip like a needle on a record. Ghosts, quite likely, are created as a result of an emotional ending.

"This does not mean they were kicking and screaming in frustration, but rather that something significant was holding them when they were alive. For some it is great love. Ghosts of children sometimes remain out of love for their parents and their desire to stay with them and vice versa. Sometimes lovers will remain entwined forever. In other cases, these people have died horribly from sickness, disease, or even war. With the ghosts I've spoken to over the years, the shared experience has been one of regret or loss or great love and the desire to clear up unfinished business."

As the old man spoke, Nora looked at each one of her ghostly companions and saw the thread as it existed. Peepers was constantly searching for his lost Adelaide. Reno had been cut down in his youth far too soon. And Andrew…

"I tried to save you," Andrew said quietly to her. "It was killing me, and I fought against it with everything I had. I did everything I could to stay with you and protect you."

"I know you tried to save me," Nora said. "And you did. It didn't get me." Then she touched the mark by her eye. "At least not all of me."

Charlie shifted in the doorway, and Graves turned to look at him. Nora hadn't told either of them what happened to her that night, though if either read about her in the papers they would have a good guess that she was talking about the monster who attacked them. She felt her cheeks flush as she imagined they would make fun of her or dismiss her account, but neither of them was smiling or looking at her like she was a wounded animal. Her chest relaxed for the first time in what felt like forever. It was almost as though she could breathe again. If there was anyone in the world who would believe her, it might be these two.

A rude orderly and a crazy old man. Still, better than nothing.

Nora looked back to Graves, who turned over the palm of his hand and showed her the small, mostly faded purple scar on his hand. He stood up gingerly and shuffled over to where she was sitting. He bent down and lightly touched the palm of his hand against her scar, and she felt the heat generated between them. A look of relief passed his face, and though he lifted his hand gently away, Nora got the sense that it was a true effort of will for the old man to have done so. When Graves removed his hand, it glowed faintly purple.

He unbent his back and looked around the room, and this time Nora knew that he could see her friends. He smiled at each one in turn and nodded respectfully. Then he blinked once, twice, three times, and Nora could see that the mark on his hand had faded once again, and her friends were invisible to his clouded eyes.

"They like you," he said once he sat again. "That will be useful. You will need it."

"Useful? Why?" Nora asked. "I don't want this ability. I want it gone. People think I'm crazy."

"Well, I can't help you with that," Graves said. "People think I'm crazy too."

Nora held her tongue and thought about reminding him about the 'bashing' incident on his front lawn but ultimately thought better of it.

Besides, he had said the ability would be useful. That she would need it. She didn't want it, much less need it.

"Why do I need it?" she asked, though she feared what the answer would be.

"Because you are marked," Graves said. "Because the Revenants and their masters cannot allow it. You have seen, and now you must be stricken from the world."

"What are you talking about?" Nora asked, feeling the panic rise in her chest. She looked at Charlie, who was avoiding her gaze. "What is he talking about? What the hell is a Revenant?"

"The creature who gave you that mark," Graves said. "It lives on the border of living and the dead. It blends in with your kind and preys on them. It sucks out your soul, using the energy to fuel and sustain itself. The more it consumes, the more powerful it becomes. Very few encounter a Revenant and live to talk about it. Most who do either believe themselves incredibly lucky or else bear the mark we share as a constant reminder. We have always worked to keep them in check and limit their activities."

"We don't always succeed," Charlie said quietly from the corner. Graves looked up at him sadly and nodded. There was a shared pain between them and not really her business, but she wanted to know anyway.

"Who is 'we'? You keep saying things that don't make sense!" Nora was becoming more and more agitated. She was getting answers, kind of, but they weren't to her liking at all. None them contained a quick and easy solution that let her get back to life as normal. Why was it so hard to get someone to just push a button and solve all of her problems? Wasn't that the way life should work?

"We bear the mark, and we share the burden. Your mark suggests that you fought back. It's how you got your gift. Once the Revenant starts to feed on our energy, it leaves itself open to attack. If you can interrupt that attack, and few manage it, then part of the Revenant's being is expelled like a bursting balloon. Our bodies can't process that energy the way they can, so we are left marred instead. Our minds process the trauma and take in the foreign matter, making us just a little bit like them. That's where the Vision comes from."

Nora had just been told she was part monster or had contracted some kind of supernatural STI. Her hands trembled, and she did her best to set down the shaking teacup. She kept looking around the room, hoping for a camera crew to pop up and tell her it was all just a prank. She started to breathe quickly and felt the blood pound in her head.

Charlie came over and sat down beside her, much to Andrew's disgust. "Hey," Charlie said calmly. "It's okay. Just take it in slowly."

Andrew sat down on her other side. "Ignore him," he said. "Just focus on me. We can figure this out together."

Reno and Peepers, meanwhile, shifted uncomfortably behind them.

"You aren't meant to have the ability," Graves continued, seemingly oblivious to how upset Nora was becoming. "That's why the Revenant will hunt you forever. There are few ways out of that business, but they lead to a far darker destination than you could ever dream of. A dream that would see you scream but never wake up, let me tell you!"

"Graves…" Charlie said warningly.

"It will not stop," Graves continued. Anger flared in him. Deep anger born of experience. "You have seen it. They are mandated to work in secret and to keep that part of the world away from prying eyes. You have been marked by it, and it will come to collect what belongs to it. It will take everything from you!"

"Graves, seriously, stop!" Charlie said, much louder.

"You must fight, or you will die. If it takes your soul, all of your energy, then I'm afraid that's it for you. I don't know if there is a heaven, but for the souls trapped by a Revenant, I'm quite sure there's a hell. There's no escaping that prison. They live forever, and you suffer for their goddamn pleasure!"

"Graves!" Charlie shouted.

"Enough!" Andrew yelled at the same time.

"Did it take any from you?" Graves asked Nora, suddenly full of concern. "Did it drink anything or did you hurt it immediately? This is critical. Wisps are no laughing matter."

"It… I don't know… I was cold," Nora said with a sob.

"Unfortunate," Graves said knowingly. "No matter how much it got, you're stuck. It's tied to you, then. Now and forever. It is in you, and you are in it. Now you'll have a Wisp, goddammit. I hate those things. I will never forgive!"

"We don't know that," Charlie said. "Maybe things will be different this time. It doesn't have to be the same."

"The same as what?" Andrew asked. "What aren't you telling us?"

"I don't want it," Nora interrupted as she pushed herself away from the chair. She began pacing the room, and her breathing was laboured. If she didn't calm down, she was liable to have a heart attack. "I can just ignore them if I have to. The ghosts. Then this Revenant thing will just leave me alone. I won't say anything!"

Graves just shook his head sadly.

"I won't say anything!" she screamed at him. Andrew stepped in front of her and futilely tried to hold her. He raised a hand to touch her face, and she recoiled in shock and anger. "Get away from me!"

The mark on her eye flared, and a beam of energy pulsed out of it and blasted right through the tips of a couple of Andrew's fingers, sending them scattering like ashes in the air. Though dead and supposedly beyond pain, Andrew screamed at the attack and fell backward.

Nora was horrified at what had happened but didn't know what to do. Graves looked shocked, Charlie was trying to grab her hand, while Reno looked completely uncertain of where he should help. Only Peepers looked oblivious since he was now intently looking at an old cuckoo clock.

"Andrew, I'm so sorry!" Nora said. She took a step toward him, and he flinched. It was small, almost imperceptible, but it was there. Andrew was afraid of her. It made her sick to her stomach. It all did. She turned and ran out the door.

"Nora!" Andrew called after her to stop her, but it was already too late.

Outside, Nora ran down the street. She didn't want to be special. She didn't want to be hunted. She didn't want to fight. She didn't want to have Vision, or whatever other garbage she was being fed. She wished that her stupid doctor had just given her the meds and that she was at home and doped up. Instead she was a crazy person and a coward who was half blind from the tears.

Gradually she slowed down and found herself walking aimlessly down Gordon Street. Tired, both physically and mentally, she crossed the bridge over the Speed River and headed for the little Waterflow Cafe on the edge of the river. It was a place she used to come to with her parents when she was little and wanted ice cream. They would get their cones, hers always a delicious French vanilla, and they'd sit on the back of the river and watch the ducks swim by. After, they'd go across the covered wooden bridge into Riverside Park, where she would play for hours.

She didn't want ice cream, but she did want something comfortable and familiar. She bought a scoop of vanilla and wandered over to the bridge and watched as the sun began to dip in the sky. *Soon it'll be dark*, she thought. She hoped that she could sleep soon, get some rest, and wipe the day's events away with one broad stroke. Maybe all of this was just some big side effect of paramnesia and it would be over.

Then she thought of Andrew again and how she had hurt him. She didn't know what to do. The boy she loved was dead and haunting her. He wanted to help her, despite what had happened to him, and instead she hurt him even more. Nora began to cry again, and her tears dripped into her melting ice cream.

If her eyes had been clear, she might have noticed the ambulance that pulled into the parking lot of the Waterflow Cafe and sat there idling. After a while it pulled out and drove away.

CHAPTER 11

Enough mistakes had already been made. The Revenant's first instincts had been to rush out and grab the girl when she saw her alone on the bridge, but by waiting an extra couple of minutes she saw that it would have ended in disaster. The Waterflow Cafe was a popular spot in summer, and while none of the patrons had yet walked around the back to the bridge, it was too risky that someone might do just that at any moment. Even if no one came, the girl might cry out to send people toward them, and that would compound the issue. The debate was firmly settled when the Revenant saw a small, portly little ghost shuffle over to the building and around the corner to the back.

No, it was all too exposed. Rushing had gotten the Revenant into this mess. It was time to be smarter and think things through. The situation had only gotten more complicated with the involvement of what looked like an old man, possibly a Seeker, back at the museum. Their kind was a nuisance. They mostly made more noise than actual trouble, but the Others were specific in their direction to remain undetected, and bringing the old man into the situation would make things really hard to deal with properly for a multitude of reasons. Taking the girl on here and now, so close to her allies, increased the personal danger level for the Revenant. One girl on her own was nothing, but the girl, a host of spectres, and now likely a Seeker were another thing. Something burned in the back of her mind to be particularly wary of this one.

It was a problem, but not one that couldn't be solved. Though the creature was loathe to do it, it knew that if the girl was getting help, the Revenant needed to get help as well. There were ways to compel and enhance others who might do the dirty work. She smiled and almost laughed at the simplicity. How do you kill a girl without being seen? You send someone that no one can see to do it. The girl had already helped out in that regard by kicking up a fuss in the media with all the talk of ghosts and monsters. No one would be surprised if she suddenly went crazy and started shouting at invisible things all around her. Many would see it as a kindness that she was finally put out of her misery.

The Revenant started up the ambulance and pulled away from the Waterflow Cafe. The plan was there, but the timing was critical. The girl was alone and not looking to leave any time soon, so the faster the Revenant got the help she needed, the faster this whole ordeal could be left behind her. She wouldn't pass up opportunities should they present themselves so clearly.

What she needed was to find a ghost with the right qualities and temperament for the job. The only place to look for a lost soul such as that was the abandoned circus at the edge of Exhibition Park in what was slated to be a construction site. It had been popular back in the fifties and sixties with the kiddie crowd. Performers from across Canada and the United States made their way to see the revolving door of acts. You had entertainers, you had charlatans, and of course the rides and games that gobbled up every spare dollar. Gradually, the glitz and glimmer of the place had become passé and kids grew up into different interests. By the time the eighties and nineties came around, video games paved over the great outdoors and kids stopped coming. The only things left now were the tattered remains of the central pavilion, and off in the distance there was the merry-go-round and the tracks of the old kiddie steam train that toured the perimeter near the new park. Where once it was a sparkling jewel, now it was a boarded-up tenement. Teenagers still dared each other to enter the building, but they quickly rushed out again, chased by imagined shapes in the darkness. Squatters, likewise, never took to the place. It had a roof over its head that would keep out the elements, but the soul of the place still thrummed angrily at having been abandoned. There was nothing of substance except the vermin within it.

Although, the Revenant knew, that didn't mean it was empty. Those kids fled and laughed at their fears, though the shapes they saw were real enough. Squatters couldn't stay because eyes were watching them and greedy hands were all too ready to take anything of consequence from them as they slept. She arrived and appraised the place. It was as ruined as ever and boarded up. She left the ambulance and casually walked over to the door. She ripped off the wooden planks covering it and revealed not emptiness but a teeming metropolis of angry and bitter souls, any one of which would suit her purposes just fine.

They all looked her way as she entered, but then most did their best to go about their endless business. The pavilion was a ghostly marketplace and slum, divided up amongst the souls that called the place home. Off to the right, a makeshift bazaar had sprung up where ghosts traded knickknacks or items raided from homes, most of which were useless to the dead (though many of them were just as useless to the living). To the left was a bar common area. The only spirits were nonalcoholic, however, and mostly the ghosts just milled about and yelled at one another as they went through the motions.

The action the Revenant craved was dead ahead. In the centre of the pavilion was the circus ring itself where the show never stopped. The Revenant began walking toward the centre and found a wide path was laid out before her. No stranger to hard times, most of these ghosts knew the risk in coming too close. Though others like herself preferred their souls fresh, it wasn't unheard of for a hungry Revenant to suck down an old soul. It was like drinking stale water, or perhaps even closer to salt water, but it still got the job done. Just because you were dead didn't mean you had nothing to lose, so these ghosts wisely stayed away and kept one eye on her wherever she went.

As the Revenant got closer, she could hear the roar of the crowd. The ring still had its share of marquee performers, despite the circus days being long gone, though it occasionally entertained fights and other competitions. The whisperings of the souls she passed revealed that the Strong Man and his tiger were being featured tonight. She heard words like 'cruel' and 'vicious,' which sounded like an ideal combination to her.

She reached the edge of the crowd and watched. The ring announcer, dressed in a wretched long coat and a ripped hat, yelled to the crowd for silence. "We have a special treat for you tonight, ladies and gentleman. Performing for you is none other than Cyril the Strong Man, scourge of Russia, who in his life was capable of lifting three grown men over his head without breaking a sweat! He never backed down from a challenge, no matter how dangerous. In fact, it's how he met his end! Welcome, one and all, CYRIL THE STRONG MAN!"

The crowd cheered madly as the ghost of a huge, bald, muscled man entered the ring. He was well over six and a half feet tall and had muscles bulging out of every part of his body. He took only a cursory notice of the crowd, though when he did many gasped. His face might has well have been a mask with a ghastly smile frozen in place. There were claw marks that tore up the right side of his face, beginning with the long gash by his mouth that gave the illusion of a smile. His eye above it was milky white and wide open, as the eyelid was mostly torn free. The other eye, clear and focused, didn't blink or show any emotion whatsoever. The announcer, clearly intimidated, stared a bit too long at him before daring to continue.

"He's an impressive specimen, isn't he folks?" the announcer said, his voice wavering. Watching, the Revenant had to agree. Everywhere the man turned, the crowd took an involuntary step back.

"The last challenge in life pitted against him was to fight, with only a small blade, a fierce Siberian tiger named JAX!" With a flourish, the announcer gestured to the opposite side of the arena, where the ghostly form of a large tiger entered. Now this was a surprise to the Revenant. Few animals ever manifested in such a way, their souls being made up of a different kind of energy, and never before had she seen one like this. The beast had a limp, and the Revenant could see something stuck in its back. It had a thick silver chain around its neck and dragged a length of it behind.

Once the crowd finishing *oohing* and *ahhing*, the announcer continued. "As you guessed, folks, it was this last challenge that finished both of them off… but not before each got their licks in. Jax raked his claws through the flesh of the Strong Man's face, but not before Cyril drove his blade into the beast's back. They grappled and thrashed, neither one giving in, until both finally succumbed to their wounds. Tonight, they will fight again, but not against each other… oh no, tonight they will take on any challengers together. For in death, Cyril and Jax became bound to one another. Now they are the most ferocious team in the afterlife!"

With that, the tiger pounced at Cyril, who grabbed the beast by the head and wrestled him to the floor. Cyril grabbed at the chain link collar and pulled the animal's head straight before pulling the blade out of the cat's back. The great cat howled in pain and anger but was no longer limping. The animal took up position next to Cyril and roared as Cyril lazily dropped a loop over the cat's neck and then wrapped the rest of the length of free chain around his wrist before both roared at the crowd. The crowd roared back in approval.

The first 'contestant' to face the pair was another circus ghost. The man juggled ethereal knives and tossed them at Cyril. Before the blades could connect, Jax leapt through the air and snagged them in his mouth. Too stunned to react, the ghost failed to notice Cyril lunge toward him. The big man grabbed him in his hands and lifted him over his head. Cyril pulled the man taut and turned towards the tiger. He shouted at it, and Jax jumped up and with his paws and claws shredded the man in two. Cyril tossed one half to the right and the other, the legs, went casually sailing into the crowd.

"Not to worry, not to worry!" said the announcer merrily. "As we're all dead here, our contestant will gradually find a way to pull himself back together. Please return all parts of him if you find them. No souvenirs, please!"

The next contestant had his head crushed between Cyril's massive hands. The third was chased and had his spine torn out by Jax's paws and claws. The crowd was loving every minute of it, and the more the Revenant saw, the more she was convinced this was her man.

"Who's next?" asked the announcer. "Who is brave enough to fight Cyril and Jax?"

A ghost with most of his teeth missing, half of his head shaved, and a tattoo of a tear under his eye wafted in front of the Revenant and sneered at her. "Well?" he said rudely. "How about you? You gonna do something or stare?" When she didn't respond, he took that as a minor victory and laughed, though few backed him up. Most of them looked warily at the Revenant. Those were the smart ones, she realized. They knew what she was. This idiot clearly did not. "Out," he said simply when she didn't respond. "We don't serve your kind here. You want to see a show, go to a movie. Coward. Ha!"

Another ghost wafted closer and attempted to pull his friend out of the way. "Scotty, man, you don't know what you're doing. Come on."

"Nah, man, these people gotta know where they stand. They can't just come in here like this. And she can see me, so she can hear me." Scotty looked back at the Revenant. "Or should I feed you to the man and his tiger?"

The Revenant, bored now, looked past this fool and to Cyril and Jax, who were eyeing her indifferently. "You," she said, addressing Cyril. "You are with me."

Cyril, like many others, was watching the exchange outside the arena. He laughed at her arrogance, a horrible sight given the state of his face, and the crowd eventually joined in nervously. "And why would I be doink that?" he asked in a thick Russian accent.

"Hey, he ain't doing *nothing*," Scotty sneered as he waved his hand in her face to get her attention. His eyes widened in surprise when she shot out an arm and grabbed him around the neck, something he didn't know she could do. He whimpered in fear and tried desperately to get away. His feet scrambled for purchase, but they kicked uselessly against the ground. The crowd backed away from the two of them immediately, some of the ghosts fading to mist in fright. Cyril said nothing but continued to watch appraisingly. Jax paced back and forth at his feet until Cyril jerked the chain and the great cat sat still.

"Didn't you mention feeding?" she asked, finally looking at Scotty. "I could use a snack." Her face transformed, and she opened the slits on her cheeks wide. Not content to just draw in the man's soul, she relished tearing his essence apart bit by bit as he screamed and was absorbed into her body. Not quite satisfied, she grabbed another soul close by and began to repeat the process as she slowly approached Cyril and Jax. The crowd began to scatter, but not before she managed to grab a third soul, a woman, and began to stuff her into her face.

With the last screams of the absorbed souls abruptly cut off, she stood face-to-face with the Strong Man. "You asked why," she said and took pleasure in how the man, despite his gruff exterior, flinched slightly when she spoke. "Because I can give you something in return. I can make you strong again."

She reached out with both hands and cupped his face. Cyril's eyes widened in alarm, fearing that he was next to be consumed, when instead the slits opened and she began to breathe all of that freshly absorbed energy into him and the cat at his feet. Slowly, the faint blue light of his body began to brighten and become less opaque. He could feel the ground start to solidify under his feet. He felt the pull of muscles again and the stress of sinew.

For the first time in ages, Cyril felt truly strong and would do what he must to keep it that way.

CHAPTER 12

Nora leaned against the side rail on the bridge and watched the sun kiss the horizon while her ice cream cone melted largely untouched by her side. The setting sun was a reminder that it's important to stop and take notice of beauty when it is right in front of you, instead of speeding past the moment.

She remembered one time when Vee had taken her to a party out at Elise Campbell's house in the country. It hadn't been the blowout that Vee had claimed it was going to be. It was quite the opposite, in fact. It was Elise, Ken, Abrar, Atiya, Chris, Peter, herself, and Vee for the most part sitting around a fire and listening to Ken pluck away at his guitar. None of them had spoken. It felt like a rule, some sort of pact they had agreed to beforehand. They were quiet, they listened to the music, and they watched the fire. On the way home, Nora had been looking out the window while Vee chatted away about movies, music, and everything in between. It was then that Nora had noticed the stars, barely visible through the window and shielded by Vee's headlights. Nora asked Vee to pull over, and she did so without argument.

Outside, it was magic. They looked up to the heavens, and Nora saw more stars than she could count. It was more than she could ever remember seeing before. It was a blanket of possibility that was blotted out by the light pollution of the city she lived in. Here was an ordinary beauty covered up and kept secret from most of the people she knew. Vee grabbed a blanket out of her trunk, and the two girls spread it across the hood and windshield and then lay down to look up and wonder at the universe.

Looking at the sunset now, Nora felt that same wonder. There was a world here that existed just below the surface of what she saw every day. It was a miracle she could see and talk to Andrew, especially since many people would give everything they ever owned for a chance to speak to someone they had loved and lost. She felt ashamed and guilty for rejecting both Andrew and this 'Vision' out of hand. It wasn't Andrew's fault. At the time he was being attacked, she would have given anything, even her life to help him. How could she do any less now?

Things were different, she knew. How could they really have any kind of relationship when they couldn't even touch? There would be no wedding, no children, no laughter around the house. To the outside world, it would be a lonely old woman who talked to herself about a love long lost. Pining for a lost loved one was a sad way to live.

"I checked inside that lovely store just before it closed a few minutes ago," came a small voice beside her. "But I didn't see my Adelaide. I *did* see a lot of ice cream. I miss it."

Nora felt doubly guilty then. Guilty because she had forgotten about Peepers and his endless search for his own lost love, and she had just been criticizing the practice in her own mind. She also felt bad because of the way he stared sadly at the puddle of ice cream. It was a small pleasure forever out of his reach, and she had taken it for granted. Nora turned to look over her shoulder and saw that he was right and that the Waterflow had closed. The customers had all left and the street was quiet. Even if she wanted to get more ice cream for the little guy, she couldn't.

"I'm sorry," she said, looking back at his sad face. It was an apology for everything and anything she could think of. There was no limit to her regrets at the moment.

"Me too," Peepers said with a sigh. Nora was surprised. It was the first time the little man ever seemed to properly acknowledge something said to him.

"Why are you sorry?" Nora asked.

He cocked his head and considered this while wringing his little hands. "Because I lost her. I don't know where she is. Or maybe I'm lost. If I find her, I'll tell her I'm sorry."

"It's not your fault. Things happen. People die and move on. It's just the way it is. Maybe you just need to let her go."

"Is that what you're doing? Are you letting go?"

Little bugger. Nora felt trapped by her own line of thinking. He was right, after all. By her own advice, it was time to let go, or at the very least accept what was. Judging by Peepers, his search, and her own inner turmoil, she knew that it was far easier to give advice than to take it.

"No, I guess not," she admitted. "Though I want to."

"I don't," Peepers said. "Why would I want to let go of the thing I want the most?"

"Well, because holding on to it isn't helping. It doesn't let you move on."

"I don't want to move on. I want Adelaide."

For some reason she thought back to the dog she had as a child, Barney. He was full of energy, always barking, and happy to be with you. Then one day Barney got old. It was so quick that Nora almost gasped with the realization. Then her father told her it was time for him to go and asked her if she wanted to say goodbye. She couldn't, though. How could she say goodbye to the thing that mattered most to her? Instead she had continued playing and went off into the other room. She never saw Barney again and always regretted not taking the time to put things right. To find closure. Maybe all we need in life is to find a little closure, though, unfortunately, many people don't get the opportunity.

"I know what you mean," Nora said. The silence rang out between them as she watched his small, sad face. It was then that she knew what she had to do. "I'll help you. I'll help you find Adelaide."

Peepers didn't look at her, but as he nodded his appreciation a few ghostly tears of gratitude appeared on his face. "Thank y…"

Large, feline teeth appeared at his shoulder and tore off a chunk of his ghostly essence. He screamed, and Nora scrambled back in shock at what she was seeing as a huge, pale blue tiger bit down into Peepers' shoulder again before shaking him from side to side, and then tossing him off the bridge and onto the bank below them. Nora's eyes darted from the tiger to the little man below, just long enough to see that he wasn't moving.

"What are you?" she yelled at the tiger. "How is that possible? Did you kill him?"

A thick, calloused hand grabbed her by the back of the neck and yanked her rudely off her feet. She grabbed at the hand with both of hers and tried to pull the impossibly strong fingers off her neck while kicking out toward the tiger to keep it away from her. It snarled at her, and bits of Peepers' ghostly essence dribbled from its jowls.

"Kill him? Nyet," answered the man who had her by the neck. "Kill you? Absolutely. It is demanded."

Before she could question him further, he pinned Nora against the side of the bridge. She barely managed to get air into her lungs before it was all forced out again.

The man punched her, a glancing blow in the kidney before he lifted her over his shoulders and then dropped her onto the ground. The tiger leapt in and bit at her arm. It failed to get a grip, though it left a good scratch on her forearm when she pulled away.

Weeping, she attempted to run but could only manage to crawl. How stupid had she been? The old man had warned her that there was danger, and she had run from the only people who could possibly help her.

A foot planted itself against her side and shoved hard. Instead of just rolling over, the force of it sent her careening into the rails once again. She moaned softly, but the sound was cut off when her attacker grabbed her and once again lifted her off her feet.

She got a good look at him that time. The man was huge, whoever he was, both in terms of height and his strength. His face, half of it, was horrific and terrifying. She tried to scream, but only a thick cough came out as his arms tightened around her. Despite her fear, she could also see that he was different from other ghosts she had seen. If the pale blue tiger hadn't been obvious enough in its colouring, this man removed all doubts.

He was a ghost and yet thicker than others she had seen. Brighter. He had more substance to him. This was something new. "You. . ." she choked out. "A ghost?"

The man laughed at her and did not release his grip. If anything, he squeezed harder. "I was but am more now. I am Cyril the Strong Man. If I plan to keep being this way, and I am plannink, then I am demanded to end you. Nothink personal," he said with a thick Russian accent.

Nora wanted to know more, but it was getting harder and harder to think. The oxygen was being cut off from her brain, and spots began to form at the edges of her vision. Cyril had won and just needed to wait her out, but he squeezed harder anyway. The bones and tendons were stressed to their maximum, Nora knew. Another moment and her bones would start to break.

He can't win! Don't let him win! The anger welled inside her, and she concentrated it all into one last, defiant stare. All her frustration, regret, sorrow, and hope were poured into that look. She felt her face tingle, and her vision cleared enough that she could see the man's scarred face widen in surprise just before the purple bolt of energy shot out of her face and exploded against the scarred side of his.

He dropped her, and she gasped for air immediately. She looked up and saw him reeling back, a great link of metal wrapped around his wrist and his feline companion looking at him in confusion. The great man stumbled and fell backward over the railing. The tiger clawed at the ground to try to find purchase and anchor itself, but it was pulled by the neck. For a moment, the tiger was a counterweight to the ghost thrashing beneath it, but the angle was all wrong, and the animal was whimpering from the strain. Finally, instead of fighting against the weight, the tiger adjusted itself and let it be taken down with its master. Both fell into the water below, though neither made a splash.

Nora knew she had to run and get as far away from this pair as possible, though she didn't want to leave Peepers behind. She spared a look over the side of the bridge and saw him lying on his back below. He looked up and saw her and somehow heard the unasked question but waved her off. She was still going to go down to help him but didn't know how. Her hands would just pass right through him. A little further upstream on the opposite shore she saw the tiger paddling toward it and dragging the half-headed man, who was thrashing about wildly and screaming. Unfortunately, the pair were going to wind up on the shore closest to the road, which meant going that way would be suicide.

"We are coming for you, girl! Jax has your scent! He has tasted your flesh and will have more of it!" Cyril screamed from the river. Blue 'blood' gushed and floated around his head in the water while some of it drifted off into the air. "I will take your face as payment for my own. Blood will have blood!"

That settled it. Ignoring the many aches and pains in her body, Nora ran off the bridge and toward the park, hoping to lose the deadly pair in the trees or find a crowd of people to blend in with. The sun was now mostly hidden from view and with the Waterflow closed and the customers gone; there would be no help in that direction anyway.

Within seconds, the trees became both her ally and her nemesis. Any help the remaining trickles of daylight would have provided was rendered moot in the thick grove. The occasional shaft of light cut through, but mostly Nora was running blind. She stumbled and fell, cursing herself for being careless before getting up and running again. Behind her in the distance she could still hear Cyril yelling, and his voice was getting louder. They were coming for her.

Nora continued running until she found a path in the woods. Staying on it would make it easier for her to run, but it would also give her pursuers the same advantage. Running in the dark was even less appealing because she was as likely to kill herself by accident as Cyril and his tiger were with their hands or claws. Choosing the lesser of two evils, she pushed down the path and looked for anywhere she could hide or get help, but it was nearly deserted.

Nearly, but not completely empty. Up ahead she saw a man jogging toward her, and she cried out for help. "Please! You have to help me!"

Immediately, the guy rushed over. "What's wrong?"

"A man and a tiger are after me!" she said. The man kneeling beside her blinked but took it in stride. It was clear from the expression on his face that he didn't believe her.

"Oh, okay," he said, the panic replaced by curiosity, though he did at least look around. "Well, you're safe now. No more tigers. See? They're all gone."

Well, the hell with it, Nora thought. She tried to push past him and keep running, but he blocked her passage with his arms outstretched in an attempt to get her to calm down.

"Slow down!" he said. "I'm not going to hurt you. What's your name?"

"Get out of the way!" Nora yelled. "You don't understand! I have to get away!"

"You're safe. Nothing can hurt you here," he said. As if pulled by an invisible rope, the man was suddenly jerked away and tossed into the bushes. He screamed and tried to run back to the path when deep claw marks suddenly shredded his back and shirt. He immediately went limp and dropped to the ground, revealing the tiger that had attacked him. Nora watched in horror as the tiger sank its teeth into the man's calf and dragged him slowly back into the undergrowth. A smear of blood on the trail was all that was left of him. Nora backed away, her mouth soundlessly moving as she tried to deny what she had just seen.

Cyril crashed through onto the path a moment later. Without hesitating, Nora turned and ran.

BACK AT the shore by the bridge, Peepers knew he was in trouble. What was worse, it was going to be much harder to find Adelaide now that he could barely move. Nora had promised to help him! It was a moment of great relief, and now she had left him, and much like Adelaide, he feared she would not be coming back.

Imagine his relief when he saw the nice man from the hospital wander onto the bridge above him. Beside him were the two other nice youngsters who he had been spending time with. He waved and called out meekly until one of them spotted him.

Reno was the first to reach him. He jumped off the bridge and floated down, his essence puffing out slightly with the impact of landing. "Peepers, man, what happened to you?"

Peepers tried to talk, but it seemed part of his throat was missing. How silly!

Charlie rushed down and tried to help Peepers, but he didn't know what to do. Anywhere he placed his hands on the man, they just brushed right through.

"Where's Nora?" Andrew said.

Peepers again tried to talk, but it came out a weak gurgle.

"Peepers, man, what did this?" Reno asked.

Charlie positioned himself so that he could look into the little ghost's eyes. "Look at me. It will be okay. We'll help you. But first, you need to help us. Did you see Nora?"

Focusing, Peepers nodded.

"Good! Is she okay?"

Peepers nodded, but then hesitated and shook his head. Finally, he shrugged.

"Was it the Revenant? Did it come for her?" Andrew asked.

Peepers shook his head.

"It was something else?" Charlie asked.

Peepers nodded and held up two fingers.

"Two somethings, guys," Reno said, looking around wildly for any sign of Nora. "This isn't good."

"Where is she?" Charlie asked again. "Which way did she go?"

Peepers pointed in the direction of the woods, and Andrew took off immediately. Charlie called out for him to stop, but Andrew was running up the side of the bank to the bridge above. "Dammit," he said. He looked uncertain about what to do. Peepers was in trouble, but he was also already dead, so it was hard to see how he was going to get much worse. Nora was in danger, though Charlie hoped she at least was still very much alive.

"Go, man," Reno said as he cradled part of the ghost. "I got this. And if there are things hunting Nora, I can help with that too. I have friends who deal in this sort of business."

"What kinds of friends?" Charlie asked.

Reno grinned. "The best," he said. "This is the sort of thing they live for... no pun intended."

It was good enough for Charlie. He ran off after Andrew to aid in the search for Nora. He hoped he wasn't too late.

CHAPTER 13

I t was fully dark out now as the cold lights in the park sputtered to life.
They illuminated the path and supposedly made it safer for people walking
at night, but right now Nora thought they might as well be a spotlight
that pointed out her every movement. For the moment she had lost her
pursuers. Cyril was busy trying to wrestle that poor man's body out of Jax's
mouth, and she had used the opportunity to escape. She couldn't hear them
now, but her breathing was so loud, she worried it would give her away.

She decided to risk a moment of rest just off the path. She panted
heavily and tried to control her breathing so that she could listen and see if
they were still coming. While she couldn't hear footsteps or the cat's growl,
she did hear something else. It was faint but still undeniably music, high-
pitched and slightly irritating. She knew the music well. She had visited the
place often enough as a child.

Riverside Park, like many of the green spaces in the city, had its
playground attractions. Tonight, it seemed, the attractions were still running
because she could hear the merry-go-round in the distance. If it was on and
playing, it meant people and safety. Or at least she hoped that's what it would
mean.

Deep in the woods beside her, she heard a branch snap. Then another.
She didn't have much time and didn't waste any more resting. She was up
and off toward the music in a heartbeat.

As she got closer, any chance of hearing her pursuers was lost entirely.
The music gave way to voices, flashing lights, and a small crowd of people.
An early summer fair had sprung up, complete with carnival games, deep-
fried food, and, most importantly, there were people.

Nora ran over to the crowd, glancing over her shoulder as often as she dared, and did her best to blend in. Not a minute later she saw her pursuers emerge from the path. Cyril was still gingerly touching his damaged face while the tiger was sniffing at the ground in search of her scent.

Though she was blocked by a constantly moving wall of people, the tiger still knew exactly where to look. Its head came up, and as it locked eyes with her, the ears on its head lay flat and it opened its mouth to show its many teeth. Feeling the tension, Cyril let go of the leash, and the cat bounded toward her immediately.

Nora turned and started to push her way through the crowd, despite protests from the annoyed carnival-goers. "Look out!" she screamed at people who looked at her as though she'd lost her mind. "Get away! There's a tiger!"

One or two people screamed and started to run, but they didn't know where to go and then laughed at themselves for being so silly. A tiger! As if. Others turned in amused circles, looking for a supposed tiger, but there was none to be found. Jax continued to come closer to her, slinking around legs and not touching anyone as it eagerly swished its tail.

A small child, no older than five, walked in between the two of them. He held a battered blue cotton candy swab and looked at Nora with curious eyes. The cat, not caring even a little, opened his mouth and approached the boy, ready to remove him one way or another. Nora, not daring to wait, reached out and shoved the boy out of the way, which sent him sprawling and resulted in loud, wet tears. Jax leapt, missing Nora by inches, and knocked over a popcorn stand, sending several people crashing to the ground. All eyes turned angrily to Nora.

"What the hell is your problem?" a woman yelled at Nora as she ran for the crying boy. The popcorn vendor, similarly annoyed and covered in his wares, began to approach her while calling for the police. To them it was a prank gone wrong. No one knew or cared that Nora had just saved the boy.

Explaining would do no good, Nora knew, so instead she ran and bypassed the line at the merry-go-round while ignoring complaints from the parents queued up. She pressed a few dollars into the bored carnie's hand, ducked into the ride, and tried to hide behind the animals. It was a terrible strategy. Everyone in line was staring at her. A few had pulled out their phones to film the crazy girl.

Beyond them she saw Jax pawing his way out of the popcorn and Cyril shove past two people to get to the ride. The people he shoved fell over themselves and each blamed the other, not having seen the Strong Man at all.

"All of you! You have to run!" Nora shouted at the gathered parents and their children. Most of them ignored her and were now filming her with their phones. How could they not see the danger? Neither Cyril nor Jax were like any other ghost she had seen, so surely someone here must be able to.

"No more running, I am thinkink," Cyril said as he stepped onto the ride. "No more breathink. No more screamink. Only you will be quiet now, da?"

"I don't think so!" Andrew yelled as he drifted through a carriage beside Cyril and slammed right into the big man. It was a dramatic entrance, but futile. Cyril didn't move an inch. Instead he reached down, grabbed Andrew by the neck and leg, and tossed him out into the crowd, where he dissipated into the sea of staring strangers.

Charlie appeared, moments later, on the far side of Cyril, and he tensed up to fight. Cyril looked at him and snorted before turning back to Nora and approaching her slowly.

"Get away from me!" Nora yelled.

"What can I do?" Charlie called to her.

"Nothing!" she said. "You have to go!"

"Dude," said a man standing in line with his daughter. "You heard her. Just, like, take off. She doesn't want to be around you."

Charlie looked at the guy as though he had two heads. "You don't understand," he said. "She needs help."

"Clearly, buddy, but not from you."

"Just... mind your own business," Charlie said and then he started toward Nora but found his progress blocked. The man in line was holding him back, and the more he fought against them, the more others joined in and held him back as well. More of them called out for him to leave the girl alone, and soon he was being pushed and shoved back and away from Nora, which left her all alone to deal with Cyril.

"No one left, I am thinkink," Cyril said, laughing. "Now, you are for me." He reached out with his massive hand, and Nora tried to bat it away only to have it pass through him harmlessly. "Neat trick, no? I am touchink you, but you are not to be touchink me."

"Is that so?" Nora asked, trying to sound more confident than she felt. She thought back to the bridge and tried the same technique. She focused all of her emotions and stared as hard as she could at the man.

Cyril blinked once. Then twice. "Are you tryink to be havink a starink contest with me?"

"You'll get it in a second!" Nora said and tried again. Still, nothing happened. It was getting embarrassing.

The Strong Man roared with laughter and turned Nora so that she could see herself in one of the suspended funhouse mirrors. "You look stupid!" he said, catching her reflection. "And your purple face is not so purple now. You're out of juice, and so you are beink out of time."

Hope died in her chest. She closed her eyes and waited for the end.

A gunshot roared out, and the big man took a stumbling step backwards. Cyril roared in anger as he felt at his forehead, only to find that the pale blue had turned transparent in a perfectly rounded circle. That was new! He then jerked back spasmodically as a volley of machine gun fire began to tear into his body, sending streams of pale blue out behind him.

"Eat lead, dirtbag!" yelled a ghostly blue man in a 1940s-era mobster outfit. He pulled the trigger on his machine gun, and once again transparent bullets began to spit out of the thing at a furious pace.

Cyril lurched backward, uncertain of what to do or where to go when he tripped over an object on the ground and fell onto the grass. He looked to see what had tripped him and watched as it was lifted off the ground and reattached under the dress of a teenage girl in a prom dress. "Don't look at my leg, you pervert," she said and slapped him. Cyril staggered back, not from the impact, but the absurdity and shock of it all.

Jax, meanwhile, was having issues of his own. The ghost of a fat man in an army uniform leapt onto the surprised cat and pinned it under his weight. "Hello, kitty!" he yelled. "I have a message from the army. You are now dishonourably discharged! DISMISSED!" He then grabbed at the ghostly blade in the cat's back and twisted it sharply. The cat howled and dropped immediately to the ground.

Lastly, a cute little ghost girl walked over to the cat with her mongrel ghost dog. The tiger looked at her and roared, but the little girl was unconcerned. She punched the tiger square in the nose, which made it blink in surprise. "BAD KITTY!" she yelled. "Scraps, sic 'em!"

The dog obliged and began nipping at the flanks of the cat. The tiger, not knowing what else to do, backed up and whined in confusion. It looked to Cyril for help, but the Strong Man was ducking the flying bullets, now half of his head fully returned to its original ghostly state, along with a good chunk of his body. The cat turned and fled.

"Coward!" Cyril screamed at the retreating cat. "You will pay for this!"

"You have other things to worry about," Reno said as he emerged from the crowd and charged toward Cyril. When he was close enough, he jumped up and planted both feet into the man's chest. In life, Reno had the build of a pro rugby player. In death, he still had more than enough mass to shove Cyril off his feet.

On his back, Cyril pushed Reno off to the side. Reno hopped to his feet and planted them firmly in the grass to get ready for a second attack. Cyril, ready to fight, saw the mobster approach and rest against a giraffe on the merry-go-round while pointing his weapon at him. The girl in the prom dress stood beside the mobster with her arms folded. The little girl and her yapping dog approached with the fat man in his army uniform. Beyond that, Andrew warily approached, ready to join in where needed.

"Your move, chrome-dome," said the mobster as he readied his gun. "Maybe you oughta take a powder, huh?"

Cyril narrowed his eyes and considered his options. Finally, he stood up and stared at the group. "This is not beink over, you understand?"

"Bye, bye, mister meanie!" said the little girl. Her dog yapped at him.

Cyril turned, reluctantly, and began to walk away.

Nora, meanwhile, was too stunned by all of this to say much. The people at the carnival were trying to talk to her and were beckoning for her to get off the ride now that Charlie was gone. Some of them wanted to help her, but a lot of them just wanted to get on the ride. Many of their kids were whining and crying.

In typical fashion, that's when the police showed up. The mom of the kid Nora had pushed over and the popcorn vendor had ratted her out. Coupled with her storming of the merry-go-round, the police had little choice but to arrest her for being a public nuisance. Several people pointed at her and the word 'crazy' reached her ears more than once. Charlie, who had finally been let go, was pleading with the police on her behalf, but they just weren't having it. They placed her in a police car and were gathering a few more statements before they took her to the station.

Andrew didn't leave her side the whole time. He sat in the car and tried to say soothing things to her, but it was all noise. She was battered, bruised, tired, and now a criminal. It hadn't been one of her better days.

Reno looked all kinds of smug when he walked over and inserted himself between her and Andrew. "Told you I had friends!" he said with a smile.

"Tell them thanks," Nora said weakly. "Peepers?"

The smile dipped from Reno's lips. "I got him to safety, but I don't know what's wrong with him. I don't know what to do. I've never seen someone... scattered like that."

"Thanks, Reno," Andrew said. "We'll figure it out."

Nora nodded grimly. "Or we'll die trying."

CHAPTER 14

The Revenant was called to the scene, of course. Being an EMT meant that she was always where the action was happening, even at a carnival where a young girl had lost her mind and was pushing around little children. She was happy to go and collect the body of a certain teenage girl.

But there was no body to collect. She clenched her fists in anger.

There were bumps and bruises all around at the scene, but nothing that couldn't be solved. She stood at the edge of the crowd and watched until she saw what she was after. Finally, it appeared. A small, blue tail swished around the corner of one of the pavilions. As she was no longer needed, the last of the boo-boos having been kissed and other such nonsense, it was nothing to stroll around the corner to where the big man and his cat were licking their wounds.

When Cyril saw her, shame flushed his cheeks, and he averted his eyes. "We will do better," he said meekly.

"I know you will," the Revenant said.

And then he screamed.

A short time later, the Revenant walked back toward her ambulance, filled with anger and frustration. The oaf had failed miserably, but at least her cover was intact. There was that much at least.

The flickering lights of the police car caught her attention as it drove slowly by. She made the briefest of eye contact with the girl inside, whose eyes widened in fear and recognition. In response, the Revenant smiled at her and then watched the car until it faded from view.

It wasn't over yet.

PART 2: BARGAINING

CHAPTER 15

"Is it getting any better?"

Nora had been staring off blankly and hadn't registered the question at first. She smiled slightly, sighed, and adjusted herself on the uncomfortable leather couch. She'd had to endure Dr. Westlake more than she would have liked to over the past twelve days, but she figured it was a small price to pay for what her family had been told was a 'public meltdown' back at the fair.

Nora's parents had come to pick her up at the police station. Luckily, she still retained some of her public sympathy and notoriety over the accident that killed Andrew, so they were willing to let her off with a warning after getting a promise from her dad that she'd get some help. Nora's mom had a sad smile on her face and seemed almost afraid to hug her, like she was fragile and would break. Nora wanted to tell them the truth, but the truth was... well, the truth was nonsense, wasn't it?

At home, her brother hung around the periphery of whatever room she was in and seemed to be struggling with how to approach things. Finally, Tom, in his own lumbering way, made his approach and actually succeeded in cheering her up a little bit.

"Always gotta stand out," he said with a grin. "Why are you so ab-Nora-mal?"

Despite herself, she laughed and threw out a weak punch that hit him in the shoulder. After that, he wasn't afraid to come near her. In fact, he made a point of hanging out as much as possible. They started watching movies together and chatting like real people. It was an unexpected side effect of tragedy, Nora thought. It brought families together like nothing else. Her brother didn't even say anything when she missed out on going to his high school graduation ceremony. They all came home after, and he sat with her and turned on the television. He skipped all of the parties just to be with her. She didn't know if this new truce and bond would hold, especially since it was partially built on a necessary deception, lest she be thrown in the nuthouse, but she wouldn't be the one to break the treaty. Tom even trusted her enough to bring Casey home one night to watch a movie with them, his eyebrows daring Nora to make a joke the entire time. She didn't.

Vee treated the incident like it was a minor blip in the road. She was a rock star like that. As far as she was concerned, Nora could do no wrong. It was hard not to love loyalty like that. Vee told Nora that if anyone asked her about what was going on, she just said that Nora was working through things and was just fine. Like Tom, Vee was just there ready to talk or ready to sit and just be around. Nora was grateful for the company.

Living company, anyway. Ever since the night in the park, Nora hadn't been able to see as well as she normally did. Well, the 20-20 vision was still there, but the ability to see the undead had diminished. This wasn't overly helpful, since it reinforced the idea that maybe she *was* crazy, but each night, as soon as it was dark enough, Andrew would appear at her window sill and say, "Hello, Nora Angel," and remind her of the new status quo. She didn't know if the Vision would return as strongly, but perhaps that was for the best. She hadn't been attacked, nothing had been following her, and life was almost back to normal.

She knew it couldn't last. Charlie would meet up with her every now and then in the park to give her updates on Peepers and the others. Occasionally she could be talked into going to see them. Every time he warned her and repeated the concerns that Graves had raised about the Revenant.

"It's not over," he said. But she ignored him anyway, because she so desperately wanted it to be. That was Future Nora's problem. She could deal with it then. Present Nora just wanted to watch movies with her brother, his girlfriend, and her best friend in the whole world before going upstairs to hang out with her dead boyfriend.

Oi, this was complicated.

"Well?" Dr. Westlake repeated. This was the last part of the new normal. The police had specified that Nora needed help, and she allowed her parents to send her back here. It made it easier to meet up with Charlie, considering he worked at the hospital and her parents were constantly keeping a wary eye on her.

She thought she would have taken more pleasure in seeing Dr. Westlake again and making him squirm over the fact that he had dismissed her initial concerns and rejected her plea for medication. It was the first thing he had offered her when she came back. She accepted the pills but flushed them in the toilet as soon as she got home. The man truly was a quack.

"Better," she offered. "A lot can happen in a couple of weeks."

"The pills are helping?" Dr. Westlake asked. It was more of a statement, really, and it made him seem arrogant, as though it was some kind of foregone conclusion. He was too convinced of his version of reality to be able to help her. She wondered, and not for the first time, if there weren't a number of so-called crazy people out there who weren't crazy at all but had been labelled as such by people like Westlake who couldn't properly understand them. She wasn't crazy, after all. Hopefully.

"Yes. I think so. I'm sleeping better."

"Great. And no more daydreams about ghosts, tigers, or anything else like that?" He chuckled a bit as if to suggest they were in on some sort of inside joke together. She'd made the mistake of telling him the truth in their first meeting but actively worked to deny it ever since. Now Westlake treated it like some sort of funny run-in. A comedic mishap of sorts. It pissed her off, but she kept her cool.

"Nope," she said. "Though I still think about going out on a date with a famous actor, becoming fabulously wealthy, or being able to travel around the world. Those all still sneak into my thoughts from time to time."

"Ha!" he said, though without much actual humour. He clicked his pen and wrote something down. Nora was exasperated immediately. Could it be this guy couldn't take a joke? He flipped up the notepad, his customary gesture for announcing the end of their meeting, and put it down on the table. "Well, those are the good kind of daydreams. We can keep those up. Just so long as we know they aren't real."

"No problem," Nora said. She then put her arm around an invisible person next to her. "Taylor Lautner and I can keep a secret." She then fake kissed him and saw that Westlake's eyes were super-wide. He was reaching for his pen and notebook. "Kidding!" she said quickly and loudly. "Seriously, I'm just kidding!" Dr. Westlake relaxed and nodded with a slight smile, which suggested he didn't entirely believe her. "It's okay. I would never date Taylor Lautner. This is Kit Harington, Jon Snow from *Game of Thrones*."

Nora laughed at her joke. Dr. Westlake didn't. As she got up to leave, she heard the click of his pen behind her.

THE LIE had come easily enough to her lips that it made Nora wonder if more than just her vision had changed. Seeing Dr. Westlake made sense since she'd already established a relationship with the man, but it was really the convenient access to Charlie, his car, and the other acquaintances she had gathered in recent weeks that made it a prime location. Nora told her parents that there was a group meeting after her appointment with Westlake, where she spent time with other people like herself who were suffering various kinds of trauma. It wasn't a complete lie, since all the ghosts she knew certainly couldn't be said to be whole and healthy, but it was a shallow justification and she knew it. Charlie would meet her at the end of her appointment, and they would sneak off while Nora's mother or father waited patiently in the parking lot. She felt scummy about doing it, but circumstances unfortunately dictated that she go against her better judgment.

Tonight, Charlie showed up with Andrew in tow. Since meeting up with others like himself, Andrew had cheered up considerably. He still visited her nightly but seemed less focused on her and her alone. It was odd that in death Andrew had started to get a life.

She grimaced at the thought. Nora was adjusting, but she could feel it pulling her a bit farther away from Andrew instead of closer to him. Sometimes she thought she made little internal jokes about him to try to cauterize the wound. She put on her best smile as they walked up but was sure both guys would see right through it.

But of course they didn't. Boys are like that.

"Hey, Nora Angel," Andrew said happily. "Your burned-out chariot awaits."

"Hey!" Charlie protested. "Leave her alone. I'm telling you, that van is a *classic.*"

They all slipped out the back entrance, far from the parking lot, and piled into Charlie's van. The gears slipped and groaned, but Charlie still managed to coax the vehicle to life. It was a short trip from the hospital down the hill and into the core of the city. From there they moved past the clubs, restaurants, bookshops, cafes, and other attractive options to the deserted bus station at the edge of downtown. It was a place no one went to, not even the teenagers looking for a cheap thrill in an abandoned husk, because it was pretty rank. People just let it be.

Their loss, thought Nora.

She loved the place and all of its charms, though that wasn't the case the first time she showed up. After spending the night in jail and being subjected to a Westlake pen-clicking session (he clicked so often, she thought he was having a seizure), Nora had practically begged Charlie and Andrew to get her away from it all. She meant Hawaii or someplace exotic, but Charlie had taken her to his van and driven in silence until they got to the terminal. She looked at him doubtfully, but he explained that the people who saved her were inside and wanted to meet her.

"But I don't want to meet them!" Nora said, terrified. "Look, I'm thankful that a ghost and his tiger didn't kill me, but I've had enough. I don't want any more of this crap."

"Don't be an ungrateful brat," Charlie snapped.

"Hey!" Andrew put in. "Don't talk to her like that. She's been through a lot."

Charlie turned off the engine and pulled out the keys. He turned around and gave them both such a look of anger that for once in her life Nora kept her mouth shut. "Don't talk to me about suffering. You think I

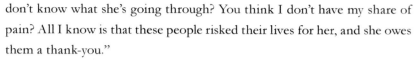

don't know what she's going through? You think I don't have my share of pain? All I know is that these people risked their lives for her, and she owes them a thank-you."

Nora muttered softly to herself.

"What did you just say?" Charlie asked angrily.

Nora looked at him petulantly. "I said 'how can they risk lives they don't have'?"

Charlie shook his head at her. "You still don't know a damn thing, do you? Stop being selfish and spoiled, and maybe you'll learn a thing or two. Starting with gratitude."

He got out of the van and stalked off toward the building. Nora sat with her arms folded and stared out the window at nothing. She was determined not to give the rude orderly any sort of satisfaction. He could go hang out in his dead terminal all night for all she cared.

"Nora Angel," Andrew said. Nora started a bit; she'd forgotten he was still there. "I don't want to say it, but he's kind of right." He put up his hands defensively when she turned to face him. She must have looked pretty scary for him to recoil like that. It was the realization that she was about to lose her temper that focused her mind and calmed her down. "Look, he's a jerk. I think we agree on that. But those people did help you. I've been talking to them and hanging out with them. They're good. And hey, we're going to need all the help we can get."

"We?" Nora said. "It's not you that thing is after."

"Not anymore, anyway. Remember? It got me first. Anyway, I'm in it for the long haul," Andrew said. "Till after-death do us part."

She rolled her eyes and couldn't stop the smile from coming out. God, he was corny sometimes.

Nora allowed herself to be led into the building and was instantly in awe of what she was seeing. The inside of the Peter Cullen Bus Terminal was about the most amazing place she had seen in her life. It had all the style and charm of an early 1920s terminal with cathedral ceilings, red suede couches, ornate glasswork, and gas lanterns hanging on every wall post. The plants and weeds had sunk their teeth into the place, and now vines and bushes sprang up next to benches and offices. Rather than tear down the place and make it ugly, time and nature had made it beautiful. Even the dark corners made the place warm and inviting. The old enclosed bay where the buses used to pick people up and drop them off was tall and imposing with the creeping rust looking like rosy latticework. The ceiling, somewhat crumbling, had a large chandelier that hung at an awkward angle but still glowed with a warm light so that everyone could see their way clearly. Under it was an old, rusted-out double decker bus, the words 'sight-seeing' scratched and faded, but it still held its charms, unlike Charlie's mess of a van. Inside the bus, Nora saw the ghost of the little girl press her face up against the glass in excitement.

"Nora's here!" she squeaked excitedly. The hollow yap of a small, ghostly dog followed the announcement as the girl bounced up and down. "She's here!"

Nora began to smile and then screamed when a huge, fat ghost pushed out of the shadows to her right and sent dust particles flying through the air. He roared or yawned, Nora wasn't quite sure, but the effect was the same. She backed into a doorway, away from the ghost, and her glance flicked over to Charlie to get some indication if the thing was friend or foe.

"Get outta my office, ya lousy dame!" shouted a man behind her. Nora turned to see the mobster ghost, his feet up on his chair, giving her an annoyed look. Nora stammered to say anything at all, but no sound would come out. Tired of waiting, the ghost picked up his tommy gun and fired off a series of shots that sent Nora screaming and scrambling back out of the office. "Scram, I said!" he yelled after her.

Nora backed out and then fled from the fat ghost, who was still pulling himself together. The ghost dog was now yapping at her heels, and the girl was hopping down out of the bus. A tired-looking teenage girl in a prom dress, her one leg visibly dragging, followed behind her. Nora ran, looking for any kind of exit, and went headlong through Reno, who had both arms out to try to stop her.

"Slow down!" he shouted, but it was too late. Nora ran right through him and smacked into a pole, nearly knocking herself out.

Dazed and confused, Nora tried to focus, but it was so hard. She thought she could hear voices. Television? In her head? People? Too hard to think. She drifted off again.

"Not too bright," she heard a girl say. *That's rude*, Nora thought. Then she drifted again.

"Did she deaded?" asked the young girl. A reply, but Nora couldn't hear it. She drifted again.

"I was just kidding!" complained a man.

"I was stretching!" said another.

Finally, there was silence for a long time, and Nora slept.

When she woke up, there were a number of pale blue faces staring down at her. Nora fought the urge to yell and willed herself to blink. She managed the first, but not the second.

"You have the ability to wake the dead, you know," Reno said with a grin.

"You snore a lot, Nora," said the little girl. "It was scary and loud. Like a dragon! ROAR!"

"Who are you people?" Nora asked.

Reno smiled at her. "These are my friends that I told you about. Together, we call ourselves the Deadish Society."

"Deadish?" Nora asked.

"Yeah, well, you know," Reno said sheepishly. "We're dead, but not all the way dead if we're still here. We haunt, we bop around, we talk, we play, but we don't eat, sleep, poop (I miss a good poop), so we aren't technically alive, but we also aren't all the way dead. Just a little bit dead. Kind of dead. One foot in the grave, one foot ready to go to a rave. No? Living-lite, so to speak. Not totally dead. Just dead… *ish*."

Nora looked at him blankly.

The other ghosts looked at each other and shifted uncomfortably. "What?" Reno asked them. "It's a good name!"

"I told you it was stupid," said the prom girl.

"No, it's not!" Reno protested. "It's clever. It's funny because it's true. On-the-nose humour!"

"It ain't funny," the mobster said. "Putting my gun up your arse and pulling the trigger, now *that's* funny."

"That's disgusting!" said prom girl. "*You're* disgusting!"

"I like it," said the little girl. The dog yapped beside her. "So does Scraps. We're Deadites!"

"Dead-*ish*," corrected Reno. "You have to say it right!"

"Leave her alone," prom girl said angrily. "She's just a little kid."

"She's been dead for a hundred years!" Reno shot back. "She's older than both of us!"

"Enough!" bellowed the fat ghost. "I will not have my soldiers turn on themselves. It's undignified! Now stand to and let the girl be! Fall in line!"

"We aren't soldiers, you twit," muttered the prom girl, but she quieted down anyway.

"Nope, we're better than that," Reno said proudly. "We're family." The mobster snorted derisively at that.

"Nice to meet you, I guess," Nora said. "Though I don't know your names."

"Roll call!" yelled the fat ghost. He stood at attention, and his belly shook around his army uniform. A button above the gut looked like it was on the verge of exploding outward.

The little girl was first up. "I'm Scarlett," she said shyly. "I like dolls, and you, and playing, and dogs, and sunshine." The little dog yapped at her ankles. "Yes, and I like dogs. Did I say that? This is Scraps. He's mine, so *back off, bitch.*"

Nora was startled at the abrupt change in the girl. "I'm sorry, what?"

Reno interjected quickly. "Don't mind her. Scarlett is an old soul... literally. She died a girl but has been around at least a hundred years. Sometimes she can be a bit... touchy."

"I like you!" Scarlett giggled to Nora.

"I'm Isabel," said the prom queen. "Recent addition."

"I recognize you," Nora said. "You died last year. Car accident, right?"

Isabel scowled. "Yeah, car accident. The same kind you had."

"But I wasn't in an accident," Nora began. Then she realized. She wasn't the first victim of the Revenant. "Oh. I'm so sorry."

"Lost a leg but gained an accessory," Isabel said as she pulled loose the phantom limb and hefted it like a baseball bat.

"Cool trick, lady," said the mobster with a grin. Isabel gave him a withering look and returned the leg to its proper place.

"Rocco, behave," said the fat ghost.

"Well, that's my name given, isn't it," spat the mobster. He doffed his cap in her direction and revealed more of his face than Nora had seen before. She guessed he was in his mid-fifties when he died. "Rocco," he said. "King of the Bootleggers before I was fitted with cement shoes back in Hamilton. Good gig, that was."

"Bootlicker?" Scarlett giggled.

"Boot*legger*," Rocco stressed. "As in liquor. Alcohol. *Spirits.*" He emphasized the last word and chuckled at the pun. "I had other interests as well. Gambling. Prostitution. No big deal."

"You're disgusting," Isabel said in a huff.

"Stand down," the fat army ghost said with a wheeze. "I'm Sergeant Lee O'Malley, Canadian Armed Forces. Call me Sarge. I head up this little group."

"Says you," Rocco sneered as he hefted his gun.

"I said stand *down!*" Sarge bellowed and swiped his fat hand through Rocco's face, sending both the ghost and his essence tumbling away. Rocco reappeared farther down and started firing his ghost bullets at Sarge. They ripped through and sent the mist scattering, but it was clear there was no damage done. The two of them continued to fight and argue, though, and since both were already dead, it seemed pointless; neither was getting hurt. Scraps barked and ran around them in circles. Scarlett began to shout after the dog and the men, but they all ignored her. Isabel sat on the periphery looking bored while Reno rubbed his eyes with his hands in embarrassment. Andrew, Charlie, and Nora all stood looking dumbfounded.

"Hey! What about Peepers?" Nora asked into the cacophony. "Is he okay? Can I see him?"

They all stopped rather abruptly and looked awkwardly at each other. Something had happened to the little man, Nora knew, but no one wanted to tell her. She waited until Reno came forward and took her to him.

All of that had happened nearly two weeks ago, and Nora still shuddered each time she thought about poor Peepers. It had been a grim end to her introduction to the Deadish Society. Seeing the little ghost, Nora pledged to come to the bus terminal on a regular basis and worked the details of her lie with Charlie so that her parents wouldn't send out the police searching for her. She was never able to stay more than an hour or so, but she got used to them quickly and liked their company. Cullen Bus Terminal was becoming a second home. If she admitted it to herself, Nora would have to say that she was actually starting to be happy for the first time since Andrew had died.

She should have known that the good times weren't going to last.

CHAPTER 16

Nora started treating the Cullen Bus Terminal like it was her own personal space. She brought in a ton of fairy lights she bought at IKEA and strung them up all around. When the Deadish complained, she pointed out to them that while they were dead and beyond the need of such comforts, that she was still very much alive and would like to see where she was going. They grumbled and complained, particularly Rocco, but all of the issues seemed to disappear once the twinkling lights lit up the room with new life and warmth.

Nora dusted, tidied, and soon the place was almost passable. She learned that the bus was the main place that they gathered, but each ghost had his or her own area that they haunted. Rocco stuck to the main office and wouldn't let her or her 'woman's touch' anywhere near it. Sarge preferred hanging out below in what he called his 'firing range.' Nora wasn't allowed to go down there, and after hearing the shouts, bangs, and thumping that happened, she didn't want to. Scarlett, Scraps, and Isabel hung out in the bus for the most part. Nora assumed at first that Isabel was acting as a surrogate mother to the little girl, but it soon became obvious that it was the other way around. Scarlett spoke and Isabel obeyed. The little girl acted sweet and innocent, but there was a deep seriousness in her eyes that let Nora know that if anyone messed with her family, they'd have to contend with this tiny force of nature. Nora knew from experience that size, particularly in a mother, didn't mean much. Her own mother could be scary beyond reckoning, and Nora was half a head taller. Tom had hidden in his closet one night to avoid their mother after wrecking one of her prized plants by pouring a can of pop into it instead of water. Aside from that crew, Reno, their newest inducted member, seemed to like the ticket counter area.

Cullen was more than just a hang-out. It was still a real, bustling terminal in many ways. Other ghosts from the neighbourhood flittered through on a regular basis, like workers on a busy commute, though none of them lingered for long. They would come to share stories, laugh at jokes, and give updates on the quality of local hauntings.

A good haunt was something to take pride in, Reno told Nora one day. Each ghost spent most of his or her time in a place as a way of staking out territory and sometimes would make their presence known to the living. The reasons for a haunt were various. According to Reno, with a lot of time and effort a ghost could impact or manipulate not only their own body structure and change its form briefly, but an adept ghost would also be able to interact with objects in the real world. Most of them were terrible at it or couldn't do anything at all, but with a lot of dedication and effort some were able to move objects, keys, or other small items of value that drove the living nuts to discover had gone missing. Reno said some ghosts were honing skills, but many of them were just jerks.

Most ghosts didn't bother the living and weren't interested in interacting with them in any way. A lot of supposed hauntings weren't purposely designed to scare people but were simply by-products of sharing the same space. "Think about it like this," Reno said. "At home, you're watching television and your brother walks in front of you. You yell at him and tell him to take a hike. He wasn't trying to be a pain in the ass, he was just passing by. That's what a lot of hauntings are."

Some ghosts, like Old George, an elderly Scottish gentleman who wandered through from time to time, were in the haunting game for the shock value and would gladly share their tales. "One place I was in I would make sure to open and shut doors loudly in the bathroom while people were taking a shower. They'd get angry and take a peek at who was interrupting them. No one there, of course. They'd get out, check the closed window, check the locked door. While they were in there, if they was alone in th' house, I'd run up and down the stairs quick as ye like, and they'd open up and see nobody home. Drove 'em nuts.'"

Jennifer, a pimply-faced teen girl, liked playing with doors. "One girl kept trying to sleep, so I kept opening the door to her room. She'd get up, close the door. I'd open it. She'd get up, close it, check that it was shut, and go back to bed. I'd open it. She'd slam it shut! I'd open it again. Eventually, she was so freaked out, she bailed and went to her friend's house!"

A creepy older ghost with a hue so dark blue it was nearly black passed through from time to time. Nora avoided the ghost and shuddered at his haunting tactic. He would stand in doorways and stare at people until they saw his outline, and then he'd vanish. Sometimes he'd get right up close to their faces and wait until they opened their eyes. He seemed to take no pleasure in it, certainly no amusement, and Nora didn't dare ask him why he bothered.

In short, the ghosts of Guelph were a lively community. Instead of being teachers, doctors, electricians, bank managers, factory workers, writers, or anything else that occupied the living, the ghosts were content to keep on being. Some, like the librarian in the Heritage Room, haunted a place because it was familiar and gave them something to do.

"Even dead people get bored," Reno said. "And they get bored more easily as well! No meals, no sleep, nothing else to do. I'm surprised more people aren't actively haunted."

Reno hung around the high school most of the time but was crap as a poltergeist or even as a low-level haunting, he admitted. He was working on it, though. He'd try to bounce a ball in the gym, run up and down the hall at night, or close doors, but he was terrible at all of them, and most people thought it was either the wind or the rats. Sometimes it *was* both, and he realized he was competing with rodents. Eventually he had met the Deadish through Isabel, who passed through the school one night, and figured there was a better way to go about his business in the afterlife but hadn't totally made up his mind about what he was going to do. Haunt or hang? It was a tough call. When he first met Nora, he was actually trying to scare her. He felt terrible about it after, of course, saw that it wasn't going to pay the bills, and was why he worked so hard to help her out afterward. "And now I have a friend!" he said cheerfully.

Some of the bangs and noises that wake people in the night are from ghosts just going about their business. People are more sensitive at night, apparently, and can hear things in their sleep that their waking minds would dismiss or explain away. During waking hours, teenagers were kept away from Cullen because of the racket created by Sarge in the basement and the pops and echoes made from Rocco's gun. But at night when it was dark and people in their homes were asleep, the people would be startled by ghosts scaring dogs, making cats howl, causing lights to flicker, or trying to move things. Reno said there were some who were trying to raise the subtle hauntings to the level of an art form.

Not all ghosts enjoyed the afterlife, however. Most of them hated it, in fact. They were trapped in between life and death for whatever reason, and if they stayed too long they eventually forgot what it was they were trying to do in the first place. The Deadish were together because it was convenient but also because it gave them something to focus on: each other. Ghosts who were alone or searched for what they were missing for too long were often a lost cause.

Ghosts like Peepers.

With each visit, Nora made sure to stop in to see him. The Deadish had taken him in against his weak protests that he had to return to the hospital in case Adelaide came looking for him. They put him up in a waiting room in the back, where he lay and moaned constantly. None of them were too sure what to do; even Charlie, who had experience in this area, said he'd never seen anything like it. The marks that the great cat had left on him hadn't gone away. Peepers wasn't pulling himself back together. If anything, he was getting worse. *How can what is already dead be dying?* Nora wondered.

Graves didn't know what to do either, which was the most disconcerting thing. Charlie assured Nora that Graves was looking into it, but the old man had so far found nothing that worked.

"It's the first time I've seen him focused in years," Charlie said grimly. "Ever since... well, it's good, anyway." There it was again. The untold story. Nora let it be.

Peepers was always grateful when she came in. "Adelaide?" he would ask. "Did you find her?" Nora felt terrible when he asked this question because each time she would tell him no. His face fell a bit, but he would at least then be able to chat about this and that. He quite liked Isabel and Scarlett, who were looking after him, but it was clear he was afraid of Scraps. Each time the dog barked, the little ghost flinched as though it was going to bite him. Perhaps it was a bit of PTSD: post-tiger stress disorder.

The best benefit of all was Andrew, however. He still came to see Nora each night until she fell asleep, but it was probably boring watching her sleep all night and deafening to listen to her snore. She learned from Reno that Andrew had been spending more and more time with the Deadish Society and Isabel in particular. Nora felt a rush of jealousy and relief when she heard that but didn't know which emotion was valid, if either, and so it was something else she pushed aside. She would have to be careful about that, she realized. Too much avoidance isn't good. If there was one thing she had learned from all this it was that you didn't want to live life with a boatload of regrets or unfinished business trailing behind you.

It wasn't all sweetness and light, however. In the brief time she and the Deadish had together there was always time for plans. The Revenant had been oddly quiet, though they were all convinced that even if the creature didn't know where they were at first, it had to know by now. They had never tried to make their location a secret. Sooner or later, one of the ghosts who passed through the terminal would talk to the creature or one of its agents, and they'd be found out. Knowing it was a matter of when rather than if kept them wary and on high alert, but the longer it went without an attack, the more relaxed they had become. Relaxed was dangerous.

The biggest concern was Cyril and Jax. The Deadish Society had seen what had been done to Peepers, and that worried them. Before Cyril, none of them had seen a ghost that opaque, much less one with the ability to permanently inflict damage on them or interact that solidly with the living.

It meant that Nora was a high-value target and that the Revenant meant business. When it came back, and there was no doubt it would, they would all need to be ready.

They just didn't know what to do. Mostly it involved setting up escape plans to get Nora and Charlie out of there unscathed. They looked to Graves for more information, but all he would say was that he was looking into it and tell them nothing substantial.

Time, she felt, was not on her side.

There was something else Nora had been keeping quiet from all of them ever since that night in the park. She didn't want to worry Charlie or Andrew, so she didn't mention that with each visit she was having more and more trouble seeing the Deadish. They got a little less loud and little less vibrant in their blue hue. She would have been thrilled at this development at the start of her ordeal, but now it was like she was losing a part of herself.

"I'm just tired," she said out loud to reassure herself. She sat up in the rafters of the Terminal, a favourite viewing spot, as she watched the Deadish and the visiting ghosts mill about below.

"Okay, but don't fall asleep up here, Nora Angel," Andrew said as he sat beside her. "It's a long way down and a permanent trip to night-night time."

She looked at him and melted inside when he smiled at her, then felt sadness rush in when she remembered that smile used to be followed by a kiss. Not anymore, though. "I miss you," she said. She didn't have to explain. He knew what she meant. He sat down beside her, so close that she should have been able to feel the warmth of his body. Instead, it was just a slight shiver as the mist gently scattered away.

"I think about our night together all the time," he said after a while. "It was the best night of my life."

"How can you say that?" Nora said sadly. "That was the night you died."

"I can think of worse ways to go out," he said with a chuckle. "At least I got to see you sleep, even if only for a couple of minutes. Mostly because of how loud your snoring was."

She snorted despite herself. They sat together in silence.

"It was the best night of my life, too," she said after a while. "I know I told you this at least a hundred times, but I don't know that you could ever truly know just how much I was in love that night."

"I knew."

"It filled up every part of me. Every inch of me wanted to explode with the joy and the knowledge of it. I would have screamed it if I could have."

"The snoring was more than enough to let me know how content you were."

"Stop it. I'm serious. I loved you."

"Loved?" he asked, a blue-hued eyebrow raising. "Past tense? I guess I'm a permanent past tense now, aren't I?"

Nora didn't know what to say. She hadn't meant to say it like that, but now that the words were out, she didn't know if she could deny they were true. Her feelings were there, but the situation itself was messed up beyond belief. "I don't know what you are," she finally said.

Andrew nodded.

"I know you are the first person I have ever loved," she said. Tears were filling his eyes, but he said nothing. "I know that you mean more to me than anyone else in the entire world. I know that my heart wanted to spend the rest of our lives together."

"Stop," he said quietly.

"Andrew," Nora said.

"Please, Nora Angel, just stop," Andrew said, putting up a false brave face that she saw through immediately. "You did everything you could to be with me. I saw that. We fought for each other and to stay together. By some twisted miracle, we still are. But even though I'm an inch away from you, I'm a whole universe away from being able to be with you. You are all I think about, and considering I don't sleep anymore, that's a lot of time to think.

"There was nothing more in my life that I loved more than you," Andrew said firmly. "*Nothing.* Part of what that kind of love entails is the knowledge that sometimes love isn't enough. That love, true love, means giving up the thing that you want most in order for the other person to be happy. I know we can't be together. Not like we were."

"But I want to!" Nora protested. "I want you!"

"No," Andrew said sadly. "You want a memory. And you can only hold me as tightly as you can a memory."

"Maybe there's some kind of way, something that Graves knows that can help us?" Nora suggested. She wanted some sign of hope. Some way of putting off the break-up, the official version of it, from happening right here and now. She wiped her tears away and turned to look at Andrew.

But he was gone. Totally, completely gone.

Nora called out for him, sure he had drifted off below, but when she looked, the place was totally empty. Only her fairy lights lit up the darkness. There were no blue hues. Nothing.

As quickly as she could, she climbed down from her perch and frantically searched for her friends. She called out for each one of them, begging them to come out of hiding. She even dared to put her head into Rocco's office, but it was empty. She cried and screamed at them to come out and see her. She collapsed in a sobbing heap outside of the double-decker bus.

Charlie, who had been outside attending to his rust bucket, came back in when he heard all the yelling. "Nora, what is it?" he asked in a panicked voice. "What's wrong?"

"They're gone, Charlie!" she sobbed. "They all left me!"

"Who left you?" he asked. "What are you talking about?"

"Andrew!" she called out. "Come back! Scarlett! Isabel!"

"Nora, you're scaring me. Stop this!"

"What if the Revenant got them? They're all gone, and it's all my fault!"

Charlie held her face in his hands and locked eyes. "Nora, I don't know what you're talking about. They're all right here. We're all right here. Even Andrew. They're looking at you right now. Can't you...?" The word he was going to use was 'see,' but he stopped short. Looking at her face, the scar by her eye was a plain and faded white, just like any other old injury.

She had lost her Vision.

CHAPTER 17

*L*et the *smug little bitch enjoy her temporary victory*, thought the Revenant bitterly, and not for the first time. It had been petty, but the Revenant allowed herself to be seen by the girl as she was driven away from the park that night after beating the Strong Man and his tiger. She had wanted the girl to know that it wasn't over, that she was still out there, and that she would be coming for her soon. She wanted her to constantly check over her shoulder, to cry herself to sleep, and to lose her mind with fear.

However, it seemed that more caution was called for now than she initially realized. More patience. God, how she hated the word! When the Revenant had powered up Cyril and his cat, Jax, she figured that would be the end of it. She had certainly enjoyed watching the small ghost get skewered while the girl was battered about. She had to restrain herself more than once at the beginning from partaking herself. It was only the wrath of the Others that stayed her hand.

But then the girl had fired that blast from her eyes. That was new. That was unexpected. It took Cyril's face, not that he needed half of it anyway, and sent him over the bridge. What should have been a quick killing on a very uneven playing field suddenly proved more dangerous and treacherous than she realized. Watching the rest of the event, including the ill-timed interference by the girl's ghostly allies, also unexpected and unknown, convinced the Revenant that patience was called for.

Yet patience was not something the Revenant was known for. It was infuriating. She had waited nearly a year to feast and now this nonsense was delaying her further. She gave up some of her own power to a moron and a cat only to watch them get spanked like naughty children. Rushing in to a confrontation now was not only ill-advised, it could unravel the Revenant itself, not to mention the secrecy the Others valued so much.

So the Revenant let the girl go.

She watched her as best she could, but it was hard to do so while maintaining her daily cover as an EMT with the hospital. The Revenant knew where the girl lived, but with all those bright, living souls it was too much of a risk to rush in there, though if the Revenant had to wait much longer she was going to do just that. Maybe it would be best to just kill them all and pin it on the girl. No one would be surprised.

Yet there were other parts she was less certain of. She knew where the girl lived, where she went to school, and that she frequented the hospital, but there were long stretches where the girl seemed to disappear. The Revenant assumed she was with her new allies, but so far her best efforts had not yielded results.

While Cyril and Jax writhed under her watchful eye in her lair, the Revenant paid several more visits to the circus to see if she could uncover any useful information. The ghosts there knew better now than to mess with her or get too close, so they gave her a wide berth. Getting information proved difficult at first, but the worries of the dead are easily taken care of if you offer them a taste of the good life.

"Speak if you know something," the Revenant offered the watching and wary crowd. "A gift will be offered."

For days the offer was repeated and none accepted. The whispers came fast and furious about what this so-called "gift" might be. Rumours sprang up. Curiosity was at an all-time high, but no one seemed eager to be rewarded, given the fate of the last man who accepted her offer.

On the twelfth day, a ghost answered. He was cloaked in black, darker than the night around it, and his voice was hoarse from lack of use. He seemed disinterested in recognition or reward and spoke without further prompting. He claimed to have told a tale or two to the girl the Revenant was asking about.

"Where is she?" the Revenant asked.

"Cullen," the ghost whispered. "Bus terminal. Downtown."

"Tell me more," the Revenant said and beckoned the old ghost forward.

"Not much to say," the old ghost muttered. "She's gotten boring, anyway. She can't see properly anymore."

Now this was news. "What do you mean?"

"She's lost her ability to see us," the old ghost said. "Or at least it isn't strong. We come and go now to her. Like shadows in the dark. I know something of shadows."

"Is that your name?" the Revenant asked. "Are you now just a Shadow?"

"I am nothing. I cast no light."

"You will with me. Come forward to me and accept your reward."

"No reward needed. What could you offer me anyway?"

"Why not find out?" the Revenant asked. She touched him, and the darkness grew firmer and whole. She pushed him back, and he stumbled before falling to the ground and kicking up dust all around him. He looked back at her, his eyes wide and moist for the first time in ages.

"Anyone else know anything?" she asked. "Would anyone else like to be rewarded and brought into my fold?"

The crowd needed no more convincing or proof. The old ghost, or Shadow as he was now called, had actually kicked up dust and interacted with the world. The thought of being able to touch, to taste, to feel again was more than appealing to the throng. It was like being offered water in a desert. Warmth in the harshest of winters. It was the gift of light in the absolute darkness. The roar of voices was deafening, and what little light there was in the room became blocked out by the raised hands.

CHAPTER 18

"Aw, come on!" moaned Tom as he walked into the living room and saw Nora perched in her same spot on the couch, staring at nothing. "Are you sitting around here again? Why do you have to be such a *bore-a*, Nora?"

Nora said nothing. The truce between her and her brother was still standing for the most part. His shot at her now was meant to get her fired up, not angry. Some faraway place in her mind appreciated the effort, but she didn't have the energy to respond. Poor Rorschach pawed at her leg for attention as well, but even that didn't get through to her.

She was aware of the irony. This dull life was what she had been craving since the start of this insanity. Now that she had some grasp of what it all was, even making friends despite her own attitude, she felt it slipping away. Her Vision was fading fast, if not already gone. The ghosts in the terminal flickered back into existence every now and then, but it was more like seeing out of the corner of your eye than actually being confident you saw something.

She missed them. She may have looked loony tunes talking to herself while walking down the street, but she knew they were there and that counted for something. She thought about what would happen if she told Westlake about all of it. She'd be locked up for sure.

Not even Vee could snap her out of her current funk. Her best friend had been surprisingly patient with Nora through all of this, even though they hadn't been spending as much time together as they normally would with all of Nora's visits to the terminal. Vee was compensating by hanging out with Kapalini more often as she hadn't managed to patch things up with Kia, even though things with Peter had fizzled out with the other girl as well.

Today, Vee brought Kapalini over with some iced capps while they talked about the ongoing friendship freeze with Kia.

"Seriously, Vee, you really need to make up with her," Kapalini was saying.

"I know I do," Vee intoned as if by rote.

Kapalini sighed loudly. "So why don't you?"

"Mostly because I left it so long. We both did. How do I even know she'd want to talk to me? I feel awful about it all, though part of me is still mad that she started going out with him in the first place. I mean, it's none of my business, but a heads-up would have been nice. Am I wrong on that?"

"Just get over it," Nora said out of nowhere. Both Vee and Kapalini were staring at Nora with wide eyes. Nora was surprised as well and was trying not to look around to see who had just said that. It had been all of three seconds, and she still couldn't believe the words had popped out of her mouth.

Vee looked super embarrassed.

"Okay?" she said, too nicely, though Nora could see that it stung. Vee might be her best friend, and Nora could say anything to her when they were alone, but it was kind of an unspoken rule that you didn't make the other feel bad in public.

"Sorry," Nora said, apologetically. "I just mean that while Kia might have broken a friend rule about dating your ex, she didn't do it to hurt you. She adores you. At this point, you're both just punishing the other needlessly. You do so many good things, so let forgiveness be another thing you're good at, okay?"

The silence was palpable. Vee looked torn about what to say next. Nora's statement was a clear message, however, and not meant unkindly. Vee finally nodded.

Nora opened her mouth to speak when there was a knock at the door. Rorschach started barking his fool head off and tore out of the room to eat whoever had approached. In the distance Nora could hear her mother rushing to answer the door.

Rorschach kept barking, despite the constant requests from both Tom and her mother to stop it. A moment later, Nora's mother appeared in the doorway to the kitchen. "Nora, sweetheart," she said. "There's a man here to see you. He says he was referred by Dr. Westlake? He's from the Culshaw Institute, which I've never heard of, but he seems sweet enough. Do you know...?"

She left the question hanging in the air and raised a questioning eyebrow at Nora. In that eyebrow, Nora thought she saw hope in her mother's eyes that this was something that was going to "fix" her little girl and get her back on the right track. Nora felt a pang of guilt at everything her parents had been going through over the past couple of months. Life may have been interesting for Nora, but it was hell for them. They only wanted to help her. She didn't like lying.

At least she didn't have to fake enthusiasm. Nora was thrilled that Graves was here to see her (who else could it be?) and perhaps give her some answers and direction. She hadn't seen him, or anyone else from her new group of friends, thanks to her Vision fading, in quite a while and she was looking forward to being able to talk about things with another person without fear of a padded room following the discussion.

"Sure, Mom, I'll talk to him," she said. The enthusiasm must have shown on her face because everyone in the room took the hint. Unasked, Kapalini gathered up her stuff and mumbled something about waiting in the car while Nora's mother went back to the front door to escort the miracle worker into the kitchen.

Vee coughed at that point and started to busy herself to go. "We'll talk later, okay?" she said quietly.

"Wait," Nora said. She got up, moved over to her friend, threw her arms around her, and hugged her tightly. Maybe too tightly, but Nora had a lot of pent-up love to get out of her system. Even though she may have upset her friend, she wanted Vee to know how much she loved her. Vee's arms hung limply at her sides for a moment before she relented and hugged back.

"Jerk," Vee said with a giggle into Nora's ear.

"Jerk," Nora said back. Just like that, everything was fine.

Graves walked in and took in the scene with his usual furrowed brow. Though indistinct, Nora caught a glimpse of McCrae's ghost wafting in behind him. Every time she thought she could focus on him, however, he faded from view. Vee gathered her stuff and smiled at Graves and his wild hair as she let go of Nora and started to walk past him. "Hi there," she said. "Your hair is kind of crazy!"

"Vee!" Nora said, hugely embarrassed. "Manners!"

"Oops!" said Vee, who blushed furiously. "I mean, crazy, but cool? I don't know?"

"Thank you, my dear," Graves said with a wink. "I do indeed have wild locks. It's because I'm a party animal from dusk to dawn.'"

Vee was absolutely delighted. "Oh, Nora, I like this one! He's lively! Call me later, okay?"

"I will," Nora and Graves said at the same time. Vee just laughed as she went outside.

Once she was gone, Nora and Graves sat in a comfortable silence for a moment or two. She offered him a drink, and he gladly accepted a cool glass of lemonade. After a few sips, Graves moved closer to Nora and put his glasses down on his nose to get a better look at her scar. "May I?" he asked as he reached toward it. Nora nodded, and he gently traced the scar with his fingers and inspected her closely. It was the kind of thing someone else might find creepy, but Nora found it warm and reassuring. She felt like someone was finally caring for her.

After a moment he nodded as if in answer to a silent question and then he gestured toward the backyard. "Let's talk," he said. "I expect you have questions."

Sitting down gingerly on the lawn chair with the ice in his lemonade clinking, Graves lifted his chin to the sky and basked in the warm summer morning light. Some of the age seemed to come off him in that instant. Nora suspected that he spent a lot of time indoors at the museum from how pale he was.

She sat in the old swing opposite him and twirled her toe in the dirt at her feet. She hadn't sat in this swing in at least a few years and was surprised at how it brought back memories and feelings that she would have sworn were long gone. She could feel her father's hands on her back pushing her as she swung back into them. She could picture Rorschach as a puppy tearing back and forth under her feet. She even remembered the exhilaration of jumping off the swing when it was nearing the apex of its forward swing and flying through the air until she came to a rough landing several feet away while laughing her head off.

"This is what it's all about," Graves said as he closed his eyes and raised his chin to the sun. "Light. Warmth. A few moments of respite in a world that goes by you in a blur. *This* is what people should live for."

"It's nice," Nora agreed. "Feels simpler."

"Indeed," Graves said. He looked down at the sweating glass in his hand and swirled the remaining mixture before swallowing it all at once. He relished the drink and savoured it. Then he burped loudly. Nora tried not to laugh. He was still a bit nutty. "Now let's get to the complicated," he said pleasantly.

"Okay," Nora said. She watched Graves shakily put down the glass and dry his hands on his pants.

"You've lost your Vision," Graves said. It wasn't a question, so Nora didn't respond. "You've also lost some of your drive and fire, I see. Missing some piss and vinegar. Charlie tells me you've stopped visiting with him and the others. No, no, don't bother to deny it. One foot in that world and then the rug is pulled out from under you. I've been there as well. Still am, in many ways."

"So you understand," Nora said.

"Yes," Graves said solemnly. "And no. You see, I have a little more experience in these matters. I can help you, should you so choose."

"You can?" Nora felt hope rising in her chest. She had started to give up on the idea that she would be able to see her friends again. Not being able to see Andrew was painful. Not being able to talk to those who understood her left her feeling alone and vulnerable, especially with the Revenant still out there somewhere. The way she was now, she wouldn't be able to see an attack coming. She kept expecting to suddenly be dead, her loved ones wondering where the claw marks had come from, and have that be the end of it. Maybe she would be able to see them again!

Graves eyes suddenly went dark and cold in response to her joy. "This isn't a kindness, young lady. I'm not doing you any good. In fact, I'm condemning you. Damning you to the life that I had and that I spent many a good year and many a good brain cell on that in the end has left me with nothing. I'm offering a life that has taken the only good thing from me and left me with a bitter taste in my mouth. It's a living hell, so don't look so damn eager to grab on to it."

Nora was taken aback at the anger and despair in his voice. It scared her, but she was determined to go forward. She was confident that she could handle whatever he had to say, or at least that's what she told herself. It kind of sounded like an ad warning about drunk driving where the person who has had too much to drink swears they can still drive. She just had to believe that wasn't true in her case. *God, isn't that what drunk people say as well?* She pushed the thought away as best she could.

"Tell me," she said. "What have I got to lose? At this point, I'm dead either way. At least this way I might have a fighting chance."

"The telling is difficult," Graves sighed. "The showing, however, is a bit easier. You are aware that Mr. McCrae is here with me, are you not?"

"I can't really see him," Nora said. "Just in passing. Out of the corner of my eye. I blink and he's gone."

Graves nodded as if it made perfect sense. "The Vision isn't gone, you see, but it works much the same the rest of the human body and mind work. If you don't sleep, you become tired. Sluggish. You can't think as quickly as you normally would, no?"

Nora nodded. "Like I'm moving in slow motion."

"Exactly. If you don't exercise, you become more fatigued. If you don't eat, you become hungry and then weak."

"So you're saying I need to eat something?" Nora asked.

"I am saying you need to *nurture* yourself," Graves clarified. "The body and mind need more than just food and shelter to flourish. They need comfort. Love. Support. Guidance. All of these things you need in order to live and function properly. If you wish to build a muscle or your capacity for love and understanding, you must use them regularly and find ways to encourage them along. Survival is not enough, nor is it the point of life. We need connections, all of us."

With that, he reached his hand in front of him and grasped an invisible object. If she stared at the spot directly, all Nora could see was a crazy old man shaking the hand of an imaginary friend. Nora focused on Graves himself and did her best to avoid looking at his hand. Here, at the edge of her field of view, she could make out a distinctly blue human shape and saw that Graves was holding the forearm of John McCrae.

The contact lasted for little more than a couple of seconds, but Graves sighed heavily and let go, looking a bit younger. His eyes were a little more focused, as though he had just woken up from a well-deserved and much-needed nap. "What was that?" Nora asked in wonderment.

"Friendship," Graves replied simply. "Hard-earned, honestly meant, and freely shared. Though sometimes he's a bit mouthy." He laughed at this joke and winked at the empty space in front of him.

"He did something to you, didn't he?" Nora said.

"Something *for* me," Graves clarified. "You see, Mr. McCrae gives me some of himself as a means to fuel my Vision."

"You're... *eating* him?" Nora asked, horrified.

"Absolutely not!" thundered Graves. "Do you eat your mother and father every time they hug you or tell you they love you? No, they are feeding you. They are nurturing you. They are giving of themselves freely to make you happier and whole. It doesn't cost them anything beyond time and effort, not that they would see it as a cost at all.

"If you grieve, does contact from your friends or loved ones not give you the strength you need to stand? The energy that is transferred is real, even if it isn't something valued or explained by science. It is good, and it is fuel for the soul. As long as we are not greedy or selfish, this is a fountain from which water will eternally spring."

"So his energy is giving you strength. It's what allows you to see?" Nora said as she began to understand.

"It's limited, but yes. Mr. McCrae and I have spent so much time to ourselves that our bond has become quite deep. His is the only soul energy that I take into me, which is why he is the only ghost I see these days. We have been through the wars, he and I, and spent our share of blood together. I will accept his energy, his friendship, but not that of others. I am too old and too spent for that. The little I get from him is enough to let me see him. For that, I am content. It's too dangerous to go further. I should know."

Nora knew it was dangerous ground and might provoke him into leaving or clamming up, but she was too curious. "What danger? What aren't you telling me? You keep hinting or teasing about all of these horrible things, but you won't come out and just tell me."

"Because I don't want to," Graves snapped.

"Then why are you here? Why even bother telling me anything? What is the point to you even still being alive? Why not just give up and die?" Nora yelled. She wanted to rage and to hurt this man whom she didn't even know just to have some power over someone.

She could tell he was fighting a war within himself. His face turned purple with the effort of keeping whatever it was inside bottled and contained. "Don't you think I haven't thought about that?" he asked quietly. "Don't you think I haven't tried? Mr. McCrae wouldn't let me. Charlie wouldn't let me. I have hope, however stupid and pointless it is, and it wouldn't let me go either. Now you are here, in front of me, and my own damn sense of honour won't let me."

"I didn't ask you to come here," Nora said coldly.

"Put out your hand," Graves said without emotion.

"Why?"

"Just do it."

"*Why?*" Nora demanded.

"So you can live!" Graves shouted. "So you can live where my... where others can't! It's your damn turn, so stop being so damn stubborn and shove your hand out!"

Nora stared daggers at him. She wanted to throw him out and be done with all of it. She was tired, but she was too curious. She held out her hand to no one or nothing in particular that she or anyone else could see. She was aware that anyone looking at her would think she had gone crazy.

At first nothing happened. Then there was a cool, pleasant sensation that flowed into her fingertips. Then into her hand, her forearm, and then past her shoulders. Around and around it went until it wrapped itself around her body. She wanted to cry at the joy and relief. She let go of tension she didn't know she was carrying as that invisible hug consoled her and told her that everything was going to be all right. For the first time since Andrew died, Nora really allowed herself to let go and grieve. She cried for her loss, and she cried for her own pain. She pulled on that energy then felt it rush into her. The sensation had gone from opening her mouth to catch snowflakes to putting her mouth next to a tap and sucking water in greedily. The thirst and hunger she felt was being quenched and greed was replacing it. She wanted more and pulled it in as fast as she could. It never seemed to be enough.

The cooling sensation snapped suddenly and quickly, and Nora was jolted back to her senses. Graves had just slapped her. Her hand was still outstretched, but the fingers were clenched so tightly that she thought they would break if she kept up the pressure. Gradually, she calmed herself and relaxed her fingers to the point where she was able to flex them and feel the blood start flowing again. Breathing slowly, she opened her eyes. She did her best to prepare herself for what she might or might not see.

In front of her stood John McCrae, bright blue and vibrant, smiling sadly down at her with a deep understanding. He said nothing, merely nodded, and moved off to the far end of the yard. He looked exhausted.

From the way she followed his movements, Graves could see that her Vision was back. "My apologies for the slap. I needed to interrupt you before you went too far. He has given you a gift," he said. "It was his idea, his to give, though it will cost him for a while."

"Have I hurt him?" Nora asked in a whisper as she rubbed her aching cheek. She felt a flush near her right eye and resisted the urge to look in the mirror to confirm what she knew deep in her gut: that the purple colour had returned to her scar. "I couldn't stop. I didn't want to."

"He's fine, or he will be. He is beyond physical hurt at least," Graves said. "His essence is diminished from sharing with us, but it will come back in time. Much like time heals all wounds, time will see him grow stronger once again. But you see the danger now. You see the risk."

"What would I have done to him if you didn't stop me?" Nora asked.

"You would have lost yourself," Graves said. "You would have started your journey to being one of *them*."

"One of whom? Can I control it? Do I need to keep doing that in order to see? What does this energy come from?" Nora thought she had questions before, but now they came faster than she could think of them.

Graves was a patient teacher, however, and waited for her to be calm. "I will answer your second question first. Yes, you can control it. You need to think of it as a gift and only accept that which is freely given, and only take what you must. All relationships should work this way, though from what I've seen on my television lately, there are few that do. You do not need to do this often, rarely, in fact, if you merely wish to keep the Vision. Over time, years, it will gradually fade and become harder to use if all you want to do is see. Getting energy from a variety of places will keep you fresh and clear, but if you focus on just one person, as I have done, then it becomes more specialized. If you spend it, though, you will need to get it more often."

"Spend it?" Nora asked. "Like when I blasted that guy on the bridge?"

Graves nodded. "I will admit that I don't know much about this aspect of Vision, having seen so few examples of it in my own life and having directly experienced it myself only once long ago. It takes a special sort of person to be able to do what you did. How much energy that takes, how often you use it, all of these are things you will have to work out over time if you are fortunate enough to get it."

"And my first question?" Nora asked.

Graves hesitated and looked off toward McCrae, who was watching quietly. McCrae nodded and gestured. Graves cleared his throat. "You stand at a crossroads, young lady. You have a choice between fighting against evil or becoming it. If you take in too much energy, if you crave it and allow yourself to hoard it, then you become the very thing that is hunting you. Mr. McCrae gave you his energy freely as a gift. It was his compassion, his mercy, his love for me that allowed him to do this. Since it was your first experience with sharing energy, it surprised you and got the better of you. Instead of accepting what he had to give, you became hungry and greedy. You were ready to steal to get what you want, to rush the process, to take without giving. You were ready to take from him because you could. To take too much without permission is to start your journey toward becoming a revenant."

Nora's eyes widened in surprise.

"They were human once, like you and I, though seeing the depths to which they are capable of going makes me sometimes rethink that assessment. Whatever the origins of their masters, the Others, the revenants are former humans who have had their greed transform them into these creatures. They don't care who they hurt so long as they have what they want. They want a meal, they want pleasure, but they don't want the commitment, the structure, the patience, or the work involved in maintaining a real relationship. They want food and care nothing for what they leave behind."

"But they feed on living people," Nora said. "Not ghosts, right?"

Graves shook his head. "It is the progression of the illness, of the greed. They begin much like you and I. They are able to see the other world and derive satisfaction from the interaction. Then they take more and more than they need to be a part of that world. They take more and more so they can dominate it or control it. When that becomes insufficient, when water is not a substitute for a buffet, they turn to the living. Your body, right now, is merely a shell for the spirit inside. Only that spirit right now is richer, fuller, and tastier because it isn't tainted by death. Your spirit, your energy, is the best of all because it is thick and rich. Those who become revenants discover that energy and feed on it to the point where real food no longer sustains them or drives them. Life no longer touches them in the same way. They may have flesh and blood for bodies, but the energy inside them is stolen from others and keeps them alive and moving."

"They sound like vampires," Nora said.

"They are," Graves said. "I wouldn't be surprised if they were the actual inspiration behind the creatures, which are, incidentally, fictional."

"So if I take energy in, I'll become one of them eventually?" Nora asked. She felt under her eye and was repulsed at the thought that she might want to consume her friends one day. She wouldn't have believed she was capable of it before, but the brief contact with McCrae had her drinking in the energy almost against her will. Logic and reason had flown out the window. She had been acting on a near-instinctual level. If Graves hadn't been there to stop her, she would have sucked all of John McCrae in and looked for seconds. She shuddered at the thought.

"No," Graves said, appraising her. "I don't think you will. The revenants gather energy because they are hungry. They steal their food and gather it so that others will starve. You, my dear, are not that kind of person. I've heard about you and your compassion for the ghost called Peepers. You give other people strength and you inspire loyalty. Look at how the Deadish respond to you and care for you. Look at how Andrew follows you and tries to protect you. Look at how Charlie watches you. I know that look."

Nora snorted. "Charlie? Are you serious? He hates me."

"You and I both know that's not true," Graves said with a wink.

"There is nothing like that going on," Nora insisted. "Believe me."

"As you say," Graves said. "Anyway, there are other ways to get soul energy that require patience. Allow it to be given to you through compassion, love, support, and forgiveness. It's about acceptance of that love, feeling worthy to receive it. In some cases, it's also about moving on. A spirit will give their energy to their loved one, often those without Vision at all, to give them the comfort and support they need to continue to live their lives. It's true that we take those who pass on before us with us wherever we go. When a person dies, that energy is never truly lost. It gets passed on. You can be cynical and say it goes into the power lines, but instead I believe it goes into the people left behind who were loved. You should take this energy and live life to the fullest while revelling in the joy of what was and what will be. Then, when it's your turn, pass it on to the next person. You may not be able to see them, but you feel them in your heart always where it matters the most."

"It sounds beautiful," Nora said.

"It is," Graves said. "That's the way it should be. For a revenant, however, it's about control. They hold on to this energy, to this love, because they can or because they're afraid to let go. *You must learn to let go,* do you understand me? It does no one any good, the living or the dead, to dwell on a past that cannot be brought back. Revenants, damn them, get so caught up in the possession of all of these souls that they lose themselves. I don't just mean that figuratively, I mean that they barely remember who or what they were before. They become machines of greed. Try as you might, and I have tried, these things forget who or what they were. Their first victims are really themselves.

"Their other victims, the ones they feed on… they're a different story. Sometimes you see them. The person they consumed, that is," Graves said in a hushed voice. "The revenant lets them free to see what they've become. Breathes them out of those gills. Lets part of their spirit out in the world once again. But twisted. Most in my community don't believe in them, but I know they're real. I've seen it.

"Wisps, to clarify, are soul fragments that are taken but not fully absorbed by a revenant. The original host body that served as the source of the Wisp may or may not still be alive. It matters not to a revenant. They keep and house some of these souls, and their own bodies and minds twist and bend them like a partially digested meal. Then they can be freed at will by the creature and sent to do its bidding."

"Wait a minute," Nora said. "Are you saying that part of me is in that thing?"

"Yes," Graves said. "I'm afraid so. We leave a part of ourselves with every person who plays a significant part in our lives, but in the case of a revenant it's a literal truth."

"What about Andrew? Is he in that thing? I need to know!"

Graves wasn't sure what to say here. "You must understand that I don't know everything, even if you think I do. He was absorbed, that much is clear, but his ghost is still free because of your interference. Part of his essence escaped, but I don't know how much. Was it the majority? How much is needed to remain oneself? I don't know how much of either of you is in the creature."

"Can I get him out? Can I get myself out of it?" At that moment Nora was ready to go on the offensive. She would track down the thing and be rid of it, free Andrew, and save the day.

"Yes," Graves said. Nora started to get up, but Graves motioned for her to sit back down. "The Revenant could release your Wisp, and Andrew's, but I'm not sure you'd want it. It is more a part of the creature now than it is you. The Wisp could rejoin the original body it came from, but at a cost. The Wisp might be able to take control or continue the work of the Revenant, having been infected by it, and slowly convert the host body to match the parasite. I have seen it happen. No one in my order would believe me, but I've seen it. I still think there must be a way to cleanse the soul fragments and rejoin it with the rest of its essence. It would be good if we could set the soul free of a Revenant, even if the body it came from is already long since doomed. There has to be a way.

"But I couldn't find one. I was disgraced. My order cut ties because of my theories. I've not even told Charlie that they abandoned me. I don't think he could take it."

Graves began weeping then, uncontrollably. Nora eased herself off the swing and put her arm around the old man. McCrae watched on, quietly, and bowed his head in sadness.

"This one," Graves said after a while. "This revenant after you seems young. It's too eager, for one thing. Killing people, the ghosts it sent after you, all of it, smacks of immaturity. I sometimes wonder..."

"Wonder what?"

"Wonder who?" Graves asked. "Can I help you? Do you have my badminton racket? It's an heirloom. There was a slate it came with as well. It's long gone."

Nora blinked in surprise. When she looked into the man's eyes, she could see that he looked at her as though she were a stranger. She raised an eyebrow toward McCrae.

"He lasted longer than I thought he would," McCrae said sadly. "It comes and goes. He's tired."

"Who's tired?" Graves asked. "Where am I? I want to go home now."

"Can I give you a ride home?" Nora asked him.

Graves looked at her, and his eyes lit up. "Yes, young lady, you can. I would like that. Say, you're quite a looker, you know."

"Thanks, sir, I appreciate that."

"I know just the young boy for you," Graves said with a smile. Then he frowned as he remembered a forgotten detail. "Oh, no, of course he's taken. Isn't he? He's not, now. Wait. Oh my, what's going on?"

"Don't worry about it," Nora said. "I have my eye on you." She gave him a quick kiss on the cheek, and he hooted with pleasure.

She got him into the car and drove him home. McCrae floated quietly in the back, and the three of them drove in near silence. Whatever Graves had been through in his life, it had left him broken. Nora felt a huge amount of pity for whatever it was the man had gone through and also a tremendous amount of respect for still pushing forward with his life. She could see why Charlie cared so much about him.

She wasn't surprised when she pulled up at the house and saw Charlie sitting on the front porch, waiting. He looked relieved when he saw Graves, and he rushed over to open the car door. Graves swatted at him immediately and told him to get off his lawn and that he wasn't buying any crap today, but between Charlie's patient voice and McCrae's familiar presence, they managed to get him into the house.

A short while later, Charlie came back outside and saw Nora waiting by the car. He walked over to her and leaned next to her, his eyes focused on the ground the whole time. "Thanks," he said.

"No problem," she replied.

"You can see again, huh?" he asked. "He showed you how. I didn't think he would. Not ever again."

"Why not? What happened to him, Charlie? What aren't you telling me?"

"You aren't the first person he's helped," Charlie said with a sigh. "It used to be a point of pride with him to guide the younger generation in the fight against the forces of evil. I think it was something he romanticized. Heck, all of Hollywood does it these days. The goal is not to kill vampires anymore, but to become one of them. If only they knew."

"I certainly plan to burn my copies of my vampire novels when I get home," Nora said. She looked at Charlie to see if he was smiling, but there was no hint of it on his lips.

"My parents were killed by a revenant," Charlie said bluntly.

"Oh," Nora gasped. "Oh. I didn't know. I'm sorry."

"Thank you," Charlie said. "I was young when it happened. I fought the thing, tried to pull it off, but it didn't save them." He pulled up his sleeve to show the purple mark on his arm. "But I got a present all the same. It gouged me, and I swiped at it, and now I have my own scar to forever immortalize my childhood trauma.

"It's also how I met Graves. He found me in a child psych ward, muttering about demons and monsters, and he knew what had happened. Everyone else had written me off, even my aunts and uncles, but Graves brought me home with him. Taught me everything I know. I had a family again. The three of us were really happy together."

"The three of you?" Nora asked.

"Yeah," Charlie said. "Me, Graves, and Alice. His daughter. My... friend."

"I didn't know he had a daughter," Nora said, surprised.

"Emphasis on the word 'had,'" Charlie said angrily. It wasn't directed at her, but at the memory. Whatever it was, it was so painful that he looked like he would break. "Anyway, we'll talk soon. I have to go to the hospital. My shift is starting." Before she could ask him another question, Charlie hopped into his destroyed van and coaxed it to life. "Hey," he called out to her. "I'm really glad you can see again. I like the mark. Purple suits you."

She felt the flush in her cheeks, and before she could decide what it meant, Charlie drove off without another word.

CHAPTER 19

When Nora arrived back at the Cullen Terminal early the next day, she wasn't expecting such enthusiastic applause. All of the Deadish, Andrew, and the regular visitors to the terminal were there and shouting and cheering. Most of them tried to give her a hug or high-five her, but of course they just passed through. It was the thought that counted. There was even a weak banner strung up over Reno's ticket counter that read "Welcome back," though it looked pretty sketchy. She was wondering who had made it when Charlie sheepishly stepped forward.

"Not my best work," he said shyly.

"You did this?" Nora asked. It was an odd gesture coming from him. She had figured by now that being nice wasn't something he was capable of.

"I helped!" Scarlett broke in. She was below, at Nora's knees, holding on to a struggling Scraps. "I told him what to write."

"Thanks, Scarlett," Nora said before looking at all of them. Rocco tried to look totally disinterested as he polished his gun while Sarge hoisted up his large belt to keep his pants from falling down. Isabel smiled sweetly at her and shrugged by way of apology in case their welcome was a little too much. Reno was busy moaning to anyone who would listen about the lack of cake and how much he missed it. It all made Nora smile. She felt more at home here than at her actual home. "Thanks, all of you. It's really nice. I'm glad to be back."

Nora looked around for Andrew and found him standing at the edge of the crowd. They hadn't had a chance to speak since their last conversation. Were they broken up? Were they even still together at that point? From the way he kept his distance, it was clear that Andrew didn't know what their status was either. That would be Future Nora's problem, Nora decided. Right now it was time to enjoy being back.

"Now we can take the fight to them," Sarge boomed. "I'm eager to take on that big man again."

"I've got more than a few things to say myself," agreed Rocco. "And so does my gun."

"Slow down, guys!" Reno said. "She just got here. Once she's ready to go, I'm sure she'll give the word. Let's just enjoy the party. Even if there isn't any cake. What I wouldn't give for some freakin' cake!"

"Enough about the cake!" Isabel shouted at him in frustration. Scraps started barking at that point, and then they were all off and arguing. Nora couldn't help but laugh in delight.

While they were all distracted and having fun, Nora slipped off to go and check on Peepers. The little ghost was where she left him, lying down, looking even worse than before. His hue was so transparent that parts of him were indistinguishable from the surface underneath. His eyes lit up when he saw her.

"Adelaide?" he asked. Nora's heart broke at the question but also at the weakness of his voice. He was very hoarse.

"Not yet, but I'm looking," Nora told him. He nodded, satisfied, and relaxed.

"Are you feeling better? I was worried," Peepers asked.

"Ha!" Nora laughed. "You are the sweetest man. I should be asking you how you're doing!"

"I'm okay," he said. "I have some new friends here who look after me. Your sweetheart, Andrew, is particularly kind."

Nora winced on the inside but held the smile on her face. "Yes, he is. He's amazing."

"You'll need him, won't you?" he asked. "When you have to fight those things again? Oh, I wish you wouldn't. I don't want to lose you like I've lost my Adelaide."

"I don't know if I can fight them," she said truthfully.

"Why not?"

"Because it would cost too much to do what I need to do. Remember when I blasted that man on the bridge?"

"Of course. You saved yourself and probably me. It was very exciting!"

"Well, that used up a lot of the energy I have in me. I found out that in order to do that again, I have to take energy from you guys. From my friends. It's what lets me see you."

"Okay," Peepers said. Without hesitation, he lifted his hand out and reached for her. This little ghost, with nothing left within himself, was offering himself freely and without hesitation. It was sacrifice on a level she had never witnessed. *This*, she thought, *is what true love is. Not romance or passion, but sacrifice.* She wanted to reach out and take it. She craved it in a way that shocked her. She also knew that if she did this, it might be the last thing he ever saw, and she couldn't bear to see hurt and betrayal in his face if she couldn't control herself.

"I can't," she said, swallowing hard. "Thank you, but I can't." She explained to him what had happened to her before with John McCrae. What it could mean to them all if she couldn't control it. All of her fears and anxiety rushed out at once.

When she was done talking, she saw that his hand and determination hadn't wavered once. "Let me help you," he said. "I can't help Adelaide. I can help you. I don't mind."

She started crying because she was so touched. "No, Peepers. Not you."

"Then me, Nora Angel," Andrew said from behind her. "Let me give you what you need."

"Me too," Scarlett piped up.

"It'll be an honour and pleasure," Sarge said.

"Yeah," Reno agreed. "All of that."

"We'll all help," Isabel said.

"Not me," grunted Rocco from behind. "Youse may be nice to look at, but I like all my bits and bobs where they are, thank you."

Isabel sighed in exasperation. "Really, Rocco? You're going to take a stand over *this*? You aren't going to help?"

"What's in it for me?" asked Rocco. "A one-way trip to her belly if she can't hack it? Nah, I'm good over here."

"YOU'LL DO IT AND YOU'LL LIKE IT OR I'LL TEAR YOUR FOOL HEAD OFF!" Scarlett screamed at him. Rocco nodded in agreement as fast as his head could bob up and down. Scarlett looked back to Nora and was immediately sweet again. "See? We'll all help."

"It might not be enough," Charlie said from the doorway. "The kind of energy that you'll need... even if everyone here gives you some of theirs, it'll cost them for a while, and they may not be as effective." Rocco snorted as though this was obvious. "Besides, it might be enough for a blast, and then you could go 'blind' again. You'll need a lot. And you don't even know how to control it. Even if you can control it, do you even know how to let loose another blast? Way too many variables."

Nora was relieved, though she tried not to show it. That meant she wouldn't have to risk her friends or anyone else. She was free and clear just to maintain what she had.

"No problem," Reno said. Nora's heart dropped. "We canvass for volunteers. If the people in this room aren't enough to juice her up, then we go looking. I bet there are lots of souls here at the terminal who would be willing to donate. There are souls at the school, too."

Charlie was nodding reluctantly. "And at the hospital."

"Not to mention the cemetery," Sarge added.

"And the mall!" Isabel squealed in delight. When everyone stopped to look at her like she had two heads, she went defensive. "What? There are ghosts everywhere. Might as well do some window shopping while we're out."

"See, Nora Angel? We're going to solve all our problems," Andrew said. Nora wasn't sure if he meant just the Revenant or something more. Once again, a problem for Future Nora to sort out.

THE IDEA was solid in theory. Grab some ghosts, get some juice, do it kind of like a blood drive or something. It wouldn't be a big deal at all.

Well, it was a big deal. In fact, it was chaos from beginning to end. It screwed Nora over in more ways than she could count. If she had a time machine, could go back and stop herself, not only would she but she would also slap herself silly as well for even having considered it.

Inside the terminal, there were less than five or six ghosts still hanging around after her welcome. They were all willing to donate, though both they and Nora were terrified that it was going to go to crap. It didn't help that she emphasized over and over again that it could go to crap. Finally, Charlie had to pull her to the side and tell her to stop scaring the dead people.

With the first contact after that, an older portly ghost named Alvin, they both closed their eyes and prepared for a shock like a finger jammed into an electrical outlet that would fry them both. Instead, Nora took her time and was overly cautious as she probed around the pulling sensation. Slowly, very slowly, the cool feeling in her fingers that she had felt before started working its way into her fingers.

Nora wanted to grab and pull on that energy flow once it started, but she forced herself to be more passive and accept only what was sent. Instead of rushing through a meal and gobbling everything up, she savoured it and allowed herself to dwell in the moment. With the second, third, and fourth person she found it getting easier to control. She got the hang of Acceptance, as she named it for herself, and was all that much better for it. She let herself be wary of the fact that she was never full and wanted more. That awareness kept her grounded.

She enjoyed the process. It was kind of like communion in church. Nice, peaceful, relaxing. She could do this. It was getting easier. It was good.

Then she went out in public to get more, and that was where her troubles began.

CHAPTER 20

The Deadish insisted on going with her everywhere she went for her own protection. The problem was that they were overly enthusiastic, both in the realm of protecting her from potential rogue spirits, but also in the drive to get ghosts to donate. At Isabel's insistence, they went to the mall first. She clapped in glee and hopped up and down on her one good leg.

Isabel's spirit had a bit more potency than most, being so recently dead. She still had a bit of strength and was able to move objects a little and knock things over. According to Reno, she was prime haunting material at the moment, and he'd been trying to convince her to go out with him to spoke some locals and irritate people from their old school. So far she'd rebuffed him and kept her talents to herself, but her teenage brain got overwhelmed at the first window display. What happened next wasn't subtle.

"Oh my god, I have to have it!" she squealed at the shoebox mountain display. Andrew was with them and just looked bored out of his mind. There were an array of amazing looking shoes, Nora had to admit, though they were all way too expensive and many of them looked incredibly impractical. She was happy to just look and admire when Isabel threw part of herself through the window. Nora yelped in surprise, startling some of the living people milling around her. She tried to pass it off as excitement over the shoes.

Through the window, Nora could only watch as Isabel, in her over-eagerness to browse, managed to knock over a pair of shoes. Then another. So far no one else but Nora and Andrew had seen this. The last thing Nora wanted was to draw attention to herself.

"Isabel!" hissed Nora. "Stop it! You're going to make a mess!" Isabel's head, however, was on the other side of the glass and she couldn't hear. She was a little too far gone in the realm of bliss to care.

"She's happy," Andrew said with a shrug and a smile. "It's too bad she's dead. I wonder if she'd get a discount because of the missing leg if she were alive? Or would she consider it a two-for-one sale? Ha!"

"That's not nice," Nora said sharply. A little girl had been walking by and was pulling her dolly behind her. She lifted up the doll and inspected it to see what she was doing wrong. Her father gave Nora an odd look and pulled his daughter along after him.

At that moment, a pimply-faced teen ghost bounded over the railing on the floor above her and crashed into the fountain below, though his form barely made a ripple in the water. Moments later, Sarge was right behind him, screaming "CANNONBALL!" as he dropped like a boulder on top of the other ghost and crushed him.

"What are you doing?" Nora yelled at them. Sarge looked surprised to be yelled at, especially by an insubordinate, but not as surprised as the shoppers who were wondering why this odd girl was yelling and who she was yelling at.

Another ghost came running around the corner with Scraps at his heels barking and snapping. Scarlett was hooting and yelling for the dog to hurry up and catch the man.

"Scraps!" Nora yelled. "Bad dog! Leave that man alone!"

People were now starting to be concerned, and Nora noticed one woman tap on the arm of a security guard. Behind her, Isabel pushed over another pair of shoes. If she wasn't careful, it was going to be Riverside all over again.

"These are great!" came Isabel's muffled voice.

"Okay," Nora said to Andrew. "People are staring at me, so you go and get them. This is not the way to get help! They are harassing these people, even if they are dead! I need volunteers, not prisoners!"

Andrew raised his hands in surrender. "Fine, fine. But you better get Isabel."

"Why?" Nora turned around and saw that Isabel, now mostly in the display, had pushed more shoes and boxes out of the way. The entire tower display was now hanging on by a thread. If she didn't stop her, Isabel was going to knock the whole thing over.

Nora rushed in and pushed past a clerk, who asked her if she needed any help. Nora offered a terse "No, thank you" and went to the front display, where she proceeded to scold it. "What are you doing?"

"Are you speaking to the shoes, ma'am?" asked the concerned clerk.

"What? No," Nora asked. "Sorry." She looked back to the display. "Get out of there!"

"Do you want me to get something for you?" asked the clerk.

"Come on!" snapped Nora. Isabel just laughed and plunged back in.

"Do you want me to get some*one* for you?" asked the clerk, now genuinely worried.

"Now!"

"Now?" the clerk asked, looking around for support. Finally, she rushed off out of the store. Nora paid her little attention.

"Fine!" Isabel said, though she wasn't moving. Nora reached over to her, futilely, because she couldn't actually grab the girl, and her arm brushed a shoebox, just faintly.

And the whole display came crashing down, Nora's arm outstretched in the middle of it, as all the people walking by in the mall stood there staring at her through the window, including a tired-looking security guard and the clerk Nora had unwittingly sent to fetch him.

"WHAT DO you want to tell me about it?" asked Dr. Westlake as he clicked his pen.

"It was nothing," Nora said. "A misunderstanding. I just wanted to look at a pair of shoes."

"And then you were arrested," Westlake said.

"No! Not arrested. I was never arrested. I was detained and then asked to leave the mall. For at least a year."

"Hmmm," Westlake said. Pen click. God, she was going to shove that pen up his ass if he kept doing that.

"The report said you were shouting at people and things that weren't there. Is this a recurrence? Are you still having trouble separating dreams and reality? Is it the paramnesia?"

"*No*," Nora said. "*Definitely not.* I'm feeling much better. In the mall, I just thought I saw someone I knew."

Dr. Westlake sighed. "Listen, Nora, I'm not here to judge you, and I don't want you to be afraid of me. This is a safe place where you can say anything." Nora doubted that. It was a safe place to say something if you wanted to get locked up. "I can't help you unless you're willing to talk to me."

"I swear, I'm fine," Nora insisted. "Everything is getting back to normal."

"YOU ARE *so* not normal," Vee insisted as she accepted the cup of coffee. Vee offered to get her out of the house, which had become a little more tense since the mall incident, and her parents had reluctantly agreed. They relaxed and chatted, and it was nice to feel normal for a change.

"I agree," Rocco spat from behind her. "You're nuts."

As usual these days, she hadn't gone out alone. "Shut up," Nora said.

Why did it have to be Rocco today?

Vee laughed. "It's not my fault. You're the one who had to have a new pair of Toms!"

Try as she might, Nora couldn't help but snort. She hated it when she did that! The more she tried to cover it up, the more it kept happening. Vee started laughing too, which made things worse. Nora slowed her breathing and calmed down. She lifted the white hot chocolate with extra whipped cream up to her mouth and couldn't hold it. She snorted again and blew foam all over the table. This made Vee laugh even harder, and she slopped some of her coffee. Of course, once again, people were staring. This time, though, they probably didn't think she was crazy. Or at least not the kind that needed police attention.

"We look crazy," Vee giggled as she wiped up the spill. "We're making a mess!"

"Don't use the 'c' word, okay?" Nora said.

Rocco rolled his eyes and looked bored. He shifted from where he was sitting, reached over, and promptly dipped his finger into Nora's cup.

"Hey, don't do that!" Nora said, giving Rocco the evil eye. Vee looked at her as she was cleaning, and Nora smiled awkwardly.

"We made the mess, we should clean up the mess," Vee said. "The people who work here have to put up with enough, don't you think?"

"Totally," Nora said. She shot Rocco a meaningful look. "We should be on our best behaviour."

Rocco laughed as Vee raised an eyebrow at her and grinned. "Well, maybe not our *best* behaviour. Not all the time, anyway. You have to have a little bit of fun, right?"

Rocco took this as encouragement. He stuck out his leg and began to mime tripping people and then yelling "SPLAT" as he imagined them falling over.

"That's not appropriate!" Nora said. She was speaking to Rocco about his behaviour, but Vee was obviously confused.

"What are you talking about? I just mean going out late, bending a few rules. Road trip shenanigans. You know… the usual."

Rocco snorted loudly and then spat a giant wad of ghost goo into a bowl of soup at the next table.

Nora had enough and snapped. "That's disgusting! Stop it at once. Have you no shame?"

Vee looked really hurt and confused. "Are you serious or joking? I can't tell. What has gotten into you?" she asked. Rocco was laughing his fool head off, but more people in the cafe were glancing over at her now. Nora stared at Rocco, who was still laughing. He finally held up his arms in surrender.

"Sorry," Nora said, focusing properly on Vee. She had been so preoccupied that she hadn't really been listening. The look on Vee's face made Nora feel doubly guilty. "Seriously!"

"You are *so* not normal," Vee said, still playful, but a hint of worry had seeped into her voice.

"Just don't tell my parents, okay?" Nora said. "They'll send me back to the shrink. It's just... I don't want to let anyone down. I can't upset my parents. Please don't say anything." Once again Nora found herself lying to her best friend, or at best bending the truth. The Deadish meant well, but staying safe was turning into tiring work. Vee smiled once again and nodded, ready and willing to be there once again for her friend. The scales were totally imbalanced, and Nora wanted to shift the conversation to Vee and her life. That Vee was letting Nora steer the ship so much lately was only part of why Nora loved her so much.

"Scout's honour, I won't say a thing!" Vee said.

"You aren't a scout," Nora pointed out.

"And my honour has been questioned more than once," Vee agreed.

"Not likely!" Nora said with a smile.

They laughed at this and Nora asked about Vee's latest project. Neither of them noticed Kia, a few tables over, still hurting from not talking to Vee for so long, as she dialled Nora's home number.

"I HEARD there was some trouble in the coffee shop," Dr. Westlake said.

Click.

"No, there was no trouble," Nora said as she ground her teeth in frustration. "Just a girl who used to hang out with us called my mom to say that I was acting up."

"So you weren't yelling at your friend?"

"What? No. We were just goofing around."

"And spilling drinks?"

"Yeah. It's not a big deal. People spill stuff."

"Are you having motor control issues, Nora? Maybe some exercises would help you to steady your hands. I have a pamphlet here somewhere. Might just be stress. It's totally normal."

Nora's eyelid twitched as she accepted the pamphlet. It full-on fluttered when she heard the damn pen click again.

THINGS AT home were starting to become tense. After the coffee shop, Nora had to explain why she was caught talking to herself in the park. One night, Tom followed her to an old bus station and watched for a little while as she was chatting with what looked to be an empty bench with a potted plant on it. Her parents had been called later that week to the local cemetery by the gravedigger who watched her move from plot to plot while chatting up the residents.

"Nora, what can we do?" her mother asked pleadingly one night when they went out for dinner.

"Mom, I swear. I'm fine. It's just a few hiccups," Nora insisted. Her father shook his head at this. Tom had been sent out of the house for their little "talk" with a few bucks in his pocket while the rest of them went out for something to eat. She had seen it coming a mile away, of course, but had hoped it was just going to be a nice outing. It was really hard to concentrate, because Reno had tagged along and was looking enviously at everything she put in her mouth.

"I miss drinks so much," he said sadly about her Dr. Pepper. When it was time for dessert, a chocolate brownie, he groaned in envy. "Is it good? It looks good."

"Is it something we did?" her father asked for the hundredth time.

"No," she said, answering both Reno and her father. "Look, seriously, I've had a bad year. I think we can all agree on that. You guys have been amazing and supportive. Things just haven't been smooth for me, that's all."

"But you're still seeing things, aren't you?" her mother asked. "That's what your doctor said, anyway. I like him, by the way. He seems very nice. Very detailed. He takes incredible notes, you know!"

Nora rolled her eyes. "I know."

"Seriously, we just want to help you. You look stressed out, sweetheart," her dad said.

"Dad, I'm okay. I just have a lot to think about."

"I can tell," he said with a supportive smile. "I can see your thought-spot going a mile a minute. Don't let this paramnesia stuff get to you, okay?"

She snorted at this. When she was just a baby, there was a spot on her forehead that was a little bit indented. Whenever she looked up or around, it looked like it was caving in. Her dad named it the "thought-spot," and now they used it as a reference whenever one of them had something troubling them or really occupying their minds.

"It's going, but only because you guys are stressing me. *All of you,*" she said, this time glancing pointedly at Reno, who was now trying to lick her plate to get the melted ice cream. Her parents looked back and forth between each other, clearly at a loss.

She knew they wanted to help her, but it wasn't something they could fix. There was no magic wand. Telling the truth would only make it worse.

Finally, her parents stopped pressing the issue. They did what they thought was best, Nora knew, and instituted a rule that said she had to stay put at home, where they could keep an eye on her. She was grounded until they either felt she was good or the mighty Dr. Westlake gave the all-clear. Until she was whatever passed for normal, there would be little to no freedom. There was also an unspoken threat that there was a next step that they were willing to take, but it never came up.

Not until she didn't give them a choice.

CHAPTER 21

E ach incident in Nora's quest to gather soul energy so far seemed to result in a quick trip back to that quack, Dr. Westlake. He had upped her medication in response (which of course she wasn't taking) and made their sessions mandatory. Like her parents, he danced around the suggestion of having her go somewhere to "gather her thoughts," which was code for "psychiatric ward" as far as she could tell. No one seemed ready to trigger the nuclear option yet, so it was all just talk.

She told the Deadish about this and in the nicest way possible asked them to kindly stay away. Whatever protection they were offering wasn't necessary, since no one had attacked ("Because they know we're there!" Sarge protested), and they were going to do more damage to her life and reputation than good. Charlie offered to be her muscle, so to speak, which calmed everyone down. Only Andrew looked sullen at the suggestion. They still hadn't found time to really talk, but there was a truce of sorts between them. They could chat about random things as long as it didn't veer into the realm of the personal.

Even though she could sometimes barely stand Charlie and his smug attitude, and she was terrified of that death trap of a van of his, she saw the benefits. Now she had a buffer in terms of conversation, so it didn't look like she was talking to herself. If anything odd happened, he would be there to explain it away. It just looked like two young people being goofy, if anything, and that seemed to appease most people.

All of her hunting and gathering expeditions, however, hadn't gone unnoticed. The undead community, though not overly social, was small enough that word was getting around about what she was doing and what she was after. Though she hadn't attracted the attention of the Revenant and her group, not that she was aware of, she was at least relieved that nothing bad had happened yet. All the same, Nora started to become more and more uneasy each time she left her house. Tonight, as she waited in the stillness on her porch, she felt like she was being watched. It was just a tickle on the back of her neck. She looked around for the familiar blue hues or other clues that she was being followed, but all she saw was darkness and shadows.

She strained her eyes into the corners of her yard but saw nothing. There was a light breeze that made the bushes move and the leaves dance, but once the wind quieted, so did the leaves. Nothing came at her.

A low rumble and wheeze around the corner let her knew that her ride was almost there. Charlie's destroyed van limped its way around the corner and stopped a couple of houses down. It was quite distinctive, not to mention noisy, so Nora had asked him to park away from the house so it wouldn't attract any attention. She took a quick glance back at the house to make sure no lights had come on. All was quiet.

The only time Nora could safely get away from home these days was after everyone had gone to bed, but she felt pretty bad about it. She had never once in her life needed to sneak out of her own home. Her parents trusted both Nora and her brother to be mature and responsible. They never had a curfew but an understanding that if they were out past midnight they would call home. Nora had once asked why they didn't have a curfew. "You don't need one," her dad said. "As long as you show respect, you'll get respect. If there are rules that need to be made, then they will be. You guys are great, though." It was one of those things that made her really love her dad. He wasn't the kind who was waiting with a fake shotgun to attack boys she brought home. He was of the opinion that if he did his job and raised her right, she was smart enough to make her own decisions and find the right person. He supported her, no questions asked. Her mom, too. Actually, her whole family was great. Even Tom, obnoxious though he was. And now here she was going against the one rule they had finally put in place. To Nora, it was the ultimate disrespect she had shown for people who were just trying to help her. If she was able to put all of this behind her, she vowed she would make it up to them somehow.

But tonight she and Charlie had work to do. The two of them were going to go to the hospital for Charlie's night shift, when the ghosts were more active. The place was a revolving door of energy, so it was a good place to camp out and try to gather some. A few ghosts had been receptive to sharing so far, more than any other place they had been, and there were still a lot of floors to explore. Her goal was to gather until she was either full or at least had as much ammo in the chamber as possible before she had to pull the Vision trigger.

At the hospital, it was nice and quiet. Only a skeleton crew of nurses and doctors worked the floor, so they were free to move about. They had to watch their voices, however, as the silence at night made for easy eavesdropping, and they didn't want to wake the patients.

She had just finished talking with an elderly pair of ghosts, both of whom had shared with her, when she heard the bang from within the auditorium. Being afraid of ghosts was now a thing of the past, so she wasn't at all hesitant to go into the big space to see what was going on.

When she opened the door, her heart started beating faster anyway. Ghosts may not be a problem, but a looming and oppressively dark place woke the fear in her chest. A memory came to her unbidden. She remembered when she was younger that she always used to sleep with her door open. It was nice and easy to get in and out or to make herself heard if she had to call for her parents. That changed one night when she could hear a gentle scratching on the carpet in the hallway, like someone shuffling back and forth. She wasn't sure that's what it was, but the more she listened the louder it seemed to get. Whatever it was never appeared in her doorway and never entered her room, but the terror became so great that she called out.

"Mom. Dad," she yelled. Only it wasn't a yell. It was barely a croak. She was so scared that her voice failed her. She tried again and again, but nothing would happen. That croak was quiet enough that her worry shifted and she was worried she would attract attention of what was in the hall but fall far short of her parents' sleeping ears. Finally, she broke through her terror and yelled for them. Her voice gathered strength and got louder and louder. Her father came, tired and frustrated, but still loving and patient. They went into the hall to confront her fear together, but of course there was nothing. From that night on, Nora slept with the door closed just in case. What was really absurd was that for years after, and occasionally to this day, she still hesitated in the middle of the night to open that door and go out of her room if everyone else was asleep.

Back then, it had been the fear that it was an alien or a ghost in the hall. Now that she had no fear of ghosts and was reasonably sure aliens weren't hanging out in the hospital, she knew that there was nothing to really be afraid of in the room. At worst, it could just be a patient who was lost. The bang came again from inside the room, so she summoned her courage, stepped deeper inside, and listened.

Nothing. Silence.

"Hello?" she called out. Her own voice echoed back until quiet once again filled the space. She was about to turn around and leave (really, run away) when she heard a faint bang come from the back of the room. At least, she thought it was the back of the room. The noise echoed in the space, making it impossible to say exactly where it came from.

Every horror movie she had ever seen in her life warned her against going deeper into the place. Somewhere, an audience was watching what she was doing and screaming out that she was an idiot.

"Hello?" she called again. "Is someone in here?"

She made her way to the centre of the room as best she could. She screamed when she walked into a chair she didn't see and sent it crashing to the floor. She picked it up and laughed at her own silliness. She sat in the chair, leaned back, and closed her eyes.

Not five feet in front of her, there was a loud bang as another chair was sent flying across the room. Nora's eyes flew open, and she could barely make out the shapes of the other bits of furniture in front of her. She leapt to her feet just in time to have the chair she had been sitting on whisked away and tossed up all the way onto the second floor. She bolted toward the main stage, only to have a table explode into pieces in her path. She skidded to a stop and ran to the left and was tripped up by another chair. She fell down to her hands and knees, which saved her from being crushed by a storage crate that went sailing over her head.

"Where are you?" she said defiantly into the darkness as she rose shakily to her feet. "Come out, you coward!"

"I *am* out," whispered the darkness. "You can see me all around you." The voice came from every corner. Nora couldn't tell if it was behind her or in front of her.

A hand pushed her from behind and sent her scrambling forward. She turned around to fight but was slapped in the face instead. She swung her arm wildly behind her to try and clip the thing, whatever it was, but it sailed freely through the air.

"Not there!" taunted the whisper.

She picked up a chair and threw it in front of her. "Come out and fight, you bastard!"

"Not there, either!" laughed the whisper.

Nora stopped then and tried to think. Whatever it was, ghost or not, she was wasting time fighting the darkness. She tried to push whatever soul energy she had toward the mark by her eye. Even if she missed, she wasn't going to go down without a fight. She tried to will it to come, to direct the energy inside her, but nothing was happening.

"*Here I am!*" came the voice directly into her ear.

The darkness pulled Nora's hair and then kicked out at her legs, sending her crashing to the floor. Nora screamed in terror. She tried to lift her legs but found they were pinned down by a crushing weight. She tried to raise her head up, only to have it pinned back down onto the floor. "*Good,*" the darkness whispered. "Fight me if you can."

Nora pushed and pushed against the darkness but felt like she was being crushed. She did everything she could just to sit up, but nothing was happening.

There was no easing or relaxing, but the pressure was suddenly gone, and Nora popped up so fast she was sure she pulled a muscle. She gasped and looked around as the room laughed back at her.

It was playing with her.

"Enough games! What are you? Did that bitch send you?" Nora spat.

"'Everything that we see is a shadow cast by that which we do not see,'" said the whisper.

"Great. Except what are you talking about?"

"No sense of history," said the whisper dolefully. "No respect for the greats. That was Martin Luther King, Jr."

"Enough!" Nora yelled.

She was slammed from behind and sent flying to the ground. She bit her lip and felt the warm blood trickle down her chin before it dripped onto the cool floor. She wiped her chin and got to her feet.

Her anger was leading to increased focus. She was NOT going to be taken down by something she couldn't see. She felt her cheeks flush, and then the scar by her eye began to throb ever so gently. The throb became a pulse, and finally, blessedly, a faint purple light flickered on to fight back against the darkness.

The mark acted like a flashlight of sorts, though weak. Wherever she turned her head, the darkness receded as though beaten back. Her confidence grew. Her surety that this was just another trial that she would overcome took over as she prepared to destroy whatever was coming.

The laughter had stopped. The silence was thick. Nothing came at her or bothered her. Maybe the light itself was enough to beat this thing. She stood at the ready, but a full minute passed and nothing happened. She relaxed her stance and turned to leave.

"BOO!" screamed an ink-black face, appearing just inches from her own. The scar pulsed and a quick beam shot out, missing the thing by a narrow margin. It cackled as it receded into the darkness beyond. "Not enough, girl. Where there is light, there is also SHADOW."

"Fine by me, 'Shadow,'" Nora said bravely. "Step into it. Show me what you're made of."

And it did. The darkness pulled itself into being in front of her and formed into a man, older than she expected and bent at the shoulders. The darkness swirled about him and onto the floor like an oversized trenchcoat.

On his head was a thick-brimmed hat. The most surprising thing was that Nora actually recognized him.

"You," she said. "You were at the terminal. You told me ghost stories."

"I did," he said. "I was. Until I wasn't. I found another place to go."

"What you found was her, wasn't it?"

"Perhaps, perhaps not. What I found gave me strength. Gave me substance. It was a taste of the light you toss around so casually. I don't fear it. I want more of it."

That was interesting. Nora's blast was something that hurt Cyril back at the bridge, but he certainly wasn't interested in having more of it. Why would this old ghost be interested? Was there more to what she could do with the soul energy? "You want some?" she said with swagger she did not quite believe. "Come GET some!"

The ghost swirled and expanded quickly, but the centre mass, just ever so slightly darker than the rest of the room behind it, remained focused in the middle, with arms outstretched as he lunged toward her. Nora let go then, and the blast from her eye peeled the darkness back off of the thing, and it flickered and burned like ashes from a fire. Shadow screamed and recoiled. Apparently he didn't want the light after all. In place of his black arms now were two faint-blue stubs that had been cleared of the taint.

Nora pressed the advantage and sent out another couple of pulses until the thing was on the run. She pushed him back into the corner, where he found he couldn't escape. The gift he had been given that allowed him to cling to the darkness apparently came at the cost of being able to move through walls. That was just fine with Nora.

Finally, he was pinned, and despite the ink-black face, Nora could see he was scared. "Answers," she said through clenched teeth as the purple energy cascaded out of her scar. "You weren't like this before."

"*She* did it," he said bitterly. "That purple shit you spray out of your eyes. Only hers came slowly. A trickle rather than a blast. Filled me up. Gave me focus. Gave me strength to mess with you. Mess with *all* of you." He spat at her feet.

"All of us?" she asked, filled with fear. "All of who?"

"Oh, yeah," he said with a grin. "Starting with your family. We've been watching you. I've been watching you. I had orders to hold back, but I couldn't resist tonight. I couldn't stop myself. I can't stop myself. I don't want to stop. It's been so long since I could touch. Since I could *kill*. They're next. Your family. Then your friends. Then anyone you've ever talked to or bumped into at a supermarket. But you... you get to live to watch them die. That's the price for interfering."

"Don't worry," she said, matching his grin. "I pay my debts. And I tip well." His smile faltered. With that, she blasted him again, deep in the centre of his chest, and kept up the focus. The black cracked, and orange light flared out. He was screaming as the light tore through him and filled him up until the burst apart. The room was momentarily lit up until the shadows came back as the charred remains floated down to cool on the floor.

That's when she noticed that she wasn't alone. Ghosts were up on the balcony and at the edges of the room. How long they had been there and how much they had seen, Nora wasn't certain. They all looked at her with a kind of awe. Slowly, one of the children approached her.

"You beat it," he said wonderingly.

"I guess so," Nora admitted.

"It's fading," he said and pointed to her scar. She gingerly touched it and knew she had used up a significant portion of what she had taken in. From the amount of sharing that she had been going through lately, she expected to have much more left in the tank, yet if the Revenant attacked her tonight, it wouldn't be much of a battle. She had thought she was nearly ready for a fight. Had that fight happened, she would have lost and lost badly. Shadow might have done her an unwitting favour.

She looked down at the little boy ghost. He nodded at her with pride. "You can win," he said. "You can have some of me."

He offered her his hand, and she took it gratefully, noting that a line of ghosts had formed to share with her. It wasn't just soul energy that passed between them as well, or at least not what she mainly experienced. The throbbing in her head eased, the blood stopped dripping from her chin, and she felt better, more alive, than she had in ages. She felt healed, somehow.

Whole. More complete. Around her, the ghosts in the room became more distinct.

Nora gently took what the little boy had to give, and when his blue faded too much and he grimaced, she slowed the flow down to a mere trickle. Before she let go of the connection, she remembered how Shadow had said the Revenant had poured energy into him in a way that made him stronger. She willed herself to stop the flow and tried to reverse it ever so slightly. The boy's colour at once brightened, and he stood a little taller and smiled at her. Once she broke the connection, the little boy bounded out of the room and came back a short time later with Charlie in tow. He looked in wonder as Nora was sharing back and forth with the many ghosts in the room along with more and more who came for their turn. There were questions in Charlie's eyes, but they would have to wait until later.

Nora knew then just what she needed to do with this new ability.

HIS EYES flew open with more spark and energy than she could ever recall seeing before. Nora could see that he would be up and even running within a few moments. "Coming to get you, Adelaide!" Peepers cried out in joy.

Everyone else was crying, though. Even tough guy Rocco in the corner let out a fart of an emotion in the form of a sniff. It was hard not to be happy. There was Peepers, full blue, brighter than any of them, and he was whole again. His body was back together, and his eyes were as big and wide as ever.

After quickly filling Charlie in on what had happened to her during her fight with Shadow and telling him not be concerned about all the blood on her shirt, she then refused to tell him why it was so important to get back to the terminal as soon as possible. She had similarly ignored all questions from the Deadish Society once they arrived. She went into the room, found Peepers all but gone, and held her hand over him. She pushed the light into him bit by bit as they all sat nearby, watching the ghostly flesh reattach, smooth over, and then brighten up the little soul they had all become so fond of. It was as close to a miracle as any of them had ever witnessed. They were stunned.

She sat back smiling but exhausted and closed her eyes. When she opened them, she thought she had done something wrong, because everyone was half as bright as they normally were; even Peepers had lost some sheen, though he was blindingly bright compared to the rest of them at the moment. Her hand went instinctively to her eye, and she felt within herself that she was nearly spent. If this was her last action, however, Nora was content. She did at least one good thing with this power.

None of Andrew, the Deadish, or Charlie were pleased with her, despite the fact they were thrilled to have Peepers back up and raring to go. All of the blood on her might have had something to do with it. It didn't matter that it wasn't flowing any more. All of that blood was hers. And it could have been much worse. "That was a silly thing, Nora Angel," Andrew said to her when they were alone. "I can't have anything happen to you, do you understand? Nothing is more important to me than you being safe."

"You can't keep me safe, though," Nora said. "And more than that, it isn't your job. I'm not some weak little girl who needs protecting. I took on Cyril and beat him. I was attacked by a damn shadow, and I beat his ass as well. Both things I managed to do without you."

Andrew looked hurt and backed off. "You think I'm happy about that?" he asked angrily. "Look at me! I'm DEAD. I don't want this for you. I lost my family. I lost *everything*. I can't lose you. Not the way I'm lost!"

She reached out for him, but her hand passed uselessly through his. "I know. I get it. I know what you did for me. I know how much you love me. I know how much I love you. But sometimes love isn't enough. You can't blame yourself for anything that happens to me, any more than I can blame myself for what happened to you. Sometimes life is a bitch."

He laughed at that. "Yeah, sometimes it is."

Charlie coughed to interrupt them. "Listen, I don't want to break up… whatever this is. But it's almost dawn. I have to get you home."

"Go on," Andrew said to her. "See you tonight?"

"Of course," she said with a wink. "In your dreams."

"Just the good ones," he said.

"Okay, enough pervy double-talk," Charlie said. "Your highness, your chariot awaits."

"That thing is going to result in me getting a tetanus shot," Nora said. *"That van is a classic!"*

AS THE dawn started to break, Charlie cut the engine half a block from her house. He sat back and looked at her for a moment before his head dropped. He mumbled something at her.

"What was that?" Nora asked.

"I'm sorry," Charlie repeated, a little bit louder.

"For what? I mean, I can totally think of a hundred things that are wrong about you that you need to apologize for. The first being this van."

"I'm sorry for tonight," he said seriously. "I wasn't there. I shouldn't let you go off on your own."

Nora sighed. What was it with boys thinking that girls needed them around for protection? Guys had such fragile egos, it was unbelievable. "It's not your fault. I can take care of myself."

"I know you can," he said. "You've proved that. More than once. I just mean that I let myself down by not being there, and as a result, I let you down. However much of a pain in the ass you are, I won't let you down again."

She was taken aback by the sincerity and earnestness in his voice. "Okay," she said. She didn't know what else to say. "I should go."

"Right," he said. "Go on. See you later. Be careful as you get out."

"You admit it? That your van could cause injury?"

"What are you, some kind of cheap TV law firm? No, I just don't want you to scratch the paint. I have it just the way I like it."

"It's already scratched!"

"No, it's a purposeful design. It's found art. Go on, scram. Wait!"

She paused mid-exit. Was this going to be more awkward apologies? "Make up your mind," she said.

"Pfft. Your shirt," he said with a gesture. He reached in the back, grabbed one of his, and tossed it to her. She raised an eyebrow at him. "Well, you can't go in there looking like you were in a pie-eating contest, Davey Hogan! Get changed."

"I'm not changing in front of you," she said.

"Who asked you to? Besides, like I'm going to get excited to see Nora the Explora flash me. Get in the back."

She ground her teeth but didn't argue the logic. She hopped in the van and took off her shirt. As she pulled Charlie's shirt on over her head, she couldn't help but notice how good it smelled. Not just clean, but *good*. She looked silly in the thing, since it was much too big for her, and she wasn't pleased at the small thrill she got from wearing it, but he was right about not taking chances by walking into her house looking like she'd just finished slaughtering a deer.

"I didn't think that shirt could look worse," he said with a grin.

She rolled her eyes and got out. She watched him drive away before turning and heading down the street to her house.

When she got there, the place looked nice and quiet. She eased up the rock near the front door, found the key she left, and put it into the lock. She wasn't worried about the door making any noise, but she didn't want to wake Rorschach and have his bark rat her out.

Before she fully twisted the knob, the door flew open, and both her mother and father were standing there glaring at her. They were in their bathrobes, their hair a mess, and Nora's mother's face was a mess, giving away that she had been crying.

"Oh, fan-crapstick," Nora said.

CHAPTER 22

As the van rumbled away down the street, the Revenant took in all that she had just witnessed. It had all been so clear earlier: take down the girl, destroy her companions, move on back into the shadows.

Now it was more complicated.

Why was it more complicated?

Something nagged in the back of the Revenant's skull. Some lizard-brain warning was going off that things were spiralling out of control. There was no logical reason to think this. The attack at the hospital had gone just fine, as far as the Revenant could see. It had been early and ill-advised, but informative all the same. The girl was getting stronger, but she could also be easily separated from her friends, and she didn't have that much power inside her. Her control of it was dubious at best. The Revenant could win with a war of attrition… send out one powered soul at a time to wear the girl down until she was either dead or close enough that the Revenant could sneeze and watch the girl expire.

So what was the problem?

Was it culling the ghosts? No, that was going well, at least for the Revenant. For the few souls she had given a bit of juice, far more were simply absorbed totally. Even when the saps figured out that she was taking more than giving, they still lined up. They were willing to take their chances. Hope had long gone out of most of them. Few of them had any loved ones still living and were looking for any way at all to end the existence.

It made sense to her to want a quick way out. Bafflingly, there were still people in this world who wanted to live forever, but that was more of a curse than a gift. Who would want to live forever? You live while all of your loved ones die off? Watch everything you know slowly disappear? It's not like you could stop working or finding a way to support yourself. Life would drag on and on and on and on and on, ad infinitum. Eventually, humanity would die off (likely due to boredom), and you would be the only thing still alive. Billions of years would pass. Heat death of the universe. Just you on your lonesome floating in the abyss. For some of these ghosts, the grandeur of immortality in the afterlife had stretched only a few years after their loved ones were gone, and they quickly realized they wanted no more of it. If there was no heaven to welcome them, then taking a chance at finding a better way to exist was worth the risk of oblivion. Either option was more appealing. Either get on with it or stop the bus entirely.

It was almost too easy.

So if that was easy, what was giving her pause now?

Was it just the girl? The need to finish the business at hand? The Others were patient; they had learned that skill over the centuries, but the Revenant knew that patience could be exhausted. It would be too, instantly, if they knew what the Revenant was doing with the local spirits. Too much risk over one simple girl, they would say. The counter-argument against leaving her be was that the girl could still be a problem now that she was getting the hang of her abilities. She was still a threat. The amount of energy may be minor, but if she was able to pull more of it into her and direct it properly, then the Revenant knew that a stray blast could still end her fledgling existence. And then who was to say she wouldn't take the next step up the supernatural corporate ladder?

Was it because she was being trained? That she was getting stronger?

Ah, there it was. Or closer to what the issue was, at the very least. The girl shouldn't have been a problem, but she was learning. She was getting stronger. It wasn't being done on her own, either. She was getting help from the dead and the living alike. That was a bridge too far. The risk of detection was increasing at a rate that was out of control. If The Others found out and got involved...

But that wasn't it. Not all of it. Something else pulled and screamed at her to see, but she couldn't.

As the van cleared the corner and the girl made it to the safety of her front door, the Revenant decided to pick one trail and see where it led. It would either console or confound, but it was time for action. She started up her vehicle, stolen from an impound lot, and followed the beat-up van.

A few twists and turns, a stop at an all-night drive-through, and the van pulled up and seemed to die in front of the museum she had seen the girl at before. The pulling feeling at the corners of her mind was still going, racing, screaming for attention, but she couldn't put the pieces together. It didn't make sense!

She nearly screamed out loud in frustration when the door opened, and she saw an old man and a ghost answer. The old man was clutching a badminton racket, which made him look insane, but the Revenant saw that he had an air about him, a quality of sorts, that she knew deep in her gut meant one thing: adversary.

Fear clenched at her and surprised her. Fear was not something she had felt in a long, long time. Oddly, she wanted to sob as well. What was going on with her?

Enough. Enough. *Enough.*

Let it be done, she decided. She would gather so much energy that would put the girl's efforts to shame. Then she would empower a few to help thin out the herd. Then she would find the girl, her friends, her family, anything and anyone else in the way and get rid of it. Let it all be gone. She'd face the consequences later. She'd take on the Others themselves if she had to.

The noise in her brain was deafening, and the quiet needed to come back.

It all had to go.

CHAPTER 23

Nora sat opposite Dr. Westlake and had said nothing for at least the past five minutes. He sat opposite her and just looked back at her, waiting for her to say something or do something. She cleared her throat, and he clicked his pen.

"Could you not do that?" Nora snapped.

Dr. Westlake raised an eyebrow and looked at her while absently scrawling on his notepad. "Not do what, Nora? What is it you think you're seeing me do?"

Oh, so that was the game. Nora's parents had been furious at her late-night outing, and though she swore that was the only time it had happened, she clammed up when they pressed her for details. The bruises, the ruffled hair, and the "I don't know" wasn't at all sufficient. They took this as confirmation that whatever paramnesia was in theory was translating in a real and brutal way to Nora's waking life. It was one thing to be embarrassed in public, but it was another thing entirely to come home looking like the newest member of the cast of *Fight Club*.

There had been a lot of anger at first, then confusion, then tears. Her brother watched all of this from the stairs, not saying a word. That was the worst part for her, because her brother normally never shut up. He just looked at her with dead eyes.

In the end, the decision had been to go to see Westlake first thing in the morning. Nora didn't have much choice but to agree, and now she was sitting opposite this idiot who looked eager, greedy even, to hear whatever details she was going to give him. She had gone from a pity-case teenage girl with a dead boyfriend to a potentially psychotic girl who was having public meltdowns and now was out all night and coming home looking like she'd been dragged the whole way. She looked at him and saw that he was barely concealing the smile playing at the corner of his mouth. What a prick.

"I think I'm seeing a third-rate opportunist and wasting my time," she said coolly.

He looked like he had been slapped, then clicked the pen and jotted something down. "The only one wasting time is you, Nora. Everyone just wants to help you."

"Yeah, but you're not helping. All you're doing is clicking that stupid pen of yours and making me self-conscious when you write stuff down every time I open my mouth. Do you not get how distracting that is? It's weird. Creepy, even. It doesn't make me want to open up."

"I see," Dr. Westlake said. He made no move to put the pen down or alter his own behaviour in any way. Apparently, only people on the other side of the fence were in need of improvement. Nora fought the urge to roll her eyes. "What does make you want to open up?"

Nora sighed in frustration. "Not you. Not coming here. Not having to deal with questions all the time. I'm fine. I just need some time to process things. I'm not in a fight club. I'm not doing drugs. I'm not out having sex every night. I don't even drink, for god's sake." She almost said that she was boring, which would have been true before the accident, but that would have been a lie now. The rest was true, for whatever it was worth.

"Then where are you going at night?" he asked.

She bit her lip so hard, she thought blood would come out. "Nowhere," she said through gritted teeth. "I don't remember."

The pen clicked again. This time, however, he paused mid-pen-stroke and peered at her over the top of his glasses. He hesitated and then decided to lower the pen. It was a good thing he did, because if he kept writing Nora wasn't sure which of the openings on his body the pen was going to be shoved into.

"Okay, then," he said. "Well, you're in luck."

"I am?" she said wonderingly.

"You are. There is an institution that contacted my office this morning just before you got here. The treatment it offers and specializes in makes it an ideal place for you to go for recovery. I am assured that the staff are experts and the facility is out of this world. I discussed it with your parents, and we agree that this is your best option," Westlake said.

Nora was beyond furious. Even though she saw it coming, the sting of it all, the sense of betrayal, was way too much. "No!" she yelled. "You are not sending me away! I'm not crazy! I don't need to be locked up. YOU CAN'T DO THIS!"

There was a knock at the door, and an orderly poked his head in. "Everything okay in here?" he asked. Nora turned to scream at him to get out and choked a bit when she saw that it was Charlie.

Dr. Westlake looked relieved not to have to be dealing with a screaming girl, though he pretended to be annoyed at the intrusion. "Excuse me? You can't just come in here. I'm in session!"

"Sorry," Charlie said, though from his tone it was clear he wasn't. "I got a call to come down and pick up a patient for transfer to the Culshaw Institute?"

"Well, yes," Westlake said. "But now is not a good time."

"Wait," Nora said, a touch too eagerly, clueing in as to what was going on. "Him? Is he here for me? Culshaw? Me?" That was not the best sentence she had ever spoken.

Now it was Westlake's turn to look confused. "Uh, well… um. Yes, but, we, uh…"

"I'll go," Nora said. She stood up abruptly and collected her things. "Now?"

"Oh, uh," Westlake stammered. All of this was spiralling out of whatever control he thought he had over the situation. Nora was loving it and thrilled to see that his pen had fallen to the floor unnoticed. "There are forms. Your parents…"

"They agreed, didn't they?" Nora asked sweetly. God, she was loving this. "This was their idea?"

"Well, yes, but…"

"Great. Tell them I'm going. But I'd like a few days, at least a week, to get settled before I see them. Okay?" That would be a good buffer. Doctor-approved, safer for everyone. A lie, but a convenient one. She owed Graves a great big kiss when she saw him next.

"That, uh, seems reasonable. I'm sure that will..."

Before he could finish his sentence, Nora was out the door.

WHEN NORA got to the Terminal, now redubbed the Culshaw Institute in her own mind, there were more ghosts there than she had ever seen before in one place. It was just like a busy day at Union Station in Toronto or at Grand Central Station in New York. Ghosts moved about with purpose. Some stayed and talked, others moved in and out at a regular pace. It was a hub of activity again, even if to a regular Joe off the street it looked as abandoned as normal. At best, the living might notice the building making more "settling" noises than usual.

As Nora made her way inside, she was greeted often and warmly by the throngs. None of them impeded her, and all were respectful, even though there was an undercurrent of expectation. They were waiting for her to say or do something, though none of them knew exactly what. It was exciting and it was interesting, something that most of the souls there hadn't experienced in a long time. Nora even spied the old librarian from her school walking about. When the ghost saw her, she gave Nora a wink and jokingly put a finger to her lips to shush her.

"There she is!" Reno sang happily as he bounded through his ticket counter and rudely shoved past both Isabel and Andrew. "Miss America!"

"This is Canada, idiot," Isabel said sharply. Andrew was behind her and snorted at this, but Reno ignored them both.

"All hail the conquering hero!" Reno yelled.

The ghosts at Cullen Terminal stopped and applauded then, loud and fiercely for her. Sarge popped up out of the basement, looking large and imposing as usual. Rocco leaned against the doorway to his office for a moment or two before looking bored and going back inside. Scraps was

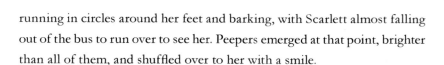

running in circles around her feet and barking, with Scarlett almost falling out of the bus to run over to see her. Peepers emerged at that point, brighter than all of them, and shuffled over to her with a smile.

"Welcome back!" he huffed. He hesitated and held off as long as he could before he leaned in and whispered, "Adelaide?"

Nora shook her head, and he nodded quickly as if to ward off her apology.

"Hey, Nora Angel," Andrew said as he stepped forward. "Welcome home."

"I can't believe you did this!" Nora said. "All these people!"

"Anything for you," Andrew said with a smile. "Haven't you gotten that through your head yet?"

"And to be fair," Charlie said behind him, "it was really me who did it. Graves, too, of course. The whole 'Culshaw Institute' thing. He put the seal of approval and lent an air of authenticity to the duplicity — how he put it."

"It was my idea," Andrew said.

"My legwork," Charlie said.

"Hey, no talk about legs." Isabel pouted.

"I'm thankful for *all* of you," Nora said. "I mean, I'm not happy about lying to my family about staying at the 'Culshaw Institute,' but I'm glad to be out of there. Anything to get them out of harm's way."

"Well, they ain't totally out of harm's way, ma'am," Sarge boomed. "We got spectral agents stationed outside of your primary domicile to keep a vigilant watch in case of a surprise attack by the enemy. The bean counters estimate a significantly less likelihood of attack, however, now that you have been relocated."

"I'm the bean counter!" Reno beamed. Sarge looked annoyed. Isabel swatted Reno upside the head. Sarge looked less annoyed.

Nora took a moment to take in the busy terminal. "How did you get all these ghosts here?"

"They heard about you, Nora," Scarlett said. "Then we told 'em to wait until you got here! I said you are really good at playing and really nice to dogs and that you will help people and you helped Peepers."

204 BRIAN WILKINSON

"She said that," Peepers agreed cheerfully. "And if they tried to leave, she threatened them with many words my Adelaide would not have approved of!"

"I *encouraged* them," Scarlett clarified. "Scraps helped!" The dog, once again at the girl's feet, barked in acknowledgement. "Now they're all here for you."

The enormity of the statement hit Nora like a ton of bricks. She had never in her life felt so important. So *needed.* Without any fanfare or ceremony, ghosts approached one by one, often casually, and donated what energy they could. Some ghosts were far too diminished, having spent too long in the afterlife without solving their unfinished business or finding other ways to move on. They were sad and lonely but still willing to give. Nora had more than enough energy, and many more ghosts who were around and willing to share, so she gave out the soul energy to these surprised, forgotten individuals. The confusion would leave their faces, and clarity would come with an increase in their overall hue.

The act of giving made her even more popular. It showed that she was kind, thoughtful, and loving. Whatever collected energy it cost her to give, she was getting back a hundred times over from the many who did not need it back. Soon she had to stop, not because she was full, but because she was tired. Andrew politely asked them all to give her a bit of rest while thanking them profusely at the same time. The old ghosts wandered off with the new having found themselves a part of a community once again. It was sweet.

Charlie eventually came to get her. He led her off to one of the many rooms at the back of the building she hadn't visited and was pleasantly surprised to see that it had been fixed up. There wasn't much to be done about some of the decay of the building, but there was a new bed in there, a night table, a fresh set of clothes, and even some flowers. "Wow," she breathed.

"I know it's not much," Charlie said, clearly embarrassed. He was looking at the floor.

"It's perfect, Charlie," she said. "Thank you." She leaned over and gave him a kiss on the cheek. He blushed furiously. It wasn't like him to be so kind and generous. There may have been prodding from the Deadish, but he was still the one who had done all the work. It was amazing. It made her once again rethink her initial evaluation of him. He was even sort of cute. Nora noticed more than one muscle when she had leaned in for the little kiss.

"Hey," Andrew said sharply from the doorway. "Not interrupting, am I?"

Charlie pulled away from Nora like he'd been burned. Andrew stood his ground and blocked the only exit, but Charlie quickly and firmly went right through him to escape and then paused a moment before he left. "We should talk," he said. "I'll come back in a little bit, after you've been settled. About the Vision. Other stuff. I'll help you how I can." He may have been embarrassed about the situation, or maybe he felt as confused about everything as Nora did, which would account for how awkward he was coming across. Andrew just folded his arms and glared at Charlie until he left.

"He's not so bad," Nora said.

Andrew's eyes went wide. "*Now* he's okay? I thought you hated him. What was he doing to you, anyway?"

She laughed. "He wasn't 'doing' anything. I just figure that a guy who does all of this for a girl who treats him like crap can't be all bad."

"I told him what to get," Andrew said petulantly.

"I know you did," she said, smiling at him. "Thanks."

He was clearly waiting for more, but she didn't know what to say. There were a thousand things and yet also nothing all at once. She missed him, but she was also having a hard time with him the way he was. For one thing, he was entirely too focused on her now. When he was alive, he had school, his family, and his future to look forward to. That was something they could share together. Now it just felt like he was constantly watching her to see what she would do next. It was starting to feel oppressive.

"What's wrong?" he asked. "What's going on with us?"

"Nothing," she said. "Everything. I'm worried about you."

"Me?" Andrew said with a laugh. "My health has been better, but otherwise I'm okay."

"No, you're not. I don't know what to do to help you. I can't help you. You're always trying to look after me, but you're, like, *always there*... and... well..."

"I need to get a life?" he joked. He laughed, but there was no real humour in it.

Finally, she nodded.

"Ouch," he said. "Well, odds are against that."

"I just don't know that I can be what you want me to be. What we should have been."

"I know that."

"Do you?"

"Yeah, I do. But what else am I supposed to do?"

"I don't know."

"Neither do I."

The silence hung between them.

"I want to help you. Protect you. I'm useless everywhere else," Andrew said.

"Don't say that."

"I am!" he insisted. "Look, you think I'm overly focused on you. Well, maybe I am, but it's not for lack of trying to find something or someone else to care about. You never even ask me about my family."

She winced. He was right, of course. The subject never really came up. Nora was so preoccupied with her own family and her own business that she failed this one basic task of paying attention. She had made a few overtures after she got home after the accident to go and see his parents, but they were grieving, and she was the crazy girl in the news. They stared at her like she was an alien one minute and then like she was a fragile piece of china after that. They cared about her because her son cared about her, but now what was she to them? She and Andrew hadn't been together all that long, they weren't married, they didn't have kids; they weren't even living together. She was someone her son dated. It was awkward, and they had nothing to say to one another. She stopped going to see them and stopped asking Andrew about it. She had moved on.

He, however, didn't have that same luxury. She cursed herself for being a selfish fool.

"You're right. I've been way too selfish. I should have been paying more attention. I really am sorry. How are they?"

Andrew sighed and sat down. "They're awful," he said. "For a lot of reasons. Their son is dead. I can only imagine what that must feel like. To have the thing you raised, the person you loved more than yourself, suddenly gone from your life…

"I went home a lot, in the beginning, usually after you fell asleep. My mom was always up when I went to see them. She would sit in the same chair the by the window and stare outside. She wasn't eating. She wasn't sleeping. At best, she would cry. I would try to talk to her, to let her know I was okay, to hold her, to… anything. But I'm this," he said, gesturing to his incorporeal form.

"So what could I do? My dad wasn't much better. He fixed everything in the house, even the things that didn't need fixing. He went to work. He made dinner. He was a flurry of activity around my mom, who wasn't reacting to anything."

"Oh, Andrew, I'm so sorry," Nora said. She should have been better at seeing the pain he was in.

"But then," Andrew continued. "Then… one night, about a month after I died, my father lost it. He was screwing in a lightbulb and the thing popped in his hands. Blood all over the place. He starting throwing things and smashed up anything he could get his hands on. That woke my mom up, all right. She came over to him and tried to calm him down. She just kept hushing him until he started to cry. Then they both held each other and cried, right there in the living room. They cried until they sobbed, and it was all out of them.

"Then they got up and cleaned up. And not just that night, but every day since. The house, themselves, whatever was around. There was no talk, no agreement, but they started again."

"Started what?" Nora asked.

"Living," Andrew said simply. "They started living. I went to see them the other night after avoiding them for a couple of weeks. They're gone. My grandmother was there chatting on the phone, and I overheard her. My parents both took a leave from work, and they've gone travelling together. They have no return ticket, no end date in mind, they're just going to see the world. Together. And it's awful."

"Why?" Nora asked. "That sounds wonderful. They found each other again."

"Yeah," Andrew said, wiping away a ghostly tear. "By leaving me behind. I know it's selfish, but the mourning made me feel important. I know that they're healing, and I want them to heal. But I don't want them to leave me behind. I want to go with them. But they can't even hear me."

Nora nodded. Andrew was clinging to her, not only out of love, but because she was a firm connection. She could see him and hear him. He knew that they were separating, that they were moving on, similar to how his parents had, but to him it was another act of leaving that he couldn't control. He didn't want to cause her pain, but he was afraid.

"They can't leave you behind, even if they wanted to. You can't leave love. You take it with you, however it exists," Nora told him.

"I know," Andrew said. "Thanks." It was a polite gesture, but she could tell he still felt hollow. Sometimes, telling someone things will get better in time when they are hurting the most is a waste of time. It may be true, but the pain at that moment makes it a lie. Whatever she and Andrew were or were going to be, they would need a bucketload of time to find out.

Outside, they could hear Charlie talking with one of the ghosts at the terminal. His voice got louder as he approached. Nora thought he was talking louder than normal, no doubt to give her and Andrew time to collect themselves. It was another sweet gesture by the scruffy orderly on a list that was getting oddly long. God, why did life have to be so confusing? Why did he have to suddenly start looking just the tiniest bit cute?

"Ready to go?" Charlie asked when he popped his head into her room.

CHAPTER 24

C harlie pushed Betsy the Beat-Up Van as hard as he could as they went down the undulating Stone Road out past the city limits. It was nice to be out in the country with the warmth of a summer evening all around them. It was still hot, but more of a comforting blanket than an oppressive heat. It was a world comfortably at rest after a hard day at work. This was the time of day and the time of year she liked best. She could walk all night and not be cold or even tired. Time seemed to stand still on a good summer night. It was when you tended to make the best kinds of memories with friends or family. Even with your senses. There was something about a fresh rainfall evaporating off a hot sidewalk that reminded her of summers at home when they would dance around in the unexpected warmth of a sun-shower.

Going down Stone Road now was another sense memory. It reminded her of trips she would often take with her family all the way to the end of this road to where the Mustang Drive-In was located. They would roll their car in, pick a spot, and the kids would run off to the playground at the front until it got dark enough for the movie to start. Then they would run back to the cars, friends parked next to each other, and sit in lawn chairs while eating popcorn out of grocery store bags that the dads had popped before the trip. The first movie was always aimed at the kids, and she was lucky if she could stay awake for even part of the second.

She looked over at Charlie as he absently stared out the front window and wondered if that was where he was taking her. It would be a nice break, but what kind of break was it supposed to be? Surely it wasn't a date?

She was a little surprised that the notion of a date with him wasn't unappealing.

But no, he pulled off about halfway to the drive-in into a laneway that she knew well. They were at the Oak Ridge Campground, a popular summer destination for kids, with lots of activities, trails, and part of the now-infamous Speed River flowing through it. It was late, and all the camp kids were gone for the day, so the place was totally empty and very isolated.

Once the van was choked off, the place was deafening in its silence until her ears slowly started picking up the cricket song in the night. She breathed deeply, taking in the rich air, and found that she was at peace for the first time in ages.

Charlie fumbled for the cellphone in his pocket as it began to buzz. He pulled it out and held it to his ears for a moment, but he pulled it away without speaking. "Lost the signal," he said. He frowned as he checked the caller ID. "Graves. Probably calling to check in."

"Do we need to go and call him back?" Nora asked.

Charlie shook his head. "Nah," he said. "I get lots of calls from him. Too many, really. I'll call later to let him know that we're still in the land of the living." He looked out of the car and gestured at the empty camp. "Been here before?" Charlie asked casually.

"Yeah," she said. "I used to come here for camp with Vee when we were kids. She hated it, said it 'didn't mesh well with her complexion,' but I loved it. I was always out in the woods, getting bitten by mosquitos, falling down, and getting bruises. I haven't been here in ages."

"I come here to think, sometimes," Charlie said. "We're only minutes from the city, but it's far enough that I feel like I'm in a different world."

Nora laughed. "We are in a different world, you and I. Not the one I grew up in, that's for sure."

"True," Charlie said. "That's why we're here. Let's talk about that different world. I'll tell you what I can and answer what I can. Anything you like."

"Anything?" Nora asked. "What if you don't like the question?"

Charlie bit his lip and took a deep breath. "Anything," he repeated, though he sounded unsure.

"Go ahead," Nora said. "Start."

"Let's go for a walk," Charlie said. He gestured off down the path to the river. The light was fading in the distance, but they had more than enough to guide them. Charlie brought a flashlight just in case, even though she knew the place well enough to get them back in the dark.

For a while, Charlie just talked and she listened. At first the details he would share were random and haphazard as he tried to find the proper footing to tell her his story. He was searching for context and would pull on threads as they occurred to him.

Charlie's story was sadder than she expected, though she knew based on the odd hint that his past wasn't sunshine and roses. He was an only child, his parents both dead and gone years before. It had been an accident, so he'd been told, though he knew better. There had been a Revenant there, and that was how he had gotten the mark on his arm. He didn't go into much detail, he said, because the whole thing was a blur. Graves had found him and took him in, and at some point, though he was being hunted much like Nora was now, Graves came back bloodied and bruised and told him it was done. Charlie expected to be sent away after that, but Graves never brought it up or suggested it. Charlie thought it was pity at first that Graves kept him, but the old man never seemed to have anything but love in his heart for this lost boy. Then one day Graves came outside while he was playing and saw Charlie standing there with a blue figure beside him. It was McCrae. Graves asked if Charlie could see him. The boy looked at McCrae, nodded, and smiled.

At this point, Graves started teaching him about spirits and the spirit world, even taking him with him when he went out to fight things that went bump in the night. According to Charlie, there was a lot more out there besides ghosts and Revenants. Nora had only experienced the tip of the supernatural iceberg. "There are many more worlds than this, and not all of them have residents who like to play nicely." This made Nora shudder, and she decided not to ask about that just yet. One thing at a time.

Charlie talked about more adventures that he had with his adoptive father, but a few times some of the details seemed to suggest that there was more to the story that wasn't being shared. He kept mentioning "we" and "us," and to the untrained observer someone might think he was referring to himself and Graves. But there was an unspoken third party in the mix.

"Who are you talking about?" she asked. She knew the answer, but it was clear Charlie needed to say it. Nora was certain he brought her here to talk about it and just needed the prompting.

"You know who," he said sadly.

"Graves' daughter," she said.

"Alice," he breathed. "She was like my sister. She was more than that. Much more. She was…" And then she understood. Graves wasn't the only one who had lost someone irreplaceable. Alice had been his girlfriend.

"A revenant took her," he said. "We think, anyway. She had Vision as well, a by-product of being the daughter of the notorious Graves Culshaw. Her mother, Graves' wife, had been killed years before while 'on the job,' and somewhere along the line Alice had developed the talent and was introduced into the family business. Alice had a long-suffering history fighting the good fight. Graves brought me into the fold, taught me the tricks, and Alice and I became a team in more ways than one.

"Anyway, one day she was gone. Alice had been hunting a revenant, so she said, as we all had been hunting things just like it. She got a tip that one had been seen at the old Valiant Star factory and went off. She left us a note. Can you believe that? Like she had popped out to the store to buy some groceries. 'Gone hunting,' it said. 'Bought a pizza earlier. Leftovers in the fridge if you're hungry.' The worst thing about it was that it wasn't even strange or alarming. That's just how life was then. Go out for a taco and take out a creepy-crawly. Then catch a movie. Man!"

They stopped at the river's edge, and Charlie picked up a few stones. He tossed a few in the slow-moving waters until they were all gone and then picked up another handful. "She didn't come back," he continued. "Graves played it off like he wasn't worried. She'd done that sort of thing before, you see. But he was worried. How could he not be? That was his daughter. Despite the life he had led her into, he loved his daughter and would do anything to protect her. He would never allow anything bad to happen.

"We went looking for her, of course. We found her car, her gear, and signs that she had been there. But the factory was empty. Signs of a fight of sorts, but no Alice. Nothing. We hit up the spirit community, made a lot of noise, and turned up a few leads. One ghost pointed us in the direction of the thing that took her (Graves and I both refused to believe she was dead), and we were off," Charlie said.

He brushed his hands on his pants. "We found it," he said with anger in his voice. "Saw it skulking around in some dark, dead building. You couldn't really even see the thing, but you could hear where it was shuffling around. Once or twice I caught a quick glimpse of it when it passed a window. Enough to see that it was filthy and that those gill-things were moving a mile a minute. Graves wanted to take it slowly. Come up with a plan. I was just so *mad*. He shouted at me to stop, but I couldn't and wouldn't hear him. I rushed in and attacked. I put everything I had into making sure that thing was destroyed. I know I hit it, pushed it, and kicked it, but I don't remember doing it. I only know I did because of the bruises on my knuckles and the soreness of my muscles that appeared in the days after. At that moment, though, I was just so mad. I could barely see it both because of the dark and how angry I was. Too angry. Not that it did me any good. It barely had to lift a finger to knock me down. I had a concussion so bad that I was in bed for the next three weeks.

"It would have killed me as well, if Graves hadn't arrived then. He came in and fought the thing off. They fought their way out of the building, and I heard screaming. At first from the creature, then from Graves. I struggled to my feet and came outside to see Graves on his knees in the dirt. On his *knees*, man. Never seen that before or since," Charlie said.

He shook his head in wonder. "But he got it," Charlie said with a smile. "He got the thing. Said it just exploded, and that's what had hurt him. But we got the thing that killed Alice."

"Killed her?" Nora asked.

Charlie nodded. "Graves got that much out of it before he killed it. He just kept saying 'she's gone' and 'she's lost' and 'what have I done?' I don't think he's ever gotten over the guilt of bringing her into this life. He wasn't the same after that. Only gotten worse, as well, as you've seen for yourself."

Nora moved over and sat by him. The Charlie she knew, the orderly who kept pestering her, was gone. Now she saw a guy who had seen too much in his short life. She looked at him with new eyes and fresh understanding. She wanted to hug him and hold him. She wanted to cry with him and cry for him. She reached out and grabbed his hand. It had been the gesture of one friend to another, but his fingers curled around hers, and her heart fluttered an extra beat.

"I gave up the life that night," he said after a while. "I moved on. Learned to let things go. I became a worker at the hospital because I wanted to help people, both living and dead alike. It's a good place for that. Not everyone who dies becomes a ghost, but a lot of them do, and as best I can I pass on messages for them. I usually go with the whole 'before they died they said x, y, z' kind of thing, and it brings a lot of comfort to their loved ones. For some ghosts, it's all they need before they're able to move on."

"You've seen it?" Nora asked. "Ghosts moving on? What happens? Where do they go?"

"Don't know," he admitted. "Somewhere better, I hope. They just kind of glow a bit brighter. They look scared at first, or uncertain, then without fail each and every one of them smiles. Then they're gone. When they go, though, a bit of their light spreads out." Charlie let go of her hand then, something Nora immediately felt sad about, and pulled up his shirt to show the mark on his arm. "And this takes some of it in. This is how I manage to keep my Vision up. To be honest, I never liked doing it Graves' way. I take mine in passively, like a plant soaking up sunshine. It's all I've ever needed."

"What about for offensive attacks?" Nora asked. "Like my eye?"

"*That* is weird," Charlie said, shaking his head. "I've never seen that before. I asked Graves, but he threatened to spank me when I brought it up, so I have no idea what he knows about it. I've never had that talent or even been aware of it, so taking in more energy never made sense. No, for me, I love working at that hospital and showing people in their worst moments a taste of hope."

"And being obnoxious to people who are living," she reminded him.

"Not to all of them," he said. "Just the moderately attractive ones."

"Moderately?" she asked teasingly. "Really, now."

"Listen," he said. "You are a good person. You've always been a good person. You have the kind of strength that inspires people. Not many others have that, living or dead. You inspire people. Hell, you inspired me to get out of retirement. Just don't get me killed, okay?"

"Deal," she said. "Get your van fixed so that you don't kill me, okay?"

"It's a *classic.*"

ON THEIR way home, Nora felt certain that something had changed between them. They had gone from being acquaintances trapped together by circumstances to... friends? What were they now? She looked at him again and tried to figure out exactly what she felt for him. It was nothing like what she felt for Andrew, that was for sure. That was love in its purest form. Teenage love. Ideal love. Charlie was much more frustrating in many ways, and yet somehow he exerted this kind of force. It was a bit like a magnet... if you were aligned the right way, you were attracted, but he flipped it so often that she was repelled in equal measure. What did she want here?

"Know what I want?" Charlie said as his eyes lit up. Nora got excited for a moment, thinking they were on the same page, when she followed his gaze out the window to behold... a mini-golf course. The Pergola sat perched on the edge of town just off the 7th Parallel road. Despite how run-down parts of it were, it was actually a pretty decent spot, especially now that it was night and the place was lit up for moonlight golfing. The course was fun and inventive, and the soft-serve ice cream was great. Nora laughed and nodded. Charlie pulled Betsy, wheezing and choking, into the parking lot and was out his door faster than an excited toddler.

Within minutes they were clutching the worn putters that they got from a haggard-looking attendant named Harold and began knocking brightly coloured golf balls around like kids again. To Nora, Charlie looked lighter all of a sudden. He was more free. Dancing around all over the place. It seemed as though just talking to her had removed an invisible burden that had been keeping him down. Even the rough edges that usually accompanied his tone and gait had been lifted away, giving Nora a totally new look at the mysterious orderly named Charlie Ignis. He was kind of cool, actually.

Charlie got excited at the next hole and ran off to the swinging pole at the end of it. He pulled it back and let it fly as the wood swayed back and forth over the hole. Nora lined up her shot and putted as gently but firmly as she could. The ball went straight for the hole, but the merciless pole came out of nowhere and knocked it away. She moaned in frustration as Charlie cackled in delight.

When they finished up their game, Charlie happily bought both of them an ice cream cone, and they ate in amicable silence on a picnic table surrounded by the twinkling lights of the Pergola.

"I totally feel guilty," Nora said and blushed as Charlie raised an eyebrow. She had meant to say it was because they were out having fun while everyone else was back at the Terminal preparing for an epic showdown, but as she looked at Charlie and felt that pang again, she knew it was also guilt because of her ties to Andrew.

Luckily, Charlie took it the first way and let her off the hook. "Everyone needs to have fun now and then," he said. "Even grumpy girls and ornery orderlies. Nothing to feel bad about. We are behaving, aren't we?"

"We are," she said with a smile. "To us! To behaving!"

He laughed at that and lifted his ice cream in a salute before then popping it right into her nose. She screeched and threw her ice cream at him, but he was already off and running, so she missed completely. It was a waste of exceptional ice cream. Nora just laughed instead and started to wipe her face clean.

"I thought we were behaving!" she called out.

"I never agreed to that!" Charlie said in between bouts of laughing.

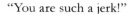

"You are such a jerk!"

He came back to the table and propped himself up. "Yup," he agreed. "That's me, the jerk. I kick ass, take names, break hearts, rip farts, and then I don't call the next day!"

"You are beyond gross," Nora said before looking longingly at her lost ice cream. "I really wanted that!"

"I'll get you another one. Though you may not want to eat too much; you can always use some as a face moisturizer." He began to laugh again at his own cleverness. "But our crazy antics have reminded me that I owe Graves a phone call. He's probably worried by now."

"Tell him that I hate you," Nora said playfully.

"He won't believe me," Charlie said as he got out his phone and began scanning for a signal. "He thinks we're perfect for each other. He told me that you actually like me! I mean, *like* me, like me. Can you believe that nonsense?" He finally fished the phone out of his hands and looked up into her eyes and saw that she wasn't laughing with him. His smile faltered just a bit, but not in a bad way.

"Right," Nora said quietly. "Nonsense." They were sitting very closely now, she realized. Closer than she expected but perhaps not as close as she wanted.

Charlie's breathing got a bit heavier, and his eyes grew a bit wider. His phone buzzed repeatedly, then as it reconnected to the network at he glanced down at it. "Oh my god," he said.

The tone was not a pleasant one, and whatever moment they were about to share was now over. "What is it?" Nora asked.

"Missed calls from Graves," Charlie said. "At least five of them."

He dialled so quickly that he made a mistake and had to start over. His hands were shaking, and he had to take a deep breath to steady his nerves. Finally he managed to do it, and they sat waiting as the phone rang once. Then twice. Three times. Four times. Graves wasn't answering.

Finally, the phone picked up and there was silence on the other end.

"Hello?" Charlie asked. "Hello? Graves? It's me, Charlie. Hello?"

"Where were you when you were needed?" answered a voice that Nora knew well. The Revenant. "He called you and called you, but there was no answer."

"Who is this?" Charlie demanded. "Where is Graves? What's going on?"

"You're too late." The beast laughed. "Too late again. Always too late."

"Too late for what?" Charlie yelled but there was no answer. "TELL ME, DAMN YOU! TOO LATE FOR WHAT?"

"Graves is dead," stated the Revenant simply. "I killed him. Don't worry, though. You'll see him soon. After all, you're next."

Then the line went dead.

CHAPTER 25

The smell was the first thing that hit her when they entered the museum. Even though she had gotten used to it now, the sense memory of the accident kept coming back to her, hitting her like a ton of bricks. The foulness of it and the way it permeated everything. Then there was also the undignified response of a body that had drawn its last breath. Coupled with the way they found him, sprawled on the floor and his blank eyes, oddly calm-looking, staring at the ceiling in a forever-stare, Nora wanted to vomit.

Charlie was still on his knees beside the body of the man who had essentially been his father. His fingers danced and twitched midair as if looking for something to hold on to or a place to start to reverse what couldn't be undone. His whole body shook with the trauma, yet no tears or words would come.

Nora hung back, trying to forget the smell and wanting to say something to Charlie or take some sort of action, but the paralysis had hit her as well. Until today, the whole thing had been a surreal experience, and even though it had personally impacted her, the time in the hospital and the days of consciousness/unconsciousness had allowed her to build up a buffer of sorts. It had been like watching a movie with the characters acting their parts. Even though she went through the same trauma with Andrew not long ago, this was harder to bear for some reason. Maybe it was the lack of hospital medication and the soothing voices of her family. Maybe it was because this time she should have known something like this was coming. There had been enough threats and enough violence that sooner or later there was going to be a casualty. But Graves? After everything he had been through, it just felt so wrong.

It was still surprising, though. It was something they knew was coming. They all saw it a mile away, and yet she was still surprised.

She stood in the doorway and looked desperately around for something to cling to that would give her something to do. Some way to be useful. Charlie was now cradling Graves' head, sobbing quietly, which made Nora feel like a horrible voyeur. She went into the kitchen just to try to give them some privacy for a moment.

Absurdly, to her at least, she began to put on some tea. She poured the water and plopped the kettle on the stove and then stood back to watch it boil. She thought of the old saying, "a watched pot never boils," and hoped that it was true. At that moment, Nora would have been content to stand and stare at that pot until the end of time so she wouldn't have to face whatever was going to come next.

"That," came a hoarse voice, "is exactly what I had in mind."

She spun around in surprise and saw John McCrae, slashed, arm severed, and faded to near nothing propped up in a chair in the corner. Around him she could see signs of a struggle and parts of his being spread across the room, including his arm resting apart from the rest of his body on the table in front of him. Nora cursed herself for forgetting about the ghost and rushed over to help him immediately.

He weakly protested at first, but she poured some of her energy into him anyway. His glow brightened up a bit, and some of the worst damage began to repair itself. Before she got much further, not even making it to his arm, McCrae broke the connection and insisted that she not continue. Nora could see he didn't want it. Whatever had taken Graves from him had also killed him a second time. Whatever came next, be it heaven or oblivion, was where John McCrae was intending to go.

"I need him," McCrae whispered. "Where is Charles? I must speak with him."

"You can tell me," Nora said. "I don't think Charlie's in a talking mood right now. I... I don't know how to tell you this."

McCrae nodded. "It's okay," he said. "I already know. Of course I know. But Charles does not. Not all that he needs to."

Nora bit her lip and looked back to the other room. Slowly, she went in as though she was afraid of disturbing anything, even the dust in the room. Charlie had put a blanket over his friend, covering everything, including his face, and was leaning back against a wall, where he stared at the body. The smell assaulted her once again, and Nora felt bile rising in her throat. She choked it back down.

"John needs to talk to you," she said.

Charlie looked up at her, nodded briefly, and pushed himself to his feet. He walked into the kitchen and saw what had been done to McCrae, not even knowing how much worse it had really been before Nora got to him, and tears ran down his face. Charlie reached out to try to console the man, and the ghost acknowledged the effort, and the two men sat down and cried with one another. The kettle was whistling, so Nora went over and removed it from the burner before going out into the backyard to give them some privacy. She very nearly went back into the living room but remembered what was waiting there and knew she wasn't ready to deal with that on her own.

It wasn't long before she heard a shout of surprise and anger from inside the house. She turned to go back up the stairs but Charlie thundered out, nearly knocking her over, his eyes wild with anger and confusion. "We have to go!" he yelled.

"What?" Nora asked, confused. "What's going on? What about Graves?"

Charlie never slowed his pace toward his van, but he did stagger a little when he heard her say Graves' name. "We'll deal with it later," he said.

"Shouldn't we call someone?" Nora asked. "The police? What about John? Charlie, you're scaring me!"

At this, he did turn, his eyes full of fury. "You *should* be scared!" he yelled. "This isn't a game, Nora! At what point are you going to wake up? Graves is *dead*. John is nearly gone. Peepers was torn apart. Are you forgetting about Andrew? Aren't you paying attention?"

Nora clenched her teeth. "Of course I'm paying attention," she said. "You stupid bastard, *of course* I know what's going on!"

"Oh, sorry," Charlie said rudely. "Then you've already thought about the fact that if she... if... Graves and John... then who else might it go after? Where do you think we should be?"

Nora flushed in anger. Mostly at herself, because he was right. She had been so focused on the scene behind them that it didn't occur to her they might not be the only casualties.

Charlie softened, if only a touch. "Look, we need to go. If what John told me... *we need to go, Nora.* Before it's too late. Graves..." He looked back at the house and choked up a moment before looking back at her. Numbly, he took out his phone and called 911. He said that he heard a noise come from inside the museum and that he was worried about the old man inside, but no one was answering. He didn't give his name and hung up quickly. He looked ashamed of himself. A moment later, he turned to Nora. "He isn't going anywhere. Not tonight. Let's do our best to make sure he's all we lose. Okay?"

"What did John tell you?" Nora asked.

"Let's just go. We'll find time for that later," Charlie said.

"Are you sure?"

"No," he replied honestly. "But it's the best you're gonna get."

"Fine," she said, though it really wasn't. "Let's go."

THEY COULD see the spectral energy being tossed around a block before they even arrived at Cullen. Charlie never slowed down once to appreciate the fireworks. He pushed the rusted pedal to the rusted floor and Nora held on tight. They spun around the corner and came face-to-face with a mob of blue bodies running away from the scene. Charlie didn't slow down at all but instead plowed right through the mob, sending a shower of scattered blue forms into the wind behind them. He lined the van up for the boarded-up main entrance and gunned the engine. Nora screamed and braced herself as the van slammed through it and crashed into the ticket counter on the inside, where more blue forms were scattered about.

Within seconds, however, they were back and nearly indistinguishable from one another as floating arms and legs collided into a single mass before reluctantly separating. If it was chaos on the outside, inside the terminal it looked like the end of days. In every corner of the room there was fighting going on, and it was impossible to say who was winning. The forces of the Revenant were easy to spot, since they looked more solid than most, though none of them had the extra thickness of Cyril or Shadow. The Revenant, if Nora had to guess, was going for quantity over quality in this case. Judging by the intense fighting and screaming, it might be the winning strategy.

Nora kicked at the door to get it open, but it was wedged against the counter. Charlie had hit his head on the wheel when they collided with the building and was now trying to shake it off, but there was a trickle of blood from his scalp going into his eye. From her limited vantage point, Nora quickly focused on the members of the Deadish, all of whom seemed to still be in the fight, in part thanks to her growing skill with manipulating energy and the boost she had given them earlier. It was what was giving them a fighting chance in this situation, as the ordinary ghosts of Cullen were getting cut down and torn apart by the invaders. Some were standing their ground regardless of the disadvantage, but many were fleeing out the way Charlie and Nora had come in. She couldn't blame them. It was a slaughter in here.

Isabel was on the balcony and swatting intruders with her leg. Where it connected with the thicker blue forms, it left a slight indentation. When she connected with the same spot on one of her attackers a second time, it knocked that extra layer of protection the Revenant had given them off. The ghost still advanced to attack, but Isabel saw it wasn't invincible.

Below, Rocco was firing nonstop into the crowd pushing into the back entrance. He was screaming, though his voice was cut off by the volume of his gun. The waves of encroaching ghosts would stagger, but as impressive as he was with his weapon, he couldn't get them all. They were about to reach him when an explosion in the crowd sent a mass of blue scattering away courtesy of one of Sarge's homemade spectral grenades.

"Boo-yah!" Sarge thundered as he tossed another. Nora's energy had given even their weapons a bit of punch. The next explosion sent more bodies scattering, the thicker ones leaving a trail of goo in their wake. It would have been pretty if it weren't so violent.

Scarlett and Scraps were in the mix as well. They had no obvious weapons to power but had found other ways to compensate. Both of them had become ridiculously strong as a result. Scraps had his mouth clenched on the leg of the one of the invaders who made the mistake of ignoring the dog. A second later, Scraps whipped his head and tore the leg clean off. The dog tossed it into the air, where Scarlett snatched it and then used it like a baseball bat to smash the one-legged man clean through the building wall, leaving only a smear of ectoplasm where he'd gone through.

Nora wanted to get into the mix, but no matter how hard she kicked at her door, it wouldn't budge an inch. Reno slowly reformed by her door, having apparently being an accidental victim of their entrance. Part of his thickened essence was missing now, but he reached out and grabbed at the handle with his good hand. He had been practicing interacting with real-world objects long before Nora had powered him up, and now he could actually move things with some skill. She pushed and he pulled until the door opened enough for her to squeak out.

"Good of you to join us," Reno said. He gestured around the room. "Pick a fight, any fight," he said before he turned and lunged at the nearest enemy.

"Wait!" Nora yelled after him. "Where's Andrew?" There was no answer from Reno, who tangled with his opponent, then fell through the floorboards to the level below. Nora looked around to find Andrew, but there was no easy way to tell him apart in the chaos.

One of the Revenant's powered-up ghosts saw her and began to charge. She turned and looked at him calmly, her eye glowing brightly. He barely had time to look surprised before a tight burst of light shot out of her and blew the head completely off his shoulders. She turned and began to sweep her light through the room, obliterating more than a dozen ghosts in one burst. The invaders began to hesitate while the Deadish redoubled their efforts to better press the sudden advantage.

They might just win this, Nora realized, just before she was clubbed on the back of the head and sent sprawling to the floor. Unseen claws raked at her back as she tried to crawl forward, and she was grateful that her coat was keeping her skin intact, though it wouldn't hold for long. She screamed loudly in frustration and in pain.

"That will be enough of that, I am thinkink," said a thick Russian accent. Cyril stood triumphantly behind her. His great tiger, Jax, opened his jaws wide as it prepared to rip out her throat.

Scraps jumped up at that moment and bit the tiger's flank. The beast roared and snapped at the intruder, but Scraps was much too quick and had already retreated out of range. A gunshot from Rocco took the animal in another leg, causing it to leap back. Nora used the opportunity to get to her feet and fire a bolt of energy toward Cyril.

The Strong Man had learned, however, from their first encounter and was already moving. He lifted a sheet of drywall from the floor to block the blast and tossed it her way. Nora scrambled to get out of the path of the object and noticed with grim satisfaction that the wall piece took out one or two of the Revenant-powered ghosts instead. Rocco continued to fire after Cyril, narrowly missing each time.

More and more ghosts continued to arrive at the back door, where Sarge was currently putting up a fight. Big as he was, Sarge was quickly becoming overwhelmed.

Nora sent a blast toward the back door to help ease the pressure while Isabel leapt down from the balcony to help out. Cyril used the distraction to hurl more debris at her, the dust getting into her eyes and mouth causing her to choke and cough. She fired blindly then, getting a yell of protest from Scarlett, who had nearly been caught in the blast.

Nora cursed herself for being careless. Having power was great and all, but it did her no good if she hurt her friends. She did her best to keep on fighting, but the constant pulses she was blasting out were causing her to lose energy quickly. She impulsively reached out and grabbed one of the Revenant's forces, a feral-looking woman, and pulled the excess energy into her own body. The woman looked terribly sad and sank to her knees when Nora was done. Now just a normal ghost, she was effectively out of the fight. There had been a moment when Nora wanted to absorb the woman entirely, but an image of Graves flashed through her mind, and she managed to stop herself. As it was, she was horrified by what she had done. She felt justified in the action since that ghost meant harm to her and her people, but at the same time the idea that she felt okay with it made her worry even more.

She pushed it aside. She'd have to deal with that later.

Now that Cyril and Jax were in the mix, the other side was slowly becoming more organized. The advantage that Nora gave them was balanced by the arrival of the Revenant's enforcers, and along with the steady stream of new arrivals, it was plain to see that it was only a matter of time before they were overrun. Scraps had been doing well at keeping Jax occupied, but the tiger finally got lucky and snapped up the little dog whole in its mouth before tossing it aside. Scarlett screamed and ran to get her dog. Nora thought Scraps was now more dead than dead-ish, but after a moment he weakly got to his feet and limped toward an open-armed Scarlett. The girl's concern for her pet was nearly her undoing as well, as a ghost started approaching her from behind. Nora sent a blast through it, but the little girl was now curled up beside her dog and out of the fight.

Rocco and Isabel were being pushed back and were now side-by-side with Sarge, who had run out of grenades and was now using a spectral shotgun. Reno appeared out of a hole in the floor and dragged himself over to Scarlett and Scraps, clearly in no condition to do much fighting. Just like that, Nora was down half a team. She spared a glance to see that Charlie was still in the van but unharmed, which was good news, but she still hadn't spotted Andrew or Peepers, the latter of whom she hoped had sense enough to run at the start of the mess.

The light in her scar fading, Nora figured she had enough for one or two last shots before she was utterly defenceless. All that energy stored up to fight the Revenant, and she hadn't even seen the creature here.

The last bullet fired out of Rocco's gun took a spook in the face at the same time as the rest of its body knocked the gun out of Rocco's hand. That was it. The Deadish were done. The silence returned to Cullen.

The Deadish closed in around Nora, and they all stood back-to-back as the enemy horde surrounded them, parting only enough to allow Cyril and Jax to walk toward the defeated group. Looking extremely satisfied, Cyril raised an arm to signal the final attack when a high, shrill whistle froze him in place. Cyril sneered at this intrusion and looked like he was going to ignore the command, but after a moment he winced and took a step back anyway.

Nora looked toward the source of the sound. Standing on top of Charlie's beat-up van was the Revenant, looking ecstatic in its victory, one hand clenched around Andrew's neck and the other hand around a squirming Peepers. Without a shadow of doubt, Nora knew they had lost. She hung her head in defeat. The Deadish looked at Nora and hesitated before they, too, surrendered.

"Enough," the Revenant said. "It's done. You are done. The silence will return. You and your friends will be gone, just like the old man, and order will be restored. I will have my place in the world again."

"Fine," Nora said. "Have your place, whatever the hell that means. Just leave them alone. They can't hurt you. Let go of my friends."

"No," the Revenant said. "I'm hungry. I'm *very* hungry."

"Then eat me," Nora said with a mischievous grin. Behind her, beat to hell though he was, Reno snickered. Nora was banking on the Revenant thinking her soul energy-deprived, but if that thing got close enough she'd be able to let one last blast through and hopefully end the whole thing. "Come on, loser. I'm ringing the dinner bell."

The Revenant sneered and hopped down, impossibly fast, from the van to the ground below. "Careful what you wish for," she said. She held out her arms, her captives still clutched firmly, and began to pull their essence into her body. Involuntarily, both Andrew and Peepers began to scream.

"Stop it!" Nora screamed at the creature, who continued to walk toward her, undaunted. Andrew and Peepers continued to fade while the gills on the creature grew brighter and brighter.

"You're too late," the Revenant said.

"Not this time!" shouted Charlie from behind it. Before the Revenant turned, Charlie slammed a rebar against the thing's back and out of her chest. Instinctively, being made of flesh and bone, the creature dropped her prisoners and grabbed at the metal pole. She turned to face Charlie, who had another piece in hand and ready to swing. Before he did, though, he looked the thing in the face and stopped mid-arc. The creature, too, went stock-still as she stared at Charlie.

Charlie opened his mouth to speak, and the Revenant backhanded him and sent him flying into his van, where he crumpled to the ground. Nora couldn't tell if he was dead or not. She started to run toward him when a spectral explosion went off in front of her that pulled her up short. Once again the room erupted in chaos and a rough arm grabbed her from behind and pulled her back. She looked to see Sarge, clutching one last grenade, nod at her before he shoved her back to the others.

Rocco gestured at Nora to follow him, and she dully saw that he no longer had his gun. She was about to ask where it was when it began to thunder behind her as Sarge picked it up to help make his last stand. Reno, clutching Scarlett and Scraps with his one good arm, was heading down into the tunnel that Sarge often used to get to his haunt below the terminal. Behind him came a shuffling Peepers and Isabel, who were dragging a very weak Andrew. Rocco was shouting at Nora and pushing her down the tunnel. She backed up past him in time to watch the Revenant grab Sarge's head with one hand and his body with another before she pulled the head clean off and then soaked in the remaining energy. Sarge was gone. Forever, this time. A thick sob caught in her throat.

Cyril and Jax blocked her line of sight as they rapidly advanced upon her. Nora powered up her eye to take another shot when the whole world went dark and the tunnel entrance seemed to implode as a result of the toll the fighting had taken on the building. Getting her footing, Nora ran as the path they were on didn't hold up well, either, and the hallway collapsed. Nora ran as hard as the others, but part of the ceiling landed on her and sent her sprawling to the floor. More dust, debris, and plaster splashed all around them in what remained of Sarge's home turf. Nora pushed a few boards off herself and started looking for a way to get back upstairs to get to Charlie but couldn't see anything through the haze in the air.

A moment later, a blue hue lit up her area as Andrew crawled over to her. "Nora Angel," he said. "It's too late. We have to go. We need to go."

"There's a tunnel down here," Rocco called out from somewhere in the fog. "Sarge showed us. An old bomb tunnel. It'll take us down to the river. If we go now, we should get away."

"But the others…" Nora said.

"Hell with 'em," Rocco said.

"*Rocco*," Isabel warned sternly.

Peepers shuffled over to Nora and looked at her with his large eyes. "My Adelaide would want you to live."

"Yeah, well, I want you to kick some ass," Reno put in.

"To do that," Andrew interrupted. "We need to *go*. We'll get him back. We won't stop until we do."

She thought about Charlie and the same vow he made with Graves. *This time will be different, however,* Nora vowed silently. *This time we'll win.*

Reluctantly, she followed them down the tunnel and went into the light.

CHAPTER 26

The tunnel had collapsed, but the girl and her companions were just feet beyond. The Revenant quickly sucked in the essence of the buffoon who had allowed his friends to escape, and then she prepared to lead the charge. That was when she noticed the world had gone still. Too still. Dust motes hung in the air. Cyril was frozen in place, and Jax was frozen mid-leap.

No, no, no, thought the panicked Revenant. *Not now!*

But now it was to be. She felt the hook in her belly as the shadows around her yawned and tugged. She was pulled back into them, a million barbs tucked into her flesh that tore her apart as they dragged her back into the darkness of the Margins beyond.

She did her best to resist, but in the end she screamed just as all did when they were summoned by the Others. The pain was beyond anything she had experienced before, and when she could stand it no longer, when death was not merely a possibility but the thing she craved more than anything, it all stopped as soon as it had begun.

Darkness surrounded her except for a small pool of light where she lay. Her torn flesh was all about her, and she summoned as much strength as she could to pull it back in and heal herself. The process was slow and agonizing, until finally the relief was total.

"It's better than you deserve," chuckled a voice in the dark. She looked up and could barely see a shadow upon a shadow. Two eyes burned in the darkness, which gave her a point to focus on.

"You... have... to.... send... me... back..." she choked out. She could barely speak.

"Have to?" said the voice, amused. "*HAVE* to?" Hundreds of throats snapped and snarled in the darkness, a cacophony of hunger and evil. He bent forward, slightly, so that only a small amount of his head could be seen. The Revenant recoiled in horror. It was a mask of skin pulled tight against his face, with ringed circlets holding it in place. The same skin was on his hands like gloves. A winged bat-creature, seemingly made of the darkness itself, settled on his shoulder. "No, I don't believe I *have* to do anything," he said so absently he might as well have been out for a stroll in the park. That's when the Revenant knew that whomever she was dealing with was beyond dangerous. She didn't matter to him. Not in the slightest. Whatever happened next was going to be to his amusement one way or the other.

"I'm close," she said. "They're right there."

"What you are, my dear, is a failure," said the face as it receded into the shadows. "Once, twice, three times… how many chances should you get?"

"One more," she croaked. "I was about to win!"

At this, the darkness chuckled and with it the hundred throats in accordance. "Perhaps," it said. "Maybe, baby. Mother may I? Polly want a cracker?" More laughter like nails on a chalkboard. The Revenant winced.

"What can I do?" she begged.

Sharply, the darkness fell silent. "You can die," came the voice.

"No," she said. "*No!* Let me prove myself!"

"Prove yourself in death. I have no more time for you. I have other matters. Other doors to explore."

"Wait!" the Revenant called. "Please!" But the darkness was quiet. Beyond quiet. Not even the snarling or snapping of voices. "I'll do anything! You can have anything!"

A rustle of wind in the shadows. "Anything, you say?" it whispered. Whether it was pleased or not, the Revenant could not tell.

"Name it," she said through clenched teeth.

"Not today," it said playfully. "Maybe not ever. You will get your 'last chance,' though only because it amuses me to do so. You are a waste of a creature, and we have spent far too long on you already. Dead or alive at this point, your value is next to nothing.

"We will send you back. But you deserve no help from us, and so we will give you none. You are stripped of all your powers. What energy you have within you is what you may take into the final battle. If you live there, then you can be welcomed back into the fold. You may continue your existence. If you die there, so be it. You have caused enough trouble. One outcome or another removes a problem for us. We do not care if you succeed. If you die, another will be sent. One who does not fail."

The Revenant knew that she was being offered a gift but couldn't keep herself from protesting. "My power? How can I fight if I have no power? The girl has allies! What am I supposed to do?"

"Fail, or don't fail," came the voice. "But you may have your allies. We will allow your two powered souls to remain with you, but you will not be able to drain another soul, living or dead, until this is resolved. Go and fight now, if you wish, but in three days the moon will be full. That is when our kind has the most strength thanks to the full blue of the moon."

"But won't the girl have more strength then as well?" asked the Revenant.

The voice only laughed. The hundred throats cackled all around her.

Before she could ask further, the hooks snagged in her gut again, but the tearing and shredding was absent. The darkness pulled into every pore, and the gloom of the terminal snapped back into focus. There was a burst of energy from the Revenant that burst outwards and obliterated every soul in the room except for herself, Cyril, Jax, and the unconscious Charlie at her feet.

"What has happened?" Cyril said, his eyes full of wonder and fear.

The Revenant nudged Charlie with her foot. He groaned slightly. That was good. He would be needed to draw the girl out. Beyond that, he was useless. He turned slightly, and she saw his face. Her cheek and eye twitched as she took in his features.

Jax growled at her feet, and Cyril snapped his chain back. The great cat backed off and looked warily at the Revenant.

"Three more days," she said absently. "Then it ends."

"Fine," Cyril said as he looked around the room. "It is appearink that we are needink new recruits."

She winced at this and thought back to what the Other had told her. She had only the power within herself to use. She had a great deal of energy stored, though it wasn't limitless. She would have to be smart and careful about deciding how to best use it.

A smile played at the corner of her lips. There was just enough for two while still leaving her plenty of energy for herself.

"No more ghosts," she said. "I have something better in mind."

The gills on her neck began to flex and relax as the smoky light puffed out. One form coalesced into a weak, smoky state that was shaky and uncertain on its feet. The other took on a clearer form until it started to become stronger and firmer. It became thicker, harder, and more substantial until the smoke pulled itself in and the creature, the Wisp, appeared and looked nearly as real as any living person.

"How?" whispered Cyril in awe. "Why?"

The Revenant smiled in response. "Three days," she said to Cyril. "Send out the word. Tell everyone you find. The endgame is about to begin."

PART 3: ACCEPTANCE

CHAPTER 27

"You have the ability to wake the dead, you know," Reno had joked two days ago without any real enthusiasm.

Reno was looking better, more firm, once Nora had gotten a chance to heal him. She and the Deadish Society were holed up in an abandoned house in an area of the city called the Ward. It wasn't posh, but they were left alone, and no one knew where they were. Nora had slept, barely, last night, and the bags under her eyes confirmed it. That she had snored was actually a good thing, a sign of deep rest, even if she didn't feel it. She smiled wanly at Reno to acknowledge his attempt at humour, but this was a day where there wasn't room for smiles and laughter. Today, they were having a funeral for Victor "Graves" Culshaw.

Peepers had gone back to the museum to collect John McCrae, who told them that the police had arrived and found Graves. As far as the EMTs could tell, the old man had died of a heart attack, and when the coroner arrived he concurred with the findings. A few people in the neighbourhood had come out in response to the flashing lights and had moved off when the stretcher and body bag came out a short time later. There had been a few questions about next of kin, and though one or two of the neighbours mentioned seeing a young man stopping by from time to time, none of them had really gotten to know Mr. Culshaw well enough to say for sure.

The funeral was to be held two days later. Graves had prepaid and arranged for his own funeral some time ago, and it all sped along quite quickly. Almost too quickly, Nora thought. It was as though the living wanted to be rid of the responsibility of caring for the dead as quickly as possible to avoid being tainted by it. No one really wanted to dwell on the fact that no matter the route they took, everyone wound up at the same destination. The Deadish Society argued about whether or not it was wise to go to the funeral, but Nora wouldn't hear of it. They were going to pay their respects. It was the least they could do. Honestly, though, part of Nora hoped that the Revenant would show up, if only so they could find out if Charlie was still alive.

Stop that, she chided herself. Of course he was still alive.

To the living, it would have seemed to be a sad affair. Nora would be there, as would a couple of the regular visitors to the museum or a few of the neighbours that Graves hadn't chased off with a badminton racket at one point or another. Through the lens of his real life, however, it was a crowded affair as close to two hundred spirits were in attendance from near and far. Beyond the few black-dressed mourners was a sea of blue… an ocean of love from the people Graves impacted the most but seemed would never join, because if Graves had a ghost, he hadn't made it known. The look on his face when Nora and Charlie had found his body had been peaceful, serene even, and instinctually Nora knew that he'd found the strength to move on. Graves had left them alone to the world.

Nora chose to adopt this as a point of pride. Rather than feel abandoned, she felt extra confident that Graves believed they didn't need him to face the challenge ahead. Isn't that what parents, mentors, and guides are supposed to do, anyway? They prepare you for the world and all of the joy and misery it can bring before stepping back, spreading their arms, and saying "have at it." That was the goal of the parent — to become unnecessary. That didn't mean they weren't wanted or missed, however. That part, Nora knew, would never go away.

Gradually, the strangers all around her at the funeral made their way off. Nora heard a couple of them mention the absence of Charlie in a disapproving voice, but she had neither the energy nor the inclination to explain. The Deadish Society stood around her, Andrew closest, and were her support, though she could not even lean on them. They were there and that was enough.

One by one, the Deadish drifted off and away, each taking a moment to stand by the coffin. Though they barely knew him, they respected him.

Finally, it was just Andrew and Nora, side by side, watching as the ghost of John McCrae limped over to the coffin for a few moments of privacy.

"I'm sorry, Nora Angel," Andrew said.

"I'm sorry, too," Nora said. "For everything."

Andrew nodded. "Take your time," he said before moving off and giving her space.

Nora waited a minute before approaching John, wanting to make sure he had as much time as he needed. The two of them stood side by side for a while in silence. It was Nora who spoke first. "I wish we had buried him with his badminton racket," she said.

For the first time, she heard John McCrae laugh. "He would have liked that," he said. He turned and looked sadly at Nora. "He's not coming back, is he?" The question was rhetorical, but Nora shook her head anyway. "Good," McCrae said in a satisfied voice. "*Good.* I'm glad. Victor lived his life to the fullest he could. The man had regrets and plenty of them, but I believe he made his peace with them. His business, or his part in the business, was finished. He's moved on."

"I'm just glad he didn't know about Charlie," Nora said.

McCrae turned to her with fierce eyes. "Now you stop that," he said firmly. "You don't know whether Charles is alive or dead. Until you know, you keep the hope. You keep fighting. It's what Victor and Charles both would want."

She nodded. "I just wish they were both here," she said.

"Now wouldn't that be an interesting conversation. 'Why are you at this hole in the ground?' Victor would ask."

They laughed a little at that.

"I'd tell him it was for Charlie's van," Nora said.

"On *that* we do agree," John said. "That thing was a death trap."

"Nah," Nora said with a small smile. "It's a classic. But don't tell him I said that."

"Your secret is safe with me," John said, chuckling. "I won't tell another living soul. Or a dead one, for that matter."

Something in his tone made Nora worried. "What do you mean?"

"You know what I mean," he said sadly. "My time here is done, for better or worse. Victor was my unfinished business. One way or the other, I planned to spend my eternity in his company. He's my best friend."

"You're moving on?" Nora asked. She looked around for some sort of sign, a light, something to cling to.

"Yes, child," he said. "With your help." He reached out to her, and she recoiled in horror.

"I can't do that," she said. "I won't."

"My time is done," he said calmly. "I don't know how I know it, but I do. Take as much as you can. Take all of me. I have a feeling that it isn't the end. I'm not afraid."

"But I am," Nora said. "It's too much! I can't take being responsible for you, too!"

"We are all responsible for our own actions and our own choices. Just as we are for the consequences. But have faith. I've accepted what's next. I only ask, I only hope, that you honour my choices. I leave it to you to protect my family."

With that, Nora nodded and reached out. The cold numbness spread into her hands at once, but it wasn't like any other time she had collected energy. Those moments had been born of hunger and need, but this one was gentle and flowing, like a long, loving hug. She suddenly had visions of her grandparents and feeling their warm, accepting embrace. She opened her eyes and rather than see a faded John McCrae, she saw the edges of him sparkle gently. The energy stopped flowing into her, and only a faint outline was left of McCrae.

"Look after them, okay?" he said. "*Both* of them." He looked all around her, not even seeing her, and then a smile was on his face. "Oh," he said contentedly. "Oh, *wow.*"

And then he was gone.

LATER THAT day, Nora found herself in a difficult situation. She was on her hands and knees, scraping through a small opening, feeling tiny pinpricks of needles scratching at her back. She wanted to call out in pain and fear, but the only way to go was forward. She had no choice. She was determined to make this work.

Finally, she managed to make her way out of the small bush she was awkwardly trying to get through. It was a thorny hedge that surrounded the King house and the closest access point to the window belonging to Vee. She'd made her way through that thing dozens of times to hang out when they were kids, but she was old enough now that she shouldn't be doing those kinds of things. She didn't want any unwanted attention, however, and Vee's parents were hardcore gossips, so this was just easier... if undignified.

Nora rapped on the window as Vee strutted around in her room, dancing her head off. Her headphones were totally cranked to the max. Anyone else would look like a dork, but Vee looked so happy that she made it cool. Nora rapped harder and harder until she figured she might as well have gone in the front door anyway for the amount of noise she was making. Finally, Vee clued in and shouted in glee when she saw her friend. She ran over, popped the window open, and practically dragged Nora in.

"Is this a jailbreak?" Vee asked excitedly. "Are you on the lam?"

"Yes, Vee," Nora said with an eye roll. "Michael Scofield is outside waiting to take us both away."

Vee actually spared a glance out the window before laughing again.

"Shhhh!" Nora hissed. "No parents, okay?"

"Okay, okay!" Vee said, but she was fighting hard to control her glee. "Why are you here? How did you get away? I am *so* sorry, by the way, about Kia. She ratted you out in the coffee shop. Kapalini told me."

Nora smiled. This was what she needed. Everything else may have been falling apart in the world, but she could count on Vee to be the balm for every open wound. "Let's get out of here," Nora said with a smile.

Not long after, they found themselves nestled in their favourite coffee shop, The Meridian, situated along a pleasant strip of the downtown core. Bookshelves lined the space that had an earthy, cabin-like feel to it. There was a large selection of tea on the menu, more than any other place she had seen, and they selected a variety to taste and to sip. They were on the cusp of adulthood anyway, but something about this place made them feel like they were settled and refined. It was perfect.

"So, tell me," Vee said as she inhaled the fruity aroma of the blueberry tea. "What's it like being in the cuckoo's nest?"

Nora bit her lip. Vee had always been the one person she entrusted with the truth. She hadn't had a chance to talk to her before she'd been whisked away, so no doubt her family or the rumour mill had informed Vee of what had supposedly happened. Andrew had argued with her earlier that going out was dangerous on its own, but telling Vee the truth about where she had gone was worse, since it put Vee herself in danger.

Sitting across from her best friend, Nora knew that the truth was what she owed her friend, whatever the consequences. "Listen, Vee, I have to talk to you."

Vee giggled in anticipation and leaned forward.

"Seriously, Vee, I need you to listen. Before I start, I swear on our friendship that I'm telling you the truth. You don't need to accept it, but it's what I have to give."

Still smiling, Vee reached out and grabbed her friend's hand. "Okay. Tell me. Whatever you say, no matter what you say, I am your friend."

Hoping that would still be true once she finished talking, Nora started at the beginning. More than an hour passed before she was done, with Vee asking only minor questions from time to time. Nora couldn't tell if her friend was freaked out or not. If Vee ever decided to take up poker, she would clean up. Her face didn't once betray what she was thinking.

"No wonder they locked you up," Vee said when Nora was done. "Cray-cray, fo' sho'."

Nora's heart fell.

"Stop that," Vee said with a smile. "I didn't say I didn't believe you. Just that you're crazy. That's some seriously messed-up stuff. You should write a book."

"If I survive, I'll totally do that," Nora said.

"Dedicate it to me," Vee said.

"I will dedicate it to you," Nora affirmed. "So, you believe me?"

"Honestly?" Vee said. "I don't know. Best I can do. I believe that you believe it, if that's any consolation. I don't really like thinking of you living in an abandoned bus terminal, though."

"I'm not any more. It was kind of destroyed," Nora said.

"Ah," Vee said. "So where are you now?"

"I don't want to say," Nora said. Vee looked offended, so Nora quickly tried to appease her friend. "No, no, it's not like that. If that thing found Graves and the Terminal, I don't want it to find you or come after us. Less risky that way."

Vee tapped her nail against the teacup as she sat and considered her friend. "So, you still see him? Andrew?"

"Yeah," Nora muttered. "All the time."

"Oh, sweetie," Vee said. There was real compassion and sympathy in her voice. "I'm so sorry. I can't imagine how tough that must be."

"It's not fun," Nora admitted. "Nor is it going well."

Vee chuckled at this. "I'm sorry," she said. "It's not funny." Then she started laughing. Hard. Nora was annoyed at first, but after a moment she started laughing too. They both were laughing so hard that tears were coming down their faces, and other customers began to shush them. "Oh, YOU shush!" Vee fired back as she continued to laugh.

"I guess it is funny," Nora said once they'd calmed down. "God, this is messed-up."

"Sure is," agreed Vee. "What about your family? What did they say when you told them the truth?"

Nora blanched. "Vee, I can't tell them. It would kill my mother and father. They already agreed to send me away. If I come home and tell them I lied about where I was staying and what I was seeing... well, what would you do?"

"Apparently," Vee said as she raised her hand to get the attention of the server. "I would buy you more tea."

"Seriously."

The server arrived and poured out two more cups. One was strawberry-flavoured, the other had a hint of vanilla. "I don't know what I'd do," Vee admitted. "But perhaps telling them the truth is a bit of a no-go. There are some things parents aren't ready to face about the world. Their kids growing up and having sex being one of them."

"Well, that's one thing they don't have to worry about with him," Nora admitted.

"No! I thought for sure you must have. Then again, I suppose I knew all along, didn't I?" Vee said with a smile. "There's no way you would not have told me by now."

Nora laughed and nodded her head before loudly sipping her cup of tea. She smiled broadly, enjoying this moment. It was a good memory to share, after all, even if Vee was overly delighting in it. The moment passed, and then she put the cup down and looked solemnly at her friend. "I owe my mom and dad so much. I just feel like I need to tell them... something. Andrew talks about his parents and how he feels like there's so much his missed out on. Charlie would have given anything for one more conversation with Graves. I'm just afraid of leaving them without having said or done something meaningful that they can carry with them."

"So go talk to them," Vee said. "You're still here. There's still time."

"Problem," Nora said. "I'm supposed to be locked up."

"Day pass," Vee said. "You get a day away from your reality."

"Nice in theory, but what if they want to see it?"

"Then show them one."

"Right. Where do I get a day pass?"

And that was how Nora found herself in a craft store fifteen minutes later with a day pass in her hands. It was made, polished, and even laminated by Vee and the helpful staff of the centre. Vee told them it was a prop for a YouTube movie they were making, even though no one asked or seemed to care. When Vee presented it to her, Nora had to admit it looked pretty good. Vee said she'd drive her home and be her backup and moral support, though Nora made her agree that at the end of the visit that Nora would take a taxi back to where she was hiding out. Vee looked a bit hurt at that but nodded anyway.

Nora's parents and brother were shocked to see her, of course, but that quickly turned to relief and happiness. They accepted the day pass story easily and didn't even look at it, despite the fact that she tried to show it to them. They led her to the living room and asked how she was feeling, the people she was with, the treatment, the food, everything at once. Nora answered each question and felt terrible for how easily the lie came each time. With Vee's help, she steered the conversation back to her family or to memories of better times. Gradually, the talk moved away from the institute and paramnesia to ordinary life.

This is where I belong, Nora thought. She looked around the room at the smiling faces, the familiar furniture, smells, and sights. She rested her hand on Rorschach's back as the dog had taken up residence by her side the moment she sat down. There was something so powerful about being at home. There was no other place like it in the world, and there never would be. Nora knew that no matter where she went, how far she travelled, whom she met, or even what kind of family she might make for herself one day, nothing would ever truly compare to this place and this moment. It was one of those rare moments when she was aware that she was coming of age. Everything seemed to freeze in her mind like a snapshot that she would carry in her heart until the day she died. She just hoped that day was a long time off.

"I love you all," Nora said to her family, tears threatening to well in the corners of her eyes. "Mom, Dad, Tom, Rorschach… thank you for being my family. I know it hasn't been easy lately, but you were all there for me in more ways than I can count. I'm proud to be your daughter. Tom, I'm proud to be your sister, even if you can be difficult and a little gross." Tom smiled at that, tears touching the corner of his eyes. She ruffled Rorschach's fur, and the dog gazed at her lovingly. "I love you, too, buddy," she said. "No matter what happens next or in our lives, I just wanted you to know that."

"We know, sweetheart," said her father. "We love you too."

"I love you," said her mother.

"Love you, sis," Tom said. "I even kind of miss the snoring. You could set your watch to it. House is too quiet now."

Rorschach farted. Everyone laughed, including Vee, who furiously waved her hand in front of her nose and even started retching. The spell broken, the moment passed, and Nora felt one burden at the very least had been taken from her shoulders.

A short time later, she used the ready-made excuse she and Vee had planned and told them she had to take a taxi back to the Institute. Offers were made by all, even Vee, to drive her, but she insisted that the best thing right now was to end the night on this positive note, since it had given her the strength she needed to face her problems head-on. That much, finally, was true.

The taxi pulled up a short time later. Hugs were given all around, and then Nora hopped into the cab. She waved goodbye as the cab pulled away, and her friend and family faded from view. She started to feel anxious right away, however, and debated whether to tell the driver to pull over so she could run back home. Maybe it would be better to be amongst those who loved her most. She wrestled with a decision and began to reach out to tap the driver on the shoulder.

CHAPTER 28

Tom was surprised and pleased when he opened the door a few minutes later and saw his sister standing there. The whole family meeting had been unexpected but also really great. His parents had been in a tailspin since Nora went away, and any attempts at restoring some kind of normalcy had fallen on deaf ears. One day he even brought over Casey, who had done her best to be helpful, but Nora's mother had started sobbing at this teenage girl in her home who wasn't her daughter and had failed to escape the room before the tears presented themselves.

Seeing Nora tonight had helped, Tom thought. He was a little resentful of how much time Nora occupied for his parents, especially since he was the one who had just graduated high school and would be going off to university in the fall. If there was a time to celebrate his life and achievements, it was now. Displaying a level of maturity that he didn't know was there, Tom managed to distance himself from the situation and take on the role of a parent. Rather than be difficult, he was helpful. Rather than be a pain to his sister, he was a friend. He thought it would be difficult or that he'd be labelled a hero. Instead, he realized that he didn't need praise or recognition to be an adult. Things were just better now. Rather than resent his sister and her problems, he looked at them as an odd blessing in disguise.

So he was exceptionally happy to see her at the door again only moments after she had just driven off. When she had gone off in the taxi, he'd fought the urge to run after it and pull her out. Having the whole family back together had been great, just like the old times, and he felt sure that if she just stayed home that they could face it all together and get things back the way they used to be.

As he looked at her at standing on the porch, he was a bit unnerved by the odd smile on her face that he didn't quite know how to take. He also didn't know why she had bothered to knock, but he invited her in immediately.

"What are you doing back?" he asked with a smile. "Forget something? Staying, maybe?" There was clear hope in his voice, but it was tinged with caution as well. He was trying to be supportive without being suffocating.

Nora didn't answer him, just walked in and took in the surroundings. Vee entered from the kitchen, having stayed behind to help clean up. "Hey, babe!" she called out and offered a friendly wave.

Nora ignored the wave and rudely pushed past her into the kitchen. Vee stumbled a bit and had to be caught by Tom. Both of them were surprised to be in physical contact with each other, and Tom's hands on her back and shoulders lingered a moment longer than was necessary.

"Rude, much?" Vee said in a way that she could have meant either Tom or Nora. Tom hoped she only meant Nora. He blushed anyway and let go, letting Vee fall to the floor, where she let out a squeal of pain.

Nora, meanwhile, made her way into the kitchen. Her father was in there, his back to her, while he was reaching up to put dishes away. She walked up behind him and without any sort of preamble grabbed a plate out of his hand and smashed it into the back of his head before he was even able to turn around. He staggered under the blow and dazedly reached up to touch the point of impact. Before he could, Nora grabbed him by the hair and violently smashed his face into the cupboard, causing the bridge of his nose to snap and blood to gush out everywhere, before she allowed him to drop to the floor.

"You okay in there?" called Nora's mother casually from the next room. The sounds of clearing away could be heard. Nora's father had always been accident-prone, so the sound of dishes breaking wasn't anything out of the ordinary. Unfazed in the slightest, Nora went toward the voice.

At the dining room table, Nora's mother was busy cleaning up. She looked up in time to see her daughter, but before she could utter a word Nora slapped her so hard across the face that it sent her flying backward over the table and into a heap on the floor. Tom flew into the room, saw his mother on the floor, and ran to restrain his sister.

"What the hell are you doing?" he cried out, but there was no reaction from Nora at all. Instead, she elbowed him in the stomach and knocked the wind out of him. While he was gasping for air, she struck him with the point of her fingers directly in his throat, and he began to choke. Not content, Nora grabbed him around the throat, and Tom began to turn a sick shade of purple.

THWACK! Nora eased her grip slightly, finally allowing Tom to gasp in a breath as she turned to look at a stunned Vee, who was brandishing a now-bent umbrella after bashing her friend in the head with it. "Sorry?" asked a frightened Vee.

Nora punched her in the face, and Vee fell back against the wall before she fell forward onto the ground. Tom, still gasping for air, felt helpless as Nora walked over and planted her foot against the back of Vee's neck. For the first time, Nora seemed to show emotion as a sly grin played at the corner of her mouth.

She began to apply pressure, Vee's scream becoming muffled, when all of a sudden she stopped dead in her tracks. Her head cocked to one side, then the other. She looked to be listening to something, but try as he might, Tom could hear nothing except the pounding of his own blood in his head.

The moment stretched, and Nora hesitated. She would put pressure on Vee's neck and then ease it. Pressure and ease. Finally, she lost whatever internal battle she was fighting and removed her foot.

Vee didn't move, just cried softly into the floor. Nora slowly kneeled beside her friend and reached out for her in a not-unkind way. Vee looked at her hopefully for some kind of explanation but none came... only one more quick punch that rendered Vee unconscious.

Horrified and terrified both, Tom looked from Vee to his sister and back again. He backed up against his mother and yelled out both for her to wake up and for his sister to stop. "Why?" he croaked out to her. "Why?"

The last thing he saw was Nora's hand reaching out toward him.

And then darkness.

CHAPTER 29

W hen Nora arrived back at the safe house some time later, she did her best to shake off all that she had seen and done in the past few hours. There would be time later to really go over it in detail and to let the enormity of it all sink in, but for now, it was time to put on her mask of optimism as she got down to business with the members of the Deadish Society.

"All in favour?" Reno asked as she entered the house.

"Aye!" chorused all the others.

"Then it's settled," Reno said happily. Everyone else clapped and smiled. Everyone was there except Rocco, who was nowhere to be seen.

"What's settled?" Nora asked. "What did I miss?"

"Adelaide?" Peepers asked as he turned around. When he saw Nora, he didn't frown as he usually did when his lost wife didn't turn up but gave her his best smile.

"It's a little embarrassing," Andrew said as he approached her through the back slaps and fist bumps.

"No, it's not," Isabel said as she gave him a kiss on the cheek. If it were possible for a blue face to blush red, Andrew would have done it at that moment. Nora noted that the kiss, while friendly, lasted a little bit longer than perhaps it should have. For some reason, this gave her a bit of comfort. "I think it's great. Long overdue, in fact."

"ONE OF US! ONE OF US!" Scarlett shouted in triumph. Scraps barked his assent at her feet.

"Don't forget Peepers, Scarlett," Andrew said.

"TWO OF US! TWO OF US!" Scarlett amended before hooting and running around with Scraps following quickly behind.

"They made Peepers and I members of the Deadish Society," Andrew told Nora. "To replace Sarge."

"No, no, no, no, no, no, no... *no*," Reno said quickly. "We do not have a limit on membership. This is because of your bravery in the Battle of Cullen Terminal (it has so been named) and... because, well, we already live together. But now it's formally done!"

"Don't I get to join?" Nora asked playfully.

"No," Peepers said. "You are not dead. Not even dead-ish. You are very much alive and bright and wonderful. I hope you never get to join. But you can be an honoured guest! Hopefully just like my Adelaide."

"Thank you," Nora said, genuinely touched. "That's very sweet."

"We needed a little something to celebrate," Isabel said. "Enough sad things for a while, don't you think?"

Nora only wished that were true. Charlie and John McCrae were gone, Graves was dead, and everything else that had happened weighed on Nora's mind. They were headed down a path of destruction that would have repercussions for all of their actions.

Andrew, ever the psychic when it came to Nora's thoughts and feelings, spoke to her fears and doubts. "Hey," he said. "We're going to get him back. We're going to end all of this. Eventually. We just need time to plan it all out. Gather more energy. Time is on our side here."

"Not anymore, it ain't," put in Rocco as he breezed through the door. Even though she'd been around the dead a lot and seen them do this often, Nora always gave a little start when it happened. Doors were meant to be opened. "Word's out. Ghosts are talkin' all over the city. Big goon and his cat are tellin' everyone they can that the Bearcat is gonna be at the Old Quebec Street Mall tonight and that if our resident doll wants to see Charlie still in the land of the livin', then she has to show up at midnight, or she'll clip him and stuff him into his very own Chicago overcoat."

"It's too soon," said a deflated Reno, who plopped down into a beat-up chair. "We need more time."

"How much energy do you think you have stored up, Nora?" Isabel asked hopefully. They all knew the answer.

"Not enough," Nora said as her anxiety began to ramp up. "*Oh god. Not enough.*"

"What are we going to do, then?" Scarlett asked pitifully.

Rocco locked and loaded his weapon, then spat on the floor. "I'm not ready for the big sleep. Well, the bigger, deeper sleep, anyway."

"So we run?" Reno asked. "What about Charlie?"

Rocco shrugged, and Nora covered her mouth in horror. It was all on her, she realized, but she had nothing left to give. Where was she going to find more ghosts to give her the boost she needed? There was no time. Charlie was going to die, and it was going to be all her fault. This time she saw death coming, unlike with Andrew, and still she couldn't do a damn thing. One by one, the Deadish Society turned and looked to her for an answer. She couldn't meet their faces, not a single one of them, and so she turned away.

"Give her some space, guys," Andrew said quietly. They all nodded and drifted away, leaving Nora and Andrew alone in the room. "Come sit," Andrew said, indicating the worn couch by the window. "It's just me."

Nora sat. "What are we going to do?"

"We're going to fight," Andrew said simply. "That's what we do, Nora Angel. That's what you and I have done for each other since the beginning. We fight through the pain. We fight through all of it to reach a better place. We don't give up. Like the line in that movie... 'embrace the suck and move the eff forward.' That night, when I died, we both fought harder than we ever thought we were capable of. We didn't win, not exactly, but I don't have any regrets about the effort."

"How can you say that?" Nora asked. "I wasn't able to save you."

Andrew shrugged. "I wasn't exactly able to save you, either. Maybe, though, just maybe, that's what real love is. It isn't about protecting and shielding the person you love from the world, because that's impossible. Life happens to you whether you want it to or not. What love is about is doing the best you can to help people get through it. You aren't responsible for me."

"Does that go the same for you?" Nora asked. "You said you stayed behind... your whole unfinished business... is about protecting me."

Andrew thought for a moment. "You're right," he said. "I don't like to admit it. Maybe that's the guy part of my brain. The caveman impulse. I can't even say it."

"I can," Nora said. "And I want you to hear me. Really hear me. You aren't responsible for me. I can look after myself. Your love meant the world to me. You helped make me who I am today. I am forever grateful for you and the role you played in my life. Nothing that ever will happen to me will change that."

He nodded tearfully. "Thank you," he said. "I wish, though... I wish that all of those statements didn't have to be made in the past tense."

"I know," Nora said. "I avoided saying them, too. Saying it like that makes it real."

"It means you're letting go," Andrew said.

"I think I have to," Nora said. "I don't want to."

They were both quiet for quite some time. Somewhere, deep in the house, they heard Scraps bark once or twice playfully. "We both have to," Andrew said. "It doesn't help to hold on to a past that can't really lead to a future. I can't keep haunting you. I can't keep using you as a reason to exist. I need to find my own way."

"And I can't use my love for you as a reason not to move on," Nora agreed. "To stop myself from living and experiencing the world."

"So," Andrew said. "This is it, then?"

"The end," Nora agreed.

"Whoa!" Andrew shouted with a forced smile. "Not the total end, okay? I may be big enough to admit that we need to move on, but there's still a little bit of caveman in me. Let's make sure we kick this thing's ass, *get some payback*, and if there's time... maybe we'll save Charlie. But I have plans tomorrow, so we'll only save Charlie as long as it doesn't interfere with whatever else I've got going on. I'm a busy soul."

Nora laughed and smiled sadly. "You are such a dork. You're *my* dork. Now and forever."

"And don't you forget it, Nora Angel," he said. "I love you, you know."

"I know," Nora said. "I love you too."

"And I love BOTH of you!" Reno said as he ran over and jumped onto the couch. His enhanced form felt an extra degree cooler to Nora as he landed, but Andrew let out a groan as the two ghosts bashed into each other. "Oh, *Andrew*," Reno said in an exaggerated falsetto voice as he pawed at Andrew. "You're so handsome! I love you! I want to kiss you!" At this, he kept trying to kiss Andrew's face while Andrew struggled to keep him away.

"Get off me!" Andrew protested in good humour. Scraps bounded up the couch next and scampered on top of both of them, alternately licking each face. "Aggh! Stop it!"

Reno took this as an opportunity, grabbed the dog, and started snuggling with it. Scarlett laughed and clapped happily in approval. Rocco, as usual, looked annoyed as Peepers shuffled beside him. Isabel watched it all with an appraising eye from the doorway. Nora noted that Isabel's gaze stayed on Andrew a bit longer than the others. Whatever her feelings were on the subject, however, Nora decided it was just time to let it all go.

AT LAST it was time. Nora checked her watch and saw that it was a little after 11:00 p.m. The night was firmly dark and the stars were out. The moon was ripe and so full that it looked huge in the night sky. The light pollution had turned it a shade of pink bordering on red, which seemed an ill omen of the battle to come.

For us, or for them? Nora wondered.

They had spent the rest of their last day, as Reno morbidly insisted on calling it, looking for ghosts for Nora to gather energy from. Far fewer were around than they expected or hoped for, partly because it was day and ghosts didn't tend to come out much in the bright light. The other reasons they thought possible was that the Revenant had either scared them away or absorbed them all outright. That last option was the least hopeful, and they all crossed fingers and toes that they were wrong.

Despite it all, Nora had a flicker of hope. The energy she grabbed wasn't much and would allow her only one or two solid blasts after she powered up the Deadish a bit to help her fend off the forces of the Revenant, but it was enough that it gave them a chance. How much of one was questionable, but if they were going down tonight, they would go down fighting. Graves would be proud.

They said little as they amassed in the living room and checked each other over one last time. With there only being eight of them, the plan was limited and would probably go to hell once the fighting started, but making a plan helped to calm nerves and give them focus. Rocco and Peepers were to find as high a vantage point as they could. Rocco would unload his guns on anything that wasn't friendly while Peepers acted as his spotter. Below, Nora would take the centre position with Isabel and Scarlett flanking her, acting as bodyguards, while Reno and Andrew acted as offensively as possible, the priority being to occupy Cyril and Jax, in order to give Nora whatever time or opportunity there was to get the job done. Simple, right?

The walk to the Old Quebec Street Mall wasn't long, no more than half an hour, but it stretched out endlessly as they padded down the street. The Deadish, as per usual, made no noise or impact on their surroundings, so to the sleeping outside world it was just one lone teenage girl out for a stroll on a moonlit night.

It was the perfect night, Nora noticed with some irony. Her favourite kind of summer night. It was cool, but warm enough that not even a light hoodie was needed. The leaves danced in the light breeze as the light from the street lamps flickered through to the ground below. A few houses that she passed had lights on, people tucked into their homes for the night who were reading, watching TV, or checking on children who had long since gone to bed. She envied these people and allowed herself to look into these houses as she went by to imagine what kind of lives were being lived.

Nora took the time to reflect on all that she had seen and done since the attack on her prom night. How much her life had changed, both for the better and for the worse. She had new friends, unlikely though they might be, and even though they had all been tested, brutally, she still had her best friend and her family alive and breathing.

Nora wasn't religious and didn't subscribe to one faith over the other. Like much of her outlook on life, however, she had hope. She figured it was better to believe and hope for God to exist and for there to be an afterlife than waste time worrying about the alternative. She would die eventually, one way or the other, so why not embrace the unknown?

Nora was shaken from her reverie as she noticed the night around her had steadily been getting brighter. At first it was just one or two, then a few groups, and now a small crowd. Ghosts of all shapes and sizes lined the street on each side of her, allowing the Deadish to pass on their march to the final conflict. They said nothing but looked at her with grim eyes full of determination.

Eventually, one or two ghosts ambled out of the crowd as she walked. They stood in front of her as she approached and opened their arms to embrace her. As she went through them, gently, small amounts of energy were donated to her. Others followed their lead, and soon she was embraced, held, hugged, and comforted nearly every step of the way.

If this is what the coming of death is like, Nora thought, *no one should ever fear it.*

She *was* afraid, however. But the show of support and the strength given to her by her friends allowed her to take each and every step. By now she was close to the downtown core and the light was everywhere. Nightclubs were in full swing, though the crowds were down now that a lot of the university kids had gone home for the summer. There were a few places to grab food still open, as well as some softly lit cafes. People were all around her now, both living and dead. The living laughed and drank merrily in the heat of a summer of night. The dead stood mutely around them in the cold of the coming fight.

She passed the cafes and left the living as she came to the front entrance of the mall. There she fought the urge to laugh. The mall was closed for the night, dark and locked up. There was no way around it. She found a large rock, picked it up, and tossed it through the window, hoping that particular pane was not alarmed. It would be the height of stupidity to be arrested in the middle of a suicide mission.

The smashing glass made a lot more noise than she expected, even drawing one or two curious gazes and cellphone snaps from drunk club-goers down the street who had heard the commotion. Nora winced and waited for the alarm, but none came.

Gingerly, she made her way through the smashed window and looked in awe at the assembled ghosts waiting within. There were hundreds. Friendly or not, they all came to a hush and stared at her as she came inside. She made her way down the steps to the lower floor with most of the Deadish Society as Rocco and Peepers did their best to discreetly slip upstairs. No ghosts offered their energy in this place. They simply stood vigil over the scene. They were the witnesses.

Nora was ready to fight.

On the landing above a giant fountain, the Revenant stood there bathed in the moonlight thanks to the atrium-style roof of the mall, Cyril and Jax beside her. At her feet, on his knees, was Charlie. Nora expected that, though whether he was alive or not was uncertain. He was perfectly still. He didn't even raise his head to look at her. On either side of him sat Vee and her brother, Tom, who looked around with wild and confused eyes. Nora wasn't surprised to see them. It was her fault they were there. She knew she shouldn't have gone home. But she did and now they were here.

Vee knew what the Revenant was, more or less, and had the good sense to keep her mouth shut. Tom didn't know what was going on. All the two of them could see was Nora standing all alone down below.

"Nora?" Tom asked in a confused croak when he saw her. "But you're..."

"Here," answered the Revenant with a gesture. A girl came out from behind the creature, and she heard Andrew gasp at her side. From head to toe, down to the smallest feature, the girl was an exact copy of Nora.

"What the hell?" Reno asked.

"Nora Angel?" Andrew said as he looked between the two of them.

"A Wisp," Nora said, remembering what Graves had told her in her backyard what now felt like a century ago. "It's me. The energy she took from me."

"Your energy?" Andrew asked. "But that thing also took some of..." From the other side of the Revenant came a smoky black figure, not fully formed, but unmistakably "...me." Andrew's wisp grinned to expose smoking teeth in its black mouth.

No matter how unsettling it was, Nora tried to focus.

"Give up," Nora said to the Revenant. "You're not going to win."

Tom, dazed and confused, tried to get to his feet. He looked from the Wisp to Nora and back. "Please... Wisp? Nora? What is this?"

With that, the Wisp smacked him in the face. Hard. Tom fell silent at once. "Not 'Wisp,'" she said. She considered a moment. "Call me Aron."

"Don't care," Nora said. "Let them go. Or else."

The Revenant cackled and stood up. Aron, Cyril, Jax, and Andrew's Wisp tightened up beside her. The Deadish Society spread out and warily braced themselves to fight whatever came next. "Or else it is," the Revenant said.

With that, the scar beside Nora's eye began to glow a bright purple.

CHAPTER 30

Without hesitation, Nora fired the first blast out of her eye right at the Revenant's head. If the creature hadn't dropped into a crouch at the exact same moment, the fight would have been over before it even started. Instead, the blast took out a light fixture behind the Revenant, sending a shower of sparks down onto Charlie, Vee, and Tom. Vee and Tom both screamed at the assault, Tom in confusion as much as surprise, while Charlie didn't stir at all. Shielding her eyes from the bright sparks, Nora lost the Revenant as it and the two Wisps bounded away into the crowds.

Around them all, the ghosts began to chant and cheer. It was a modern version of a gladiatorial-style battle that would have happened in the Colosseum. Cyril threw up his arms in celebration just as one of Rocco's bullets tore into his upper arm, causing him to drop the chain that held Jax at bay. At once, the great cat leapt off the landing and bounded toward Nora and her companions.

"Spread out!" Andrew shouted at Reno. "Don't let them near Nora!"

"Got it!" Reno agreed as he turned to face the crowd.

Isabel, Scraps, and Scarlett took up their positions at Nora's side. The dog yapped and scurried around Nora's feet but stayed far enough away that he wouldn't accidentally trip her up. They were looking into the crowd for any sign of Jax, but after the initial impact that sent ghostly mist into the air, the crowd had mostly gone still despite the cheering. There was no sign of the cat or of his movements. It was too smooth. They were being hunted now.

Above, Rocco continued to fire at Cyril, who had ducked behind the parapet. The strong man roared in pain and anger as he waited for an opportunity to escape the assault.

258 BRIAN WILKINSON

"Well?" Rocco shouted to Peepers. "Did I get him?"

Peepers shook his head in a lack of understanding. Rocco pointed to where Cyril was with his free hand and mimicked shooting. Peepers understood that they were shooting, so he nodded. Rocco eased up.

"Why did you stop shooting?" Peepers asked. "Is my Adelaide over there? That's very kind of you."

Rocco's eyes widened. "Wait, you told me I got him!"

"No, I agreed you were shooting at him," Peepers said cheerfully.

They both turned to look across the distance and saw Cyril heave a bench over his head. They barely had time to get out the way, Rocco one way and Peepers the other, before the bench loudly smashed apart where the pair had just been standing. Cheering ghosts were caught instead and were sent scattering into mist. The remaining crowd cheered even harder.

Below, Nora's guards did their best to stand watch. Reno chanced a glance over his shoulder to tell them they were all clear when Jax pounced out of the crowd and swiped at the boy's head, hard, and knocked him down. The cat jumped on him and bit at his leg. Reno screamed, reached up, and began to punch the cat to little effect. Nora fired a blast at Jax, searing his leg and causing him to back off. Even though the cat looked about to retreat, he doubled back and reached out with his teeth to grab Reno around the leg and then toss him into the crowd, where he disappeared from view.

"Isabel! Scarlett!" Andrew shouted. "Plug the hole!" Before anyone could move, a large potted plant smashed into the fountain beside Nora, sending a shower of water and dirt all over the place. More objects began to sail down at them from above, courtesy of Cyril, who was chucking anything he could find. He kept it up until a few bullets from Rocco made him momentarily back off.

Nora looked up, ready to fire again, when she was tackled from behind and taken away from her group by... herself? The Wisp kicked and clawed at her, and Nora was surprised to see that she could physically fight back. Whatever the Revenant had done here had made the Wisp into something she could touch. She spared a quick thought for her brother and Vee and worried who else this thing might have hurt while wearing her face. Then she punched herself in the face. God, it felt good.

"Nora!" Andrew shouted. He ran toward her but was clotheslined and sent to the floor. When he looked up, the room had gotten quite a bit darker. It took him a moment to realize that he was seeing it through the black body of his own Wisp.

"You will fail her… again," the Wisp said.

Andrew pushed the Wisp off and leapt at it, only for it to dissipate, and he instead found himself crashing into a mobile phone booth. The Wisp reformed behind him and punched him in the back of the head and then lifted Andrew up before dropping him onto the glass counter. The Wisp jabbed a hand into Andrew's stomach and twisted his wrist. Andrew moaned.

Isabel, Scraps, and Scarlett started to run toward Nora and Andrew, but Jax leapt out and cut off that option. The cat knocked Isabel to the side and sent her leg scattering several feet away from her. She did her best to locate it and then tried to crawl to it as quickly as possible. Jax approached her slowly, showing all of his teeth, until he let out a yelp of pain and tried to bite at his own back. When the cat spun, Isabel saw Scraps there, growling and snapping at anything he could get his teeth on. Scarlett approached the cat with a pitifully small knife that she had found.

"No, Scarlett! Get away from it!" Isabel pleaded.

"I can do it, I can do it, I can do it," Scarlett muttered to herself over and over. "BAD KITTY!" she screamed.

In response, Jax turned and looked at the little girl with fire in his eyes. Opening his jaws impossibly wide, he swooped down and swallowed the little girl whole.

"NO!" screamed Isabel. With that, Jax turned to look at the legless girl and licked his chops. Any victory was cut short as the cat yelped again from the renewed assault from Scraps on his back.

Andrew, meanwhile, was shaking the cobwebs off his own vision when his Wisp attacked him again by pummelling him in the face. In between hits, Andrew could see Isabel crawling away from the approaching cat and knew she only had a few seconds left unless he could do something. Before the Wisp hit him again, Andrew remembered that he was a ghost and didn't have to take this crap. In fact, he didn't have to let anything affect him at all. Including solid surfaces. As the Wisp brought down his fist again, Andrew let himself fall through the counter and onto the floor. Above him, the glass shattered under the assault of the Wisp, who yelled in frustration.

Andrew was already off and running toward Isabel and the cat. Too late, Jax noticed him coming as Andrew jumped into the air, feet first, and slammed into the side of the cat's head. Jax staggered back and shook his head roughly. Andrew was now on his back and at a clear disadvantage. Before Jax could do anything, though, he was hit in the head again, this time by a disembodied leg swung around by a *very* pissed-off prom queen.

"Back off!" she yelled.

From above and all around came the laughter of the Revenant, clearly audible even over the chants and cheers of the crowd.

Nora knew things were going badly. She barely brought up her arm in time to block another one of the punches by her Wisp, Aron, and then she lazily tried to hit back. She let loose a small blast that made the Wisp back off, if only for a moment, to give her time to breathe.

More laughter.

USING WHATEVER time and opportunity she had, Vee was looking around at a whole lot of nothing except for Nora fighting herself. Whatever the hell that freakish woman wanted them for seemed forgotten at the moment, and Vee wasn't going to wait around to see if it remembered they were still there. She went over and shook Tom to snap him out of it. The guy wouldn't stop staring as his sister(s)? kept hitting each other.

"Tom!" Vee snapped. "We have to go!"

He nodded but wasn't looking at her and wasn't really seeing her. Vee bent down and shook Charlie gently, but he wasn't responding. She shook him harder and harder still. Finally, Vee slapped him as hard as she could.

His eyes flicked open in shock and surprise as he did his best to take in where he was and who had just slapped him.

"What the hell?" he asked. "Who are you?"

"Vee, remember?" she said impatiently. He blinked in confusion several times. Vee sighed in frustration, since this was neither the time nor the place for friendly chit-chat. She needed him to get it together. "Nora's friend?"

"Right," he said. "Why are you slapping me?"

She rolled her eyes and turned him over so that he could take in the Nora slap-show. Of course, that wasn't what Charlie saw at all. What he saw was chaos and potentially the end of his world. He tried to get up and was grabbed from behind and lifted up in the air by, to Vee and Tom's eyes, an invisible hand. Charlie kicked and spat, but nothing seemed to work.

"And where are you thinkink you are beink going?" Cyril asked through clenched teeth. He had a number of bullet holes in him with a softer shade of blue misting out. Rocco had hit his target, that was for sure, but the damage hadn't slowed him down. "I will tell you. You are going away." With that, he tossed Charlie back through a store window. Vee screamed, which finally got Tom's attention. He stood up and decided to take action.

"Come on," he said. "We're getting out of here!"

They started to run toward Charlie, but Tom was tripped by Cyril, and he crashed into a food cart. Absurdly, Tom grabbed a ketchup bottle and turned around to spray it into the empty air. Except once he sprayed the bottle he found that the space wasn't so empty after all. Some of the ketchup stuck and resolved itself into what looked like the face of a very surprised man who was bigger than anyone had a right to be. For good measure, Tom tossed the now-empty bottle at the head of the man and watched it bounce off before landing with a hollow plop on the floor.

"What the f…" began Tom.

"Let's go!" Vee said as she pulled him along.

Back at the entrance, the drunks who saw Nora break into the Old Quebec Street Mall had arrived with a few of their friends. Word was getting around through texts and social media that a crazy girl had broken into the mall, but what they were seeing now was completely insane. Of course, they'd had a lot to drink, but still… this was on a whole other level.

The crazy girl was fighting and yelling with what looked like her twin sister, as well as a bunch of other people, but if there was actually anyone there besides the two girls, they couldn't see them. There were crashes and bangs all over the place. Benches, stores, plants, even the fountain were looking totalled. Cellphones were brought out and started recording.

Vee and Tom could see the people at the doorway and were thrilled that help of some kind or another had arrived. Vee reached out and was about to shout at them when the Revenant dropped down behind the small crowd and began assaulting them and bodily tossing them back out of the building. The thing was careful to avoid being seen as it dipped in and out of the shadows. It reached out smashed every phone, some of which were crushed, along with the hands still holding them. The people screamed and fled, the drunks tripping over their own feet. Vee and Tom skittered to a stop and began to run the other way, but it was too late. The Revenant was upon them in an instant.

UPSTAIRS, CHARLIE moaned as he tried to get to his feet without cutting himself on all the shattered glass. He carefully stepped over the shards and rested against the next pane, which was still intact. The respite was brief as an enormous hand smashed through the glass and pulled him through the falling pieces. Cyril bent down and snapped off a particularly jagged piece that he thought would help finish the job nicely. Charlie spat blood and got to his feet, where he stood as closely face-to-face with the man as he could.

It *was* face-to-face, anyway. A perfectly round hole bloomed in the centre of Cyril's forehead, and the strong man's mouth formed a perfectly round "o" of surprise.

"You got him!" Peepers yelled in glee as Cyril dropped to his knees. The impact had scattered his increased essence and his long-dead brains. He looked dead. Again.

Rocco marched over to the strong man, triumphant, with a passing nod to Charlie, and pressed the gun against his forehead. "Anything else you gotta say, punk?" he said.

"Yes," Cyril said. He moved impossibly fast and knocked the gun out of Rocco's hand with one fist and grabbed the mobster in the groin with the other. He squeezed hard. Rocco's eyes rolled into the back of his head as Cyril lifted him up over his shoulders and tossed him over the balcony and into the crowd below. "I am needink you to be away," he snarled.

Woozily, Cyril turned, still clutching his shard, and focused as best he could on Charlie. He grinned as though the match was over and victory was assured. "Now it is your turn, I am thinkink," he said.

"Overconfidence did in Rocco, too," Charlie said. "You forgot someone."

Cyril blinked in confusion before his eyes went wide, and he turned to look at Peepers. The little ghost looked utterly absurd holding a giant gun, but there was nothing funny at all once he pulled the trigger. Cyril's face was filled with so many ethereal bullets that it peeled away like an exploding watermelon. Whatever extra the Revenant had given him in terms of strength and physicality were also a weakness, because when Peepers was done and the gun clicked empty, Cyril the Strong Man dropped to his knees and then fell flat down on the floor and didn't move again.

"Payback is a bitch!" Peepers said before descending into a fit of giggles. He then looked at Charlie, mortified. "Oh, my. Please don't tell Adelaide I used profanity. Though I must admit, that was *fun*."

"Your secret is safe with me, little guy," Charlie said gratefully. "Now let's go help the others!"

ANDREW, ISABEL, and Scraps were doing the best they could to keep Jax from shredding them, but none of them had noticed the shadow of Andrew's Wisp as it made its way to their rear through the crowd.

Isabel prepared to swing her leg at the tiger again when it was pulled out of her hands from behind and caused her to lose balance. Andrew's Wisp laughed at her misfortune, and when Andrew himself turned to help

Isabel, the tiger pounced and raked at his chest. Blue mist bloomed heavily on Andrew's chest and he staggered backward. The tiger batted him again, and he fell to the floor. Andrew's Wisp held Isabel's leg and began to beat her with it. Charlie and Peepers arrived then to try to help. Charlie tried to grab the Wisp, but it puffed away in smoke, and he went right through it. The Wisp solidified again in an instant and swatted Peepers away with the leg.

Nora, meanwhile, was still going at it with her own Wisp. Both of them looked beaten up, but the Wisp was clearly enjoying the encounter. They punched and clawed at each other, all form and purpose out of it, like two animals in the wild. Nora rolled and tossed the Wisp away from her and then lay down panting heavily. She rolled the other way and started to get up but was then harshly kicked by the Wisp, who had recovered much more quickly than she had. The Wisp straddled her and grabbed Nora's hair and pulled her head back roughly so that it couldn't be hit by her soul energy blast. It then cradled Nora's head with her two arms and began to apply pressure. Within seconds, Nora knew her neck would break and she would be dead.

"ENOUGH!" came a shout that thundered and echoed through the empty mall. Everyone and everything paused in an instant in the space. No more cheering, no movement at all, just the sounds of laboured breathing and blood dripping onto the floor. The Revenant came forward then, dragging Vee by her hair while holding Tom in a chokehold. The gills on its neck were open and throbbing. Soul energy, little by little, was being sapped out of both Vee and Tom. "You will stop now," she said.

Nora wanted to blast the thing, but the angle was all wrong. She tried to talk, but barely a gurgle could escape. Instead, it was Charlie who spoke for her.

"No," Charlie said as he stood in front of the thing and blocked its view of Nora. "Oh, no," he said sadly. "*You* will stop now. It's not too late." He reached out slowly with one hand toward the thing, an act of kindness, not of violence.

What is he doing? Nora thought. But even then, she already knew the answer. She had known for quite some time.

The Revenant hesitated, not sure of what to do. The evil and anger were still there, but for the first time Nora saw a trace of doubt. It was the barest inkling of a long-buried humanity. Graves told her that revenants had been human once. It hadn't been an educated guess. He knew from personal experience.

"It is," the Revenant said quietly. Then, with more conviction. "It *is*. There is no stopping this."

"Then I'm sorry," Charlie said. The Revenant was surprised and caught off guard when Charlie brought out the wooden pole he grabbed from the wreckage of the mall and smacked her in the neck with it. The creature howled, and the energy it had been sucking in burst out and cascaded against Vee and Tom, who she then roughly dropped to the floor.

Nora used the moment to pull her head back down and fired as widely and blindly as she could at her Wisp. The blast came from everywhere and nowhere at once, and the Wisp was knocked away so forcefully that Nora was quite sure she had obliterated the thing in the process.

The Deadish, or what was left of them, were still on the defensive from Jax and Andrew's Wisp. Andrew was too weak to fight, and Isabel was doing her best to keep from being bludgeoned by his Wisp. Peepers stood on his own opposite Jax. Nora had to make a quick decision of whom to help.

The decision was made for her. As Jax approached Peepers and opened his jaws wide, a gush a ghostly blue blood flew out of his mouth. The cat staggered back and suddenly limped on his right leg. He began to hop from side to side, snapping at the air. The tiger yelped, but it came out in a gurgle. Nora saw then that all over his body there were little points that were rising and falling until finally a small little knife poked through the skin before being withdrawn and emerging elsewhere. Scraps leapt off the cat and backed away lest he was cut in the process. The little dog whined in confusion and excitement as again and again the little knife poked in and out until the cat went limp and flopped heavily to the floor. Finally, the knife popped out of the skin and made a long, clean slice, and a little girl, as whole as she had been when she was swallowed, stood shakily in the middle of the body to examine her gory work.

"*Screw you,*" Scarlett snarled.

Nora couldn't help herself. She actually laughed.

The smile turned into a determined snarl once she saw how well Andrew and Isabel were doing against the smoky Wisp. Nora fired off a blast toward the thing, and the smoke swirled away where the blast should have torn through. It laughed at her and tossed her the leg, which she ducked under. "I never really cared about you," Andrew's Wisp taunted.

This brought Nora to a stop. "What?" she said.

"You know I only told you that I loved you so I could get closer to you, right?" the Wisp asked.

"Ignore it, Nora Angel," Andrew called out. "It's lying!"

"You got me killed," it said.

"No, I didn't," she said.

"You destroy everything you touch."

"Touch *this*," Reno shouted as he and Rocco emerged from the crowd. Reno tossed a brick high at the Wisp, which swirled low as Rocco did a sliding kick into it, which finally brought it down to the ground. Reno heaved himself on top of the thing while Rocco, Isabel, and Scarlett grabbed onto the limbs.

"Blast it, ya silly dame!" Rocco shouted at Nora.

Instead, Nora looked to Andrew, who had mostly faded away to nothing over the course of the battle. She didn't have the energy within herself to restore him, take out his Wisp, and fight the Revenant. Then she realized that she didn't have to use the energy at all. It was here right in front of her.

She got down on her knees in front of the snarling Wisp, which was futilely trying to make its escape. She reached out and gently held each side of his face in her hands. She closed her eyes and breathed deeply as she pulled the entire essence of the creature into herself. Soon the Deadish were sitting on nothing but the cold floor.

Andrew smiled at her and nodded, the pride evident in his eyes. He began to fade further and was almost gone when she reached him. "You did it," he said. "You got it."

"No," she said with a smile. "I've got *you*. And now I'm ready to give you back."

All of the energy from the Wisp flowed out of her, no longer murky black but a brilliant blue that had been cleansed of the darkness that tainted it, and she poured it all back into him. Within a few moments he was not only healed but whole. Fully. She reached out and realized that even though he was still dead and lost to her, that she could feel the faintest touch of his fingertips.

The battle was not over, however. Charlie and the Revenant were still having a war of words. The Revenant retreated from him and was throwing things at him to scare him away, but Charlie pressed on more determined than ever.

"Go away!" the Revenant screamed as it attacked once more. "No more!"

"No," Charlie insisted. "I know who you are. I know what happened to you."

"You know nothing!" it yelled.

"I know your name."

"I HAVE NO NAME!"

"Alice," Charlie whispered. "*Alice*, I found you. It's not too late."

Behind them, Nora and the Deadish gathered and stood ready. The enormity of what was happening here was not lost on any of them. Standing before them was the long-lost daughter of Graves Culshaw and the love of Charlie Ignis's life.

"My god," Andrew said. "Is it possible?"

Nora nodded. She had pieced together enough of the details and hints dropped by both Graves and Charlie to already have arrived at this conclusion. It had never been expressly said by any of them who the

Revenant really was. Graves had known, though, Nora was fairly sure. He probably knew the night they first found the newborn creature. He had told Charlie that Alice was "gone" and that she was "lost" and allowed him to draw his own conclusions. The truth was that Graves hadn't been strong enough to take the life of his own daughter. Graves had let her go, and in the end it had been she who had killed him.

"You killed him!" Nora yelled. "You killed your father!"

The Revenant startled at this, and fear and shame washed into her face. Quickly, though, it washed away. "No!" it snapped. "I have no father. I have nothing."

"You have me," Charlie begged. "Your dad... whatever you did, he still believed in you. He still had hope for you. That you could be found."

"No," the Revenant insisted. "You left me."

"So you do remember," Charlie said. "Alice, try to remember!"

"Don't call me that!" she snarled. "I'm not Alice!" She struck Charlie across the face, and he fell to the ground. "I'm not yours!" She hit him again, and blood poured out of his nose. "I didn't kill my father!" She hit again and again and again.

"I won't fight you," Charlie said weakly. "I can't lose you again."

The Revenant paused at this. "He said that. The old man... my..." She shook it off and attacked again. She raised her arm to strike him but was cut off as a blast from Nora hit her in the shoulder and slammed her back against a wall.

The Revenant screamed. It was loud, painful, and all the Deadish fell to their knees. The ghosts that had assembled began to run in a panic to get away, many of them through Nora, which blocked her line of sight.

Leaping through the air and into the moonlight, the Revenant sucked in whatever power she had left and unleashed it in a blast when she connected with the ground. All of the members of the Deadish Society were blown back, much too far away to be of any use now.

Charlie watched as Alice approached Nora, and he saw the energy in Nora's scar pulsate. "No!" he screamed. "Nora, no! There has to be another way! PLEASE!"

But no matter how hard she tried, she couldn't see another choice. She had only seconds before she would be dead and then this thing would take her friends. She had one last shot in her. One last chance. She knew that Charlie would never forgive her for this, but she didn't see what else she could do.

On her feet, Nora looked at the approaching creature and felt the energy pour into her eye. She unleashed every last bit of energy she had, a second too late as a blow to the back of her head resulted in the energy smashing into the floor at her feet. A second blow made her crumple to the floor as the weight of her own Wisp brought her down.

"Miss me?" Aron said in her ear. "You can't get rid of me that easily. I'm you, after all. Wherever you go, there I am. We're a matched set." It laughed uncontrollably for a moment. "Let's face the end together, shall we? Let's pay the bill that has come due."

Aron hauled Nora to her knees and held her arms behind her helplessly. She had no energy left. The ghosts in the room had all faded away, except for the Deadish, who were dazed and out of the fight. There was no more cheering. No one left to watch. Now, the final confrontation was made up of just herself, the Wisp, the Revenant, and Charlie. The rest of the world had gone away. She had no one but herself to blame for her failure and no one but herself to rely on now to get out of the situation.

I'm on my own, she thought.

The Revenant now stood in front of her, full of smug satisfaction at nearly having succeeded in what should have been the simplest task of all: kill the girl. "It's time now, girl," the Revenant said. "You have given me enough trouble."

I'm on my own, Nora thought desperately.

"It's too bad," the Revenant said. "I see how easily you toss about the energy you have gotten. How little respect you seem to have for it. How much you take without giving. We're not so different, are we?"

The grip holding her arms stiffened, and Nora let out a yelp of pain. Her arms and shoulders weren't meant to bend so far in that direction.

I'm on my own, she cried out again in her own mind.

"You are. Just. Like. Me," the Revenant said coldly.

And at that moment, Nora realized that she was. She had the potential, just as Alice once had, to be a Revenant. To take energy that did not belong to her. To consume the world around her. To use it to her own advantage. There was, however, one key difference. Nora used power that was given to her freely by her friends and family. There was one power that was even more potent and powerful, though, that she hadn't considered or realized until just now.

I'm on my own, she thought with grim satisfaction. She felt the tight grip of her Wisp all around her and recognized the thrum and feel of the energy as her own. The Wisp was made up of her fears, her doubts, her insecurities, her failures, but also of the strength she used to fight through each and every one of them. Nora's true strength, the gift she shared with the world, was herself.

And what was her Wisp but a part of herself that she had lost touch with?

Too late, the Wisp realized what she was doing. Rather than fight to get away from the thing, Nora pulled it in toward herself, where it rightly belonged. It tried to fight, but it was pointless to resist. All at once, the Wisp was gone and Nora's scar grew brightly to illuminate the darkness.

"Nora!" Charlie screamed as he ran toward them. "NO!"

The energy poured out of her, as powerful and forceful as any blast she had ever let go. She put herself into it, with all of her anger and fear as well as her love and acceptance. She thought of Graves and how he had been able to let go of his daughter, even knowing what she'd become, to allow himself to move on. She thought of how she lost Andrew to this horrible thing that Alice had become, the hunger of the soul energy gathering having consumed her and taken her over in the throes of its addiction. She thought of Sarge, torn apart, the Deadish, beaten and bruised. She thought of her family. Of Vee. Of Tom. Of Charlie, still in anguish, begging for Nora to stop.

But Nora wasn't stopping. The energy wasn't slowing. The Revenant recoiled in horror as the cascading purple poured all over her skin and inserted itself into the gills. It crept into the ears, the nose, the mouth, and even the eyes. Nora pushed the energy so that it filled every corner of the building with the one thing the Revenant could not stand the most: forgiveness.

Piece by piece, the Revenant was stripped away. The creature mewled in pain and disgust as the darkness flittered up and out of it. Its skin crackled and burned away, leaving pale white flesh underneath. The energy poured on it until it lay down on the floor in the fetal position, trying to withstand the flow, until finally Nora stopped and all was still.

Charlie arrived and tried to understand what he was seeing. There, on the ground, surrounded by wafts of faint purple smoke, was the body of Alice Culshaw. "What did you do?" he asked breathlessly.

In response, Alice took a great shuddering breath and slowly opened her eyes. "Charlie?" she asked in confusion. Her voice had a warmth to it that the Revenant had been missing. It was filled with life. "Is that you? You came for me. I knew you would. Where's my father?"

Charlie quickly cradled her and began to rock her back and forth. "It's okay," he said. "Of course I came." He looked at Nora with gratitude in his eyes but also another thought or feeling that he wanted to express but didn't know how.

The Deadish Society limped over to take in the scene, none of them quite knowing how to take it. Nora could barely see them until one by one they each gave her a sliver of the energy they could share so that she could keep her Vision. Behind them came Tom, who was supporting a limping Vee. They both looked in wonder at each of the Deadish members, having gained Vision through the scars left on them by the attacking Revenant. Vee had a polite little scar on her ankle, and Tom had a much larger one on his upper chest.

Flickering red and blue lights appeared in the direction of the entrance, and Nora knew their time was short. Charlie bundled up Alice and started off into the shadows, while Tom managed to steer Vee away, despite her protests. They were all safely away, but the light of a police flashlight pinned Nora where she stood, and she raised her arms in satisfied resignation as her friends and family disappeared from view.

After all, she had won.

CHAPTER 31

Prison wasn't so bad once you got used to it. Nora had been locked up for about twenty-four hours and was contemplating getting a badass tattoo to show off how jaded and tough she was when a bored-looking cop called out her name and led her to the front door. Her parents were there, looking confused and worried, as was a wild-eyed looking Tom who couldn't stop staring at the ghostly desk sergeant at the entrance. Behind them was Charlie, wearing a white coat with the words "Culshaw Institute" roughly sewn into the front. He was behind them all and grinning. He even winked when he saw her.

What a jerk, Nora thought with a mental grin.

When she approached her family, Nora saw that they seemed unsure what to do, so she took the first step and gave her mom a hug, noticing that she winced when she did so. Nora took a step back and appraised them both to try to figure out what was wrong when she noticed the bruises.

"What happened to you?" Nora asked. "Are you okay?"

"Oh!" Tom stammered, coming to life when Charlie nudged him. "We were, uh, we were all attacked. Some crazy girl broke into the house after you left. She looked like you but wasn't you. I can tell you that for sure. Mom thought it was you, but she only saw for like a second. But it wasn't you. Nope. One hundred percent. Not."

"Smooth," Charlie whispered in his ear. Tom scowled but said nothing back.

"Don't worry about us," Nora's dad said. "Apparently we're all a bit beat-up, huh?" He nodded at Nora's own wounds.

"Oh, right," Nora said. "I, uh, don't really know how I got these?"

"No, you wouldn't," put in Charlie from behind in an authoritative voice. Nora's mom jumped like she'd been attacked again. "The paramnesia, Mrs. Edwards, remember? Nora had a particularly vivid episode last night. There was a mix-up with the medications. She got a dose of something that is normally quite harmless, but the reaction helped her spiral out of control. This was a very unusual development."

"Good," said a large detective who rounded the corner. A tarnished badge showed his name as Dubiansky. He was balding and tried to make up for it with a weak-looking sprout of chin hair. He put one hands on his hip while the other played with the corner of his chin hair and twirled it. It was almost hypnotic. He appraised Nora with some disappointment that she wasn't going to be any more trouble. "You seemed more or less lucid last night when we brought you in, and I have no idea how you managed to do that much damage in so little time. Personally, I suspect some of the local crowd may have had a hand in your mischief-making, but that's beside the point. Lucky for you, we got a call from the Culshaw Institute around the same time as you were being picked up that you were on the loose and needed some help. Your doctor has cleared you of responsibility, but that doesn't mean that I have, you got me?"

It was needless blustering, and Nora immediately could tell this man was a fool. He leaned in closely so that only she could hear him. "I'm watching you. Next time, you're mine."

"What was that, Officer?" asked her father.

"*Detective*," Dubiansky clarified with unnecessary emphasis. "I was just letting your daughter know that given her situation the mall has decided not to press charges, but that she'll be expected to do some community service as a way to make amends and recuperate costs."

"Fair enough," Nora said cheerfully. This seemed to further annoy Dubiansky. He ground his teeth and walked away without another word.

"It's time to go, Ms. Edwards," Charlie said formally.

Nora rolled her eyes at him and then looked to her family. "Are you guys okay?" she asked.

Her mom didn't know what to say, but she nodded and fought back tears. Her father just reached forward and hugged her.

"*Yes*," Tom answered for all of them. "Yes, we are. Don't worry about us. We've all still got each other after all, don't we?"

"Sure do, sweet cheeks," said a rotund ex-convict ghost who put his arm around Tom and made him squeak.

Nora laughed at loud and hugged her brother firmly. "Yeah, we've got each other for sure."

Once her parents left, Charlie walked her around the corner until they were face to face with his van. His *new* van. This one was a bright blue that felt like more of an in-joke than a statement. It was the same model as his old van but lacked the rust and death rattle. Nora had to admit it was a nice-looking vehicle.

"I'm going to get 'Culshaw Institute' painted on the side of it," Charlie said by way of explanation. "I figure it's the least I can do for the old man. The lawyers called me today with the details of Graves' will. Turns out he had more money than anyone realized, and he left it all to me."

"It's a classic," she said with a smile.

"You're damn right!" Charlie said with a high five.

They got into the van, and it hummed to life. Charlie gently stroked the wheel and the dashboard in the kind of way that made Nora slightly jealous. "So where are we going?" she asked. "Back to the museum?"

"No," Charlie said. "That's public property, alas. Graves was staying there because it was easy and less dangerous for him to move around. The city has reclaimed it. On the bright side, however, it turns out that Graves is the proud owner of another landmark in the city with an even more impressive historical connection. That's where we're going now. Keep in mind, it isn't pretty to look at. However, Graves had more than enough dough on him that we can afford to fix the place up."

"We?" asked Nora cautiously.

"Well, yeah, 'we,'" Charlie said. "All of us. You. Me. The Deadish." He paused for a beat too long. "And Alice, of course," he said quietly.

Nora nodded. "Let's go, then."

"Aren't you going to ask where?"

"Surprise me."

AND THAT'S how Nora first came to visit what she thought of as a second home at the Guarida Hotel. The thing had seen better days and was little more than a husk of its former glory, but at least the walls and windows were intact and there was a roof over their heads. On the main floor there was a large, open bar and a festive mood when she walked in.

The Deadish were all there, celebrating, with spirits of all kinds from around the city. Reno stood behind the bar, mixing mock cocktails and chatting up the more attractive spirits. He bemoaned the lack of an actual drink to offer and said that he hoped one day the hotel would offer cake, if only so that they could look at it and pretend to smell it. He stood up every now and then to allow Scraps to run back and forth along the counter as Scarlett chased him below and called happily after him. On the wall behind him was an old black-and-white photo of Sarge taken when was still alive.

Rocco stood beside Nora and gave a quick nod to the picture. "Charlie found it at the city archives," he said. "Gives the place a bit of class."

"Yes, it does," Nora agreed. Rocco tilted his hat to her and then went off into the other room. She craned her neck to see where he went and smiled when he drifted through the door into the hotel office.

"Nora!" called Isabel. "Over here!" Nora looked and saw Isabel and Andrew sitting comfortably in a corner booth in the bar. She smiled, waved, and made her way over.

"I'm not really a fan of this place," Isabel said to her by way of conversation. "To be honest, I think it's a bit tacky."

"It's okay," Andrew said soothingly. He looked at Nora, who was confused. "This is where she first met... her. It's where they found her date."

"Oh," Nora said. The mention of Alice was something she had so far avoided. She hadn't pressed Charlie either when he brought her up. She looked around but tried not to make a show of it, but Andrew noticed anyway.

"She's upstairs," Andrew said. "Hasn't come down since Charlie brought her here."

"It just makes me uncomfortable," Isabel said.

"Hey," Andrew said as he put his arm around the girl. She softened immediately. "What a place was doesn't mean that's how it always will be. We can make this home."

The way Isabel looked at Andrew made Nora feel uncomfortable but she let it go.

Later on, the crowd roared in greeting as Vee and Tom made their entrance. Tom looked thrilled, though still freaked out, to be a part of it all. Vee looked disgusted at the place and only warmed up when Nora told her that Charlie's inheritance would pay for some upgrades. Vee promptly started making plans like the money was her own to spend.

"Didn't want to bring Casey?" Nora chided her brother.

He looked at her and his cheeks flushed, then he caught sight of Vee again, who gave him her best thousand-watt smile. "Uh, no," Tom said. "I don't think it's that serious."

"Oh, really?" Vee asked with a grin. She sidled up next to Tom and within seconds let out one of her famous giggles. Nora made a mental note to warn both of them about hurting the other later if things got out of hand.

Nora spotted Peepers sitting at a table by himself, where he kept his eyes focused on the door. When she sat next to him, he greeted her warmly but didn't look at her. Finally he sighed.

"What's wrong?" Nora asked.

"I don't think Adelaide will be able to find me here," he said sadly. "Maybe I should go back to the hospital. What if she came looking while I was out? That wouldn't do at all."

"We'll find her," Nora said to him. "I promised you, didn't I?"

He finally turned to look at Nora and beamed at her, but his gaze shifted to Andrew, who had approached their table. There was a soft, white glow in the centre of his chest. He was staring at it and didn't seem to know what to make of it.

"Look," he said. "I, uh, wow... this feels. What's happening?"

Charlie approached and helped Nora to her feet. He looked at Andrew with compassion and understanding. "It's okay, man," Charlie said. "You know what it is. You can let go."

Andrew looked at Nora, and there were tears in his eyes. "Listen, wow..."

"I understand," Nora said.

"I had to see you," Andrew said. "One last time. I felt it after you pushed my Wisp back into me. Once we fought that... Alice... and won. I did it."

"Your unfinished business," Nora said with a sad smile. "You're free."

Around them all a crowd had gathered to watch. The room had gone quiet, though not solemn. More like people watching a couple in love at a wedding, or a child being presented to the family for the first time. It was respectful. It was beautiful.

"I can feel it," Andrew said. "I feel so light. I can see more light than I thought was possible. They're calling to me."

"Then you should go," Isabel said sadly.

"Yeah, man," Rocco agreed from the office doorway. "Time to take a trip."

"You did good," Reno said.

"You kicked ass," put in Scarlett.

"I hope you find what you're looking for," Peepers said.

The glow was brighter than ever, and Andrew took a minute to look around the room. He saw the faces of people who had, in a short time, become friends. More than that, they had become family. In life he had found love and a place that he belonged, but in death he had found a calling and a purpose. He had met the Deadish Society and become one of them. He looked at Nora and remembered a love so profound that it took his breath away. He looked to her side and saw Isabel and the notion struck him that perhaps there was still hope left in the world.

"I think," Andrew said after a moment of clarity, "I think I already have." He reached out for Nora and knew beyond any doubt that he could finally do what he had dreamt of for so long. Their fingers approached and then touched, skin to skin. He leaned in closely and kissed her, one last time, the spark of life and death leaving a tingling on both their skin. "I love you, Nora Angel."

It was their last kiss. They both knew it.

"I love you, too," she said.

"Then do this one last thing for me," he said before whispering in her ear. When he leaned back, Nora looked like she wanted to protest but instead nodded and smiled through shimmering tears. It was just like him.

"Everyone," Andrew said. "It's time to say goodbye..." The crowd started to murmur and to speak but Andrew cut them off. "...but not to me."

Still holding Andrew's hand, Nora reached out and allowed the flow of energy to make contact with another. Before he knew it, Peepers was holding her hand, and the flood of energy within Andrew travelled through Nora and into the little man. Peepers gasped and shuddered at the flow, his eyes filling with wonder and delight.

Peepers looked back toward the doorway, and his smile spread from ear to ear. The light was blinding and bent ever so slightly around a female form who had both arms out in front of her. Nora bent down and gave him a quick hug. "I told you," she said through tears. "I told you we'd find her."

He hugged her back and gave her a quick peck on the cheek. "I don't think she'd mind that I did that," he said with a smile. Then he let go of Nora and walked to the doorway, the glow within him so bright that all of them had to shield their eyes. He reached out his hand, and Nora saw someone reach out to accept it.

"*I found you*," Peepers said, his voice full of awe and wonder. The light hit a new brilliance and then faded quickly. The little ghost was nowhere to be found.

Nora turned to Andrew then, back to his normal ghostly blue, and felt her joy turn to grief. "What about you?" she said.

"I felt it," Andrew said. "I was close to heaven. I also felt that there is more than one way to get there. I'm not in a rush. I can take it slow."

He glanced over at Isabel, who was busy playing with Scarlett and Scraps and doing her level best not to look at him. She glanced over anyway and smiled.

"Slow is good," he said.

EXHAUSTED, NORA eventually disentangled herself from the festivities (which had taken on a new height thanks to Peepers being called home) and she made her way outside to the tired-looking swing on the front porch. It creaked under her weight but held as she rocked back and forth and drew a contented breath. Within seconds, she had fallen asleep.

She woke herself with a snort a short time later and heard a soft chuckle beside her. Charlie. "You have the ability to wake the dead, you know," he said with a laugh.

"So I've heard," she said with a yawn.

"What's new with you?" he asked, and they both laughed. He reached out and took her hand in his, and Nora felt a thrill of excitement run through her whole body. They stared at each other then and both felt the inevitable pull of gravity towards one other's lips. They got closer and closer until a faint thud of some object falling to the floor on the level above them broke the spell. Charlie at once moved back and looked guilty. His hand slipped out of hers.

Nora tried her best to understand how complicated the situation was. She was the one who helped make it even more messed-up, after all. Whatever it was between her and Charlie was real, she knew, but it had never been tested and had never even really had a chance to start. Alice, on the other hand, had a long and complicated history with him.

"You need to work things out," she said both to herself and to Charlie.

"I have feelings for you," Charlie said simply. "I like you. I want to be with you." He sighed loudly and tilted his head back.

"I know," Nora said. "It's okay."

"Is it?" Charlie asked. "I don't know if it is. This is just weird."

"Yeah, but so are you," Nora said.

"*I'm* weird?"

"And kind of a jerk."

"But a cute jerk."

"Yes, a cute jerk," she admitted.

Charlie grinned at her and leaned back to swing more earnestly. "So," he said after a while. "What do we do now?"

From inside, Nora heard the laughter and happiness of her friends. She thought of Vee and Tom. Of Peepers and Adelaide. Of Scarlett, Scraps, Rocco, Reno, Sarge, and all the rest. She thought of Andrew and Isabel.

"We let go and live."

CHAPTER 32

A little over a month later, Nora found herself in Dr. Westlake's office for what she hoped would be the last time. He peered at her over his glasses and constantly was making "hmmm" and "huh" noises at everything she said. Finally, he sat up straight and cleared his throat.

"Well, Nora," he said calmly. "I think we're just about done here."

"Oh, really?" Nora asked in a too-sweet voice. "Next week?"

"No, I mean I think we're fully done here."

"Oh my!" Nora said. She was laying it on thick. "You mean I'm cured, Doctor? You did it? You saved me?"

"Well," Westlake said, blushing furiously. "I don't know about 'saved.' That's a strong word. But I think you've got the tools now to get yourself through life. You haven't had a bout of paramnesia in nearly a month now, correct?"

"I think it might actually be closer to five weeks!" Nora said in fake excitement.

"Oh?" Dr. Westlake asked. He clicked the pen and dropped it a second later as though it had been smacked out of his hand. He looked around for it to try and grab it, but it was nowhere to be found. He looked to Nora for some sort of assistance, but she just smiled sweetly and vacantly at him as though nothing had happened. "Right," he said refocusing. "Good. Yes. You haven't seen any more ghosts, monsters, or anything supernatural of the sort, correct?"

Nora adjusted herself on the couch as Reno gleefully finished kicking the pen farther away from the doctor. Andrew, Rocco, Isabel, Scarlett, and Scraps all made themselves comfortable as they sat around her.

"Nope," Nora agreed with a smile. "Can't say that I have."

EPILOGUE

Nora's eyes flickered open sometime after midnight. They adjusted slowly and purposefully in the darkness. Carefully, her body adjusted itself until she sat on the edge of her bed, her toes stretching and working themselves into the carpet beneath her feet.

Standing awkwardly, Nora's stiff legs took her tired body over to the closed window. Numb fingers played at the latch until it was undone, and then aching arms took over to push it open. Cool night air wafted into the nostrils in deep draughts while the rustle of leaves provided the music of the evening.

Satisfied, the legs carried her back to bed and the arms pulled up the covers. *That was good* came the fatigued thought. Before sleep came, one side of Nora's mouth slowly slid up into a horrific grin.

This is going to be fun.

AUTHOR'S NOTE

This book is for my daughter, Nora, who was not yet born when I first started writing it in the summer of 2014. All that I knew for sure was that she was coming, that she was going to be amazing, and so she needed an amazing story to carry with her throughout her life.

There are so few things worth leaving to our children as we make our way through our lives. Before my son was born, I looked around my home to see what it was that he might want to take with him many, many years from now (hopefully!) when I'm gone and realized that there wasn't anything that truly meant something. So for him, and now for her, I wrote stories that featured them as characters. For Owen it was *Battledoors* and for Nora, *Paramnesia*. These books are an expression of who I am, my imagination, and my unending love for my kids.

For my daughter, I hope for her to grow up to be a strong, intelligent, capable woman who is not afraid to experience adventure in all of its forms. I hope she feels free to love, to grow, and to see the world for what it can be, not what others want us to see. The Nora in this book has the ability to see beyond the surface of her world into the bad parts but also sees the incredible beauty that is hidden right beside it.

The Nora of my life is one of the most amazing people I know. She is full of passion, energy, and displays endless amounts of love for the people in her life. I already love her more than she will likely know, and this story feels like such a small thing next to the mountains of love I feel for her. I hope she likes this book. This is *her* book, after all, though hopefully she won't mind having shared it with you.

This book would not exist without the tireless support of my loving wife, Catherine, my incredible son, Owen, my dog Toby, and the continued enthusiasm and support of my mother, Edith, and my father, Graydon.

My family of supporters who love and believe in me include but are not limited to my brother Graydon and his wife, Tammy, my in-laws, Peter and Rhonda, my brother-in-law David and his wife, Libby, my Uncle Brian and his wife, Barb, the entire Mitchell clan, and my good friends Jeremy, Josh, Jamie, Paul K., Vicky, Nicole, Mark, Taina, Eric, Meredith, Sydney, Kyle, Via, Amanda, Dave, Lois, Wendy, Ellie, Patti, Aaron, Christa, Chris, Tom, Paul H., Jack, Jalen, Reno, Ali, Robin, the D.A. Novel Club, the staff and students at the school where I teach, and so very many others who all inspire me every day to be the very best man I can be.

I want to thank the incredible team at Blue Moon Publishers, including Heidi, Talia, and my unbelievable editor, Allister, who told them to take a chance on this unknown writer and who offered advice and guidance every step of the way. I also want to thank Scott Carter, the DJ to my Edgar, who acted as my guide and sounding board. He believed in me before I believed in myself, and that made all the difference.

Lastly, I must thank the city of Guelph, my hometown. All of the locations in this story are based on the real buildings and places in the city, though you'll have to forgive me for taking some liberties for the sake of storytelling. Some of the places in *Paramnesia* are long gone, others aren't where I've suggested they are or have been renamed, and some are painted in the rose-coloured glasses of nostalgia.

Given the subject matter, it seems more than appropriate to thank those who have already made the journey. Thanks to my Grandma Ada, Grandpa Cyril, Grandpa Victor, Grandpa Ed, Nana, Uncle George, Aunt Louise, Jack, Lucas, Mike E., Tony, Alex, Danielle, Julia, Uncle Mike, Rooter, Truffle, and to my good friend Lionel who knew what it meant to appreciate the view.

ABOUT BRIAN WILKINSON

Brian Wilkinson was born in Guelph, Ontario. He completed a Bachelor of Arts degree in English Literature at the University of Guelph in 2000, received a diploma in Journalism from Humber College in 2004, and finally graduated with a Bachelor of Education degree from the University of Toronto in 2007. He has been a high school teacher and librarian since 2007, where he has mostly taught English and now works to pass on a deep love of stories as a head librarian.

He has worked in various capacities for the *Toronto Sun*, *Eye Weekly*, the *Toronto Star*, *Kidscreen Magazine*, and the online comic news site *Comixfan. net*. His love of comics led to a writing job at Marvel Comics, where he co-wrote *X-Men: The 198 Files*.

He currently lives in Toronto, Ontario, with his wife Catherine, their son, Owen, their daughter, Nora, and their very loud dog, Toby.

Find Brian on Social Media:
Official Website: bewilkinson.wordpress.com
Twitter: @The7thParallel
Instagram: bewilkinson77

BOOK CLUB GUIDE

1. There's an old quote from Alfred, Lord Tennyson, that reads, "It's better to have loved and lost than to never have loved at all." Considering Nora's relationship with Andrew, do you think she feels the same way? How about Andrew?

2. One of the major themes of the novel is about letting go, whether in terms of love, friendship, or death. Discuss how this theme applies to any of the characters in the story and how their journey toward acceptance has progressed.

3. Nora's best friend, Vee, shows unyielding loyalty to her best friend. Discuss what impact you think this has on Nora as a character and do your best to relate it to someone similar in your own life.

4. Which member of the Deadish Society would you most like to hang out with? Why would you choose that particular character and what would you do together?

5. Everyone in this book seems intent on helping Nora (and some are more successful than others). If you knew someone in real life who was struggling with similar problems, what might you say or suggest to them in order to help them?

6. By the end of the novel, Nora is by herself, though it seemed at times that her love with Andrew might endure or the new spark of (whatever) might catch on with Charlie. Being a strong, independent young woman, Nora doesn't need to end up with either of them, but if you had a choice, would you pick Andrew, Charlie, or someone else entirely? Discuss.

7. Andrew gave up his chance at the afterlife so that Peepers could be with Adelaide. Why do you think he made that decision? Was it the right thing to do?

8. What sort of reunion do you imagine Peepers had with Adelaide?

9. With the exception of her brother, Tom, and her best friend, Vee, at the end of the story, Nora has kept the truth of what she has been experiencing from her friends and family. Was this the right thing to do? If she had told them what she was seeing, how could she have done it in a way to convince people she was telling the truth?

10. In the epilogue, Nora doesn't seem to be herself. Why do you think this is, and how might this impact the next book in the series?

WRITE FOR US

We love discovering new voices and welcome submissions. Please read our submission guidelines carefully before preparing your work for submission to us. Our publishing house does accept unsolicited manuscripts but we want to receive a proposal first and if interested we will solicit the manuscript.

We are looking for solid writing—present an idea with originality and we will be very interested in reading your work.

As you can appreciate, we give each proposal careful consideration so it can take up to six weeks for us to respond, depending on the amount of proposals we have received. If it takes longer to hear back, your proposal could still be under consideration and may simply have been given to a second editor for their opinion. We can't publish all books sent to us but each book is given consideration based on its individual merits along with a set of criteria we use when considering proposals for publication.

Head to www.bluemoonpublishers.com to learn more.

THANK YOU FOR READING
PARAMNESIA

If you enjoyed *Paramnesia* by Brian Wilkinson, check out these exciting young adult titles from Blue Moon Publishers!

The Battledoors Series by Brian Wilkinson
Battledoors: The Golden Slate
Battledoors: The Black Spyre

The Immortal Writers Series by Jill Bowers
Immortal Writers
Immortal Creators
Immortal Suspects

The Hit the Ground Running Series by Mark Burley
Hit the Ground Running
Flow Like Water

The Nefertari Hughes Mystery Series by Bethany Myers
Asp of Ascension
Diadem of Death
Medallion of Murder
Relic of Revenge

And don't miss the next book in The Deadish Chronicles: *Hypomnesia*!